ABOVE

THE BROKEN SKY CHRONICLES

ABOVE

BOOK 2

JASON CHABOT

TURNER

Turner Publishing Company
Nashville, Tennessee
New York, New York

www.turnerpublishing.com

Above: The Broken Sky Chronicles, Book 2

Cover design: Maddie Cothren
Book design: Glen Edelstein

Library of Congress Cataloging-in-Publication Data
Names: Chabot, Jason, author.
Title: Above / by Jason Chabot.
Description: Nashville, Tennessee : Turner Publishing Company, [2016] |
    Series: The broken sky chronicles ; book 2 | Summary: In a
    post-apocalyptic world that exists in two planes, does Elia, without Hokk,
    have any hope of returning to Above and rescuing her family, and, without
    Elia, will Hokk become just another lost soul roaming the endless plains
    of Below?
Identifiers: LCCN 2016017925 | ISBN 9781681626048 (pbk.)
Subjects: | CYAC: Science fiction. | Survival--Fiction.
Classification: LCC PZ7.1.C468 Ab 2016 | DDC [Fic]--dc23
LC record available at https://lccn.loc.gov/2016017925

9781681626048

Printed in the United States of America
17 18 19 20 10 9 8 7 6 5 4 3 2 1

Dedicated to my wonderfully inspiring
nephew and niece, Jack and Kate

I am a very fortunate uncle!

Chapter 1

ENDLESS DRIPPING MIMICKED THE SOUND of a gentle rain, though not a single drop fell from the churning clouds. Instead, these lazy droplets trickled over the mossy edges of emerald lagoons that formed steps up the mountainside. Each steaming pool dribbled into the one below, all fed by a basin at the top where boiling water percolated up from its underground source.

Cloaked by a foul-smelling mist hanging over the hot springs, Elia removed her clothes and carefully climbed the slope to the higher pools. She reached one where the temperature was just bearable and slipped into the crystal clear water. Her limbs seemed to dissolve with the warmth. Soaking her body had become an early morning ritual, a moment alone, a chance to soothe her sore joints from the previous day's work, and to rub the dirt and perspiration from her skin.

Elia dipped her head forward under the water. It plugged her ears and muffled everything as if she were half-asleep and dreaming. She drifted weightless. Every muscle was relaxed. When her lungs demanded oxygen, she floated on her back and inhaled through her nostrils. Opening her eyes, she gazed drowsily at the swirling vapors. The mist reminded her of the clouds she had fallen through to Below so many weeks before; the lagoons were reminiscent of the scalding water Cook used to pour into her washtub in the palace laundry.

The thought of that detested laundry room, buried deep underground, triggered more memories of her previous life: the two soaring towers of the Mirrored Palace; clotheslines strung on rolling green hills where white linens blew in the breeze; sunshine; the market; the uphill bicycle ride with her mother after work, bumping along the forest trail until they reached their home on its own small island, drifting at the end of a suspension bridge. It all seemed an incredibly distant reality, lost to her forever.

Immersing her head once more, Elia scratched out the grit buried in the roots of her hair — hair that had grown almost an inch since she had singed her scalp bald. She had transformed herself that first night with the Torkin marauders, matching her appearance to the person she would become. She could never go back to being the girl she used to be above the clouds.

As she lifted her head out of the water, the cold air refreshed her face. Elia licked her lips and tasted old eggs. She stood up and moved several levels down to where the pools were cooler. Though naked, she didn't worry about being seen. It was still very early. She always left her bed long before any Torkins were awake. Men from the village soaked in the hot springs during the evenings, while their wives and daughters could only bathe here in the mornings. Yet Elia made sure to finish before *anyone* arrived so she could avoid the huddled conversations and hostile glares from the other women.

The undergrowth rustled nearby. A satisfied snort followed. Elia turned to see Nym sniffing around. "Are you going to join me today?" Elia coaxed as she held out her hands, steam rising off her skin.

The fox only glanced at her for a moment before his nose was on the ground again, his huge, batlike ears standing erect, twitching to pick up the slightest sound.

Elia skimmed her palms over the surface of the water as she watched him. The animal had become a faithful companion, as committed to her as he had been to Hokk, the young man who had discovered Elia after she fell into this strange realm. Though Hokk had chosen to knock her unconscious rather than introduce himself, he had eventually demonstrated the same concern for her well-being that he'd consistently shown for his fox.

Suddenly, Nym's head whipped up. He froze. A growl rumbled in his throat. They were not alone.

Unnerved, Elia stepped out on the opposite side of the lagoon, crossing her arms over her dripping body as she moved quickly to retrieve her clothes. She no longer wore the shabby gray dress of a lowly palace servant, but the same clothing as the Torkin men with whom she labored in the fields — attire that singled her out from the rest of the women, just like the nature of her work and her shockingly short hair.

Elia bent low as she pulled the long tunic over her head, all the while keeping her eyes on Nym. As she was about to step into the pants, a small flash of yellow zipped straight toward the fox.

Nym yelped. Struck in the hindquarters, he tried spinning around to see. His back legs gave out almost immediately, but not before Elia caught sight of what had impaled itself in his fur.

A dart! *With yellow feathers!*

"Nym!" Elia shrieked as she frantically splashed back through the water, arms flailing to keep her balance, her trousers still clutched in one hand. Such a short distance to cover, yet by the time she crouched beside him, the fox had collapsed on the ground, unconscious.

In moments, he would be dead.

Elia yanked the dart out of Nym's leg, but knew it was too late. While crossing the prairies to return to South Village, she had learned from Roahm the difference between the darts. The ones with white feathers were dipped in a toxin that put victims into a deep sleep. Yellow, however, meant death. Torkins hunted with yellow-feathered darts because their poisoned tips could stop an animal's heartbeat in seconds.

Choking with sobs, Elia carefully raised Nym's head but was unable to tell if he was breathing. She could feel no pulse, though her hands were shaking too much to be certain. She scanned the surrounding vegetation for a glimpse of their attacker, but the light at this time of day was still dim, and she could see nothing through the mist.

Thwtt. Thwtt. Thwtt.

Three more darts found their target, this time stabbed into Elia's flesh. Two in her arm, one in her leg. Each had yellow feathers.

A piercing howl, like a death cry, escaped her lips. Instantly light-headed, she staggered backward into the lagoon. She desperately pulled at the projectiles while their tiny barbs tore her skin. As tears ran down her face, Elia squeezed the puncture marks, forcing out blood, hoping to expel the venom, though anxious that the fatal chemical was already traveling through her veins.

Perhaps she had acted quickly enough.

Not so. Her legs buckled beneath her and she fell to her knees, the water reaching to the middle of her chest. Her vision blurred. She tried to hold her head steady — then discovered the fourth dart sticking in her neck!

Her body now contained too much poison to cope. She was gasping. How many more breaths did she have left? Still, her instincts fought against death, and she crawled toward the front of the pool. She couldn't allow herself to slip under the water and drown.

With a final effort, she heaved her torso up onto the outer ledge, her lower half still submerged. Balancing there, Elia was able to prevent herself from falling into the pool below. As she felt her mind fading, she stared at her arms dangling lifelessly, the warm spring water trickling down her hands and dripping off each fingertip.

This is how they would find her corpse, she thought, with her trousers floating beside her lifeless body.

A surge of heat enveloped Elia, and then she closed her eyes, certain it would be for the last time.

Chapter 2

ON A REMOTE DESERT ISLAND of Above, Tasheira crested the peak of a colossal sand dune. Its long, snaking ridge divided bright sunlight on one slope from deep shadow on the other. Sinking up to her ankles on the shaded side, Tasheira's feet were immersed in coolness as if she had plunged them into water.

Before descending, she looked behind and wiped an arm across her sweaty forehead. The surface of the desert, marred only slightly by her tracks, was rippled like a fingerprint. Sand blew up the steep incline, and she shielded her eyes, squinting to see Marest. No sign of her. Yet Marest was sure to keep following. It was her duty.

Nothing before had ever drawn Tash so far into this wasteland, not even sleigh racing with her cousins. Now, separated from her father's camp by mountains of scorching sand, she worried about finding the way back. The continuous wind would soon obliterate any trace of their path across the Isle of Drifting Dunes.

Keep going. Something is out here!

Marest thought Tasheira was crazy, though as Tasheira's attendant, she would never dare say it. Certainly, the nervous twitch in the girl's lips and the raised eyebrow had given away her true feelings earlier in the morning, shortly after dawn, as Tash stuffed extra pillows under her bedsheets to create a convincing lump.

"Perhaps, Miss Tasheira, we should have others join us," Marest had suggested. "What about inviting along your cousins?"

"No, I want to do it on my own."

"But is your father at least aware? He'll expect to see you when he returns."

"I can't risk him trying to stop me. Besides, he won't be done digging until dark," Tash replied as she finished dressing, twisting a red turban around her head to contain her thick mass of curls. "We can turn back by midday if there's nothing to find."

Thankfully, Tasheira's cousins, Fimal and Neric, had shown no indication that they suspected her plan. They were going to be busy today anyhow since Baron Shoad had requested his nephews help out again at the dig site. The camp would be dull in their absence, so if Tash hadn't secretly decided last night to embark on this adventure, she would've had nothing to do all day except play tiles with Marest or watch the other servants work. She'd already read every book she had brought to camp and had foolishly forgotten to pack her piccolo to practice away the hours. And while the tethered sleighs had gone untouched for days, their sails often filling with a tempting breeze, Tasheira knew she'd feel no desire to race on her own without the added spark of competition.

Tash and Marest snuck out of camp before the others awoke, traveling by foot rather than in a sleigh, which somebody would notice missing. Though Tash hadn't asked for her parents' permission to leave, she hoped her father, the Baron, who was an explorer by nature and a collector of ancient artifacts, would understand her need to investigate. And her mother definitely wouldn't mind, hidden away in her silk cabana, kept content and drowsy by a haze of incense as she counted down the remaining days of her husband's expedition.

Now, as the blistering sun climbed toward the middle of the sky, Tash continued to the base of the dune and sat down in the gradually shrinking shade to rest her legs. Grains of sand trickled into the waistband of the baggy linen pants she had pilfered from Fimal earlier, while he slept. The outfit was scandalously inappropriate, but so much more practical than the frills and cumbersome layers of a dress. She could get away with it since nobody was around to disapprove, yet a part of her wished someone besides Marest could see her wearing it.

A grin blossomed on Tasheira's face as she imagined her mother's shock over the trousers; the smile grew even wider when she thought about how much it would drive Fimal crazy if he knew Tash was searching out here on her own. She couldn't wait to tell him. Like his uncle, Fimal was passionate about discovering things, and lately, he had become increasingly ambitious — competitive even — about someday making a significant discovery of his own. Not surprisingly, he was just as intrigued as Tash about the possibility of finding something worthwhile in the desert, especially after they had witnessed the extraordinary sight last night.

Neric, however, had naturally been skeptical.

"You'll only find charred remains, if anything," he had informed them.

"Yes, I bet you're right," Tasheira replied casually, suppressing her excitement after she noticed Fimal's eyes sparkling with possibilities.

"But something could have survived the impact," Fimal suggested. "Maybe we can convince the Baron to investigate."

"He'll never agree," Tash responded quickly and firmly, hoping to kill the idea.

It worked. Fimal dropped the topic with a discouraged shrug, though Tash could tell it remained on his mind for the rest of the evening.

And no wonder! What they had witnessed had been an exceptional display. The cascade of illumination — a sight so mesmerizing and so utterly exceptional — triggered much lively debate after the flickering lights had faded, when columns of smoke trailing up into the air were all that remained. Even the Baron shared everybody's amazement.

The shattered moon had been glowing as usual, stretched across the night sky, when a piece of it directly overhead suddenly flashed with a blinding light. Falling slowly at first, as if struggling to break free from whatever force kept it floating, it burned brightly, scarring the atmosphere with its scorched path. Smaller pieces broke off in bursts, like hundreds of shooting stars, each sparkling just as brilliantly with its own tail of fire and smoke. The blazing fragments fell faster and faster, streaking against the sky's darkness as if chasing each other to finish a race.

Tasheira dropped her dinner plate and scurried up the nearest sand dune, hoping to get above the camp for a better view. Many of the smaller pieces had already fizzled to nothing by the time she reached the top, but the larger ones kept falling. The flaming masses arrived, roaring through the air like torches in the wind. Most dove into the sea of clouds lapping at the island's edge, but one huge, fiery piece landed far in the desert. Seconds later, the ground shivered with a faint, radiating shockwave.

As far as Tash could tell from the conversations afterward, no one else had felt the actual impact. That's why convincing her father to abandon his beloved project to find out what had come to rest between the drifting dunes would have likely been unsuccessful, even if Tash had asked. The gnawing possibility of unearthing something new below the sand's surface at his beloved dig site meant he would not tolerate distractions, especially since the family would soon be leaving to return to their regular life back home. But if Tasheira herself could find just one piece of the moon and then bring it to her father . . .

Marest's silhouette appeared above the top of the dune. Tash looked up. Her attendant, burdened by the skirts of her uniform, slid down the embankment as small avalanches of sand loosened with each step. Marest was a few years older, and compared to Tasheira, she had a delicate frame and features, as if she were the one with noble blood.

Marest was breathing hard. Wisps of hair were plastered to her sweaty face. As she lowered herself to the ground, Tash rose to her feet, impatient to continue.

Her attendant frowned. "Let me get you some water first," Marest offered. Reaching into an embroidered satchel, she pulled out a waterball and passed it to her mistress.

Inspecting it, Tash removed a piece of lint before placing her lips on the quivering surface. The waterball shrank as she sucked a mouthful of the fluid, but the globe neither broke nor released a single stray drop. Once satisfied, she handed it back, and Marest brushed off the sand left by Tasheira's gritty hands before quenching her own thirst.

Tash didn't bother to wait. Instead, she started hiking across undisturbed desert.

"It won't be long before it's noon, Miss Tasheira," Marest called after her. "Maybe we should start retracing our steps. The sun's only going to get hotter." This was the closest a servant could get to complaining.

Tash turned, but continued to walk backward. "I can't give up now. Don't worry. We still have enough time." She spun around and began running, kicking up sand with her toes as she broke free from the dune's shadow and charged into the sizzling sunlight beyond.

She scrambled up another slope. At the top, where the wind blew a sheer veil of sand into the air, Tasheira stopped to scan her surroundings, and wiped away a moustache of perspiration. Pointing into the distance, she shouted down to her attendant below. "I'm going that way!"

"I'm right behind you," Marest yelled back, but Tash had already descended to the other side.

• • •

A crater marked the spot. Another hour of searching had finally brought Tasheira close enough to actually see it. Despite the distance that still remained, Tash was amazed by the crater's size as she gazed out from the peak of another large dune. And while she could not see what sat at the bottom of the pit, she knew what she'd find. A piece of the moon!

Nothing could stop her from racing forward — neither the heat nor the expanse of sand she still had to cover. Yet it was exhausting to run across the shifting desert, and before long, Tasheira's lungs were heaving. Her skin was rubbed raw where fine grains of sand clung to her sticky body beneath her clothing. She tried to ignore it all. Soon she would have evidence for the Baron and a story for her cousins.

But only a few paces from the edge, her knees locked, and Tash skidded to a halt. She could finally see exactly what had come to rest at the base of the crater.

This was not moon rock.

Chapter 3

THE POUNDING OVERWHELMED ALL OTHER senses. Elia's skull felt barely able to contain the throbbing, as if her heart had been transplanted into her head.

Slowly, she distinguished sounds, then registered painful light when she was suddenly rolled over and lifted. She squeezed her outer eyelids shut; for some reason, her inner eyelids did not close to shield the brightness.

She began swinging from side to side — one person was carrying her by the ankles, another under the armpits. The motion made her nauseous. She moaned and did not stop until she was finally lowered to the cold ground with a blanket placed over her trembling, wet body. Someone mercifully shaded her eyes with his hand.

Elia listened to low, distorted voices blending together into a confusing hum, until the voice of one man stood out, his mouth right next to her ear. "I promise. This will pass soon."

Though Roahm's words were meant to be calming, she detected anxiety in them. He knew she was dying. He was keeping her comfortable for the last moments of her life, offering reassurance that she would pass away quickly and the pain would end.

"We need space," he said to the others, his voice suddenly angry. "And the tent should be dark. Everyone out!"

She heard shuffling feet, and then the leather flap closed softly over the entrance. Roahm lifted his hand from her face and she dared to fully open her eyes. Faint light filtered through the tent's seams, and at first, she could only see Roahm's silhouette.

"Hold strong, Elia. Help will be here soon."

"I'll be dead," she croaked.

"No, your body's just resisting. It doesn't want to wake up. You've been sleeping too deeply."

Reaching out with a limp arm, Elia clutched Roahm's tunic, but had no strength to pull him closer. "I've been . . . poisoned," she whispered, the ache in her head making every word excruciating. "They want . . . to kill me."

"No one's trying —"

"Yellow feathers!" she gasped and let her arm collapse. Her watery eyes were adjusting and she could now make out Roahm's face. He was frowning.

"Yes, I saw the darts, but it's not what you think," said Roahm. He seemed shaken. "Someone must have switched the toxins."

"Why?"

"I don't know. Probably some fool's idea of a joke."

"Or a warning," Elia wheezed, struggling to steady her breathing.

"You're wrong. Things have been getting better. Haven't you noticed how the villagers seem to be more accepting?"

Yes, she thought she had noticed it too, in small ways, but this morning's attack changed everything. "I'm a threat."

"You're not."

"Surely your father . . . must think so too." Her words were raspy. "You simply . . . gave him . . . no choice . . . but to accept me."

Roahm stiffened. He could have an unpredictable temper. "The Chieftain made up his own mind," he said sternly. "He agreed to keep you in South Village and that's how it will be. Though you're obviously not one of us, you work hard and contribute as much as anybody. Others are starting to recognize that too."

Was it true? Roahm had been assuring her for so long now that she had begun to believe him. But he could be wrong. After all, they hated *her*, not him. Perhaps as the Chieftain's son, his perspective was skewed. Or maybe, because he was only a few years older than Elia, his youthful arrogance blinded him, and he wasn't as wise as he thought.

The tent flap was thrown open, and the light made Elia cry out. Roahm quickly covered her eyes again. "Please, let's keep it dark in here!" he bellowed.

"Forgive me." Their visitor covered the opening and then hobbled forward, accompanied by curious jingling sounds. "I hear someone's been poisoned." It was the voice of an old woman.

"She's had an overdose of sleeping toxin," replied Roahm.

"An overdose? Who's suffering?"

Roahm uncovered Elia's face. "The girl from Above."

"Oh. Her." The sudden change in tone was obvious.

Elia squinted, trying to make out the woman's features. She had a heavily wrinkled face and wore a bison hide over her shoulders. Charms made of wood and carved bone hung from her neck and wrists. She carried a woven basket, which she placed on the ground.

Roahm turned to the medicine woman. "We must counteract the toxin right away. I still need her in the fields today, and then later tonight at the banquet. I want her to be strong again as soon as possible, as if nothing happened."

"I can offer no solution."

Roahm's eyebrows pinched together. "That can't be true. Juniper root syrup has always been the remedy."

"Yes, normally it works fine, but if this is an overdose —"

"Then just give her more."

The woman was reluctant. "I don't have much, if any, I'm

afraid. We can't be wasteful."

"Nonsense," Roahm shot back. "Let's see what you have." Before the woman could prevent it, Roahm yanked her basket toward him and started rummaging through, tossing aside bundles of herbs, dried flowers, strips of bark, and an assortment of containers. He removed a plastic water bottle filled to the top with a cloudy brown concoction. "How could this not be enough?" he demanded.

"My mistake," the woman replied, respectfully bowing her head.

Roahm twisted off the cap and held the bottle to Elia's lips, tilting her head up with his other hand. A slimy substance, both sweet and peppery, oozed onto her tongue and coated her throat as she swallowed.

"You'll be surprised how quickly this works," Roahm murmured as he raised the bottle for a second sip.

"No!" The medicine woman grabbed Roahm's arm.

"No?" he challenged, whipping around on her with an enraged look. "She'll need more than a mouthful!"

"She must take it slowly," the woman reminded him. "Only one gulp at a time. Then wait. If she drinks it too fast, she'll throw it all up."

Roahm's anger vanished. "Yes, that's right. I remember." He gently lowered Elia's head and smiled down at her. "I once suffered like this myself. A stray dart hit me when friends and I were practicing with a blowpipe. The syrup made me feel so much better, I swallowed as much as I could. But then I threw everything up and the pain started all over again."

Though her head continued to pound, Elia could sense the trembling in her body subsiding. She hugged her chest. "I think it's already beginning . . . to work." Her voice still sounded weak. "I'm shivering less."

"See, I told you," said Roahm, placing a hand on her forehead. "By the time you finish the bottle, you'll feel like normal and you can join me in the fields. Shouldn't take longer than — what would you say?" He turned to the medicine woman. "About an hour?"

"Yes, approximately."

"Good. She'll be back digging before anyone really notices her missing." His eyes narrowed. "And if I leave now, can you stay with her and make sure she takes a regular dose?"

The woman nodded. "As soon as the girl can handle another."

"Perfect." Still clutching the bottle, Roahm got to his feet, but something beside Elia caught his attention. He crouched again and reached over her. "This stuff should work equally well on an animal, I would guess."

"An animal?" Elia rolled herself on one shoulder, just enough to turn her head. A ball of fur was curled up beside her. Blond fox fur. And those huge ears. *Praise the sun!*

"Nym!" she exclaimed, her body sagging with relief.

The fox was sleeping peacefully, his tongue lolling out, his chest rising and falling with each breath. As she watched, Roahm gingerly pried open the fox's muzzle, poured in some medicine, and massaged Nym's neck to coax the liquid down into his belly.

Roahm grinned. "There. Little Nym will be up and around in no time too."

"Thank you," said Elia, squeezing his hand.

Roahm squeezed back and then stood to address the old woman. "The Chieftain will be very pleased to hear how generous you were with your medicine."

"Of course," she said, again bowing slightly, but with a grimace on her face.

Roahm left the tent, taking special care not to let in too much light.

As soon as he was gone, the medicine woman held up the bottle for Elia. "Ready for more?"

When Elia nodded, the woman's callused hand lifted her head. She dug her fingernails into Elia's scalp like sharp claws.

Elia gulped a mouthful, yet the bottle remained pressed

against her lips, allowing more and more of the syrup to pour in. Struggling to swallow and fighting for air, Elia tried to pull away, but her strength was no match for the woman's. Her throat felt like fire. Her stomach churned. Only when she gagged, spewing the sticky liquid from her mouth, did the medicine woman release her hold.

Elia choked a few more times and wiped away the drooling mess from her chin.

The old woman scowled. "You've had enough anyway." Though the bottle was still half-full, she tipped it over the ground and drained its contents, watching the syrup soak into the dirt. She tossed the empty plastic container at Elia. "Keep that as proof you finished every drop. Don't even think of telling him any different." The woman picked up her basket. "And it's plenty warm enough in here," she added, yanking off Elia's blanket. "So you won't be needing this either."

A chill immediately gripped Elia's body, yet she didn't whimper or allow herself to shiver. She did, however, want to leap up, shake the old hag by her sinewy throat, and scream, *I'll tell Roahm what you've done! You'll pay for this!* But Elia kept quiet. While the woman would most certainly be punished, the other villagers would likely distrust and loathe Elia even more.

Elia's hateful stare bore into the back of the woman's head as she hobbled out and flung aside the front flap, deliberately leaving it open. Elia covered her sensitive eyes. Though the light of Below was feeble compared to the sun's intensity above the clouds, the toxin was affecting her reflexes. Peeking through her fingers, Elia blinked rapidly until, finally, the protective membranes of her inner eyelids slid across her vision like a transparent curtain.

Sitting upright, a belch bubbled up her throat, bringing with it a revolting taste of peppercorns. Her stomach cramped as if preparing to vomit, but she focused on calming the urge. *Keep the medicine down.* That's all she would get. Roahm had made it perfectly clear she had to recover quickly. By now, most of the villagers had probably heard what had happened at the lagoons, so Elia wanted to join them in the fields as soon as she could manage. Proving her strength and resilience was more important than ever, especially with Torkins out there who would prefer to see her dead.

Chapter 4

HALF-BURIED SHRAPNEL LITTERED THE sand, forming a ring around the bulk that had smashed into the desert island. Tash stared, unable to identify the blackened object. Whatever it was appeared almost . . . manufactured.

She hesitated. Should she wait for Marest?

Tasheira gazed into the huge crater again, scratching her furrowed brow. *Don't hold back. Marest will only try to talk you out of it.*

Carefully making her way down the slope, Tash picked up the first piece of debris in her path. It was more than a hunk of scorched metal. She flipped it over and was surprised to find a layer of dense, yellow foam bonded to the bottom. She could pick it away with a fingernail. Puzzled, she tossed the scrap onto the ground, now even more eager to investigate.

Moving closer, her footsteps slowed and then she stopped. Tasheira felt dwarfed by the object that loomed above, covering her completely with its shadow. Over three stories high and three times as long, it looked like a piece of an enormous wheel — or something that had broken off from a massive gyroscope, since its shape resembled a toy Tasheira's cousins used to play with as kids. The outer shell of the structure was severely ravaged by the intense heat of its fiery freefall from the night before, and its crushed ends had melted and cooled into solid bubbles of metal.

Tash flattened her hands on its surface. The hull was cold and gritty. Soot dirtied her palms. She walked along its length to the middle where the object had ruptured upon impact, propelling its spray of wreckage. The tear in the main fuselage was widest overhead, and enough to expose an interior that had apparently survived the landing.

Tasheira was intrigued. Maybe she could climb higher — even get inside!

Finding a foothold, she started to pull herself up when she was suddenly yanked back to the ground.

"Please, Miss Tasheira!" said Marest, holding on to her mistress's shirt. "This is too dangerous!"

Tash spun around and slapped her hand away, leaving a black smudge on her attendant's sleeve. "Don't tell me what to do!"

"I'm not. I only want you to be safe."

"And what around here doesn't look safe?" Tash challenged with a wave of her arm.

Marest swallowed nervously as she surveyed the area. "It's just not what I expected we'd find."

"We were looking for a piece of the moon."

"Yes, to bring back to camp, but this is not . . ."

"This is better," said Tasheira, turning away from Marest as she attempted once more to climb the curved side.

"But what is it?"

"That's what I want to find out."

Yet Tash was only ten feet above the ground when she started second-guessing her decision to climb higher. With Marest standing below, anxiously picking at the collar of her uniform, Tasheira could allow no sign of her wavering confidence. Instead, she focused on the cavity, which beckoned with possibilities.

The ascent was treacherous. The ragged metal of the torn hull groaned and bent with her weight. She placed her hands carefully to avoid cutting them open on sharp edges. Halfway up, her footing slipped as a piece broke away. Marest yelped. Tash pushed with her one steady leg, pressing herself against the side, blindly reaching for anything to grab. Her fingers wrapped around a hunk of foam, but it only crumbled in her grip. She grunted and snorted soot through her nostrils, feeling an instant slick of sweat cover her body as her remaining leg buckled.

"Swing over to the right just a bit more!" Marest called out.

Tasheira listened and stretched as far as she could. Her foot found a ledge. The ledge held firm.

"Don't go any higher," pleaded Marest.

Tash did not respond. She rested her cheek on the cool metal and calmed her breathing. Once collected, she gazed above, found the next crevice, and continued scaling the side.

Full sunlight bathed her as she reached the top. It was flatter here and easier to stand. The hole beside her was also wider. Tash dropped to her knees and leaned over to peek inside.

The structure appeared to be hollow. And for the most part dark. Only a narrow shaft of the sun's rays filtered inside.

"What do you see?" Marest asked in a muffled voice from below.

"I don't know yet," Tash mumbled, pulling herself out. She would have to widen the hole further. Looking around, she noticed sections of exposed foam where the metal had peeled back. She kicked with her heels, but the pieces did not fall through. They were attached to panels that tiled the inner walls. Nevertheless, she found a loose piece and struggled to pull it away, finally succeeding. More light entered the opening.

Again she dipped her head inside. Her pupils took less time to adjust. The darkness had receded. She looked carefully — and gasped.

It stuck out beyond the edge of the shadows, reaching past the rubble toward the shimmering pool of light that now shone down.

A large white glove. A person's hand.

Chapter 5

THE NAUSEA CAME IN WAVES. Elia stomped on the shovel again and watched its blade slice through the soil. She was supposed to be digging to help rebuild the damaged field, but at the moment, she could not scoop up any earth. Instead, she rested her head against the handle and struggled to stay standing. A short break was all she needed. If she didn't regain her balance, she would topple face-first into the dirt.

"How are you feeling?" Roahm inquired.

"Normal. Like you promised," she lied without looking up.

Roahm came over to examine her. "Are you sure?"

"I'm fine."

He leaned in close so only she could hear. "No, you're not!" he snapped. "And you can't be so obvious about it when others are watching."

Standing near the edge where the terrace dropped off, Elia shot a sideways glance at the field below. Several farmers were staring up at them. Their expressions were cold. Any one of the men could have been the Torkin who shot the darts. Elia stepped back so she couldn't be seen.

"Keep working," Roahm insisted.

"I will. I just needed that moment's rest for the dizziness to subside," replied Elia as she thrust her shovel into the ground once more. The blade hit a buried stone, and the toll of metal striking rock echoed between the hills. It was a sound Elia had heard countless times over the past few weeks, made by many farmers, as if the mountains were being repaired by a team of sculptors.

Roahm had explained that it originally took over a century of work to chisel the surrounding hillsides into the winding staircases that now climbed to each peak. Like layers of green ribbon, the narrow tracts of land were flat, yet wide enough to grow crops, with barley the preferred choice. From any slope, the view was stunning, and Elia always found it captivating, even that first time when the fields still showed scars of the fires set by those "metal-faced demons" who flew down from Above.

The attack by the Imperial Guards had come when the crops were ready for harvest, so the timing couldn't have been worse. Rain hadn't fallen for several days, which meant the stalks were dry. The fires spread quickly. Even now, villagers continued to talk about the mountains set ablaze, everyone panicking to save the fields. Each time Elia heard an account, she thought back to Hokk's unforgettable story of the towering inferno that had engulfed a skyscraper in the City of Ago, all started by his carelessness. The devastation had taken the lives of others, while burdening Hokk with grief and guilt. Now, like Hokk, Elia had also been the cause of fiery destruction. In their efforts to find Elia, the Imperial Guards had inflicted revenge on the innocent Torkins of South Village.

The fires around the village were eventually extinguished, but due only to another misfortune — torrential rain that poured down the hills in rivers, flowing over the edges like waterfalls until the terraces collapsed and mudslides washed away the lower fields. After Roahm and his men returned with desperately needed food and supplies, reconstruction began immediately. Much had been accomplished. As nature's unstoppable growth helped erase evidence of the flames with a

carpet of budding greenery, the Torkins rebuilt shelters, reinforced terraces, and sowed fields with the very seeds that Elia
had helped to steal.

It had been her idea to ransack the seed supplies back in
Ago. If not for Elia, these farmers would have had nothing
to grow in their soil. Had she not earned at least some trust?
Some forgiveness?

While lying in wait within Ago's surrounding ruins, Roahm
and his men had watched, truly impressed, as she singed off
her hair. By demanding they draw Torkin symbols onto her
skin to match their own, Elia was not only able to join their
ranks but ultimately to lead the raid through the city's underground tunnels, before escaping into the grasslands with the
invaders as the city crumbled and burned.

None of the men looked like warriors anymore, except the
few who were required to remain on the prairies to protect the
borders. The rest, living in South Village, had stopped scorching
the hair off their scalps. The black designs on their bare chests
had long since washed away and they wore plain tunics as they
worked. They had no reason to prove their fierceness at home
— only farmers were needed here. Elia hoped that by working
tirelessly with them, side by side, to rebuild the fields and grow
food, she would eventually win the men over once again and
alleviate the fear of their families, who perceived her as dangerous. She had just never expected it to be so tough to do.

On their journey across the prairies after the raid, Roahm
had warned her. "You should know what to expect when we
get there. I suspect most of the villagers will be suspicious of
you. Strangers have never been allowed within Torkin territory."

"Why not?"

"Too risky. It's safer to simply dispose of them."

"You mean kill them."

"If that's what it takes to protect our villages."

So then what of me? Elia had wondered.

That same afternoon, they had ridden their bison into the

patrolled foothills of the Torkinian Mountains, a massive range that tore out of the grasslands, reaching ever higher for the clouds the deeper they traveled. They continued riding for two more days, slowly following steep, unmarked trails through a labyrinth of rock, before their procession finally reached the lower steps of South Village.

Elia was nervous when she was presented to the people, even more so when the Chieftain challenged his son's decision to bring an outsider within their borders. "Why didn't you leave her on the prairies to die?"

"That would have been wrong. Our spoils of war — the food and livestock — are all useful over the short term, yes, but these"— Roahm hoisted a bag of seeds —"these are what we need to rebuild and survive. And we have them only because of this girl from Above."

The Chieftain had reluctantly given in, but although his word was final, the villagers never stopped staring at Elia.

"I'm surprised they find me so strange when I'm not the first person to fall from Above," Elia had said the next evening after her first full day of work.

"They've forgotten how the other woman used to look," Roahm replied.

"Why? What's changed?"

He shrugged. "She doesn't stand out as much anymore." He thought for a moment. "I guess her skin's paler, her hair darker like ours. We never see her down here in South Village anymore; we only hear the stories. Now people just think of her as that crazy half-wit, not the person who survived a fall."

They called the woman Koiyin. She was fascinating, an oddity, and she kept to herself. Koiyin lived in the more isolated hills of North Village, where she was originally discovered. She had dropped from an island of rock floating in the sky and had fallen into a bank of fresh snow, triggering an avalanche. The Torkin rescuers, who witnessed the incident, pulled her out and were amazed she hadn't perished.

"What's snow?" Elia had asked Roahm when he first told her the story. *Snow* was a word Hokk had never mentioned.

"It's like rain," Roahm explained. "Frozen rain that drifts down from the clouds. It's cold, and when it lands, it collects on the ground and everything is covered with white."

Elia didn't doubt what he said was true; she just couldn't imagine it. Since her own fall to Below, she had come across much that her mind could have never fathomed by description alone. Some things had to be seen with one's own eyes to be believed or understood.

"Don't worry," Roahm had offered. "We'll come across snow eventually. I'll make sure to show you when we hike up to North Village."

Elia was still eagerly waiting for that to happen. Not that she cared about seeing snow for the first time — she dreaded experiencing anything colder than rain. Rather, she was especially keen for Roahm to deliver on his promise to introduce her to Koiyin. If Koiyin represented the last remaining link to her old life, then Elia wanted to meet the woman as soon as possible, regardless of her eccentricities. Not only would it help Elia keep the memories of her home and family alive, but she hoped that bonding with someone who understood what it was like to live under sunshine and a blue sky would enable her to better cope with the lonely prospect of spending a lifetime among the Torkins.

Elia had heard of Koiyin's constant paranoia about people from Above flying down to find her, yet no Torkin had ever fully understood her concerns until, eighteen years after her fall, the Imperial Guards arrived on their winged stallions and set fire to the fields. Of course, the villagers had assumed the crops were burned to flush out Koiyin; however, the Torkin warriors returning from Ago quickly spread the truth that the guards were actually looking for Elia. How unfortunate this fact had to be shared. It changed everything.

Hopefully, with time, the Torkins would forget or at least accept Elia. And that's why she toiled in the fields, why she pushed herself so hard. Roahm was convinced that if she was going to have a life with these people, she needed to contribute just as much. Or even more.

So she dug. She hacked at the earth. She kept her head down and her arms moving at a pace to match Roahm's. The exercise and increased blood flow seemed to be helping. She could sense the effects of the toxin diminishing. Elia was built for this type of work, her sturdy body capable of enduring hours of labor. She had grown stronger since her fall from Above, both physically and in spirit, from all she had experienced and survived. And although food was heavily rationed, the regular meals helped immensely to give her strength. If not for Roahm, she likely would have received nothing. He made sure she had enough to eat.

At first, she hadn't known what to expect from him. His moods were difficult to anticipate, and while his boiling rage could catch her off guard, he was often quiet and pensive. While crossing the prairies, usually drenched by the rain as they rode their soggy bison, he quickly shed his warrior persona and Elia had grown more comfortable around him, whether he was riding beside her, sharing his food, or telling her stories about the life she could expect in the mountains. Now, back home, his expression typically reflected the seriousness expected of a chief's son, though his face was capable of flashing a huge smile that could change his entire look.

Elia guessed he was a few years older than her — maybe not quite twenty, but roughly the same age as Hokk. Like all Torkin men, Roahm had leather straps lashed around his arms and leggings, and a sickle tied to his waist. Matching the blade was a curved slice of metal that pierced his eyebrow, a symbol of rank shared by few as young as him. Several older men boasted multiple piercings. The Chieftain had the most, with metal adorning both eyebrows.

At this evening's banquet, Roahm would get his second piece of jewelery. Elia was not looking forward to witnessing its insertion.

Still digging, she glanced at Roahm. "Are you nervous about the feast tonight?"

"Nervous?" He didn't pause or look up. "I'll certainly have a good appetite."

"I mean the piercing you'll get afterward."

Roahm stopped working and straightened his back. "I'm ready for it."

"Still, it must be painful. Does it bleed?"

"Usually quite a lot." He noticed her face cringe. "But it stops. The bleeding and the pain always stop. Eventually!" he said, his face brightening.

That smile again.

Even when he was happy, Elia couldn't stop worrying about his plans for her. If things didn't improve, he might come to despise her for the complications she had brought to his life. As the Chieftain's eldest son, Roahm had always been admired by the villagers, but he couldn't escape bearing the blame for Elia's presence in Torkin territory. While his reputation remained intact with most villagers — there were rumours circulating that Elia had bewitched him — Roahm probably knew his long-term credibility rested solely on Elia proving her worthiness to live among them.

"I think we're done here," said Roahm. "Are you ready to move on to the next field?"

"I am," said Elia, tossing a last shovelful of dirt, then wiping her forehead.

"Let's climb higher."

Elia held back. She didn't see Nym. Her eyes darted in all directions. When had she last seen him? The little fox had recovered quickly from the toxin and had followed her into the fields, that much she was sure of. But then what? No matter how far his curious nose took him exploring, Nym always came back throughout the day to check on her.

I shouldn't worry, she thought. Yet while Elia knew the fox would be able to follow her scent, she couldn't bear to lose him. She already suffered enough regret for deserting Hokk in Ago, and leaving him for dead. Ever since, Elia had been carefully watching over the fox, almost as a way to console herself. She was protecting something Hokk had cherished and she thought of him every time she ran her fingers through Nym's fur.

Beside her, Roahm took a step away to start climbing. Elia reached out and touched his elbow. "Hokk, wait," she said, still surveying the terrain. "Have you seen Nym?"

Immediately, she felt his arm pull away. She turned to look at him. Her stomach became stone. While Roahm's smile could be dazzling, Elia found it very unsettling to see it gone in an instant.

"I'm so sorry," she gasped, raising a hand to her mouth.

Fury burned behind his eyes.

Elia swallowed. Her throat was tight. "It's just that I was thinking . . ."

Roahm turned his face away. "I know what you were thinking," he said, his voice seething. "And I've told you to let that all go."

"I have," Elia whispered, not sounding convincing.

She had called him Hokk twice before. The first time, he didn't mind; he even laughed when she told him who Hokk was. But it had happened again shortly after they'd left the prairies to climb into the hills. Looking back across the grasslands, Elia had seen an island floating in the clouds, and when she tried to catch Roahm's attention to tell him how much she wanted to someday return to Above, she mixed up their names. "My name is Roahm," he had fumed through pinched lips, squinting with anger. "Don't confuse me with that savage." Elia was startled by his reaction to what seemed an innocent mistake. "Getting back up there will never happen," he continued. "Forget about that place. You are lost to it. Learn to live with us. Learn our ways, or you will drive yourself insane. And if you lose your mind like Koiyin, then all of this effort will have been a waste, and there'll be no reason to keep you around."

Elia's resolve was strengthened by his bluntness. She had thought about his harsh words often since then, and though difficult to accept, he of course spoke the truth. She needed to face reality — he had simply pushed her along faster than she was ready.

Elia never mentioned Above again. If she saw an island suspended overhead, she didn't let Roahm see her wishful stare. It was easier just to ignore whatever drifted in the clouds because it saved her the pain of memories. Roahm could never comprehend the loneliness she felt for her family and former life.

It was so different with Hokk. He knew how desperately she wanted to return to Above. He understood her anguish. How could he not? As a young boy, Hokk had been banished from his city, condemned to suffer alone on the prairies. A criminal. No guarantee of survival. Years with little human contact. And after waiting so long, nothing had improved when he finally returned to Ago. He'd learned not only that he wasn't welcome, but that he no longer belonged — that he didn't even want to belong. He was at home, but homeless. Lost, though he knew every street, every ruined building.

Elia remembered her last image of Hokk — standing above, staring down at her through the hole leading into a tunnel under the city, his face grim. He had sealed the opening to protect her, but then what? Where had he gone from there? Injured, and with dogs hunting him, he would have attempted to hide. Did he get away? Was there anyone to help him?

No. He didn't survive. He couldn't have. Try to accept that.

Elia hated to consider him dead. She tried not to think about it, yet whenever she did, she was always reminded of her mother. Had Sulum struggled with the same thoughts about her daughter when Elia fell? Wasn't this a form of death too, ending up in Below, the final resting place for garbage and corpses tossed from the edges of floating islands? Opi, Elia's grandfather, was buried under the City of Ago, and her grandmother, Omi, was likely no more than a crumpled, decaying heap somewhere on the grasslands. The only family left to Sulum would have been a husband with a dead mind, and a son being trained to have a dead conscience.

What had become of all three of them? Had they been imprisoned? Were they even alive? Elia doubted it. Ever since falling from Above, she had feared that her own disappearance had very likely implicated her family in this whole mess, leaving their fate in the hands of ruthless Imperial Guards. It all began that unfortunate day when Elia discovered a blue ribbon tied to a bone in her laundry tub while working underground in the Mirrored Palace. It was supposed to be a sign, somehow connected to her family, yet before she could learn more, Mrs. Suds had been brutally arrested and hauled to the dungeon. Then, days later, a lady-in-waiting had given Elia an intricately carved wooden box containing a telescope that had been smuggled out of the palace. The woman warned Elia that certain people in Above would stop at nothing to track down the instrument because of its mysterious ability to reveal damaging secrets about the monarchy. Elia never doubted the dangers that the instrument could bring, especially after witnessing the lady-in-waiting's violent death and then being hunted down herself by guards across the prairies of Below. How she had managed to survive it all, she had no idea.

So consumed by her thoughts, Elia didn't realize Roahm had turned back to her. He must have seen the grief on her face because he held out his hand. Only then did Elia's head clear. She looked up. His expression was softer. Apologetic.

Elia had a sudden urge to shout, to cry, to explain, but stopped herself. It might make him angry again.

"Don't look so worried. Nym will find us," Roahm said in a more gentle voice. "And if he doesn't follow our scent, then the smell of cooking meat will surely draw him to the feast."

"Yes, of course," she said quietly.

"Certainly nothing will keep *me* away from the food!"

Elia studied Roahm's grinning face. For so many weeks, she had admired his smile, but had she ever seen a similar one on Hokk? A spontaneous, carefree, joyous smile?

No. Never. Certainly not a smile that wasn't infected with sorrow. And although this realization made Elia sad, she felt worse to admit something else.

She was no different from Hokk.

Chapter 6

ELIA FELT THE STARE BEFORE she was fully conscious of the eyes upon her. A tingling sensation made the hairs prickle along her arms. Though she wasn't cold, she shivered and shifted in her seat as she scanned the crowd of revelers. Then she spotted the man.

He hung back on his own, the orange glow from the bonfires illuminating his skin against the shadows. With his hair singed off and black designs drawn on his bare chest, the warrior looked threatening, yet nobody was paying him any attention. He had probably just returned from the prairies, rotating out of his duties to protect the borders and showing up in time to enjoy the feast.

So why did he have to keep staring?

Elia nervously watched him out of the corner of her eye. He wasn't eating. If he had already finished his meal, he still looked hungry. Occasionally, the warrior's attention shifted to the remains of the bison carcass rotating over the flames, but his gaze always came back to Elia.

She detested his scrutiny, so she stood up and moved closer to the fires. At the start of the evening, she had kept to the sidelines, relying on Roahm to bring her things to eat. She couldn't expect the Torkins to extend hospitality to her on this night of celebration. Now, sitting so obtrusively in their midst, with her short hair and dressed like a man, she expected others to shoot her looks of contempt and annoyance. Yes, some people glared, but surprisingly, most were too preoccupied to notice her. Good. But how long might that last? The food and drink were making the Torkins more boisterous, and Elia feared what they might do in their drunken state. Decide to throw her from one of the ledges rather than fill the stomach of an outsider? Roast her on a spit over the fire?

Reminding herself to control her imagination, Elia looked around for either Roahm or the Chieftain. Surely nothing would happen if either of them was in sight. She couldn't see Roahm, but his father sat with a group of people surrounding an old man who gestured wildly, recounting a tale that everyone was enjoying yet seemed to already know. Roahm's father laughed out loud above the rest.

Though Elia knew the Chieftain would have banished or killed her if not for his son's request, she still admired the man. He was not what she would have expected from someone with authority over such a large community. He wasn't fat off the labor of the villagers. His hut was the same as everyone else's, his food no different. Elia had seen him toiling in the fields, rebuilding banks, and working alongside farmers from the break of dawn till the end of each day, covered in dirt and sweat that left him indistinguishable from the rest, except for that same captivating smile that evidently ran in the family. Roahm was much like his father, and with the Chieftain to model himself on, Elia was sure Roahm would someday be an equally great leader.

Elia jumped when something suddenly brushed against her ankles. For a split second, she imagined the hands of the Torkin warrior trying to grab hold of her, just as she used to fear Scavengers clinging to the side of her island, waiting to pull her off. She quickly lifted both feet high above the ground, only to see Nym looking up at her, his tongue licking his muzzle. Elia released the breath caught in her chest and reached down, digging her fingernails deep into his fur.

"So you've finally decided to return," she murmured playfully, and the fox arched his back as she scratched. Elia wondered what he had seen on his wanderings, what life he led when he was not in her presence. She looked out beyond the edge of light that circled the bonfires —

He's staring again!

The Torkin had repositioned himself to afford a better view. Elia's forehead instantly glazed with sweat. *Leave me alone!* She was convinced this was the man who had shot the yellow darts at her by the lagoon. She glared at him. Like a cold, unblinking snake, he held her gaze. She struggled to maintain eye contact, yet failed, unable to stand the sight of him.

As she looked for another spot to change seats, Roahm sat down beside her, making her jump once again. "You don't seem relaxed," he sputtered around a mouthful of bison.

"I'm not," Elia answered quietly.

"What's wrong?"

Her eyes flicked toward the painted Torkin, but he had melted away into the crowd. "Nothing," she said, stretching her neck to see where he had gone.

Roahm held a meaty bone with juices dripping down his hand. "Have some." He tore off a piece for Elia. As she put it in her mouth, she noticed two young girls sitting in front of them, peeking over their shoulders to glare at her. One said something to the other that made them both snicker.

Elia clenched her teeth, certain of what they were talking about. How many times had she already heard it, how ugly she was, how she didn't belong. The females in the village seemed to be the worst for keeping the hatred toward her alive, and Elia suspected they whispered into the ears of their brothers and husbands to arouse their suspicions. *She's a demon herself. How can you trust a girl with such dark skin, as if she's been cooked over a fire? And her eyes! They blink closed, but still she can see you.*

Elia felt like kicking dirt at the two girls. The older of the pair happened to turn again as Roahm offered more food, so Elia grabbed his wrist, raised the meat in his hand to her mouth, and tore a large piece off the bone.

The girl scowled at her.

Stare! Elia wanted to yell at her. *Come on! All of you just keep staring at me!*

"Look how hungry you are," said Roahm, watching her chew, his voice sounding so much calmer than the shouting in Elia's mind. "This will help wash it down," he added as he handed Elia a flask.

She sniffed the opening. Barley ale. Elia had never tasted the stuff, but had seen its effects. She cautiously swallowed a gulp. The fermented brew burned a path down her throat, and she choked, her face twisting from the strange, musky aftertaste on her tongue. She forced herself to take another gulp and wondered how much her stomach could manage after the juniper root syrup that morning. But the alcohol stayed put, churning with the meat inside her gut. Several more reckless mouthfuls and she found it hard to focus her eyes.

Excited voices suddenly raised a commotion at the nearest bonfire. A number of young men — themselves flushed and stumbling from drinking too much ale — pulled apart the roasting spit and tossed the picked-over bones to the ground. Mangy village dogs, who had been waiting patiently all evening, quickly pounced on the remains and dragged them away. Nym jumped up from his place at Elia's feet and chased after his share.

The men started to slap their thighs with a loud, heartbeat rhythm.

"Here we go," said Roahm as a knowing grin spread across his face.

People stood and joined in, some with just their hands,

others pounding drums or banging pieces of wood together. Soon the very air pulsed around them.

Roahm got to his feet. Elia did the same, her concern growing. "What are they doing?"

"They want to start." Roahm's eyes widened. "It's time to get skewered."

Elia's chest tightened to hear his choice of words. She took another sip of ale.

The rhythm's tempo grew faster. Elia's heart kept pace. The Chieftain appeared and motioned for Roahm to follow. Along the way, he selected a few other men from the assembling crowd to join him at the fire. Including Roahm, five Torkins stood beside the Chieftain as he raised both hands. The pounding beat ceased with his signal. Everyone paused. Though the fires continued to crackle, even the wind seemed to wait for his words.

"My people," the Chieftain boomed, swinging around with his arms still in the air. "My people, tonight we feast to celebrate success. To celebrate survival. To demonstrate our respect and gratitude for the men who have returned from the prairies to families that need them. To a village that would be extinct without them."

Villagers nodded their heads. No one spoke. Drinking and eating stopped so all could listen to their leader.

"Almost a month ago, our very existence was uncertain. We were threatened by enemies, by weather, by a lack of food. But we banded together, as we have done many times, and we struggled on. Think of what we've been able to do over these many weeks since our men have come back. Homes and fields have been rebuilt. New crops planted. Everyone has sacrificed, but now we are safe. Or at least as safe as we can be." The Chieftain's voice changed, sounding grim. "A sense of security should be enjoyed and appreciated but it's never guaranteed. We must always be careful. It can disappear in an instant."

How many people shivered with his warning? How many imagined again the masks of the Imperial Guards, polished to a mirror shine, as they descended from the clouds on horseback? An attack from the air had been unfathomable to Torkins, who had always kept their territory so isolated.

But did any of these villagers, especially the returning warriors, ever give a thought to what had been done to the people of Ago? The ill-fated inhabitants lived underground, neighbors clustered together in tight spaces, looking out for one another, but all of them clueless about the advancing Torkins who had surrounded their decaying city. Elia had been one of those marauders, taking from others for her own needs and protection. The Agoans — Hokk's people — had suffered a similar fate to the Torkins, if not one far worse, when their buildings were looted and set ablaze on the same morning that an island of Above plowed through the city's core. Could the citizens rebuild after such devastation? Feed themselves? It had been so easy for the Torkins to forget about them and their individual lives when they retreated into the prairies. Ultimately, it was a ruthless lesson. Survive, whatever the cost. Enemies are always lurking.

Elia suddenly remembered the painted warrior. He could be anywhere, trying to get close enough to kill her. Lowering the flask from her mouth, she spun on her tiptoes, trying to see past the people who had pressed in on all sides. He wasn't lingering at the edge of the shadows and she couldn't see his bare chest or bald head anywhere. His absence was as worrisome as his presence.

The Chieftain summoned two young women, both sisters of Roahm, to approach the fire. The youngest held out both hands, which were covered with a red sash. Curved blades lay on top, each just two inches long. The older sister held a stick that she ceremoniously thrust into the embers. When she removed it, a flame danced on the end.

"Tonight, we acknowledge five men in particular. Their recent efforts have brought honor to themselves and their families," said the Chieftain. "These men dared to cross borders and risk their lives on our behalf."

The Chieftain picked up one of the small sickles between his fingertips and stuck the pointed end into the flame held steady by his daughter. Before his fingers could burn, he pulled away and turned to the first man to be pierced. "To mark your honor and our gratitude," he said, pinching the man's eyebrow and raising the blade.

Elia cringed as he impaled the metal through the Torkin's skin. The man barely flinched. A roar and applause erupted from everyone except Elia, who nervously took another long drink from her flask. No more than a couple of mouthfuls now sloshed in the bottom.

On down the line, the Chieftain repeated the same procedure. Each recipient received his piercing with minimal signs of distress. Elia marveled that Roahm, who would be the last, seemed perfectly calm, especially when the third man was pierced and drops of blood dripped onto his cheek. But the villagers applauded without alarm and the Chieftain continued until it was Roahm's turn.

"To mark your honor and our gratitude," he said to his son.

Elia turned away just as the metal shard stabbed Roahm's eyebrow. The crowd shouted their approval louder than before. Daring to look, Elia felt stomach acid rise into her throat.

Blood was spilling down Roahm's face. He made no attempt to wipe it away. And as if his father had not even noticed, the Chieftain continued to speak. "One blade for bravery, and a second one for leadership."

A second? Elia glanced at the young girl who had been holding the blades so stoically. Yes, there was one still left. Roahm hadn't mentioned any expectation of receiving two piercings tonight, but the Chieftain was obviously trying to reinforce his son's esteem in the eyes of everyone assembled.

"Wait!" said Roahm, stopping his father's arm before he could make the last cut. He wiped blood out of his eye, smearing it across his face, and addressed the crowd in a manner identical to the Chieftain's. "Thank you for this honor, but I am not deserving of a second. Not tonight, anyway. Yes, we had success, but my men and I were fortunate. We changed our plans when opportunity shone upon us. When we heard of the devastation in our village, and the loss of our crops, one person stepped forward with a solution."

"Oh no," Elia murmured, raising a hand to her mouth.

"It was something we could never have done by ourselves. It was a huge risk to lead us into the center of the city, but it made all the difference. And we have to be willing to accept her. You must join me on this."

No, no, no! thought Elia.

"So the person who deserves this last piercing is really not me, but —" Roahm spotted Elia in the crowd. "But that girl. Elia!"

All heads turned. Elia froze. It was too late to duck out of sight.

People stepped aside as Roahm approached her. Though his face was beaming, he looked macabre, as if he had been crying tears of blood. He held out his hand, also bloody, but Elia couldn't move . . . couldn't think.

"You must," he whispered, barely moving his lips, his own eyes widening with encouragement as if he expected her to run away.

That's exactly what she wanted to do, but she resisted. How should she respond instead? The alcohol was messing with her thoughts. Could this be the opportunity she needed? Singeing her hair had produced the desired result back in Ago, but the effect had not lasted long. Getting pierced could make an even better impression. It would demonstrate her strength and bravery. For a tribe that revered its warriors, it would be an honor to receive this piercing. But would it ensure her acceptance?

Elia glanced at the villagers around her. Every face looked expectant. Everyone recognized the significance of this moment. They were all waiting for her decision.

She mustered her courage. "I accept," she announced with bravado before striding defiantly ahead of Roahm to where the Chieftain was standing with his daughters.

Elia watched as Roahm seared the blade in the flame. She caught sight of a few eager faces in the crowd. They were waiting almost hungrily. Barbarians lusting for her blood?

Roahm approached, his expression serious. He pinched her eyebrow and raised his other hand above her face.

Their eyes locked.

Then his hand swung down. Searing pain sliced through her skin. She clenched her jaw. Her body shuddered. The hot metal pierced her flesh as blood spurted from the wound.

Roahm stepped back. His face broke into a smile, and just seeing it allowed Elia to relax enough to take a breath. However, blood began clinging to her eyelashes. She wiped it away and blinked to clear her vision. The sight of her trembling fingertips wet with her own blood made her stomach heave, and she struggled to hold everything down.

"To mark your honor and our gratitude," Roahm said, clearly pleased with her. He began clapping his hands above his head with the same rhythmic beat that had started the night's ritual, and the sound grew as villagers joined in. The energy of the celebration was building to its earlier intensity.

But then Elia saw a blur of yellow coming toward her. A dart! It didn't cut through the air as if shot from a blowpipe. Instead, someone had simply thrown it in her direction. The blunt feathered end hit Elia in the chest before bouncing off and falling at her feet. Nevertheless, the shock of seeing it made Elia yell out, startling those around her and sending a ripple of alarm through the revelers.

"Who did this?" Roahm raged as he shielded Elia, then pushed his way into the crowd like a territorial bull.

People jostled and argued under the effects of too much alcohol, trying to determine the culprit among them. Accusations flew. Shoving among some of the younger men turned to fighting, and their women tried to step in and separate them.

Elia wanted to get away. Warm blood was still running down her cheek, and she felt ready to vomit. She turned and raced off. Though no one followed, the shouting from behind made her afraid that she was being chased. She ran faster, moving blindly.

As she tried glancing back at her imaginary pursuers, she suddenly collided with an object blocking her path.

The object grunted.

Head reeling, Elia tried to focus. The light from the bonfires was sufficient to make out the Torkin warrior standing before her.

They stared hard at each other as Elia, weak-kneed, held on to him, struggling to keep her balance. She wanted to yell for help, but for some reason found herself unable. The fierce warrior opened his mouth as if to speak, but before he could, his bald head jerked up. Somebody was approaching behind Elia. The Torkin pulled free from Elia's grasp and quickly backed away into the shadows.

When Roahm reached Elia, he held her up by the shoulders. She was shaking. Her legs felt wobbly as if the bones had been removed.

"It's fine. It's over," Roahm said, turning her toward the celebration that had resumed. "The troublemaker who threw that dart just now was caught and has confessed. He's too drunk to know any better, though he's insisting he had nothing to do with what happened to you this morning. Whether or not that's true, his stunt tonight was unacceptable and nobody is impressed."

Elia was only half listening to him. She craned her neck around. "But who was that other man?" she asked, her words slurred.

"Who?"

"That warrior."

"I didn't see anyone."

"He's been watching me." Her lips and tongue felt heavy. Exhaustion was pulling her to the ground.

"You've had too much to drink yourself." Roahm frowned.

"No. He's was staring at me earlier. All evening. I think *he* was the one who attacked me at the lagoons."

"Really?" Roahm looked behind and paused. "If so, we can track him down later. Try to forget about him for now."

She couldn't. Her cloudy thoughts lingered on the painted man. As they walked back toward the bonfires, Elia tried breathing deeply to rid her mind of its dizziness. This was important. Think clearly. Though the Torkin had said nothing and his face was unrecognizable, something about him seemed familiar. She had to figure out why.

His eyes? Perhaps, but she would never have forgotten such frightening, piercing eyes. His touch? No, she was the one who had grabbed him, holding on to his arms to stay standing. Actually, his skin had a surprising feel to it, cold under her hand, gritty as if it needed to be washed. But there was something more. The skin above his wrists was thick, wrinkled in patches as if caked with mud, or . . . badly scarred.

Like the scars from a burn!

Elia immediately flung herself around, breaking free of Roahm's arm across her shoulder. Her eyes strained to see him, but Hokk had disappeared into the surrounding darkness.

Chapter 7

HOKK FLED THE BONFIRES, CHARGING up the carved stairs that connected the fields. He didn't care where he was going.

She doesn't know who I am!

Just a spark of recognition would have eased his mind. Elia's eyes haunted him now, the terror behind them, the confusion. Yet it was worse than that. Not just the blood on her face, but the squinting, hazy look as if she couldn't fully wake herself up. Or she was terribly sick. How bad was it if Elia couldn't even stand properly?

Hokk stopped to scan his surroundings. Though his eyes could make out things around him in the dark, this was not like riding across the prairies at night — here he faced the real risk of falling off a ledge or colliding with something.

Climbing higher was pointless, so Hokk darted onto one of the narrow fields, his feet sinking into the freshly tilled soil. It would be too difficult at this late hour to find his way back to his usual hiding spot, so his only option was to wait for dawn, fully exposed on this stepped hillside.

The laughter and shouting that echoed between the mountains from the bonfires below seemed to taunt him. Hokk looked down, but he could not pick out Elia from the others. It felt wrong that she was not with him. He should have grabbed her in that instant, not waited for her to realize who he was. If only he had said a few words to reveal himself. Unfortunately, Hokk had been so astounded to see Elia charging toward him from the crowd, as if she had finally recognized him beneath his altered appearance, that he had remained speechless, like a fool. And then that Torkin had arrived behind her too quickly.

He sat slumped on the ground now, his legs hanging over the edge of the terraced field as he watched the villagers. Hokk had imagined reuniting with Elia many times, but tonight it had all gone wrong. No relieved embrace as he had hoped, no joyous greeting or breathless explanation of what he'd come to deliver. He wanted another chance.

Thinking about their reunion had been his only comfort throughout his difficult journey, whether he was crossing the prairies or trekking into the mountains, trying to find cover. After his many years of exile, he should have been used to the absence of people, yet he had grown accustomed to Elia, fond of her in fact, and he knew he couldn't endure his solitude much longer. How had he done it before?

He had Nym before, that was how — the only other living thing he'd been able to count on until that fateful encounter with Elia on the beach. The day he had knocked her out cold. The day he thought a violent introduction was a smart decision.

Yet Hokk had not been entirely alone since last seeing Elia. He had left the City of Ago with two winged companions: a small donkey about a month old and a horse with silver ornaments braided into its mane and tail.

Hokk wanted his four-legged companions to stay as strong and healthy as possible because his future, just like Elia's, depended on them. Twister, the woolly donkey, was growing quickly and had learned to fly with such confidence that his hooves rarely stayed on solid ground. The white stallion's injured wing was healing well, and many new feathers had pushed through to replace the ones that had been burned when the horse tried to escape the fires of Ago. The animal was now capable of short flights, though Hokk could sense its eagerness and impatience to fly greater distances whenever Twister flapped around. Perhaps they could both feel the draw of Above, tempting them to return to their lives on the other side of the clouds. It was a world Hokk still struggled to comprehend, a realm that he wanted, more than anything, to experience for himself. Just so long as he could make a new life for himself somewhere far away from the one he had ruined.

Finding a way to get to Above, however, wasn't the only thing driving him. Hokk had also embarked on this journey into Torkin territory to find redemption for past sins. Too many people had suffered due to his obsession with fire. If he could make a difference in at least one person's life, it might lessen the burden of his guilt. He had therefore focused all his attention on helping Elia, no matter the cost, and he had envisioned the moment when he would finally be standing face to face with her, proudly showing Elia the horse and donkey he'd brought with him. Now all he needed was another opportunity to see her again.

It was amazing he had made it this far undetected. Weeks ago, after deciding to pursue Elia across the prairies, Hokk had understood immediately the importance of changing his appearance, otherwise he would never get past Torkin borders without being killed. Fire was the key. He needed to singe his hair. He needed soot to draw convincing designs on his skin. Unfortunately, he'd been forced to abandon all his belongings at the Junction, an ancient, overgrown rail yard, where he had almost been captured by his brother and Kalus, another previously exiled criminal whom Hokk had first met on the empty plains of Below. Left with nothing more than his tattered clothes, Hokk certainly had no flint to start a flame for the transformation he would need to perform.

So as he chased after Elia's kidnappers, Hokk had struggled to work out a plan. Luckily, the nasty weather forced the Torkins to slow their pace over the grasslands, and he caught up to the regiment more quickly than he would have expected. No doubt feeling overly confident after their successful assault on Ago, the Torkins had not posted lookouts for their makeshift shelters set up against the rain, and Hokk had been able to watch for his chance to strike.

That night, while a relentless downpour seemed to drown the prairies with an ocean, Hokk summoned enough courage to sneak into the outskirts of their sleeping camp. Tents flapped in the wind. Bison grazed. As an army of one, he knew he had to be fast. Get in, get the supplies he needed, then run away. This was not the time to try to save Elia. Even if he could find her, how would the two of them flee, pursued across the grasslands by a Torkin brigade mounted on bison? No, Hokk knew he had to wait for a better opportunity, rather than rush a rescue attempt and fail.

Hokk had proceeded to search the bison around the edge of the camp, hoping that not all of the Torkins' supplies had been unloaded and stored within the tents. He found several animals with sacks tied to their saddles. The bison raised their massive heads, calmly chewing as Hokk inspected the contents of their bags. There wasn't much, but at least he found a flint, some food, and a leather pouch filled with white-feathered darts. Darts were the notorious weapon of choice for Torkin warriors, though Hokk had no idea whether or not their tips had been poisoned.

With his meager provisions, Hokk had been ready to escape from the camp when suddenly, only an arm's reach away, a Torkin emerged from a tent to urinate, adding his own small puddle to the saturated grasslands. Hokk crouched low to the ground, but a moment later the groggy warrior realized he was not alone. Before he could shout for help, Hokk lunged at him with a dart clenched in his fist. He stabbed the man's leg just above the knee, then looked up to see the effect. The poison worked fast. Unable to raise any alarm through paralyzed lips, the warrior toppled over. Hokk didn't wait to see the Torkin's body come to rest on the ground. Instead, he dashed back into the prairies to find cover once more in the tall grasses.

Many days later, the Torkins finally arrived at their village. Ever since, Hokk had kept watch from a safe distance, tracking Elia's movements, afraid to let her out of his sight. If only he could lure her away or call her name. But still, he bided his time. Unfortunately, there were always too many people around, and that one young Torkin in particular kept close by her side. On several occasions, spying on her from an opposite slope, Hokk had noticed Elia stop her work to gaze out over the hills, and he had wondered whether she was looking for him — fantasized that she was. *It's me. I'm here. She wants to escape. She's dreaming about it.* But whenever an island of Above floated overhead, she ignored it completely. This worried him. Had she given up?

Then, this afternoon, he suspected he would get the chance he had been waiting for. When the villagers finished their day's work in the fields, they congregated in the valley between two of the largest hills. As Hokk watched them assemble large piles of wood, he guessed a feast was in the making, and knew he was correct when the bison was slaughtered for their roasting spit.

While the food preparations were interesting, nothing was more captivating than the bonfires roaring to life. With the *whoosh* of flames, a surge of adrenaline charged through Hokk's body and his suppressed passion for fire was fully aroused once again. Exhilaration replaced the horror and guilt in which he had wallowed for weeks. It was a self-inflicted punishment for all the damage he had caused in the City of Ago — not just the burning of the chickens years earlier, but the fires he had recently started in the Junction, which he was certain had spread wildly out of control. Tonight, however, he had been drawn to the flames like a hypnotized slave. He was amazed just how close he had allowed himself to get to the Torkins and their celebration. And then, seeing Elia there, he dared to move even closer.

His altered appearance had proven to be convincing. With the small fire that he'd been able to light earlier, using the stolen flint, he had singed his hair, and then, with the soot, he'd marked himself like a warrior. At the banquet, no one had paid any attention to him lurking on the edge of light that kept the evening's shadows at bay. The revelers were too busy with their food and drink. But Hokk knew he couldn't rely on all the Torkins showing the same level of distraction. If just one villager bothered to look more closely, the game would be over.

Now, in the darkness above the feast, a few speckles of rain landed on Hokk's bare skin as heralds to the mad torrent that immediately followed. Below him, the bonfires fizzled with plumes of smoke as people escaped to their huts. Nothing more for them to celebrate tonight.

Hokk pulled his knees to his chest. He rubbed his forearms to generate some warmth. He felt the ripples of his scars, but pushed away the memories of what had caused them. He massaged his bare feet, hoping to encourage blood into toes that were surely white. Tucked tight into a ball, he wiped his mind blank, attempting to shut down all senses as if to escape his body and the torture it would have to endure. He had mastered this skill over many similarly wretched nights. It wasn't sleep — it was his consciousness turned off. Sleeping in this weather was impossible.

A roar of rain. The trickle of water off the terraced fields. Whistling wind.

And muffled voices.

Hokk's head snapped up. The men were close. He held his breath as their voices grew louder. They were climbing the steps and only bits of their conversation broke through the drumming of the downpour.

"Could be on any of these hills . . ."

"Too much rain . . ."

"Bit farther . . ."

Hokk's eyes could not make out any movement from the levels below him.

"Chieftain says to keep the village safe . . ."

With no place on the slopes to hide, Hokk leapt to his feet, catching one last phrase before breaking into a run across the muddy terrace.

"Bet it's the same savage who followed us on the prairies . . . disguise will wash away tonight."

Chapter 8

IN THE DISTANCE, A FLICKERING light rose straight into the air, hovering high above the Baron's camp. Tasheira knew it came from a man on horseback holding a torch as a beacon. Though the flame was a mere pinprick marker against the night sky, Tash had been waiting anxiously since sunset to see it, knowing that eventually her father would discover them missing and have to send someone up — the search party would need a reference point to find their way back.

"They've started looking," Tasheira said to her attendant as she pointed to the signal.

Grim-faced, Marest looked skyward, but only nodded.

Tash cleared her parched throat. "Turns out I was taking us in the right direction all along."

Marest did not respond. She had been quiet ever since realizing they were lost.

Reading every tight muscle in her attendant's face, Tasheira felt certain she could trust the older girl's silence, which was essential for her plan to work. In the past, Marest had proven to be a very useful scapegoat for the stories that Tash invented.

They had left the crater many hours before, each carrying a piece of wreckage. Tash was convinced she knew the way back to camp, but the desert had changed, resculpted by the wind, making it impossible to know if they were traveling in the right direction. Though they had run out of water, Tasheira pushed on, feverishly intent on showing up at camp before her father returned from his dig.

They struggled through an endless afternoon, trying to protect themselves from the heat. The sun took its toll, roasting them until almost every trace of moisture was drawn from their bodies. Tash forced herself to continue trudging ahead, hoping Marest would be the first to collapse in the sand, incapable of going farther. She was. Tasheira stormed back and complained about being burdened by her, but Tash was relieved to drop to the ground as well. Shadows lengthened as the sun inched closer to the horizon, and after an orange dusk slipped into darker shades of blue and then black, the desert became chilly. The moon's many scattered pieces slowly climbed into the heavens.

Then the rider's torch appeared, shining like a star.

Now, Tasheira stood up and brushed the sand from her trousers. "Come on. Let's get moving. We should try to get closer."

"Maybe it's better to save our energy and just wait," Marest suggested.

"We're going," Tash replied firmly. She picked up the battered chunk of metal and foam she had taken from the crash site. Marest was slow to stand, so Tash held out her other hand. "Let me help you."

Surprised, Marest momentarily hesitated before accepting the offer. "Thank you, Miss Tasheira," she said. "My legs are so stiff."

"Mine too."

As she pulled her attendant to her feet, Tash deliberately allowed the large piece of debris to slip from her arm. It landed on Marest's foot.

"Ow!" Marest yelled.

"I'm so sorry," said Tash, quickly lifting away the heavy scrap of metal and checking her servant's foot for injuries. With light from the moon's glow, she could see the skin was torn and bleeding. Tasheira roughly brushed the sand from the wound.

Marest winced. "Leave it. It'll be fine," she said as she pulled her leg away.

"We should wrap it so you can walk." Tash removed her turban and began winding the fabric around Marest's foot and ankle, hoping the girl's toes would soon start to bruise. "I'll help you back, but don't worry. You won't have to carry anything this time. We only need the one piece to show my father."

The two young women slowly made their way across the desert, Marest limping and Tasheira clutching their battered souvenir from the crater. They had not managed to make much progress by the time one of their rescuers caught up with them.

Preceded by the whispering *swoosh* of its runners slicing through the sand, the sleigh flew off the ridge of a dune and soared into the air. It reached the peak of its flight, then glided down for a smooth landing before the wind threw itself into the sail once more. Straining against the mast that held it, the billowing white canvas was luminous in the moonlight. Beneath the carriage, the ski-shaped runners ran the sleigh's entire length, converging into a single curlicue at the prow.

Tash chased after it, yelling and waving her arms as she ran between the two thin lines of track left in the sand.

The sail snapped in the wind as the driver abruptly adjusted the rudder to turn the carriage around. This sent the boom swinging, and almost capsized the sleigh. It tipped up, sliding on just one runner, with the other high off the ground. The sail was released to prevent any breeze catching it, and the fabric tumbled into the carriage, burying the person below. The vessel ground to a halt, and gravity pulled the one side down with a *thunk*. The driver thrashed about as he fought his way free from under the canvas. Then out popped the head of Tasheira's cousin.

"Look who I found!" shouted Neric as he stepped onto the desert. He ran toward them. "Are you both alright?"

"I'm fine," said Tash.

"What are you carrying?" he wondered, with a nod toward the object in her arms.

"Something to prove what we discovered out here."

"Was it worth it to get so lost?"

"We're not lost," Tash replied coolly. "You're not out here looking for us, are you?"

"Of course I am!"

Tasheira shrugged. "We've known all along how to find our way back to camp. We're almost there."

"No, you're not! Not even close! Haven't you seen the beacon?"

Tash looked into the sky as if seeing it for the first time. "Oh! That's for us?" she said, feigning concern. "I hope no fuss has been made about all this."

"Are you crazy? You've been gone all day, and you didn't tell anyone."

"That's not true. I mentioned last night how I wanted to go looking. Weren't you paying attention?"

Neric frowned.

"And I told my mother this morning," Tasheira lied.

"She has no memory of it," her cousin replied suspiciously, even though everyone knew the Baroness's mind slipped in and out of an incense-induced fog, and her recollection of things was always unreliable.

Being Neric, however, he could not simply let it slip past. "Still, you should have told somebody else besides your mother that you were actually going to leave."

"Who was left in the camp to tell? Everyone was at the dig site."

"One of the other servants, perhaps."

"They don't count."

Neric sighed and shook his head with frustration. "Well,

I guess a ride back isn't necessary then if you're doing so well out here."

"But Marest has injured herself," Tash said quickly, pointing to her servant's bundled foot. "We had to travel slower because of it. Otherwise, we would have been able to return hours ago."

"I can certainly take her back with me," said Neric. "Of course, three people in the sleigh will really slow it down. We'd be lucky to return before breakfast. I'm sure you'll be fine walking back to camp on your own."

Tasheira pretended to look shocked. "Unattended?"

She would never let Neric win.

• • •

Tash and Marest flew along. Neric was somewhere far behind them, trudging back to camp on his own.

As always, Tasheira found the sleigh ride exhilarating. Nothing equaled the thrill of flying across the desert's surface, the *whoosh* of air almost cutting off her breath as it slammed into her face and howled past her ears to tangle in her hair. Fimal and Neric shared her passion, which was why the sleighs, specially constructed for this landscape, were shipped out to the camp each year.

Tash was handling the rudder. "Duck!" she called out, as a change in the wind's direction swung the boom to the other side of the carriage.

But the warning was unnecessary, since Marest had already flattened herself as much as possible. Having never ridden in a sleigh before, she was terrified, and Tash found her reaction amusing. Why couldn't she just relax and enjoy the ride?

The tents of the camp were now visible. Drawing closer to the beacon overhead, Tasheira could also see her father's excavation foreman flying up there on his light brown steed — the same horse that led Baron Shoad's entourage to the dig site and back every day. It was the only stallion allowed to remain on the island. The bleak desert could not sustain the entire team of horses that transported the Baron's family, staff, and supplies to this remote location, so the other animals were always sent back. There were barely enough waterballs for the people themselves to survive for the duration of the dig.

The number of horses assembled to get them here was small compared to the massive herd maintained on her father's estate. The family ranch, over two centuries old, produced thoroughbreds of such caliber they were always the preferred choice of any courtier, and the only ones worthy of the Royal Stables. Every year, the Baron would pick the finest specimens to deliver to the Noble Sanctuary, and the Twin Emperors would be the first to make their selection. In fact, the last time Tash had joined her father at court to sell their animals, the blind emperor Tael had taken the entire lot, leaving none for anyone else to purchase, including his brother. Decked out in his finery, the emperor had explained he wanted to reward his closest aides with the best fillies and colts for his tours of the Sanctuary gardens, since only they could describe, to his satisfaction, the beauty he couldn't see.

A few weeks from now, the Baron would be making another trip to the palace to market his livestock. Tash found it endlessly annoying that her father's reputation — and ultimately her family's overall status — was based not on his unquestionable aristocratic lineage, but on the horses he sold. It was beneath her dignity to be considered simply the daughter of a merchant, and the label was an obstacle she'd have to overcome if she wanted to rise through the ranks of the nobility. At least Tash would soon be able to take steps in the right direction — she had been invited to stay at the Mirrored Palace permanently, to become a lady-in-waiting. After assuming her new role, she'd be committed to doing whatever was necessary to outrival others, and then hopefully, before long, there would be no reason to casually dismiss her or her family as mere horse vendors. Yet the amazing opportunity to enhance her standing meant this was the last year Tasheira would be coming to this desert island. The last after so many. And, except for the sleigh racing, she would miss nothing about her old life.

No, not true. She would miss her cousins. Even Neric.

Reaching the camp, Tasheira released the tension in the sail's cords, and the sleigh quietly glided to a stop. The foreman hovering on horseback announced her safe return and summoned the rest of the search party with a startling blast from his horn. Everyone in camp stopped to stare.

Nobody appeared particularly relieved or excited she was back, except the Baroness. The curtains of her tent were swiftly pulled apart, and Tasheira's mother poked her head out. Her face beamed to see her daughter, and she stepped into the open, clutching the side of the cabana to steady herself. She let go and held her arms wide. Tash felt compelled to hug her. The woman smelled of spices, dried flowers, and smoke.

"Oh, thank goodness! You had us so worried. I've been sick with anxiety all day," her mother said with a silly smirk on her face. The goofy expression was unintentional, just her typical response, like that of a child who was unsure how to react.

"I didn't mean to upset you," Tash murmured, with a quick glare at her mother's own servant. They were always standing so close, right there! Intruding! Listening! Tash hated it.

The Baroness awkwardly stroked Tasheira's unkempt hair and patted her head. Then her body tensed, as Tash knew it would. The moment had lasted too long. Her mother was suddenly self-conscious, and her bleary eyes shifted to scan Tasheira's outfit.

"Pants?" her mother scoffed, holding her daughter out at arm's length. "People will wonder what sort of example I've set for you, Tasheira. You should change straight away."

"I want to see Father first."

Her mother's eyes flashed. "Yes. Good idea." She reached blindly for the side of the cabana, but her servant caught her arm to assist. "I'm sure you heard his voice booming across this whole godforsaken desert."

"Is he inside with you?"

"Ha!" her mother hooted.

"In his tent, then?" asked Tash.

The Baroness only shrugged. Her servant held back the drapes for her to re-enter the cabana, but she paused halfway through and looked at her daughter. "Tasheira, your hair's a mess. Do something with that too," she said with a dismissive wave before disappearing inside.

Tasheira spun on her heels to return to the sleigh where Marest was standing. She snatched the scrap of metal and stomped across the sand to a tent lying on the outskirts of their encampment. The tent was large, like her mother's, but covered in plain cotton instead of silks. The Baron's butler sat outside on a padded stool, arms crossed, patient but alert. Tash didn't acknowledge him as she pulled open the front flap and stepped through, hiding her evidence behind her back.

The Baron sat at a desk facing the entryway, his head down as he made notes in a journal. Pillows were tossed randomly on a bed, and two woven chairs hung from the rafters.

Her father's eyes flicked up but he said nothing.

"I'm back," Tasheira announced.

"I can see that," he said, continuing to write. Various artifacts were piled around him on the desktop, and Tash guessed he was sketching one of them in his notebook.

"Mother doesn't seem to remember that I told her this morning about leaving," she lied.

The Baron snorted. Tash couldn't tell if he was expressing contempt for her lie or her mother's befuddlement.

His quietness was unsettling. Either he was building up for an explosion, or considering whether to be lenient. She decided not to wait.

"Sometimes I get this urge for adventure," Tash explained. "I simply can't help myself. And I probably won't be able to prevent it happening again."

The Baron put down his pen and frowned. "I know the feeling," he muttered. "The compulsion to explore."

"Yes, exactly. And after what we saw last night, after the fiery debris that rained down, I just had to find out today what happened. I was sure a piece landed in the desert."

The Baron looked surprised. "Is that why you left? All that effort and stress on your mother to find a piece of rock?"

"That's not —"

"I forget how easily you get bored. I should take you to the dig site every now and then to satisfy your curiosity."

"No, Father, you don't understand. I found what I was looking for, but it isn't a piece of the moon." Tash revealed the chunk of metal and foam before he could say anything further.

Her father stood and came around the desk. Tasheira held the piece up for him and he took it from her hands, rotating it over and over. Several crumbs of yellow foam broke away and he rubbed them between his fingers, crushing them completely. He sniffed the remains.

"What do you think it is?" she asked.

He shook his head in bewilderment. "I have no idea." He scratched the black soot baked on the metal. "Strange that just the one side is burned."

"This is only one small piece of what actually crashed." Tash was pleased by her father's fascination.

"There's more?"

"Much more. What landed is as big as this entire camp!"

"Amazing! What a discovery you've made."

"But I can't figure out what it is. It's . . . well, it's hard to describe. No doubt it's from the moon, but it doesn't make sense."

Her father nodded knowingly. "Many things don't make sense." He handed the piece back. "I was foolish not to go out there myself to investigate. I'm proud that you did. Do you think you can lead us to the spot again?"

"I'm sure of it." Tasheira stood straight and proud.

"Then we'll have to return as soon as we're able to adjust our plans here."

"No! We *must* go first thing tomorrow," Tash said with sudden urgency. "There's more to find than just this scrap metal. There are people out there too. Maybe even survivors!"

Chapter 9

HOKK WAS WHEEZING AS HE climbed higher in the darkness and the rain. Yet he knew he'd never reach the top of the mountain. Overwhelmed by a throbbing head and spots flashing in front of his eyes, he lost his balance and fell to his hands and knees.

Hokk was confident he had outrun the Torkins, but he feared they had been close enough to succeed with a direct hit. He carefully felt himself all over for darts sticking into his flesh. Discovering none, he sprawled out on the ground.

Surely the Torkins knew he was trapped. They probably had men circling the base of the mountain to catch him no matter which side he descended.

Hokk needed a plan. The only thing he was sure of right now was that his escape would have to wait until the first meager light of dawn.

• • •

Hokk had spent hours anticipating daybreak, but unlike any morning he had ever seen before, this day did not slowly resurrect itself to its eternally overcast skies. Rather, the heavy clouds were split as if cut by a thin blade. Shafts of golden light shone down like celestial fingers trying to pry the clouds apart even farther. The angle of the rays lit only the very tops of the mountain peaks, while the valleys in between still slept in shadows. The lowest tip of a floating island of Above, its craggy mass of rock piercing through the blanket of haze like a massive stone dagger, caught the light too. All around it, the beams reached out to kiss each ripple of cloud cover until the swirling gray mass turned a glowing orange hue.

Elia's sun!

Hokk stared in awe. According to Elia, the sun was a ball of fire that traveled across the supposedly blue sky of Above . . . and there, he just saw it! Proof of the sky's existence! A sliver of blue had appeared for the briefest moment. Stunning!

The clouds closed in again. Hokk stayed frozen in place, feeling shaken to his very core. Lost in thought, imagining what an entire sky of blue might look like, he suddenly felt something moist touch his hand. Though he jumped, he knew in an instant it was Nym.

He picked Nym up, squeezing him close to his chest and burying his face in the soft, blond fur. The animal's scent triggered a rush of memories, just as it had done the day before. Hokk had been watching Elia work on a distant bank when Nym first found him, and he had clung to the fox for the rest of the afternoon as if there was a risk of being separated. Hokk had only released him later at the banquet to see where the fox would go. And Nym, of course, went straight to Elia.

How many times in the past had Nym appeared when Hokk needed him most? When there seemed no path to follow? Now, once more, Nym sat patiently beside him, waiting for his master to decide the next move.

Hokk had to act. While there was no safe direction for him to take to avoid being caught, he couldn't wait any longer. "Come on, Nym!" he urged. "Take me to Elia!"

Fueled now by both dread and exhilaration, he flew down the steps, charging toward South Village rather than running away from it. He hoped the villagers were still asleep from their late-night festivities, and that any patrols out looking for him wouldn't expect him to risk returning to the heart of their settlement.

With Nym leading the way, they soon arrived at a cluster of shacks and tents nestled in the cleavage of two slopes. Though this wasn't the main village, it still felt suicidal to traipse through their encampment. On high alert, Hokk began second-guessing himself. Silently, he and Nym climbed an incline, heading toward the shelters farther back. The fox stopped in front of one of the last. Hokk hesitated and wiped sweat from his forehead.

Was this really the tent? The one where he'd find Elia? Hokk could only gamble once. He looked at Nym for confirmation. The fox tilted his head with a quizzical look on his face as if to say, *Don't you trust me?*

Long, slender saplings were lashed together at the top of the tent and old bison hides covered the frame, stitched together and painted with faded black stripes and swirls. Entering through the front flap was riskier than sneaking through the back, so Hokk crept behind and lay flat on his stomach. He slipped his fingers into the gap between the bottom edge of the leather and the grass. Gently pulling up the siding, he slipped his head inside, careful not to dislodge any poles.

During the time it took for his eyes to adjust to the dim interior, he held his breath and listened. A body lay curled under a heap of furs. But was it Elia? He could hear light snoring that sounded more like a man's. Even the foot protruding from under the covers looked masculine with its dirty brown sole and cracked heel. Suddenly nervous, Hokk was about to retreat when the body shifted. The snoring stopped. A leg stretched and the other foot kicked out, coming straight for Hokk's nose. In a flash, he grabbed above the ankle and stopped the foot only an inch from his face. Trying to steady his nerves, Hokk focused on his pale white hand clutching the leg's smooth, dark skin. He recognized the contrast. His pulse immediately slowed and he let go of his grip as he swiftly pulled the rest of his body inside. No doubt anymore. This was Elia.

Thankfully, his noisy entrance had not disturbed Elia's sleep. Even grabbing her ankle had not woken her — she must have been sleeping very soundly. Hokk stopped moving to simply watch. She appeared so peaceful with her mouth slightly open, almost smiling, and her hand tucked up close to her lips as if whispering to her fingertips.

In no way did he want to startle her. What a sight he must be with black soot streaked across the skin of his chest and arms from last night's downpour. He imagined his face must look frightful too.

He should wake her with only his voice.

Hokk shielded her eyes with his hand. He bent close to her ear and could feel his breath bounce back against his mouth. "Elia," he whispered, pausing for a response, but detecting none. "Wake up, Elia," he said as soothingly as possible.

She stirred.

"It's me. Hokk," he continued. "I've come back for you as I promised."

"Mmm," she replied, though she still seemed far from consciousness.

But Elia was more awake than he realized. When she raised her hand to lower his, he jerked back with a start. "It's me. Hokk," he repeated quickly, worried she would yell out if she failed again to recognize him.

Yet no sooner had he finished saying his name than Elia was sitting upright with her arms around him, pulling him close. "Thank goodness," she whispered in utter relief. "Thank you for coming back." Her voice was choked with emotion. "I thought you were dead."

Compared to the previous night, Hokk was delighted by Elia's heartfelt reaction. With her body heat radiating against his bare chest, he held her in a tight embrace. One frozen ear, touching her flushed cheek, tingled as it warmed.

"You're going to get cold," said Hokk as he reluctantly pulled himself away and looked into her face. But something about her had changed. Even in the dim light, he could see that she was not well. Her head bobbed as her eyes seemed to roll back into their sockets. "Are you all right? Are you sick?" he asked anxiously.

"I think I sat up too fast," she said, her voice strained. "It's just hitting me now."

"You look rough."

"It'll pass. I think it's because last night I drank too much of something I shouldn't have. Now I'm paying for it."

Hokk was not convinced. "How bad has it been here?"

"I've been treated well." She was holding her head now with both hands.

He remembered her bloody face from the evening before. Her brow was now swollen and bruised from the piece of metal that for some reason had been stabbed through her skin.

"How could they have done that to your eyebrow?" he asked. "It's barbaric."

"I wanted to have it. To them, it's an honor."

Hokk pinched his lips, wondering how much she was holding back to save him the grief. "You should get back under your covers." He helped her lie flat again. "I'm sorry I woke you so early. I was afraid you'd be startled and not recognize me. Like last night. You looked so scared when you ran into me."

"I'm sorry. I was foolish not to realize," said Elia, clearly embarrassed. "I eventually figured it out, but of course, by then you were gone." Her face became serious as she studied him closely. "Wow, you look so different. Not how you disguised yourself — I don't mean that." She touched his cheekbone and then traced his jaw line. "You're just . . ." She seemed reluctant to say it, as if she were sad. "You look completely worn out."

"I guess I am," said Hokk quietly, glancing away while thoughts of all he had endured on his journey flipped through his mind.

"You must have risked everything to get here."

Hokk shrugged. "What do I really have to risk losing?"

"But to make it this far on your own."

"I haven't been alone."

Elia cocked her head. "You've brought others?"

"No, nobody else. Not other people, anyway." Hokk grinned now that he was finally able to say it. "I brought that donkey with me. Little, uh . . . Twister, isn't it?"

Elia sat up quickly again. "I can't . . . I'm stunned!" Then her head lolled as another wave of dizziness hit her. She reclined once more, but she was smiling. "I can't believe you were able to do it!"

Hokk's face shone with pride. "And even better than that, I also rescued a horse. One from Above. The kind that can fly. It was badly injured but has healed quickly and was able to make the journey too. So you have your choice for returning home."

"That's amazing! In fact, it's perfect! Since I last saw you, I've learned there's another woman down here like me. She survived a fall from Above, and she's been stuck for years with no way back." Elia's brow furrowed as she noticed Hokk's face fall with disappointment. "Wait, what's the matter?"

Hokk didn't want to say that his plans had suddenly been ruined. How could he admit what he had intended all along? "Who is she?" he asked, knowing he couldn't deny another person the chance of returning home when he had been so desperate for the same during his exile from Ago.

"I haven't met her yet. She's older than me, and she lives with the Torkins but in a different village. Farther north somewhere."

"And when do you think you'll get to see her?"

"I don't know. I sometimes wonder if it will ever happen." Elia placed her hand on Hokk's arm. "Please, tell me what's troubling you."

"Nothing." Gazing down at her hand, Hokk forced a smile, but fidgeted with the edge of her fur blanket. "This has all worked out as I had hoped. Now you and this woman can return to where you belong. You can finally see your family. It will be wonderful for you. But I'll find it . . . I just thought . . . it will be hard to see you go, is all."

"Yes," she replied gravely. She thought for a moment, as if considering how short-lived their time together might be, but then nodded, having apparently worked it all out. "I know . . . you should come with us!" When Hokk inhaled sharply, she assumed he was trying to interrupt, so she hurried to continue. "Just listen. It could work. Though the donkey can only manage to carry one person, the stallion can take two. The three of us could leave here together and then, before we fly to Above, we'll bring you back home to Ago."

"There's nothing for me to return to there. But I was thinking instead —"

"Then come to Above!" she said, beating him to it. She clapped her hands, obviously loving the idea. "It's so much better than Below. You'll be amazed. I'd have so much to show you, and then you could really understand. See it for yourself."

"I would like that," said Hokk, brightening. "I would love it, in fact."

"So Twister and the horse, are they close by?"

Hokk shook his head. "No, but they're well hidden. At the base of these hills, there's a very narrow, very deep canyon carved by a river that roars through the bottom. I've been keeping them in a cave that I discovered. I don't think anyone will find the spot, but what if I'm wrong? So we should go! Let's retrieve them right now!"

"Is it safe, though? You might get noticed. Maybe I should redo the designs on your skin like you had yesterday. That will make you blend in again."

"A disguise won't help anymore," said Hokk. "They've already discovered I'm here. Last night after you saw me . . ."

Hokk stopped speaking upon hearing a low growl outside. They both held perfectly still, listening. Elia's eyes were wide.

What was that? she mouthed silently.

"It must be Nym," Hokk whispered, confident enough to actually speak the words. "How much longer until everyone's awake?"

"Soon, if they're not already." She was keeping her voice low too. "I'll be expected to head into the fields shortly."

Hokk frowned. "Then we can't leave now." He scratched his singed scalp and looked around. "Maybe I'll stay in here until everyone's gone and then I can sneak out."

"You can't. Sometimes they come inside."

As if to prove her right, a man's voice called out, not far from the tent. "Elia? Are you awake in there?"

Elia and Hokk stared at each other in horror.

"Elia?" came the voice again.

"Yes?" she answered, trying to sound sleepy.

A hand outside started to undo the front flap over the entrance. "I'm coming in."

"No," Elia squeaked. She anxiously motioned for Hokk to leave through the back of the tent. "Sorry . . . I overslept," she said, her voice cracking. "Give me a moment to get dressed."

Hokk leaned forward to whisper directly into Elia's ear, and though feeling frantic, he kept his words steady and clear. "Slip away this afternoon when no one's looking. Meet me where they had the banquet last night. I'll bring the two animals so we can leave together. Will that work?"

Elia nodded. "I'll be there. Wait for me."

"Of course." Hokk wanted to say more, but instead he pressed himself to the ground and shimmied feet-first under the tent. Before his head slipped through, he took a last look at Elia, who was sitting up, clutching her tunic to her chest. And then he continued to crawl backward until he was outside.

Hokk was breathing hard as he faced the tent and crouched beside it. He could hear murmured voices within, but could not make out the words. No matter. He had finally made contact, Elia was thrilled to see him, and they had a plan. Now to make their getaway.

As he cautiously stood, Hokk heard a slight rustling in the grass. Assuming it was Nym, he started to turn when a hand reached around to cover his mouth and pinch his nostrils. The hold was so strong, he was unable to yell, unable to breathe. His head was yanked back. He tried flailing his limbs to alert Elia, but several pairs of hands grabbed him and forced him to the ground. A kick to the side of his temple knocked him out cold.

Chapter 10

ELIA HAD NEVER EXPERIENCED COLD so painful. Each breath left her lungs in heavy puffs of vapor, like traces of her soul trying to escape a body unable to protect it. Her teeth ached, and her jaw had stiffened. The frigid blade of metal that pierced her brow seemed to cut deeper into her skin like a device of torture. Her knuckles felt fused, making it difficult for her frozen fingers to grip her belongings, including the severed bison horn she had been asked to carry.

Roahm had warned her about the freezing temperature — had even suggested she wear something on her hands, which she unwisely turned down. The fur-lined coat he had slipped over her shoulders initially seemed more than enough protection, and for the first few hours of their trek, she was overheated. Now, however, the cold crept up her limbs and left behind a throbbing numbness as if death itself were inching toward her heart.

Roahm's decision to finally start searching for Koiyin had been abrupt and surprising. Earlier that morning, when he entered Elia's tent and ordered her to immediately begin preparing for the journey, she feared there was something else motivating him besides his long-standing promise to introduce her to this other woman from Above. Did he know about Hokk? Had he rushed her away to keep them separated?

Since heading out, Elia had also been worrying about not showing up at the spot where Hokk had suggested meeting in the afternoon. Perhaps he was waiting there for her right now. Or worse, maybe he thought she had changed her mind about escaping to Above. But what could she do? It was now more important than ever to find Koiyin if there was a chance for the woman to also get back home.

Yet how much farther did they have to go? From what Elia understood, Roahm hadn't planned to travel this far. North Village was their original destination, but upon arriving, they learned that Koiyin was gone. The woman had fled weeks ago when a messenger from South Village had appeared — a frightened young boy who had run the entire distance without rest, sputtering for air when he arrived to anxiously share his message that the Imperial Guards had waged an attack. Koiyin had not yet returned, and no one knew her fate.

So Roahm and Elia had continued on to find her, winding their way out of North Village on a switchback that took them deeper into the mountain range; it was the only direction Koiyin could have gone. Elia was glad she hadn't turned down the padded moccasins Roahm had offered earlier, though it felt strange to have something on her feet. Her first steps had been awkward, and she continued to feel unsure of her footing along the rocky ledge. The soft shoes sparked a memory from weeks before of her brother's struggle to wear new boots. He had received them as a volunteer Shifter, a position he had held for three years in preparation for his training to become an Imperial Guard. Under normal circumstances, he would have already assumed his new duties at the Mirrored Palace by now; but if things had gone terribly wrong for the family, as Elia strongly suspected they had, then that opportunity would have been lost to him forever.

Should she even hold out hope that he was actually alive?

Elia pushed the lingering thoughts of Rayhan from her mind. Remembering was too upsetting, so she tried focusing on the trail.

Roahm trudged ahead, bundled in his own fur coat. A backpack was suspended from his shoulders. Between them, Nym trotted along the narrow ledge, seemingly oblivious to the sheer cliff that fell away at their feet. Elia followed, carrying a sack containing the lady-in-waiting's blue dress, the gem, and the carved box with the telescope still safely stored inside. The sack had originally been Hokk's, and he had used it to conceal these items from Elia, knowing that the two of them would be summoned before the Board in the City of Ago. When Hokk revealed her belongings in front of the court's three ministers, using the items as bargaining tools to negotiate his freedom, Elia had felt crushing betrayal. He later tried with great effort to convince Elia of his true intent, insisting his ultimate goal had always been to keep her safe from Board members who would not hesitate to have her executed. Maybe a very small part of Elia had never been completely satisfied with his reasoning — until this morning, when she had learned that Hokk had risked everything to follow her into Torkin territory. Suddenly, she had all the proof she needed that he could keep his promises and could always be trusted.

Elia now wondered how much she could trust Roahm.

On they climbed. The trail became steeper and more precarious as they ascended. Elia could no longer look to the side for fear of slipping off and tumbling into the yawning chasm below.

"Are you all right?" Roahm asked unexpectedly, stopping to turn around. They had been hiking in silence.

Elia raised her head, holding back the fringed hood of her coat in order to see him. "I'm looking forward to the fire," she mumbled, surprised that words could come from a face so frozen. She licked her cracked lips and tasted the saltiness that had trickled down from her runny nose.

Though he had just asked the question, Roahm was not listening. Instead, he was distracted, gazing over her shoulder.

Elia turned too, feeling her pulse surge. Was it Hokk? Had he followed them to North Village and now along this terrible path? If Hokk had figured out where she was, he might be coming after her with Twister and the stallion.

Elia glanced at Nym, who showed no sign of picking up Hokk's scent, though she noticed the wind was blowing in the wrong direction. Her gaze returned to Roahm. Why was he suddenly so cautious? This was the first time today she had really sensed it, which now heightened her concerns.

His eyes flicked back to hers for an instant, and then again over her shoulder.

Could he read it in her face?

"I'm looking forward to the fire," she repeated, hoping to distract him.

Roahm's attention refocused and he moved toward her. His steps on the perilous trail were as relaxed as Nym's. "Let's see if it's still alive," he said with a hopeful smile.

He removed a glove and lifted the small covering over the wide end of the bison horn that Elia was carrying. Cut from a slaughtered bull, the hollow horn contained a large glowing ember that they had taken from a cooking fire before leaving. Roahm had assured her the ember could keep burning for a full day, and peering at it now, it seemed undiminished.

He carefully replaced the covering. "Good," he said, slipping on his glove once more. "If you can make it a little longer, we can get past this point and set up a camp for the night."

"Hopefully not stuck on the side of the mountain like this."

"No. We have one more bridge to cross, and after that, the landscape flattens out enough to set up some shelter. And a fire. Do you think you'll survive?"

"Of course," said Elia as she pulled her hood down over her pierced brow. "I have to."

• • •

The trail ended at the precipitous edge of a vertical drop, where a bridge should have been strung. However, nothing stretched before them. They stared at a wall of fog. It was as if they had reached the last corner of the world.

"Do we have to go back?" asked Elia with dread on her face.

"No, of course not." Roahm pointed at his feet, where ropes were tied to spikes in the ground. "The bridge is still here. It's been cut."

"Who would cut it?"

"My guess is crazy Koiyin. Probably to prevent people from following her."

Elia gazed out, but the opposite bank was not visible. "So how will we?"

"I'll get the bridge strung up again." Roahm chuckled as he saw the startled look on Elia's face. "I can do it," he added quickly. "I'll go down, find the end, and then climb up with it on the other side. Simple, right?"

Elia placed a hand on the wall of stone to brace herself as she carefully looked over the edge. She saw a ragged rock face with swirling clouds beneath. A reminder of Above. But this time without the fears of a Scavenger clinging to the side, waiting to pull her down to Below.

Roahm loosened the straps of his backpack and let it drop to the ground. He took out a length of rope and looped it around his shoulders.

"How long do you think it will take?" asked Elia.

"I'll be as fast as I can."

Roahm lowered himself and hooked his feet between the thick cords of the dangling bridge. They were lashed together so that, when hanging properly, they formed the bridge's woven flooring. Elia watched Roahm start to descend like he was on a ladder. He disappeared into the fog. The ropes groaned and continued to tremble for some time — then stopped. Elia stared down. Waiting. No movement.

She squatted on the ground and tucked herself into a tight ball, contemplating the possibility of spending a night on this treacherous ledge. She would not survive until morning.

Elia peered back along the trail. If there was ever a good moment for Hokk to reveal himself again, this was it. She concentrated hard, willing him to materialize around the last bend. If only he could show up and pluck her from this precipice. But maybe the terrain and climate had made it too difficult for him to continue. He wore so little clothing. Maybe he was waiting for her to return through North Village.

Or perhaps he had tumbled down a rocky chasm similar to the one that Roahm was now climbing into.

Elia glanced nervously at the bridge. Still nothing. Surely he hadn't —

Something overhead caught Elia's eye. For just an instant, she saw flapping wings! Several dark figures were flying high above the swirling mist.

Imperial Guards?

It couldn't be! How could they have found her in such a remote location?

Unless they had returned for Koiyin!

Her eyes wide with fear, Elia tried to make out the opposite side once more. Somewhere over there, Koiyin imagined she was safe. Had she forgotten that guards could come from the air? Cutting the bridge would do nothing to stop them, and now the poor woman was trapped, all by her own doing.

Elia cringed again to see another black figure fly past. This time, she got a better view and then laughed freely with relief. The echoing *caw* confirmed it. Crows!

The dozing fox beside her awoke and looked into the air to hear the birds' raucous chatter. Elia reached down, and with freezing fingers, scratched him under the chin as she had seen Hokk do so many times. Nym's eyelids closed with contentment until a faint sound alerted him and he raised his head a second time.

The bridge had twitched. Then it shivered again.

Elia held her breath.

Very slowly, the ropes pulled away from the cliff, stretching farther out into the murkiness. Elia pictured Roahm starting his climb, but only now thought of the weight he was carrying.

Eventually the bridge stopped rising. Was he done? The braided ropes sagged much lower than the taut bridges she had seen at other crossings. She sat patiently, watching, yet Roahm did not come back for her. After plenty of time had passed for him to secure everything and cross over, Elia began to worry. What had they discussed? Was she supposed to wait or continue on her own?

"Come, Nym," she said, making up her mind. Surely the bridge could hold all three of them if she met Roahm halfway across.

She swung Roahm's backpack around her shoulders and clutched her bag of treasures in one hand. The other held the bison horn. With a last look out into the fog, she took a tentative step onto the bridge. Then another one. The fibers creaked with the strain but held strong.

Elia would have preferred bare feet, to feel the prickly ropes beneath her soles so she could walk without looking down. Though she could not guess the height, since it was too foggy to see the bottom of the chasm, she still felt shaky as she stepped away from the mountainside. Control your fears, she reminded herself. Focus only on Roahm waiting at the other end.

Elia knew she had reached the middle by the change in the slope. She paused. Nym carried on ahead without her and vanished into the mist. As her legs absorbed the sway, she could see nothing in front of her, nothing behind. "I'm halfway across," she called out, but received no response.

Where was he?

Above her, a crow broke through the haze, surfing the crest of a strong breeze that plowed into the bridge, causing it to sway to one side, then tip back as if it might twist upside down. Burdened with Roahm's supplies, Elia lost her balance and instinctively reached out for the braided railing, releasing the bag — and almost letting the bison horn fall out of her hand!

"No, no!" she gasped as the horn's cover opened and the ember spilled out. Landing with a burst of sparks, it miraculously got caught between the knots of the bridge's woven walkway. The surrounding rope fibers, however, immediately began to smolder. Elia's throat tightened as she imagined the ember rolling over the edge into the clouds or burning right through. Or even more troubling, setting fire to everything before she could get off.

Elia dropped to her knees. *Stay calm, stay calm!* she kept repeating to herself. With the hollow horn, she tried scooping up the ember, but was horrified when she broke it in half. Using the cover instead, she tried to nudge the two smaller embers inside the container, succeeding only after several attempts.

Now to get off of this damn thing!

Elia struggled to stand and steady her legs while the bridge wobbled, rocked by rolling waves of wind. Picking up the sack, she noticed small flames where the embers had touched the rope. Since this bridge was their one route back, she quickly stomped them out, glad now to have covered feet. Only when the last few tendrils of smoke had drifted away did she hurry across the remaining stretch.

She was thankful to have solid ground beneath her once more, though her heart was beating against her rib cage like a prisoner demanding his release from jail. She forced herself to relax. The path in front of her was rough, though at least it widened out a short distance ahead. But still no Roahm to greet her.

"Where are you?" she shouted in a shaky voice as she started to walk.

Was that a muffled response?

Elia hurried forward. Rounding a bend, she was relieved to see Roahm standing on an outcropping that was flat and large enough to set up a camp. Nym was at his feet.

Again, his smile drew her to him, and unexpectedly, she found herself falling into his arms. Immediately, she regretted it.

"You're trembling," he said.

"I almost lost the ember," Elia replied. She passed him the horn. "Take it. I don't want to be responsible anymore."

His hands held hers, and he squeezed them as if trying to stop their shaking. "Your fingers are white. They're like ice."

"Can we get a fire going?" Elia wondered as she gently pushed herself away. She frowned to see the meager pile of branches he had already assembled.

"I've been looking for wood, but that's all I could find for now. There's very little out here to use."

"But I can't handle this cold any longer," Elia said between chattering teeth. She felt frustrated and embarrassed by her inability to cope when Roahm seemed to be doing fine.

One look at her anxious face, and Roahm wedged the bison horn into the crack of a rock. He opened his coat and unbuttoned his tunic. "Come closer," he said, grabbing her frozen hands. Without flinching, he placed them on his chest before bundling himself up again and hugging her to him.

Elia's face flushed. She cast her eyes down, now feeling even more awkward to be touching his skin.

But his skin was so wonderfully warm. A tingling sensation returned to her fingertips, and soon she could feel the calming rhythm of his heart beating against her hands.

"It's helping, isn't it?" he said.

"It is," Elia whispered. She felt guilty. She was glad now that Hokk had not followed to see this. Pulling away, she tucked each of her hands into the opposite sleeve of her coat, then stared at the ground. "Do you think we'll be able to find Koiyin tomorrow morning?"

"Probably," Roahm replied.

"I'll be so happy to finally meet her."

"I would have brought you to her sooner, but I wanted to make sure you had given up your crazy notion about returning to Above. I didn't want you to see her and have the idea come rushing back."

"No, of course not. I've resigned myself to all that." How little he knows, she thought. "I'm just surprised she's been able to survive out here for so long in such temperatures."

"She's probably found an old lookout post for shelter," said Roahm.

"Why wouldn't she just come back down to North Village where she's always lived?"

"You're right, it would make more sense. Perhaps we'll be able to convince her. But I warn you," he added with a grimace, "she won't be who you might expect."

"No?"

"You'll be able to tell right away. She's different. Down-right strange, in fact." Roahm could see the concern on Elia's face. "Just don't be disappointed. I can't say what state her mind will be in when we finally track her down."

Chapter 11

HOKK WAS TOSSED SEMI-CONSCIOUS into the icy water, and he resurrected as if struck by a bolt of lightning. His skin seared with pain. His chest constricted, and with every desperate gulp for air, water flooded his mouth. He flailed his arms but felt nothing to hang on to. His feet found no foothold. His head dipped under, then he bobbed again to the surface, choking. As he thrashed about, the intense cold made his limbs difficult to control. If his muscles seized completely, he knew he would sink.

While being dragged downstream by the current, Hokk made out several Torkin men following along the river's edge. They were laughing, showing no signs of initiating a rescue. A few young boys, carefully balanced on the slippery rocks, were trying to pelt Hokk with stones as he swept past.

During his days of exploring these mountains while tracking Elia, Hokk had discovered a number of different spots along the river, and with the waves churning all around him now, he knew he was in a stretch of rapids, approaching the point where the river would cascade over a waterfall. Would men be waiting for him at the bottom, eager to see his body dashed on the rocks?

Catching a glimpse above the surging water, he saw a Torkin standing waist deep in a quieter eddy up ahead, reaching out with a branch for Hokk to snag. He felt leaves and twigs graze his fingertips. He stretched to grab hold. As the man pulled Hokk closer to shore, more Torkins waded in to haul him out, wrenching his hands free from the branch. They carried him to the bank and dropped him on the gravel. Hokk scrambled to stand, yet no sooner was he upright than a fist plowed into his stomach. He doubled over with a grunt, though recovered just in time to avoid another punch. They surrounded him. He charged toward one of his captors, slamming into the man's chest, but before Hokk could pummel him, someone yanked back his arms.

The Torkins brought Hokk back over to the edge of the shoreline and, holding him by the ankles, hung him face down, just an inch above the flowing river. "Trespassing is forbidden!" one of them shouted. They dunked Hokk's head, and his nostrils filled with water. He kicked and fought to escape, and a burst of air bubbled from his mouth before he was lifted up. They held him under again, this time until Hokk was sure he would drown. At what seemed like the last possible moment, they pulled him out and he gasped for breath, snorting water and mucus from his nose.

"Why have you trespassed?"

"I'm just trying —" Hokk began to say, but they submerged him once more.

They continued this cruel, relentless pattern, asking questions, then holding him under before he could respond. He couldn't see through his stinging eyes. His lungs burned and blood raced to his head. Too exhausted to resist, his body soon hung limp.

When they saw he could no longer fight back, they stopped. "That's enough. We have to keep him alive. A little longer, anyway."

The Torkins pitched Hokk onto the riverbank, where he clung to the ground, shivering. He could barely lift his head, but when he did, he noticed men digging into the rocky soil several feet away. He was filled with dread. In a last effort to escape, Hokk began crawling toward the water.

"Watch him!" warned one of the men, and two of the young boys came to sit on Hokk's back. He collapsed, too weak to tip them off.

The Torkins worked swiftly to finish their hole, and Hokk steeled himself for what was coming next.

They were going to bury him.

"That should do it," said the man who had done most of the shoveling.

"It's not deep enough."

"Of course it is. Just throw him in there."

"He might get out."

"Have you seen him?" said the same person, pointing at Hokk still sprawled lifelessly by the river. "He's got nothing left. This hole will be fine."

They lifted Hokk by all four limbs. "No," Hokk groaned. "No." But they ignored his feeble protests.

Feet first, they dropped him into the hole. As predicted, the cavity's depth proved insufficient, so they pushed him down, forcing him to bend his knees until his shoulders were level with the ground. Dirt and gravel were shoveled in and packed around until only his neck and head remained exposed.

The perfect trap. He was entombed in his grave.

"Who's going to watch him?"

"We shouldn't have to."

"Someone might find him. She might come looking for him."

Hokk perked up. He struggled to see who was talking, but the men were standing beyond his field of vision.

"She's not in the village anymore," a Torkin replied. "Roahm took the girl away so we could deal with this guy."

Wait — away from the village? That meant Elia wouldn't be waiting for him and wondering yet again if he had abandoned her. And it gave Hokk time. That's what he needed, though at the moment, he had no idea how more time could help.

"So then Roahm's taking care of this?"

"Supposed to. But we'll bring the Chieftain here first anyway. He may have different plans than his son about how a trespasser should be punished."

Chapter 12

"I'M STUNNED BY ITS SIZE!" said Fimal, staring up at the wreckage.

"I told you," Tash replied firmly as she swept fluttering curls of hair away from her face.

Her cousin's transparent inner eyelids were shut to provide protection against the blinding midday sun. Standing with both hands on his hips, he sighed — he'd been sighing repeatedly since long before arriving at the crash site.

His obvious jealousy made Tasheira smirk. "Keep in mind, the wind has buried it even more than when I first saw it yesterday," she added.

In fact, the dunes had shifted enough to entomb one end of the massive object within a bank of sand.

"Congratulations for finding it," Fimal grumbled, followed by another heavy sigh. "I just wish I could've joined you. I should have been here too."

"I can't believe you climbed to the top. What were you thinking?" asked her other cousin, Neric.

"I was curious. Wouldn't you have been?"

"Well, I can't see how there will be any survivors inside," Neric continued. "We've waited too long to get here."

"I did my best yesterday, but it was too hard to reach them on my own."

"Them?" repeated Fimal. "I thought you saw only one hand."

"Only one *glove*," said Neric to correct his younger brother.

"Does it matter? One. Two. However many there may be, dead or alive, we have to find out," said Tasheira. She frowned as she tugged at the long skirt her mother had forced her to wear. "I'd rather be up there, though, than stuck down here watching."

Her gaze rose to the top of the fuselage where the Baron's men had pulled away enough of the foam and metal debris to widen the hole. The crew's one horse and its rider hovered above, dangling a rope that the Baron was now holding on to as they lowered him inside.

Tash could not suppress her resentment. This spot was her discovery. She should be the one investigating the wreckage, not her father. He had assumed full control of the site upon arriving, claiming it as his own. She should simply tear off her skirts, climb the metal hull to the top, and go in after him. Enough of this waiting. How would he even stop her?

"What's he finding in there?" Fimal called up to the men who were peering down into the hole.

One of them shrugged. "Hard to tell."

Hard to tell? thought Tasheira. Were there people inside or not?

"I'm going up there," she announced as she took a step closer, but Neric held her back, gripping her wrist.

"Tasheira, your mother would not approve," he said. "It's not appropriate."

Tash spun around. "Not appropriate?" she exclaimed, raising her other hand as if to hit him. "What right have you to tell me what I can do?"

Neric didn't flinch, which infuriated her even more. "You're not climbing up," he replied curtly.

Tash yanked her hand free and scowled. She despised how people had begun treating her. Actually, throughout the past year, she had noticed a definite change in their expectations about who she should be and how she should act. Certainly Neric had never been like this before. He wasn't her father. Why did he even care?

Tasheira longed for the freedoms she used to have, when she'd play with her cousins without worry, as though she were just another boy, racing the sleighs across the desert, flying kites, playing kickball, tumbling down the dunes until she were covered in dust, her hair a mess. But everything was different now. No wonder she was finding this trip more miserable than ever. And thank goodness too that this was her last year in the desert. She couldn't wait to finally live at the palace — she planned to do whatever she pleased, free from the scrutiny of her parents and cousins.

"He's ready," one of the crew announced to the man flying overhead, who then encouraged his stallion to rise higher into the air.

Expecting either her father or one of the crash victims to be lifted out, Tash gasped to see what hung at the end of the rope. It appeared to have a human shape, but it was difficult to be certain. The body was encapsulated in an entirely white outfit with excessive padding that made the limbs and torso extremely bulky. At the end of its arms were gloves like the one she had seen yesterday, while thick heavy boots weighed down the legs. Most surprising, however, was the large reflective globe sitting on top of its shoulders, enclosing the head within.

"What is it?" Fimal asked in amazement.

"It's a survivor!" said Tasheira, understanding in an instant the suit was designed for protection. Like pillowy armor, it would have provided enough cushioning for the person inside to survive a dangerous freefall.

The body was lowered to the desert to rest in the shade of a dune. Tash and her cousins raced over to watch as one of the crew members untied the rope so the horse could fly back to retrieve the Baron.

Her feet hidden by the hem of her skirts, Tash wriggled her bare toes in the sand. How thrilling to be here for the first contact, after unknown centuries, with a descendant from the moon who shared her ancestry. Tasheira shot a quick glance back at the fuselage, where her father had still not emerged, and she smiled to herself. Funny that she was the one here, waiting for the unveiling and the introduction. This was her moment, not her father's.

She peered down at the helmet, trying to distinguish the face beneath, but the mirrored surface made it impossible. All she could see were the distorted reflections of the other faces around her, as well as the blue sky and the ruthless, burning sun.

Tash grew concerned to see the survivor making no effort to move. Lying on the sand, his suit now appeared almost deflated, as if the poor person inside had shrunk from dehydration. "He's too weak. We should get him some water," she suggested, though made no move herself to find any.

"We have to figure out first how to get this helmet off," said one of the Baron's workers as his fingers searched around the neckline for a latch.

"Look. There's something written on the suit," said Fimal, pointing to a small badge on the left-hand side, just above the heart. He read out the embroidered lettering. "I - S - E - C," he said. "It must spell out his name. Isec."

Isec. Tasheira repeated the name in her mind, a sense of pride swelling within. This was the man she had saved. Soon everyone — not just her family but the Royal Court too — would know his name. Hers as well. She would be celebrated.

"There, I've got it!" said the worker. A click and a faint hiss of air marked his success.

"Quick, get it off," Tash urged, barely able to contain her enthusiasm. *Before my father gets here!* she wanted to shout.

Twisting the helmet halfway round unscrewed it from the suit. Carefully, so as not to knock the person's chin or bash his nose, the worker lifted it away.

Tasheira's hand flew to her mouth. "This can't be!" she gasped. No head!

Tash collapsed on her knees and pulled the suit toward her to look inside. She stuck in her arm, but could feel nothing other than the cool fabric of the suit's interior.

Empty. No body at all.

Chapter 13

"IT'S BEST WE DON'T STARTLE her," Roahm murmured as he halted and held up his hand for Elia to do the same.

Perplexed, Elia knitted her brow. "But she's already seen us."

"Still, we should wait. Give her space. Let her come to us on her own terms."

Elia looked up at Koiyin, whom they had just discovered on a slope about a hundred feet away. They had been following her tracks in the fresh snow for over an hour and noticed her as soon as they came around the side of the mountain. The woman now stood frozen like a crane, as if hoping to blend in with the landscape. It was an impossible feat, however, since the dark bison furs she wore made her stand out against the white hillside, where stunted trees and boulders were covered with last night's delicate snowfall.

Roahm sat on a snow-dusted rock. He still wore his backpack, and in his hands, he clutched the bison horn that had another red ember stored safely inside — they had retrieved it from the previous evening's inadequate fire. Elia sat beside him, leaving her own sack at her feet, and pulled her hood lower over her forehead. Not knowing how long they might stay here waiting, she lifted Nym onto her lap and tucked her hands under the fox's belly for warmth.

Koiyin remained motionless for a surprisingly long time before finally breaking her stance. She took a cautious step, then another, though it wasn't toward them. She crept like a feral animal, appearing to sniff the air for danger and glancing frequently in their direction or up into the sky. As if deciding they posed no threat, and seeing nothing overhead, she continued to explore the slope.

She climbed the rocky incline with a noticeable limp, whether from a recent injury or from her fall to Below all those years ago, it was impossible to know. Either way, it reminded Elia of her own mother's disability — a birth defect that had left one leg shorter than the other — and the thought of Sulum suddenly weighed her down with loneliness. From this short distance, Elia guessed Koiyin to be around Sulum's age, though she certainly didn't look like someone from Above. Not like anyone from Below either, for that matter. If her skin had ever been as dark as Elia's, it had since faded, yet the woman was not as pale as Hokk or Roahm. Her hair looked filthy and could possibly be blond if washed. Really, what her hair needed was to be shaved off entirely because it had grown into a wild mane, some parts frizzy, some matted, all tangled with debris.

Koiyin carried two large plastic bags, each bulging with more of the same bags crammed inside. Grabbing a bunch at a time, she was stuffing handfuls into holes scattered across the hill.

"What's she up to?" Elia whispered.

"She's blocking rabbit dens," Roahm replied with a half smile. "It's an old technique, but it works well."

As Koiyin roamed the slope to find every hole, she moved closer — either she was comfortable with her curious spectators or she had forgotten about them altogether. When she finally found what Elia guessed was the last burrow, Koiyin wedged two sticks into the ground on either side of the entrance and shoved a single bag inside with her fist. She wrapped each handle of the bag around a stick to keep everything in place, then she stood for a moment, admiring her work, before proceeding to climb back up the embankment.

"She isn't leaving, is she?" Elia asked, turning to look at Roahm.

He did not appear worried. "Keep watching."

The woman, however, had disappeared. They could hear nothing but the faint caress of the wind stirring the slender branches, each trembling under its thin blanket of snowflakes. They waited in silence. After a short while, Nym perked up in her lap, detecting something Elia's ears could not.

And then she heard clapping. It grew louder, followed by yelling. Soon she saw Koiyin charging down the hillside, dodging the few trees in her way. She ran and shouted like a mad woman. Only when she drew near did Elia realize why — she was chasing something. At first hard to distinguish, a rabbit was fleeing along a zigzag path. It was attempting to hide, but found its dugouts blocked.

In a blur, the rabbit dove into the last burrow, where the trap was set. The handles of the buried bag were pulled tight around the sticks, but Koiyin sprung forward in time to grab hold before everything vanished into the deep.

Once removed, the plastic gyrated wildly as the rabbit frantically squirmed within. From the outside of the bag, Koiyin grasped the animal's head, and with a flick of her wrist — *snap* — she broke its neck. The bag stopped moving. She pulled out the rabbit by its long ears and held it up for inspection before stuffing the plastic down the front of her coat.

Koiyin tensed, as if suddenly remembering her audience. She turned and paused before slowly coming toward them. She avoided eye contact and paid careful attention to her footsteps. As she hobbled closer, Elia could hear her talking under her breath, engrossed in an animated conversation with herself. She expected Koiyin to halt beside Roahm, but the woman ignored him completely and placed herself directly in front of Elia.

Her mumbling stopped. Koiyin looked up, concentrating with pinched lips. She flipped back Elia's hood and stared, allowing Elia to gaze back into a face that showed only traces of the beauty Koiyin must have once possessed. Her transparent inner eyelids were neither fully open nor closed, but stuck halfway across her blue irises, giving her a demented appearance. The skin around her eyes was heavily creased, her brows bushy, and her untamed hair streaked with bolts of gray. Three dark moles formed a triangle above one corner of her mouth and her cheeks had begun to develop jowls from the merciless pull of gravity.

Koiyin's hand reached out to touch Elia's face. Dirt was embedded under her cracked nails. "Careful, careful," the woman muttered. She traced the purple tattoo above Elia's eyebrows, then sucked on one finger to wet it before trying to rub the mark off. No success. Koiyin stepped back, but their eyes remained locked. "I know your father, don't I?"

Elia's heartbeat skipped. "Wh-what?" she sputtered in shock.

"The one they call the Chieftain," Koiyin added as she turned to Roahm.

Yes, of course, she was talking to him.

"You're right," Roahm replied. "The Chieftain is my father."

Koiyin nervously scratched her scalp. "And is this your brother?" she asked, nodding at Elia.

"No. *She's* from Above. Like you."

Koiyin's head twitched toward her shoulder. Recovering from the spasm, she looked more closely and ran her hand over the top of Elia's head, seemingly confused by her short hair. She flicked the small, metal dagger in Elia's eyebrow, which still felt tender in its wound. "I thought only boys got one of those."

"Special circumstances in this case."

"I'd like to get one for myself," Koiyin replied with a wry smile that showed one upper tooth missing from a row of stained neighbors. "I'll take yours if you're ever done with it," she said to Elia. Then her eyes narrowed and she looked back and forth between the two of them. "Wait. Careful. You're dark. Look how dark your skin is!"

"Yours was as dark too, years ago," said Roahm.

Koiyin looked down at her hands as if realizing for the first time she wasn't as pale as the people she lived with.

"I'm from Above," Elia offered gently. "I fell from one of the islands like you did. For me, it's only been a number of weeks."

"Above?" Confusion gave way to recognition and her eyes started to water. "Yes, Above," Koiyin murmured. The word seemed to trigger forgotten memories. "I'm so sorry this had to happen to you." She took hold of Elia's hands and pulled her to her feet. "But you must come with me. I've been waiting too long for this. I knew someday I would meet you."

Chapter **14**

PLEASE NOT WASPS! LET THEM be flies!

Whatever they were, they were furious. Hokk had been trapped with them since yesterday. A few hours after he was buried, a group of Torkins had returned with a large basket to put over his head. Lifting the edge, they reached inside with a plastic bottle, and Hokk had hoped for a much-needed drink of water. But no, that gesture would have been too kind. Instead, the bottle contained insects, already angry for being caught.

From that point forward, Hokk had been listening to them throwing themselves against the side of the basket, the buzzing of their wings pausing for only an instant before escalating to a more enraged, ear-piercing hum. As a form of torture, it was simple and agonizingly effective. The relentless sound threatened his sanity. Even worse, the insects would land on his lips, crawl up his nose, and drink from the corners of his eyes. He'd cringe and shake his head, but this disturbed them only momentarily and they would settle once more on Hokk's skin.

How many were there? Five could sound like five hundred. At first, he had contemplated sticking out his tongue, waiting for an insect to land, then sucking it into his mouth. Eliminate them one by one. Perhaps a good idea if total desperation set in, but he couldn't yet bring himself to do it. If these were wasps with stingers, then chewing them could be deadly.

The soil around him had been putting continuous pressure on his chest, another issue that made it difficult to control his anxiety. Since the previous day, Hokk had been drifting in and out of consciousness, even with the buzzing. He kept his eyelids closed and struggled to maintain his steady, shallow breathing. And although his limbs quickly grew stiff and numb, he would flex his muscles and then release them, shifting ever so slightly to achieve the tiniest of movements from whatever the ground would allow. He was not packed in as firmly as it first seemed.

With the fall of night, the insects had become less active, though never silent. When blessed dawn finally arrived and the morning brightened, only slivers of daylight filtered through the woven strands of the basket. Fighting his drowsiness, Hokk tried to stay alert for any change outside, any shadows slipping by, yet he could see nothing but the blur of insects ramping up their battle for freedom, more determined and ferocious than ever.

Guessing it was now early afternoon, Hokk pictured the river flowing past just a short distance away. If only he could get to it! He would relieve his tremendous thirst, then navigate along the water's edge, retracing the route to the canyon where Twister and the stallion were hidden inside that cave, its entrance halfway up the steep walls.

He let his thoughts drift back to the day he'd discovered the hiding spot — the same day he dared to fly on horseback for the first time. He had decided flying into the chasm would give him a view that the Torkins would never get on foot.

However, Hokk lacked confidence that afternoon as he pulled himself up onto the stallion's back. Could he really fly this horse? Command where it took them? Surely it was no different than riding a gazelk. Yet he wondered if enough feathers had grown back for the animal to lift a passenger. Either way, he had to risk it and find out before escaping with Elia.

ABOVE

Almost as soon as he swung his leg over its back, the horse was airborne. And Twister quickly followed suit, flying along with them. Fighting to stay balanced, Hokk watched the ground drop away as he clung to the horse's mane. Flapping its wings, the animal faltered at first, then gained enough control of its limbs to fly smoothly.

What a feeling! As if gravity no longer existed! Hokk had wanted to climb higher into the air currents, to swoop over the mountains, to find Elia and pluck her from the fields, then spiral up to Above while the Torkins stood dumbstruck.

Instead, fearing the horse would lose its strength, Hokk directed the animal toward the gorge. With Twister following, they stayed low, gliding just above the water as the cliffs narrowed in places to not much wider than the distance between each wing tip. Hokk looked for an outcropping or overhang to conceal them, but it was Twister who flew ahead and found the cave. He disappeared into it as if swallowed by the rock.

They had been using the shelter — just large enough for the three of them — for many days. Hokk enjoyed standing at its edge, watching the surging water below, its roar echoing within the canyon, a constant mist hanging in the air. Whenever Hokk left the cave to scale the cliffs to the top, he kept the donkey and stallion tied up. He took them out only at night, when no one could see, flying on the stallion to improve its strength and to practice his own riding skills.

The sound of gravel now crunching outside cleared Hokk's mind. He tensed. Footsteps stopped in front of his basket.

"So, he's under here?" asked a man with a grim chuckle.

"Since yesterday," someone replied.

Bare toes slipped under the edge of the basket, then kicked the thing over. The insects flew off in an instant, their buzz fading into the sound of the thunderous river.

Hokk looked up at three Torkins glaring down at him. The oldest was their tribe leader. The Chieftain.

"No, I don't recognize him," said the Chieftain.

105

"He's been lurking around for a while, keeping to himself," one of the other Torkins began to explain. "The people who first spotted him assumed he was one of us. But then when he chose not to eat anything at the banquet, they grew suspicious."

"Yes, that would have been odd," said the Chieftain.

"When they couldn't locate you right away, they told Roahm."

Hokk cursed himself for not taking some food. And his stomach had been so eager to taste the succulent meat, dripping with fat, as it roasted on its spit. Nevertheless, walking through the villagers, in the middle of their celebration, would have been a risk too daunting to take.

"I'm surprised you've kept him alive," said the Chieftain with a frown, turning to his men. "I would have expected him to be buried completely. Or better yet, for me to find just his severed head under this basket."

"We would have preferred the same," the second man replied, "but your son instructed us differently."

The Chieftain looked momentarily surprised before curbing his reaction. "What were his instructions?"

"To keep him alive until he had returned. To confine him so he could not escape. Where no one else would find him."

"And where is Roahm now?"

"He's gone to North Village with that girl," the same Torkin continued. "They plan to return with the crazy one who fell from the sky."

The Chieftain looked down again at Hokk. "But what does all this have to do with our intruder?"

"The girl knows him."

"Does she?"

"We found him crawling out of her tent early yesterday morning. Roahm had placed the whole mountainside under surveillance after the banquet. A number of us watched this young man sneak back into the outskirts of the village when dawn was still breaking."

The Chieftain was confused. "I can't imagine Roahm's plans," he sighed. "And I certainly don't like this situation."

The first man nodded. "We fear the rest of the village will turn on Roahm if they find out this trespasser has been spared. They may question his decision."

"As I'm doing now," said the Chieftain with a grimace. "However, I appreciate your loyalty to my son. I also thank you for your discretion. The fewer people who know, the better. And then, when he returns, Roahm will take the necessary steps to redeem himself to all those with doubts."

"What will you get him to do?"

"Roahm must set an example. This intruder has trespassed because of the girl, and whether she expected him or not, more people like him may follow. We simply can't have our territory invaded again. We might not survive another attack. That's why the girl, Elia, and this young savage cannot be left alive. They must face their death in front of the entire village. And their lives will have to end by Roahm's own hand."

Chapter 15

"I WARNED YOU NOT TO be disappointed," whispered Roahm, leaning close as they walked.

"I'm not," Elia huffed, feeling reluctant to admit the truth.

Koiyin had been limping ahead at a hurried pace, letting the rabbit dangle from her hand. Her whispered ramblings drifted back to them on the breeze. Several times she nervously glanced over her shoulder, wide-eyed, as if not recognizing the two of them and fearing they were in pursuit. Twice she broke into a run to get farther ahead, then resumed her steady gait apparently without any worries. At one point, she came back to Elia to touch her tattoo. "Careful, careful," she said grimly, her finger pressed hard against Elia's skin before flashing her gap-toothed smile and turning to lead them once more.

The woman picked up rocks along the route and stuffed them into her pockets, then emptied her pockets so she could fill them again. As if not bothered by the bitter cold, she took off her coat and tied it around her waist, only to shake it out a moment later and put it back on. Occasionally, she cocked her head as if alerted to danger, then laughed out loud. And now, coming across a dead tree, she brushed away the snow to break off a twig, which she pushed into her disheveled hair for safekeeping.

"I just feel sorry for her," Elia finally decided.

Yes, *sympathetic* was a better description than *disappointed*. It was unsettling to see Koiyin acting so strangely, her manner so unstable.

What had Koiyin been like as a young woman? Nothing about her now gave away any clues. Had her mind always been this troubled? Did anyone Above miss her or even remember her?

"I think she's leading us in circles," said Roahm.

Elia started paying closer attention. They had descended into a valley where the incline leveled off, where the trees grew denser and taller. Koiyin's footsteps were the only set of tracks ahead of them in the snow, so they weren't traveling the same route exactly. However, Koiyin had been taking frequent sharp turns, always to the left, as though slowly spiraling toward their destination.

"I think she's just making sure the area is safe first," said Elia. "That there's no one else around when she reveals her spot."

Elia was right. Before long, Koiyin stopped and beckoned for them to catch up. They had reached her shelter.

They could have walked right past it. Koiyin had built a crude lean-to against a massive rock, using interwoven branches as supports for the thick layer of leaves, moss, dirt, and plastic debris piled on top. A hole at one end was just wide enough for her to shimmy in, while the other end was sealed. Certainly a better shelter than nothing at all, which was what Roahm and Elia had experienced the previous night. They'd awoken, stiff and cold, to find their curled-up bodies sprinkled with snow.

Koiyin hid the rabbit inside her den and chased Nym away when his curious nose brought him too close. Dropping to the ground, she sat cross-legged to guard the entrance. Nym's disappointment was fleeting, however, as a new scent pulled the fox in a different direction.

It was good to rest. At this altitude, they were winded, and Elia could see everyone's breath hanging in the frigid air.

"Let's get a fire going," suggested Roahm. He surveyed the area for anything to fuel one, but since every loose piece around the site had been swept up to build Koiyin's nest, he simply yanked a few branches from its side.

Koiyin's eyes bulged as if she was worried he would dismantle her entire refuge. Rocking her body back and forth, she began anxiously scratching her scalp above both ears.

"Don't worry," said Roahm. "It's just enough to get a fire started. I won't take any more."

"Careful, careful. Watch him," Koiyin warned herself. "Careful. He's after you."

Roahm shook his head. "I'm not," he insisted.

This shut her up, but Koiyin's concern did not wane until Roahm successfully enticed a flame to grow, sparked by the ember they had been carrying.

"This fire won't last long. I'll have to find more wood," he said, nudging the ember into the horn again before standing. "If you clean the rabbit by the time I get back, we can cook your meal."

Koiyin bristled. Her eyes narrowed with suspicion as her scratching became more feverish.

"It's all for you," he reassured her. "This is your kill. We've brought our own food."

The woman watched him leave. Lowering her hands, she continued to stare after him even when he was out of sight. "Careful . . . careful. He's here for a reason," she muttered to herself.

"So that I could meet you," Elia explained.

Startled, as if having forgotten about her, Koiyin whipped around. "Why are you both here?" she demanded, beginning once more to scratch the sides of her scalp.

Elia wanted to pull away the woman's relentless hands, but resisted. Instead, she kept her voice as soothing as possible.

"Roahm explained why you had to escape North Village. But we have come to let you know it's now safe. Time for you to return."

Koiyin stopped moving, limbs tense, as she cautiously studied Elia. "But the guards were just here. How do you know they're not coming back?"

"It's been weeks now."

Koiyin slowly counted on her fingers — fingers that had strands of hair tangled around them. "I've only been gone for a couple days."

"It's been much longer."

"Not since South Village was attacked!"

"It's just so fresh in your mind, you don't realize you're wrong about how many weeks have passed."

A confused expression crossed the woman's face. "Yes. Perhaps I've made a mistake," she replied meekly. The film of her inner lids slid across her eyes as if to shield herself. She pulled her knees up to her chest and cast her sad gaze to the ground.

Realizing Koiyin's attention was shifting inward, Elia spoke quickly to prevent total withdrawal. "You said earlier you've always wanted to meet me someday."

Only the slightest flicker behind those eyes.

"Surely, though, you weren't actually expecting *me*. How could you?" Elia continued with a half chuckle. Yet something in the way Koiyin had said it before made Elia wonder otherwise. It gave her the shivers now as it had then. "I guess you'd be happy to see just about anybody from Above."

"It's been such a long time," Koiyin answered, barely audible. She looked up, suddenly seeming like a different woman. Her eyes were focused, her serious expression strained. "It's been years in fact since I've allowed any thoughts of Above." Her head twitched with an uncontrolled spasm. "Of course, half the time I don't even know what I'm thinking," she whispered, her words surprisingly lucid.

This was more the woman Elia had been hoping to meet.

"Now, today, seeing you arrive so unexpectedly has brought it all to the forefront," Koiyin added, flinching as if just acknowledging the fact itself was painful. Her damaged mind was fighting the memories.

"Haven't you always wished you could return to Above?" asked Elia, keen to dig deeper.

Koiyin frowned, trying to remember. "At first, I'm sure I must have wanted that." She started biting her lip as she grew increasingly tense. "But I also knew dangers were waiting for me up there . . . and I knew those dangers would come looking for me down here too. And they did."

"Actually, the guards descended to look for me."

Koiyin shook her head vigorously. "No! For me! You would be nothing to them."

"I have something they want," said Elia as she placed a protective hand on Hokk's bag sitting beside her. She immediately regretted the comment. Why spark the woman's curiosity? Luckily, Koiyin registered nothing, so Elia quickly continued. "What about your family? Do you ever think about them?"

Koiyin's face went rigid and her eyes glazed over. Pushed too far, too soon, she succumbed to her obsessive self-abuse, digging her long fingernails into her scalp.

This time, Elia reached forward and pulled her wrists down. "Stop. Stop this!" she insisted, feeling Koiyin's arms straining to be released. Elia persevered, however, until the woman's muscles relaxed. "You can't keep doing this to yourself!" she said, noticing the bald patches and bloody scabs on the woman's scalp.

Koiyin stopped, but her body slouched like a lifeless doll.

Shaken, Elia sat back and stared at the woman, feeling frustrated to lose the Koiyin who, just moments before, was willing to remember, willing to cling to sanity. To salvage their conversation, Elia debated telling her about Hokk's flying stallion, how it represented their one blessed opportunity to get back above the clouds. Just imagine her reaction! It might be enough to end this woman's grief.

But no. Now was not the right time. Roahm would return any moment and Elia could not yet trust Koiyin to keep such a secret.

"Shall we skin your rabbit before more wood arrives?" Elia suggested, glancing at the struggling fire. "Best to do it now, don't you think?" she asked, hoping to prompt a response. Koiyin only nodded, yet this was good enough. "I bet you're hungry," Elia added.

The woman perked up a little more. "I am."

As am I, thought Elia, knowing only a few dried morsels remained in Roahm's pack. "Can you show me how we do this?"

Drawing a deep breath, Koiyin trembled and her head twitched as if her body had just been freed from a demon who possessed it. She reached behind, pulled out the rabbit from her den, and handed it to Elia. "Hold it up by the back legs. I'll cut."

Koiyin revealed a knife hidden in the depths of her coat — probably the same knife she had used to slash the suspension bridge — and made circular incisions around the animal's knees, cutting just deep enough to pierce the pelt but nothing more. After making shallow slices along each leg, she pushed her fingers underneath the fur to separate the skin from the bone and muscle, then pulled the hide down, peeling it off as if removing a tight shirt. Koiyin cut off the head, leaving only the sleek, pink body of lean muscle dangling from Elia's hands. A slice down the middle of the belly opened up the cavity, and the rabbit's guts spilled out onto the ground.

Elia squirmed but did not look away.

"It gets messy," said Koiyin.

"I'm fine."

Koiyin paused, studying her as if with a new set of eyes. "You could almost be pretty if you were a girl."

"I *am* a girl," Elia sighed.

"Your hair's too short."

"Only because I tried fitting in with the Torkin warriors. My hair was much longer before I singed everything off."

"That would have impressed them."

"It did."

Again, Koiyin reached forward to touch Elia's tattoo.

Elia could smell the scent of the rabbit's fresh entrails on the woman's fingers. "You're really fascinated by my tattoo."

"How did you get it?"

"I received it at birth. Only certain people are allowed to have one. It allowed me access to where I used to work."

"When you worked in the palace," Koiyin stated.

Elia's mouth fell open. "That's right! How do you know?"

Instead of responding, Koiyin froze upon glimpsing something over Elia's shoulder. "Careful, careful. Quiet. Stranger approaching," the woman said, bowing her head as if trying to duck from view behind Elia.

Turning, Elia saw Roahm moving toward them with some wood. After adding a few pieces to the fire, he glanced at Koiyin, then looked at Elia and rolled his eyes.

Elia passed him the skinned rabbit. "It's ready."

"Rabbits always look so much smaller with the fur off," he said. "Definitely only a meal for one. It'll cook quickly, which is good — it's best we leave as soon as possible."

"Why? Are we heading back?" asked Elia.

"Snow's coming," he replied, gazing into the sky where the tiniest of flakes had started to drift down. "It'll get heavier soon. We should get below the freezing level before dark." He placed a hand on Koiyin's shoulder. "We're taking you with us."

Koiyin's head lurched up, and she pulled back to avoid his touch. "I'm not going anywhere!"

"It will be safer. I promise." Roahm winked at Elia before continuing. "The Chieftain fears there are intruders in these woods — soldiers from Above, in fact — and he sent us to retrieve you, to bring you back to South Village where we can better protect and hide you."

"Soldiers?" repeated Koiyin, her voice tense. "You mean guards?"

"They're back. I saw tracks in the snow not far from here where they must have recently landed. I'm surprised you saw nothing. Even more surprised they didn't find you."

Elia wondered if Koiyin would fall for Roahm's lie.

She did. Bolting to her feet, the woman kicked dirt onto the fire and hauled Elia up by the collar. "Forget the meal! We've got to leave now!"

Chapter **16**

THE LARGE, LAZY SNOWFLAKES THAT had been
floating down on the higher mountain slopes were nothing
compared to the heavy raindrops that now bombarded them.
Fortunately, the descent was much easier than the grueling
hike up, so they arrived back in South Village before nightfall.
Drenched and tired of being cold, Elia wanted nothing more
than to get under the warm animal pelts inside her tent.
Roahm, however, had other plans.

"Don't go in just yet," he said. "We still have something
to deal with."

"I don't mind sharing, if that's what you mean," Elia assured
him, having assumed all along Koiyin would stay with her.

"Not that. Come with me first."

"It's too wet. I'm exhausted." Elia opened the tent's front
flap and shoved Hokk's bag inside. Nym entered and shook the
wetness from his fur. He looked back, expecting Elia to follow.

"The light's fading. We'll keep it short," Roahm insisted,
catching her firmly by the elbow. "I'm not happy to be out in
this weather longer than I have to." He turned to Koiyin. "And
you stay here until we return," he ordered, as if the woman
were a child.

Night would soon be upon them, and Elia was not looking forward to finding their way back in the dark, in the rain, from wherever Roahm was taking her. What could not wait until morning?

At the edge of the camp, Roahm kicked the side of a nearby tent. "I'm back," he announced loudly, continuing to stride along. Looking over her shoulder, Elia saw two young men scramble out and hurry to catch up. "By the river?" Roahm asked coldly, and they both nodded.

As Elia was led across terraced hills and down steps to the lower valley floor, she sensed a rising tension coming from Roahm and his companions. It was very unsettling. Fists clenched and expressions stern, they stomped through the muddy fields as the twilight dimmed and the downpour raged on. She couldn't guess what had brought on their sudden hostility, and with each step she took, the knot in her chest tightened.

The soggy ground became more solid with stones. They had reached the river, now noticeably swollen by the rainfall. It crashed and surged around the boulders blocking its path. They were approaching an area Elia had never been to before, but if she wasn't mistaken, the steaming lagoons were only a short distance away.

Yes, the hot springs! That must be where they were headed. Perhaps Roahm's men had found evidence of the person who had shot the yellow darts.

A little farther along the rocky shoreline, however, the men circled an overturned basket sitting on the gravel beach. Roahm stooped to lift the basket, then tossed it aside. Underneath was a — what was it? In the fading light, Elia couldn't tell. At first no more than a silhouette, it appeared to be a large rock. Coming around to the front, she was surprised to see it had an ear.

This is a head! They had caught her attacker! Elia was here to identify him. Though she had seen no one while soaking in the pools that particular morning, her curiosity was now piqued to discover who this was, buried up to the shoulders.

Wiping away the rain that dripped into her eyes, Elia crouched for a better view. The face was in shadows. She squinted, trying to make out the puffy features of —

Hokk!

She gasped and lost her balance, falling onto her backside as her foot slid out from under her on the slippery stones.

As if struggling to maintain consciousness, Hokk slowly looked up at Elia. His sore, red eyes flared with alarm.

Roahm followed Hokk's gaze and saw Elia sitting on the wet ground, her hand covering her mouth. "Do you know this person?" he asked.

Elia tried to think quickly, unsure how to respond. "No," she decided.

"Why such a reaction?"

"I didn't realize there was a person under the basket." She raised her head to meet his stare.

"He was found sneaking out of your tent early yesterday morning."

Elia only shrugged.

"You weren't aware?" Roahm asked skeptically.

"I must have still been sleeping. Too much to drink the night before, and then the poison earlier in the day."

Roahm pinched his lips together, studying her with one eyebrow raised.

Feigning innocence, she held up against his scrutiny by not glancing away.

"The timing of the events is too coincidental. I'd say it's proof enough," Roahm finally said, turning to the other two men. "This intruder was first spotted in our territory around the same time as the attack on Elia at the hot springs. He's the one to blame. And he will lose his life for the crime."

Elia jolted. "I saw nobody that morning. It could have been anyone." She wished her voice didn't sound so desperate.

"But he's not Torkin. He's a trespasser," Roahm seethed. "Aren't you!" he shouted, kicking Hokk on the side of the head.

With the impact, Elia was sure Hokk's head would snap from his neck. Hokk let out an agonizing howl that brought vomit to the back of Elia's throat.

"The Chieftain has already come to see him," said one of the young men.

Roahm swallowed hard. "He has?"

"Earlier this morning."

Roahm stood straighter, bolstering himself. "Well, I suppose that's good. And does my father know I plan to have this trespasser executed?"

"Yes, something like that."

•   •   •

Roahm had escorted Elia back to camp with a tight grip on her arm as if not trusting her to return on her own. Now she sat dazed inside her tent.

Slowly, she registered Koiyin sitting opposite, waiting in silence. The woman had lit the wick in a dish of bison fat, and the light of the candle's tiny flame flitted across her aging face. She had already removed her dirty fur coat, and she looked thinner in her threadbare clothes. Yet there was more. She seemed very nervous — even a bit guilty? — as though Elia was now the crazy one to watch out for.

Maybe not crazy yet, but Elia was feeling ever closer to crossing the threshold. She felt overwhelmed by the image of Hokk buried in the ground. That swollen face. The suffering behind his eyes. How long had he been there? Hopefully no more than a few hours, otherwise his body would not be able to cope. Death could come quickly. Would he fight it or welcome its merciful relief?

Get out into that rain and save him!

Wondering if she could sneak away unnoticed, Elia cautiously parted the leather flap to peer outside. The entrance of a larger tent across from hers was wide open and there sat Roahm in full view with some other men. A small fire inside illuminated his eyes, which narrowed as he stared at her through the raindrops. She quickly dropped the flap, pressing the bison hide shut as if Roahm's piercing gaze could push through.

Options. She needed options. Elia chewed on a thumbnail and spat out the bits. Nothing came to mind. Was he going to watch her tent all night? Skip sleep altogether? Surely not. She would just have to be patient.

Elia looked down and realized her clothing was soaked. It clung to her body. Her sodden, fur-lined coat, borrowed for their trip into the mountains, was lying on the ground, with Nym sleeping on top. Koiyin's dead, skinned rabbit was nearby. Beside the carcass was Elia's sack.

Wait. The sack was open. Empty. The contents were scattered about: unusual plastic objects Hokk had collected, rope, the lady-in-waiting's tattered pale blue dress, the carved box. The lid of the box open. The telescope out, fully extended — *and in Koiyin's hand!*

"You have no right!" Elia raged. She lunged at the woman. "This is not yours!"

"Careful, careful!" Koiyin shrieked as Elia knocked her over.

"Give it back!" Elia shouted, saliva spraying from her mouth.

Nym narrowly dodged out of the way as Elia straddled the woman and began striking her again and again. Elia didn't let up, not even to see Koiyin's terrified face below her. Koiyin wailed and thrashed about between Elia's legs, trying to flip her off. Having the advantage, however, Elia wrestled both arms to the ground, pinned them with her knees, then dug her fingers into the woman's wrist until Koiyin finally released the telescope.

Instrument in hand, Elia froze. She stared at it, then down at Koiyin, who was whimpering, anticipating another blow.

I *am* going crazy, Elia thought in horror. Embarrassed, she pressed her palm against her forehead and glanced away, eyes watering. "I'm so sorry," she sputtered, wanting to say more but unable to think of anything.

How could she have just done that?

She carefully climbed off Koiyin and sat as far away as their small shelter would allow. She couldn't look over. Her actions were unforgivable. Irrational and irreversible. Whatever chance of a relationship with this woman, whatever level of trust Elia had established, was probably ruined forever.

The rain drummed against the side of the tent. The calming sound was such a contrast to their shouting moments before. Thankfully, their commotion had not summoned Roahm.

Head down, Elia began returning Hokk's belongings to his bag. Stuffing the torn dress inside, she noticed strands of Koiyin's hair tangled in her own fingers. She cringed and flicked them away, even more consumed with guilt. *This is what Below does to you! You lose your mind down here.* But to trigger such violence? It wasn't fair to hold Koiyin responsible for her actions when her thoughts were so often deranged.

Or so Elia thought.

"Now I understand why the guards were after you," Koiyin whispered.

Startled, Elia glanced up. "What?" she asked in disbelief.

Though Koiyin had scratch marks on her cheeks and one eye was bruised, she didn't cower against the side of the tent as Elia would have expected. Instead, she was petting Nym, leaning forward and gazing at Elia with intrigue, hungry for more information. "I know how it can be a struggle."

"I shouldn't . . . have attacked you," Elia said gingerly.

Koiyin gently touched Elia's arm. "It's difficult to adjust being down here. Remember, I've been through this before too. And surprisingly, my circumstances were much more similar to yours than I would have first guessed."

"You can't imagine," said Elia, wondering how the woman could show such composure so quickly.

"That's what I'm telling you . . . I *can* imagine. Your tattoo was one thing, but seeing what you carry in your sack explains so much more."

"I don't see how it can." Was the woman making things up?

"May I?" Koiyin asked, pointing to the telescope that Elia had collapsed and was about to put in the box. When Elia nodded, Koiyin expanded the telescope to its full length again. She looked through the glass at one end. "You come from a family too poor to own something like this."

Again, Elia nodded. "People have been killed for this thing." She remembered the words of Commander Wrasse when she thought she had lost the instrument to him forever. *Look inside and this telescope can reveal a truth that would topple the monarchy.*

"It holds a dangerous secret," said Koiyin, as if she had been reading Elia's mind.

Elia straightened up with a jolt. "Yes, it does! How did you know?"

"This telescope has a long history, one that has circulated for years. Probably since before you were born, I suspect. How old are you?"

"Sixteen."

Koiyin half chuckled and picked at one of the three moles that formed a triangle above her lip. "So young. And now you're left protecting something of such value."

"All I really want is to return it. To make things right."

"Careful . . . careful. You can't let it get into the wrong hands." Koiyin's head jerked with a neck spasm. She took a deep breath and rubbed her temples, but her voice was strained. "It's impossible to return the telescope now that you're stuck in Below."

"No, actually it isn't! I have a way for us to get back to Above. Both of us!"

Koiyin stiffened. She dropped her hands into her lap, and her eyes seemed to mist over. "Back to Above?" she mumbled vacantly.

"Yes!" Elia shifted closer and lowered her voice. "Someone has come to South Village to rescue me. He has a stallion that can fly us away from here!" Elia hesitated. "But he's in serious danger, and if we don't do something right away, we might lose our chance for good." She looked into Koiyin's eyes and could tell that she was losing her. Firmly grabbing the woman's shoulders, Elia tried to keep her focused. "So we have no time to waste!" she said, restraining herself from shouting. "We have to save him tonight!"

• • •

It seemed like hours since Elia had heard voices coming from Roahm's tent. She'd picked her lip raw, worrying if the timing was too soon. Or too late. But when the intensity of the downpour grew to a torrential roar, she decided to wait no longer. She peeked outside and saw the leather flap of the opposite tent sealed tight. They must all be asleep by now. Surely no one would suspect Elia of attempting to leave in such horrible weather.

"Careful. Careful," Elia whispered as she gently shook Koiyin awake in the dark, hoping the familiar word would avoid startling her.

Yet Koiyin was not asleep.

"Time to leave?" Koiyin asked in a hushed yet steady voice. "Back to Above?"

"Yes," Elia replied, wishing she had enough light to see Koiyin's expression, to assess the woman's frame of mind. "This is our chance." Elia paused. "But are you really ready for what's to come?"

"Get me out of here. I've waited long enough," Koiyin replied firmly. "Returning now is the only thing that will save my sanity."

"Good," said Elia, feeling reassured. "Then we must leave immediately and be as quiet as possible. No talking until we are far enough away."

They slipped out into the rain. Nym stayed close to Elia's heels as they crept clear of the camp. Her bag of treasures,

carefully repacked, was slung over her shoulder. Koiyin followed, carrying her skinned rabbit carcass.

Before heading toward the river, Elia took a detour to
the terraced fields, where they stole two shovels. Then they
descended the slopes along paths cut by rivulets of water. The
torrent from the skies, however, was starting to show signs of
easing, and the darkness of the cloud cover was slowly relin-
quishing itself to the struggling glow of dawn. They made swift
progress. And thankfully, whenever she looked back, Elia saw
no one in pursuit.

They heard the crashing water of the river long before the
trail opened up to its gravelly shore. Nym scampered ahead,
and Elia began to run too, heading upstream until they finally
came to the spot with the basket on the ground. Nym was
already sniffing under its rim. The fox looked up with pleading
eyes as Elia and Koiyin quickly approached.

"Hokk! We're here!" Elia exclaimed as she dropped to her
knees and flipped over the basket. She gasped and clutched
her throat.

No Hokk. She saw only a depression in the gravel as if the
rocky bank had swallowed him whole.

Chapter 17

KEEP GOING! DON'T STOP FOR *anything!*

Hokk's body ached as though he had been pummeled with clubs. His freezing feet had almost lost all sensation, and he splashed through the water, slipping and falling every dozen or so steps.

But at least to be moving! Hokk had nearly given up hope, certain he could never escape being buried in the riverbank. Luckily, after a day and night of hammering rain, the gravel around him had become saturated and the ground seemed to loosen its hold on his body. He tried to straighten his numb legs, crossed beneath him, and felt himself shift upward, ever so slightly, but enough for him to demand a burst of energy from his exhausted muscles. After repeated effort, his shoulders broke free, followed by his arms. Flinging aside the basket, he pushed with his feet and writhed about as if to escape the embrace of a squeezing serpent. Once he was fully out, he balanced on his legs, which wouldn't stop shaking, and kicked the disturbed gravel as smooth as possible before replacing the basket. No reason to make his escape so obvious.

Now, Hokk was traveling against the current with urgency, the strength of his determination making up for the physical strength he lacked. He moved through the shallow water, hoping to mask the scent of his trail in case dogs were used to track him. As he got closer to the canyon, the river narrowed and the bank on both sides became steeper, forcing him to wade through greater depths. But farther up that gorge, he would find the cave. Hopefully, Twister and the stallion were still safe inside. He couldn't imagine what he would do if they had been captured. And as the morning grew brighter, he also feared being spotted by villagers, so he had to push on.

Only when he had traveled deep into the canyon did he find a thin strip of shoreline at the base of a sheer rock wall where he could finally feel safe enough to catch his breath and prepare himself for the last leg of his journey. Unfortunately, the cave was on the other side of the channel, and the opposite bank was now covered with water. How deep, he wasn't sure. Could he successfully cross the river and reach the side of the cliff to start climbing?

Hokk knew he had no other choice. Taking only a brief rest, he continued through the rain, picking his way carefully over slippery rocks until he was upstream from the cave. Then, after leaping onto a boulder that jutted out into the river, Hokk stared at the current, trying to judge how quickly it would carry him. Would he be swept past the point where he wanted to get out?

Before he could change his mind, Hokk jumped into the frigid river. He plunged under the surface, but luckily his feet touched bottom and he sprang up with as much power as he could, erupting out of the foaming waves that carried him along. Down he went again, but now he began swimming frantically. The flow pushed him against a rock, which gave Hokk another foothold, enough for the final thrust that got him to the other side so he could cling to the cliff.

Now climb! Climb! Straight up!

He found ledges for his fingers to grab hold. He wedged his feet into cracks. Slowly, painfully, he hauled himself up the

rock face, certain at any second his frozen fingers would lose
their grasp, or his body would exhaust its last spurt of energy
and he'd fall into the turbulent river below.

Hokk groaned with the strain, and he looked up to see how
much farther he had to go. Rain dripped into his eyes. Inch by
agonizing inch, he ascended. The stone surface scratched his
bare chest and knees, and it scraped his fingers and toes raw.

At last, he thrust an arm overhead and felt nothing. He
slammed his hand down on the floor of the cave and grabbed
blindly for anything to hold on to. He felt a few loose pebbles,
a small puddle of water.

Do it!

Stretching as far as possible, Hokk touched a thin crevice
in the stone. He shoved in his fingertips, gaining a sufficient
grip, and —

"Raahh!" he yelled as he heaved his torso, then his legs, up
and over the edge. He collapsed onto his back.

Hokk felt like weeping with joy and utter exhaustion. He
tilted his head to one side and laughed to see Twister and the
winged horse staring at him from the shadows. He then rolled
onto his stomach, resting his chin on his arm so he could gaze
down into the canyon and the churning water below.

Elia was never going to discover him up here. And though
he knew he'd have to go find her again, right now he couldn't
imagine moving from this spot, let alone flying the stallion
over the Torkinian Mountains to snatch Elia from the fields.
Yes, time was running out, but first he needed to recover.

Chapter 18

ELIA SCANNED UP AND DOWN the riverbank. Could Hokk really have escaped on his own? Or had the Torkins moved him so she couldn't find him?

Koiyin dug her shovel into the gravel.

"There's no point digging," said Elia. "He's gone."

"Where?" Koiyin asked.

"I don't know." Elia looked around for Nym, wondering if there was a scent he could follow. She then debated returning to camp before they discovered her missing, but decided she couldn't — not when she knew Hokk had hidden Twister and the flying stallion somewhere within the surrounding mountains. He had said something about a cave, hidden in a canyon with the river flowing beneath. To find it, she and Koiyin would have to travel much farther upstream.

Maybe Hokk had escaped to the cave as well. He might be waiting for her there.

"I knew I'd find you here!" said a male voice from behind.

Bursting with excitement, Elia whirled around, eager to embrace Hokk.

"Though I'm disappointed I was right," Roahm added. His face was grim.

JASON CHABOT

Elia's joy evaporated. "Where is he?" she demanded through gritted teeth.

"Who?" asked Roahm, only now noticing the overturned basket.

"You know who I mean! How could you do that to somebody?" Elia shouted. "Being buried like that might have killed him!"

"All these weeks, yet you still don't seem to understand the seriousness of trespassing on Torkin territory," Roahm replied in a measured tone.

"Hokk was here to rescue me!" Elia saw surprise flash across Roahm's face, making her suddenly regret saying his name.

"That was Hokk?" Roahm asked. His startled expression twisted with a grin. "Not much of a hero to look at him."

"He's been struggling to survive out here," Elia seethed. "Who knows when he last had something to eat. And then you and your gang had to beat him up!"

"I did no such thing!" Roahm protested.

"You kicked him! I saw you!"

"I wouldn't have done that if I'd known he was this Hokk person you keep mentioning."

"Hah! I don't believe you!"

Roahm held up his hands, palms forward, to calm her. "There's no need to get so worked up. You're not thinking clearly."

"Are you insane?" Elia demanded.

"Me? How about you?"

"Just let us go! Koiyin too! Hokk's here to take us to Above, so why stop him? This way, you'll finally be rid of your wretched trespassers — every single one of us! Then won't your father be so *pleased* with you!" she mocked.

Roahm looked confused. "How can Hokk possibly take you back to Above?"

"He's brought a stallion and a donkey that can fly us away," she replied hotly, though realized again too late this was another piece of information she should have kept to herself.

132

"Do you really believe that's true?" Roahm frowned and shook his head, looking at her as if she were a fool. "How could he have brought animals all this way without anybody noticing?"

Elia scowled.

"Come on — tell me how?" he challenged.

"I don't know," Elia admitted reluctantly. She shot a glance at Koiyin, who was hanging back close to the river, then returned her gaze to Roahm. "But I trust him."

Roahm took a step toward her.

Elia raised her shovel, ready to strike. "Don't move any closer."

Roahm's face softened. "But you have to understand my position. What if Hokk has come here to spy on our villages? He might be providing information to an Agoan army hoping to retaliate for what we did in their city."

Elia paused. Yes, she could imagine how Roahm might suspect that.

Hesitating, however, had been a mistake. Before Elia could react, Roahm leapt forward and flung her shovel away. He wrapped his arms around her body. She kicked and yelled and struggled to bite him, yet he held her tight. As they wrestled, she realized he was trying to trip her with one of his legs, to get her onto the ground. To stop him, she kneed him in the groin.

Roahm hollered and released his hold. He backed away, but even in pain, he charged at her once more.

Though Elia's hand shot out toward his head, she did not hit him. Instead, she grabbed one of his eyebrow piercings and pulled. She could feel it rip through his skin as if to slice open his face. Then the blade tore free.

Roahm froze.

Elia's mouth hung aghast. She looked at the bloody piece of metal between her fingertips, then slowly raised her eyes to Roahm's face. A bleeding, gaping gash, several inches long, ran from the corner of his brow down past his cheekbone.

Roahm stared at her as if he had been utterly betrayed.

Elia swallowed hard. "I'm sorry," she whispered.

Roahm said nothing, but she could read the rage in his face.

"You shouldn't have attacked me," she explained. "What did I do to deserve it?"

"And what have I done to deserve *this*?" he demanded. "I tried everything I could to keep you safe. I stood up for you. Gave you food. Shelter. And it all meant . . . nothing!"

Elia wrung her hands. "I know," she said. "It's true. You've done so much. But if you could only —"

A loud *crack* made them both go rigid. An instant later, Elia saw Roahm's eyes roll back into his head. His knees buckled, then his legs gave out completely as he toppled to the ground.

Behind him stood Koiyin.

"Careful . . . careful," she said, holding her shovel firmly in both hands. She looked proudly at the body collapsed at her feet.

"Why did you do that?" Elia gasped.

"He's a dangerous man," the woman replied as her head twitched. "He was going to harm us."

Was he really? wondered Elia. Or would he have eventually understood and helped them?

Feeling numb, Elia looked down at Roahm. He was unconscious. His damaged face appeared lifeless, and blood pooled in his eye socket.

"You gonna keep that?" asked Koiyin, distracted by the metal piercing that Elia was still holding.

Elia refocused. "Keep what?" she asked.

"I've always wanted one," said Koiyin with a wry smile as she snatched the blade and wiped it clean on her clothing before hiding it in a pocket. She then grew serious and stabbed a finger at Elia. "He almost had you."

"No he didn't."

"You're too trusting."

"I'm not!"

"You are," Koiyin shot back. "And you must stop questioning yourself. Act, but act with conviction! Follow through and don't let doubt get in the way. Otherwise, people will make sure it's the end of you."

Chapter **19**

HOKK ... HOKK ... HOKK ...

At first, he thought his name was echoing in a dream. But then he realized that sleep had slipped away and he was half-awake. He tried to listen more closely, though his one ear was still ringing from that kick to the side of his head.

Hokk.

Someone was calling for him! The voice sounded distant and ethereal, drifting up to where he lay sprawled on the stone floor. A familiar voice. A female's voice.

Wait, it could only be — Elia!

Hokk sat up with a jolt. Hearing her call his name again, he pulled himself to the edge of the cave and peered over. Yes, there she was! She was carefully working her way upstream as he had done. She carried his old sack strapped to her shoulders, and he could see Nym's head poking out from the top. Farther behind, Elia was being followed by a wild-looking woman.

Hokk frowned. That's right. There would be three of them flying to Above. He glanced back at his winged companions resting in the depths of the cave and wondered again how they'd manage. Twister would never be able to carry the full weight of a person, certainly not across the distance they'd have to cover to get above the clouds. And although the stallion's injured wing was definitely much improved, could the animal handle *three* passengers?

"Elia, up here," he called down.

Hokk could see them both gaze overhead, searching the walls of the canyon for the source of his voice. Hokk waved, and when she saw him, Elia enthusiastically waved back. "We're coming!" she shouted, the words reverberating between the cliffs.

Hokk held a finger to his lips, gesturing to Elia to avoid any unnecessary noise. He nervously surveyed the top of the canyon, expecting to see Torkins ready to shoot their poisoned darts.

That gave him an idea. He crawled back from the edge of the cave and retrieved the few white-feathered darts he had stolen that rainy night on the prairies after sneaking into the Torkin camp. The small spears were safely stored in a leather pouch tied around the stallion's neck. He carefully removed and inspected each of them. Seeing the faint remnants of blood on one, he knew this was the projectile he had used to take down the unsuspecting warrior who had stepped outside his tent to urinate. Since there was likely no trace of toxin remaining on the sharp tip, Hokk tugged out a few of the dart's feathers so he could easily distinguish it from the others. He then returned them all to the pouch, which he secured around his waist.

He went back to the cave's entrance and looked down. They were both climbing out of the river, directly below him. Elia started climbing first, yet her progress was slow, her fingers less confident than his had been to grip the rock and pull herself higher. Her face showed the strain, but at one point, she looked up at Hokk and smiled. "I knew ... you'd be here ... waiting for us!" she called out.

Again, he placed a finger on his lips to caution her. Farther below Elia, he glimpsed the other woman struggling to ascend the cliff too.

Once Elia had almost reached him, Hokk lay flat on his stomach and stretched down his arms. "You're nearly there!" he said eagerly. He could see she was drenched.

Moments later, her hands were in his and he was pulling her higher. He rose to his knees and dragged her safely over the edge. As they both stood, Elia immediately dropped the sack and embraced him. "Thank you. Thank you," she said, her soaked chest heaving against his. Nym scrambled out of the bag and balanced his front paws on Hokk's leg, his fuzzy rump shaking with the excitement of his wagging tail.

Elia must have peered over Hokk's shoulder, because she broke free and hurried deeper into the cave, delighted to see the donkey and stallion. "You did it, just like you said!" she exclaimed as she began petting Twister. "Koiyin and I will never be able to repay you for what you've done for us!"

Hokk glanced over the side. The woman, Koiyin, was getting much closer. He could see twigs and leaves tangled in her matted hair, but he also noticed bald, scabby spots at her temples. Her head seemed to sit crooked upon her neck, and she had moles over her mouth and a missing tooth.

"Come on, Koiyin. Keep climbing!" Elia encouraged as she came to the edge with Twister.

"Stay back!" Hokk growled, whipping around on Elia. Startled, she staggered backward. "I'm sorry," he added, trying to calm his voice. "We just can't risk anything. I'm afraid Torkins might have followed you here."

Elia's eyes widened. "We didn't see anyone."

"You can't be sure. It's best you stay out of view." He nodded toward his sack on the ground. "Take my bag and tie it to the stallion's saddle so we can get out of here."

Twister stood beside Hokk and peered curiously over the edge. Hokk flattened himself again and glanced down at Koiyin. She was almost within reach.

Feeling the darts under his hipbone, he shifted the pouch and opened the flap. With his fingertips, he felt for the dart with the missing feathers. Pulling it out, he laid it beside him. Curious, Nym came over to sniff it, but Hokk shooed the fox away. Then he extended his arms down toward Koiyin. "Grab hold," he said sternly.

The woman held up a wet, grimy hand. Hokk gripped her wrist and then . . . he paused.

Surely Elia didn't *really* want this crazy woman coming with them. Koiyin didn't even look like someone from Above.

"I'm slipping!" Koiyin shouted at him.

"Give me your other hand, then!" he yelled back.

Koiyin flung up her arm, and Hokk grabbed her second wrist as she kicked her feet off from the side of the cliff. She dangled over the river, her eyes bulging.

Hokk stared at her for another moment.

And then he let go.

Koiyin screamed as she fell away from his grasp, her limbs flailing. Yet Hokk watched her for only an instant. In a flash, he snatched the dart resting on the ground and jabbed the tip into Twister's flank. The donkey let out a startled bray.

As he hurried to his feet, Hokk heard a splash in the river below. He shot a glance at Elia just as she spun toward him.

"What's happened?" Elia asked, rushing forward.

"I said get back!" Hokk demanded, pushing her ahead of him while dragging the donkey farther into the recesses of the cave.

"Where's Koiyin?" she sobbed.

"She fell!"

"We have to save her!"

"It's pointless!"

"No, the water's deep. It's possible she survived the fall," Elia shouted. "But if we don't reach her before she's pulled under —"

"She was hit by a dart!" Hokk exclaimed and then pointed to the shaft sticking out of Twister. "And the donkey too! The Torkins have found us."

"They couldn't have!" she protested, but Hokk could tell she believed him.

He yanked the projectile from Twister's side. "I just hope the little guy doesn't lose consciousness." He saw no signs of this actually happening — the donkey appeared to be fine, and

Hokk was relieved that he had assumed correctly about the dart having no traces of poison.

"What are we going to do?" asked Elia, her face shadowed with dread.

"Wait here," Hokk instructed. He inched toward the mouth of the cave and carefully peered skyward.

"See anyone?" Elia whispered nervously, having crept up behind him.

"Nobody." Hokk turned back to her with the pretense of being confused. "Perhaps there was only one. But he's seen us for sure, and he'll return to the village for reinforcements."

"Maybe he won't have to go that far." Elia quickly told him about Roahm finding them at the river, how he might have already been discovered unconscious.

"Then we have to leave now!" said Hokk with urgency.

"What about Koiyin?"

"Right now!"

"We can't abandon her," said Elia, anxiously gripping Hokk's arm.

"We'll be no good to her if we're captured too." Hokk hurried to tie Twister's rope around the stallion's neck. "We can always return with a rescue team once we've made our own escape."

"But that might be too —"

Hokk pulled Elia to the horse, then grabbed her around the waist. "Jump," he commanded. She did, and he lifted her up onto the stallion's saddle. In anticipation, the horse unfolded its wings and flapped a few times. Twister stirred expectantly too.

With Nym in one arm, Hokk hoisted himself up behind Elia, barely squeezing onto the same leather-padded seat. He kicked his heels into the stallion's ribcage, and it broke into a gallop toward the cave's entrance, hauling the donkey along with it.

Hokk tried to push Elia forward at the waist. "Stay low!" She struggled to sit upright.

"Down!" he demanded, pressing her onto the horse's back as the animal sailed free of the rocky edge.

But the stallion's wings faltered. Hokk swallowed. His racing heart seemed stuck in his throat. As the animal tilted alarmingly to one side, Elia cried out and Hokk squeezed his thighs tightly against the horse. But then its wings caught the air and, with several powerful strokes, lifted them above the canyon.

As they gained altitude, Hokk let Elia sit up, and she peered over the side. She half laughed, half cried at the same time. "We did it! We made it! I don't see Torkins anywhere!"

She turned around to glance at Hokk, but he wasn't paying attention to either her or the terraced mountains dropping away from them. Instead, his gaze was fixed on the sky overhead, on the churning blanket of gray clouds growing ever nearer.

Finally, his chance to ascend to Above.

Chapter **20**

HOKK HELD HIS BREATH AS they were enveloped by a gray oblivion. Was it the cold, heavy dampness of the clouds or Hokk's excitement that triggered his bare skin to flare with goose bumps? He watched the horse's wings flapping, but could not hear them, as if sound did not exist in this hazy realm. He saw Elia turn around to look at him. Did she want to catch the expression on his face as they burst through to Above?

Her mouth moved, but her words were lost.

"What's that?" he asked, though his question was blown away too.

Then he felt a pop in both ears.

He now heard Elia repeat, "It's already getting brighter!"

Looking down and then up, he realized this was true. They were rising toward increasing light. The air's tiny, suspended water droplets started to shimmer.

"Let me take Nym," Elia suggested.

"I'm fine," he reassured her.

"Your hands are shaking."

Hokk glanced at them. She was right. Actually, his whole body was trembling with anticipation.

"You'll want to have your hands free when we first emerge," she continued with an all-knowing grin.

"Why?"

"Trust me," she replied, taking the fox from him and holding the horse's reins with her other hand.

The intensity of the light grew stronger. As the mist thinned, it sparkled. Hokk thought he had never seen anything more beautiful. Then, in a flash of blinding brightness, they were above the clouds.

At that same instant, Hokk was forced to squeeze his eyes shut. More than anything, he had wanted to watch the scene reveal itself, but he found it impossible. Even with his eyes closed, the light was unbearable, so brilliant it glowed red through his eyelids. Instinctively, Hokk's hands shot up to shield his face.

Waves of heat began to roast his pale skin. In no time, Hokk sensed the true fierceness of the sun's rays, like lingering too long and too close to a fire.

"Blue sky!" Elia exclaimed. "I thought I'd never see it again."

Hokk lowered his hands and opened his eyes, but only for a second before they were once again assaulted by a blaze of whiteness.

"I know it's hard, but you should try to take a look," said Elia.

"There's no way I can!" Hokk groaned, both hands clamped on his face. "I don't have your protective membrane."

"No, but you can still do it. You just have to let your eyes adjust," she explained. "Separate your fingers no more than a crack to let in some light. Take it slow at first."

Sunlight filtered through the sliver of space he allowed between his index and middle fingers. His one eye burned and teared up, but he blinked rapidly, which helped ease the pain. He did the same with his other hand. Slowly, his eyes adjusted, and he could distinguish images of Above that left him spell-bound: a sea of clouds far below, with yellow light reflecting off their rippled, cushiony surface; an almost incomprehensible blue dome stretching to every point of an endless horizon; a circle of white-hot fire, floating in the middle of that dome, so dazzling that it left its imprint on his vision, even after he quickly closed his eyes again.

"Is that the sun?" he asked, trying to rub the flashing hot spots from his sight.

"It is. But remember — don't look at it directly, otherwise you'll blind yourself."

"I can see why," said Hokk. "I never believed you before." He gazed once more between his fingers. As his eyes grew even more accustomed, the sky seemed to become bluer, the soft texture of the clouds more defined. He turned and saw Twister flying easily beside them at the end of his tether. He then focused on the rhythm of the horse's wings. Their beating remained steady, though perhaps a bit slower. "So, where do we go from here?" he asked.

Elia craned her neck, scanning all sides.

Hokk caught a glimpse of her concern. "This stallion will soon tire," he warned. "We'll need a place to land."

Now, as if for the first time, she seemed to realize that their precipitous ascent from Below was going to cause problems. "I don't really know where we can go," she replied. "When we flew up from the canyon, I didn't see the tip of any islands sticking below the clouds. Not even at a distance. Did you?"

"No, I didn't," said Hokk.

"That worries me. What direction should we take?"

"I leave that up to you. It's still too bright for me to really focus on anything."

"Then I think we should gain altitude," she decided, sweeping her gaze back and forth over the clouds. "We need a better view."

But as the stallion soared to greater heights, Hokk began to feel dizzier. He rested his sweaty forehead on Elia's shoulder and could tell his body was losing strength. "I feel like . . . I'm going to . . . pass out," he wheezed.

"The air's getting thin," Elia explained. "Wrap your arms around me and try to stay alert. You'll feel much better when we go lower again."

Hokk could only mumble agreement as his mind began to surrender itself.

"There's got to be an island out here somewhere," he managed to hear Elia say, though it sounded as if she were speaking from a great distance. She started to say more, but he didn't catch the words as he fainted away.

• • •

"Wake up! Come on, Hokk. Wake up!"

Trying to revive him, Elia vigorously shook her shoulder and smacked Hokk's stubbly scalp, which was slick with perspiration.

"What's . . . happening?" Hokk asked. Whether from the searing temperature, the thin air, or the blinding light, he now had a throbbing headache.

"I've brought us lower," said Elia. "Breathing should be easier for you now."

His lungs labored less with each breath, but he still felt dizzy and the sunlight was ruthlessly frying his skin. "Too hot," he moaned, shifting his full weight forward onto Elia's back.

"Hang on a little longer, Hokk," Elia encouraged, sounding troubled as she supported him. "We're getting closer."

"To . . . what?" he mumbled, his mouth too dry to speak clearly.

"I spotted an island. We'll be able to find food and shelter."

Hokk didn't respond. So long as they could get there soon, he might be able to survive.

But they seemed to fly on without end. Every second was agonizing for him, like he was being cooked alive. He contemplated heaving himself into the clouds and plunging down to the soothing coolness and darkness of Below. Either way, he was doomed.

Even with his senses overcome by the heat, Hokk could tell the stallion was struggling too. The animal's hide was soaked with sweat. Its injured wing could not match the other for power. Hokk peeked between his fingers, and saw the horse's tongue lolling out. The animal snorted through its nostrils, and from its mouth, strings of foamy saliva flicked back at them. The poor beast wasn't going to make it.

"Brace yourself," Elia ordered, but before Hokk could comprehend what she meant, he felt a jolt travel up through the horse. Elia was able to hold on and keep her balance, although she pitched forward as the stallion's front legs buckled upon impact. The jarring collision bounced Hokk from the saddle and he fell off the animal, tumbling over and over in burning sand, where the grains seemed to dig deep into his flesh like needles. He came to rest, howling in pain. Moments later, a merciful shadow settled over him and he felt Elia's touch as she shaded his face with her hands. She then bent down to whisper in his ear. "We've made it. We're here."

Chapter **21**

HIKING UP THE SAND DUNE in her bare feet was like climbing a smoldering pile of scorching hot embers. When she reached the top, Elia cast her eyes across the desert island, hoping to find at least a speck of shade. Unfortunately, the sizzling sun directly overhead obliterated any possibility of shadows.

She didn't want to give up hope of finding shelter, though she knew their chances were bleak. As the stallion had approached the floating island, she'd seen no signs of civilization. Earlier, she had tried to sound optimistic for Hokk, but in truth, it was a miracle the horse had made it this far. Upon finally reaching solid ground, the animal had collapsed and still hadn't attempted to stand. Elia could tell it was suffering badly from exhaustion. The only thing in worse shape was Hokk, barely coping with the heat and sunlight of Above.

Elia's gaze returned to where she had left him sprawled at the base of the sand dune. Even from here, she could hear Hokk moaning in agony.

Get back to him, she told herself.

Sliding down the slope on her heels, she worried how dire his condition might become. When she reached him, she was shocked to see blisters now covering his skin. Any spot on his flesh that hadn't already developed sores was a bright, painful-looking red.

She desperately looked around. Nym was panting heavily. The stallion appeared too spent to move, but Twister started beating his wings to fan himself. That gave Elia an idea. She carefully approached the horse, who eyed her apprehensively as though she might demand another flight. She stroked its neck, cooing softly, and admired once again this remarkable, regal animal. And those silver ornaments braided in its mane and tail . . . they were so familiar. Could this possibly be the very same horse that had once belonged to Wrasse, the Imperial Commander who had hunted her across the prairies?

When the stallion finally relaxed and lowered its head, Elia raised the animal's folded wing and gently coaxed it open, stretching the limb out until it was fully extended over the sand.

Shade!

Elia hurried to Hokk. Even though he was now barely conscious, she knew this was going to hurt. While he groaned and twitched, she carefully dragged him closer to the horse, only to discover the stallion had tucked its wing up against its body again. *Damn beast!* She tried once more to spread it open. "Do it!" she shouted, but the horse resisted, swinging its head toward her with an irritated whinny and snort. It was not going to cooperate.

Frustrated, Elia threw herself onto the sand. Staring at Hokk, she felt on the verge of both screaming and crying. If the sun continued to cook his sensitive skin, he'd surely die. Hokk was bare-chested, having dressed minimally to look like a Torkin warrior so he wouldn't stand out in Below. But up here, above the clouds, it would prove disastrous. If only he had more to wear than just his leggings and that small leather pouch hanging from his waist.

After a moment's consideration, Elia jumped to her feet. She stripped naked, pulling off the tunic supplied by the

Torkins and stepping out of the pants she had worn over the past several weeks to work as one of their farmers.

Elia propped up Hokk. As gently as possible, she slipped the tunic over his head and carefully stuck each of his scarred arms through the sleeves, which were almost long enough. Since his legs were already covered, she wrapped her pants around his head and neck, leaving only a small gap for his mouth. The clothing would keep the sunlight off his body, and hopefully, in several hours when the sun had set, it would maintain his warmth against the night's cold.

To deal with her own lack of clothing, Elia untied the sack from the stallion's neck and took out the lady-in-waiting's blue dress. She unraveled the fabric from around the carved box and put the garment on. The fit was a little short, and she couldn't reach the buttons along her back to do them up, but no matter. Torn and dirty, with one sleeve missing, the dress was lightweight and silky against her skin, far better than the scratchy work clothes she had just removed or the plain gray uniform she used to wear at the palace laundry.

Returning to Hokk, she cradled his bundled head in her lap. She leaned over him and could feel the sun shining on her neck and back. She didn't fear blisters, however, knowing her dark skin was naturally well-suited for such harsh conditions. Or purposefully *modified*, Hokk might have argued, based on his theory to explain her double eyelids.

Even now, the whole concept of deliberate modification was hard to fathom, but it had stuck in Elia's mind since learning about the specially altered seeds planted in the dark towers of Ago and the enhanced chickens whose internal clocks automatically triggered their feathers to drop. She remembered Hokk wondering how somebody could possibly tell if something was natural or not, particularly when it was all that person had ever known — a valid, provocative question that was also downright troubling.

A vivid image suddenly popped into Elia's mind, something she and Hokk had seen together in a stately old building in the City of Ago. It was a stained-glass window showing two orbs surrounded by a sky of blue. One sphere was white and the other yellow, with lines radiating from its edges. Under the limitless clouds of Below, nobody in the city should have been familiar with such a vision, let alone have it portrayed on their walls. But Hokk had suggested the window was a depiction of the way things used to be in what he called "the time of the Ancients," when there was only one world beneath the sun and the moon. Could he be right? Just looking at Hokk's misery now, after a few hours in the sunlight, was proof enough that it would be hopeless for people from Below to ever survive without clouds in their sky. So wasn't it logical that Elia and Hokk belonged to worlds that had never been one and the same? Or was it the opposite? Perhaps the inhabitants from each realm had been separated for so long they had changed in ways that made living in such extreme environments possible. Either way, the only thing to determine now was whether or not Hokk could adapt to hers.

• • •

The hours seemed endless. Elia had been fanning Hokk with the lace hem of her dress, watching the dune's shadow advance as the sun shifted closer to the horizon. When the crescent of shade was large enough, she hauled him into its protective veil. She unwrapped his head. His sores hadn't worsened, but he feverishly mumbled gibberish, and when she wiped the perspiration from his brow, it seemed as hot as the sand still bathing in full sunlight.

If she had kept Hokk alive this long, then perhaps he had a chance. But how would he survive tomorrow? Her only hope was that a cool night would refresh the stallion enough so they could fly away in the morning and find a more hospitable island.

As the sun began to set and the sky turned from orange to pink, a breeze finally picked up. It fluttered the tunic Hokk was wearing, and Elia lifted it so the cooler air could blow across his chest. Nym wandered over on stiff legs and sniffed Hokk's hand. As if assessing his condition as grim, the fox licked Hokk's fingertips and curled up beside his master.

After a few minutes of watching them, and feeling increasingly tired herself, Elia saw Nym's head rise. His ears flicked and he smelled the air, then quickly stood.

"What is it?" she asked, straining to hear. She got to her feet and started climbing the dune. Nym followed. At the top, Elia paused to listen.

Shouting.

It was muffled, but she could definitely hear voices, as if people — happy people — were hollering and having fun together.

Excited, but doubting whether it could be true, Elia scanned the landscape. The sun had just set, yet there was still enough light reflecting off the shattered pieces of the moon that trailed across the sky. Then, in the far distance, she saw what looked like three white sails. They rose above the desert for a brief moment before dropping and disappearing, obscured by a dune.

Could it really be? She waited breathlessly, hoping to see —

Yes! Praise the sun! There they were again! Sleighs, racing each other as the wind billowed their sails, moving at incredible speeds. Elia watched each in turn slide up a slope, reach the crest, then soar through the air and dive behind another vast pile of sand.

So Elia and Hokk weren't alone out here! They could be rescued!

Elia wanted to chase after the sleighs that very moment, but she resisted. The three craft were traveling away from her, and with night approaching, she would have no hope of catching up. And she couldn't leave Hokk alone. The temperature was dropping, so it was best she stay with him until they could head out at dawn and start searching.

At least there was hope. They would have to suffer through just one night on their own, but by morning, all would be fine.

Chapter **22**

THE STALLION WAS DEAD.

In the early morning light, Elia dropped to her knees beside it and shook the base of one wing, hoping to rouse the animal. But the horse was not asleep. It wasn't breathing. The previous evening, with its head resting on the ground, the stallion's nostrils had stirred wisps of swirling sand with every breath. This morning, nothing. The horse was completely still.

While it seemed strange that such a large, strong animal would succumb before the rest of them, it had worked incredibly hard to get to this desert island yesterday, and dehydration had finally taken its toll.

So what did that mean for Hokk, suffering from his own ailments? How long did he have?

Feeling her stomach cramp with anxiety, Elia hurried back to Hokk's side. Though she had just left him a few minutes prior, she checked for the rise and fall of his chest. His shallow breathing was the same as it had been all night while she lay curled up next to him to conserve their body heat. She touched his forehead; his temperature had stabilized to normal, but in no time, the sun would warm the air to levels he'd find unbearable.

Elia knew she couldn't delay, yet given the new development

this morning, she would have to change her plans. She had intended to use the stallion to follow the sleighs' tracks, even if that required riding bareback and dragging Hokk behind them, with the saddle acting as a crude sled for him to lie on since there was no way she could possibly lift him up onto the horse. Because Twister was too small to carry her, Elia's only choice now was to head out on her own. She'd find the people who had been sleighing last night and bring them back to Hokk. With a bit of luck, it would only take a few hours.

Before she left, Elia made sure Hokk was as comfortable and safe as possible. As Twister and Nym watched, she returned to the horse and struggled to extend its wing. This time, it stayed open. Estimating the sun's path, she positioned Hokk where she guessed he'd get the most shade. Since she didn't want Twister following her, Elia tied him to the rope around the stallion's neck, and noticed the donkey nudge the horse as if confused by its lack of movement. Nym seemed curious too, but Elia swooped the fox up into her arms. "You're coming with me."

She then grabbed the sack and slung it over her shoulder. She had no intention, however, of bringing it with her the entire way. Climbing to the top of the dune, she instead pressed it securely into the sand. She tore off her one remaining sleeve and fastened it with a knot to the bag where the blue fabric could flutter like a flag. With so many identical hills of sand sweeping across the desert, she would need to find this spot quickly, and though she worried about leaving the bag and its contents behind, it was the only makeshift marker she could devise.

One last glance down at Hokk, hidden beneath the stallion's wing, and she set off.

• • •

Elia blamed the wind. It must have disturbed the sand since last night; otherwise, she should have found the tracks by now. Second-guessing her directions, she decided to climb one more dune before trying a different route. Elia had been telling herself *just one more* for a while now, but hadn't yet changed course; she was too apprehensive about which way she should go instead. She feared wandering out here forever.

What a relief when she finally spotted some tracks. She saw runner marks slicing across the opposite sandbank and ran toward them to make sure. She followed them up the incline, where the sails had likely lifted the sleighs into the air before they touched down again much farther ahead. There were three sets of tracks, crisscrossing each other, but at least she had something to follow.

Elia progressed steadily along these intermittent trails and strained to pick up the route whenever there was a break. From the peak of another sand dune, she gazed back until she could pinpoint what she guessed was her blue marker, no more than a speck. She then looked up to the sun to gauge its position in the sky and estimated that she had been out here for about two hours.

Stepping over the ridge of sand, Elia expected to see the runners' tracks start up again on the other side. But there was more. Elia stopped, wide-eyed.

Wreckage.

A damaged sleigh lay below her. As if it had sailed too fast or too high off the sand dune, the craft had come to rest on its side, half-impaled into the opposite bank. One of the runners was broken and dangling from the hull, and though the mast had cracked in half, the sail was still partially attached.

Elia rushed down the steep slope, almost tumbling forward with her momentum. Reaching the crash site, she saw many footprints in the sand where the driver's companions must have stopped to help after the accident. From this spot, only two sets of tracks led away.

She ran her hand over the smooth white body of the sleigh and looked up at the sail, which snapped in the wind. She noticed an insignia near the top and suspected it was the crest of a family. A wealthy family. Who else could afford to own a craft such as this, then simply abandon it in the desert? Unless they were coming back for it.

Elia fiddled with the piercing in her eyebrow. Who would she end up meeting at the end of these tracks? How might they react to her? She'd be quite a sight, wearing what remained of the lady-in-waiting's torn dress. She would need to convince them to help her — which they likely wouldn't do if they knew she was a lowly servant girl who counted for nothing.

Before she could stop herself, she dug a fingernail into her forehead where the purple tattoo was a permanent mark of her status. Tears welled in her eyes as she pierced the skin. She continued to gouge her flesh even after she felt the wetness of blood and saw it on her fingertips. The wound oozed while she tore off a long strip of lace from the hem of her dress and then tied it like a bandage around her head to cover the injury.

The pain was a small price. Elia couldn't risk jeopardizing Hokk's rescue by letting anyone find out who she truly was.

Chapter **23**

WITH ONE MOVE, TASHEIRA ELIMINATED five of Marest's pieces from the board. She smiled at her attendant. "Your turn."

Unfazed, Marest piled three tiles onto four more of the same color, then slid the stack to a new square. "I'm two steps from winning. Can you stop me?"

Tash frowned, unable to figure out the play that would give her servant a third win in a row. She was suddenly tired of playing. It was already hot, even in the shade of their silk-covered cabana, and these games always lasted too long anyway. "When are they going to serve lunch?" she grumbled as she rubbed her sore neck muscles. She had pulled them the previous night when she crashed her sleigh.

"Everyone's busy packing," said Marest.

Their sojourn on the island was coming to an end. Today was the Baron's last at the dig site, and tomorrow morning, they were expecting more staff to arrive with a team of horses to take the family back home. Tash was glad this trip was finally almost over. Just one long afternoon left to try and fill her time.

Tasheira sighed as she studied the board. She placed her hand on a green tile and glanced at Marest to see if the older girl's expression would betray whether or not it was the right

JASON CHABOT

move to make. But Marest was no longer watching the game. She was looking intently over Tasheira's shoulder.

Tash turned and squinted. Through the open flaps of their cabana and across the sun-blasted desert that surrounded the camp, she made out a figure descending the slope of a sand dune.

"Who's that, Miss Tasheira?" asked Marest.

"I have no idea," she murmured, getting up from the table and stepping outside. Her inner eyelids closed to filter out the harsh light.

The stranger staggered toward them on very wobbly legs and fell into Tasheira's arms.

If not for the dress, Tash would have guessed the person to be a boy. With short-cropped hair, and a curved slice of metal piercing her eyebrow, she appeared most unusual. The girl was dirty, with a gaunt face, and her clothing was torn, though obviously, the dress had once been a fine, stylish garment. She had a wound above her brow that had bled through a lace headband. She was also carrying a strange-looking dog with disproportionately large ears, but she released the animal as Tasheira and Marest grabbed her shoulders to keep her standing.

"She's been injured! Can't you see she needs water?" Tash shouted at her attendant.

Marest hurried away to find some while Tash led the poor girl to the shade of the draped cabana. The little dog followed them in.

"What's happened to you?" asked Tash as she got the girl seated on a cushioned bench. "Have you been in an accident?"

The girl slowly shook her head. "I can't remember."

"What's your name?"

The girl hesitated, as if even this detail was too difficult to recall. "Elia," she finally responded, though it sounded more like a question than an answer.

"And your last name?" Tash prompted.

Elia simply shrugged.

"My name is Tasheira. I'm the daughter of Baron Shoad. Perhaps you've heard of my family?" It was worth a shot asking. Judging by the quality of Elia's dress, she clearly came from an affluent background too, regardless of how she looked now or her reason for ending up here.

"No, I don't think I've heard the name before," Elia replied awkwardly.

Marest returned with a waterball, which she handed to Elia. The girl pursed her lips and sucked back the gelatinous liquid. She didn't stop until half of it had disappeared. It seemed to reinvigorate her.

"Thank you," said Elia. She wiped her mouth and then stood, pointing into the sunshine. "But it's not just me. There's somebody else who needs your help even more."

"Where?"

"He's out in the desert."

"How far?"

"Far. And I'm worried," said Elia. "He's really suffering. I'm afraid he won't survive. He's badly burned."

Badly burned?

Of course! Remembering the fiery debris that had fallen out of the sky and created such a huge crater in the sand, Tash knew exactly who they'd find. She turned to Marest. "Go to my mother. Tell her what's happened and that I've left to go help," she ordered.

"You can't leave on your own," Marest protested.

"Don't be foolish. We'll have to take a sleigh and there won't be enough room for all three of us. When my father returns, ask him to send out someone to assist with the rescue."

"But —"

"Just do it! And get a basket with more waterballs that we can take with us," Tash shouted as she dragged Elia from the cabana and toward a sleigh.

• • •

Thankfully, the wind today was not strong — Elia's footprints were visible and easy to follow. The sleigh leapt off peaks of sand and landed with a *thud* on its runners before speeding up the next slope. Tasheira was pleased to see this Elia girl was not frightened by the ride the way Marest had been. But why would she? She wouldn't have led the sheltered, fearful life of a servant.

"I'm glad to be rid of her," Tash shouted above the sound of air racing past their ears.

"Who?" asked Elia, sitting in front.

"My attendant. I find her hovering and constant worrying so irritating," said Tash, working the rudder in the back. "You've probably felt the same with your own servants, right?"

"Uh . . . of course. All the time," Elia replied, though Tasheira could sense the poor girl was struggling to remember.

About twenty minutes out, they discovered that Elia's tracks had blown away, so they stopped atop one of the highest dunes so Elia could look for the blue flag she had left behind to guide them.

"Just over there. Can you see it?" asked Elia, pointing ahead.

Tash surveyed the desert, then spotted something blue in the distance. "Yes, got it," she said triumphantly, swinging the boom so the sail could once again catch the breeze. "It won't take us long now."

As they approached the marker, Elia asked Tash to stop beside it. Tasheira plowed the sleigh perpendicular to the slope to slow down, then released the sail. Elia climbed out to retrieve the flag and an old sack to which it was attached.

"Is that your sleeve?" Tash asked.

"Unfortunately. That's all I could use."

"Makes sense if you had nothing else. It's just a shame your dress had to get ruined."

"I'm sure I must have plenty more," replied Elia.

Tash gazed into the valley below, where a white stallion was lying on the sand, its wing stretched out. A small donkey was tied to its neck. She asked Elia to give the sleigh a push so it could slide down the slope. Elia ran behind. The sleigh came to a stop and Tash stepped out onto the sand. She immediately recognized the thoroughbred pedigree of the horse and was impressed with the intricate silver bangles braided into its mane and tail.

"That's a very impressive stallion you own," she said as Elia came running up beside her.

"It's dead," Elia replied matter-of-factly, trying to catch her breath.

Tasheira flinched with surprise, then looked closer and realized it was true. What a fascinating story this girl must have. Tash was eager to learn more once Elia had fully regained her memory.

From the sleigh, Tasheira removed the basket with the waterballs inside. "So, where's this man who needs my help?"

"He's under here," said Elia as she shifted the horse's stiff wing and revealed the person protected beneath. He wore a dirty tunic and leggings, and his head was bundled in fabric. As soon as the sunlight hit him, he moaned and squirmed as if in intense pain.

"Let's free up his face so he can drink something," Tash suggested, keen to see what he looked like.

Elia unwound what turned out to be a pair of pants.

Tasheira placed her basket on the ground and kneeled beside the young man, who was probably no older than twenty. His skin was a shocking red and covered with blistering burns. She took a waterball from her basket and held it to his lips. He made no effort to drink.

"He's not familiar with those," Elia explained.

No, of course he isn't, thought Tash.

Elia's voice was tight with concern. "I don't know how we can get fluids into him if he's unconscious."

"Leave that to me," said Tash. She sucked a mouthful of water from the jiggly mass, then gently supported the young man's neck and head in a more upright position. She placed her lips on his and pushed the water into his mouth. It went down fine. She repeated this until the waterball was fully consumed. Then she studied his face for any response.

"Try to wake up, Isec," Tasheira encouraged softly. "There are a lot of people who will be very excited to meet you."

Chapter 24

ELIA STOOD PINCH-LIPPED, STEWING over how Tasheira had managed to get Hokk to drink. She knew she should be grateful for the girl's help — and she was — but how unbelievable to see Tash put her mouth against his like that!

Dressed in fine clothing, with a sturdy, well-fed physique, a mass of curly hair, and demanding eyes, Tasheira had a confident manner bordering on arrogance that clearly came from a life of privilege and pampering. Just the way the girl had treated her servant earlier made Elia thankful that Tash was unaware of her own exceptionally low rank as a laundry worker.

Tasheira took her basket over to Twister so the donkey could have a drink. Then she returned and held up a waterball. "Only one of these left," she said. "Do you want it?"

"No," Elia replied, assuming it was obvious they should save the last serving for Hokk.

Tash shrugged and proceeded to drink the thing herself, then spat a mouthful into her hands to refresh her face and wash away the dust.

Elia crossed her arms, sighing loudly.

"I know it's frustrating, but it shouldn't be too long before somebody gets here," said Tasheira. She nodded toward the sleigh. "Let's at least get Isec some better shade while we wait."

Elia wondered why Tash assumed his name was Isec, but decided to refrain from asking. It was best to avoid saying too much until she had a solid plan. Instead, Elia helped Tasheira detach the sail from the mast so they could spread it over Hokk. The material was not too heavy to suffocate him, yet not too light to blow away with the breeze.

"Of course, we won't be able to bring your horse back with us," said Tasheira, now turning her attention to the carcass on the desert.

"No, there isn't any point," Elia agreed with a frown.

"But take the saddle. And we should remove those silver ornaments braided into the stallion's hair. They're yours, after all."

Elia hadn't thought of that, but the girl was right. They had value. And why shouldn't they now belong to Elia?

Tasheira raised the hem of her dress and undid the laces of an embroidered, silk shoe before taking it off and passing it over. Elia examined the thing with a grimace. Was she expected to put it on?

"I don't think it will fit," said Elia, realizing at some point she would have to start wearing shoes if she hoped to convince anyone she belonged to a higher class.

Tash shook her head as she removed the second shoe and kept it for herself. "No, let's put the silver in here as we take the pieces off. So nothing falls into the sand."

Another good suggestion.

Tasheira removed the small bangles from the horse's mane while Elia crouched and did the same at the tail. At first, they worked in silence, but then she noticed Tash studying her. A few times, the girl opened her mouth as if wanting to say something, which made Elia nervous. What questions were brewing that might reveal Elia as an imposter?

"So, you really don't remember anything about how you got here?" Tash finally asked.

"No." Elia hoped Tasheira wouldn't sense her unease.

"Or how your horse died?"

Elia made a point of looking up and rubbing the wound on her forehead. "I honestly don't know. I suspect it died in the air and fell out of the sky. I must have bashed my head when we landed."

"Were you running away?"

"Your guess is as good as mine."

Tash paused, holding a shiny bauble over her shoe as she gazed wide-eyed at Elia. "Well, I'd say you were trying to escape, that somebody was after you because . . ." She thought for a moment. "Maybe you were being forced to marry a man you hated. Someone too old or ugly for you to even consider his proposal, so you cut off all your hair in protest."

"Yes, that might be it," said Elia, hoping Tasheira would now stop guessing.

"However, that doesn't explain why your dress is torn."

"Unless —"

"No, I know what it was!" Tash interrupted with growing enthusiasm. "Perhaps you have a secret to hide and your only choice was to escape before anybody else found out. Or . . . they did find out! Yes, that's it! Whoever discovered your secret tried to kill you before it could be revealed!"

Elia swallowed hard as she dropped another ornament into her shoe. "I'm sure it couldn't possibly be that dramatic." Tasheira's accuracy was unsettling.

"You tried to flee on your horse, but you got lost and ended up here on the Isle of Drifting Dunes." Tash glanced in Hokk's direction. "And then, by pure luck, you discovered Isec after he climbed out from his wreckage and started wandering this desert in search of help. Is that what happened?"

"This is the Isle of Drifting Dunes?" Elia inquired with amazement.

"It is. Have you been here before?"

"No, but my grandfather once —" Elia cut herself off. She had let too much slip.

"Do you remember something?" Tasheira asked enthusiastically. "Something about your grandfather? Who was he?"

"Uh … no, my mistake. Nothing's coming back to me," Elia sputtered as she recalled the polished piece of orange glass Opi had found on this very same floating island around the time Elia's father was born. She had retrieved the memento from her grandfather's bundled body after discovering him dead in the City of Ago, before Hokk suggested hiding his corpse in the tunnels beneath the streets. She had always pretended the stone was a lost jewel belonging to a princess, and she was certain it was still safely hidden in her sack.

"Well, don't worry, Elia. I'm sure your memories will come back to you soon. In fact, my mission is to make sure that happens. It's important we know the truth about you."

"Maybe I'd rather not find out," Elia said with a nervous laugh. "Maybe neither of us will like what we discover. The peaceful bliss of ignorance — isn't that better?"

Tasheira became very serious. "No. That is never better. Learning the truth about anything and everything is the noblest pursuit. I believe that very strongly. Don't you?"

"Perhaps," Elia murmured half-heartedly, though she knew Tasheira was correct. Everything she had endured since falling to Below had been in the hope of revealing truths: discovering the importance of the telescope smuggled out of the palace; unraveling the mysteries that seemed to surround the people connected to her family; and, on a much larger scale, learning the real origins of her world and Hokk's.

"You won't have to wait long," said Tasheira. "No matter what happens, we'll be able to piece things together when we take you back to the Mirrored Palace."

Elia looked up with a start.

"That's right," Tasheira continued. "Surely someone there will be able to tell us who you *really* are."

Chapter 25

WHITENESS RIPPLED ABOVE HIS FACE. It was ... fabric. A canvas sheet caught in the wind.

Shadows fell upon him. People were talking.

Lying on his back, Hokk shuddered with pain. He had never felt such agonizing sensations. Did he have any skin left?

The white material was pulled aside. Three heads appeared in silhouette, light radiating around the edges. Brightness beyond.

"We'll put the sail under him and use it like a sling." A man's voice.

"He might fall out." It was a young woman speaking. Concerned.

"I'll fly low over the desert." The man again. "He'll be fine. It's important to get him back as fast as possible for treatment."

Hands lifted him up.

He moaned.

He was lowered.

"We'll follow in the sleigh." A different female voice.

"And the donkey?" A question from the first girl.

"Tie it to my horse and it can fly back with us."

An empty sky of blue overhead. Somehow not as blinding to his eyes. Not a single cloud in sight.

Shuffling sounds.

Orders given.

The edges of the thick sheet were pulled up on either side, each corner tied to a rope. Each piece of rope merged at a point above him. A line led up to the belly of a horse hovering overhead.

Wings began flapping against the vastness of the sky.

The ropes strained.

He felt no pressure from the ground, only from the cocoon of the sling.

He was airborne again.

Then blackness and . . .

• • •

Hokk gradually regained consciousness but kept his eyes shut. He could hear someone's steady breath very close. He inhaled and exhaled to match the person's rhythm. Then he heard a grinding sound, like stone on stone.

"We'll have to make several batches to treat him," said a man with a husky voice.

Hokk opened his eyes and lifted his head. His body was stretched out. Naked. His arms, chest, and feet were blazing red, covered with festering sores. His legs were a striking contrast of white, the skin unblemished.

He was lying on a cushioned surface. The walls of his shelter were made of cream-colored cotton that fluttered with an outside breeze. He didn't recognize the two blond men with dark complexions who were standing by his side. One was crushing something with a mortar and pestle. A more mature man, wearing clothing of higher quality, gently pressed Hokk down until he was resting again on a pillow. "Just relax," he said. "We're preparing something that will help soothe the burns."

"Where am I?" Hokk groaned.

"Somewhere safe," replied the same man. He placed a

damp, chilled towel on Hokk's hot forehead. He then took the mortar from his younger companion, whose manner and attire suggested he was a servant. Scooping out a handful of greenish paste, the older gentleman began applying it, ever so delicately, over the surface of Hokk's injured skin. The cooling effect brought immediate relief.

"Father?" A girl announced her arrival only a moment before she pulled open the drapes covering an entrance.

Hokk turned his face in her direction as the older man quickly took a small washcloth from his servant and covered Hokk's exposed groin.

"Tasheira, I told you to wait outside," her father said sternly.

"He's awake!" the girl declared when she saw Hokk looking at her. She stepped inside, holding back the curtain for someone behind her. Elia entered too.

"Elia," Hokk said weakly. Just above her brow, he could see dried blood on a thin bandage wrapped around her head.

Elia blushed and gave an awkward smile. Her eyes did not seem to know where to settle.

"How are you feeling, Isec?" asked the other girl, Tasheira, as she examined him closely.

"His alertness is promising, but he's still in rough shape," her father answered on Hokk's behalf. "Once we get this paste on all his sores and give him some more time to heal, we'll be better able to assess his condition."

"But he'll survive the trip back home with us, won't he?" asked Tasheira.

Her father studied Hokk. "Depends on how he responds. His health must be very poor because I've never seen such pale skin —"

"Nor have I," Tasheira interjected. "But we can't let him die."

Her father held up his hand so he could finish. "We'll do our best. But regardless of what happens, we have to leave tomorrow when the team arrives. We don't have enough supplies to extend our stay. With this medicated paste and plenty of water, perhaps he can make it. However, I worry about the length of the journey and his comfort."

"We'll keep him out of the sun."

"But the heat seems to be a problem for him too. It will be challenging to keep him cool enough."

"I know just the thing!" Tasheira exclaimed.

Hokk saw a skeptical look cross her father's face. "What's that?" the man asked.

"We can transport him in his suit! That's what protected him from the flames when his craft fell from the moon. It only makes sense to use it again."

Chapter 26

TASHEIRA AWOKE TO THE COMMOTION of servants packing up the camp, but Elia was still sleeping soundly beside her. Rising on one elbow, Tash leaned over to look at her bedmate, whose face was pressed into the downy softness of her own white pillow.

Tasheira had been amused the previous night to observe Elia's reaction to the bed. Approaching with wonderment, the girl had timidly climbed onto the mattress as if nervous to slide her feet deeper into the silky sheets. She must have fallen asleep almost immediately because when Tash extinguished the lantern and began talking in the dark, she heard no response except the faint sound of snoring.

She decided not to wake her now. It had likely been a long time since Elia had enjoyed a decent rest in the comfort to which she was accustomed. Tash was still uncertain how much higher Elia's status might be than her own, so she wanted to offer this mysterious girl as many luxuries as possible. Elia had mentioned a grandfather — what if that man, or even Elia's father, was a high-ranking duke, or a lord with great connections who could help launch Tasheira into the higher echelons of palace society that were otherwise off-limits to her family?

Tash would receive accolades not just for saving Isec, but also for reuniting this important daughter with her rightful family — or perhaps for returning a runaway.

Tash parted the gauzy drapes that hung around her bed and slipped out from between the sheets. She put on a dressing gown over her sleepwear and quietly crept to the entrance of her cabana. Stepping outside, she discovered Marest folding clothes that had been removed earlier from Tasheira's wardrobe. Her attendant had probably been up for several hours already.

"Good morning, Miss Tasheira," Marest said with a curtsy. "I'm pleased you're awake so early. I can start packing your linens before they take apart your bedframe."

"No, you can't just yet," Tash replied. "Elia's still sleeping."

A flicker of distress crossed her attendant's face, but Marest quickly composed herself with a look of practiced patience. "Yes, of course, Miss Tasheira. I have plenty of other things I can attend to instead. In the meantime, you might like to have some breakfast," she said with a nod toward a tray of fruits and breads. The food was laid out on a table flanked by two chairs under the shade of a large umbrella. "Best to eat now before everything gets packed up for good. We expect the horses to arrive within the next hour."

Tash scanned the camp, half of which had already been dismantled. The pavilion for the servants' quarters was gone, and sitting in its place were their thin mattresses and wooden crates containing all their supplies. The kitchen tent was also disassembled — which explained the simple breakfast — though the stoves and bare shelving units still had to be moved. For the moment, they looked as though they would remain permanent fixtures on the desert.

The fabric walls of the Baroness's cabana were already off the supporting frames, and workers had climbed onto the roof beams to remove the swag of silks that formed the ceiling. Tash's mother sat nearby, shrouded in veils hanging from her sun hat. Her head rotated, as though looking in Tasheira's direction, but when Tash waved, her mother quickly turned away and snatched a piece of fruit from a tray held by her attendant.

"Good morning to you too," Tash grumbled under her breath. She gazed at her own food and wondered if anyone had thought to feed Isec. "I'll be back," she said to Marest as she grabbed a peach and a sesame roll, and hurried toward her father's tent, which was always the last one taken down.

The evening prior, Tash had lingered impatiently with Elia in front of this very tent, anxious to see Isec and to help her father with the young man's treatment. She had been told to wait outside, however, because it was *inappropriate* to enter — again, that word she hated so much! But upon hearing Isec's voice, she could restrain herself no longer. She had barged in to find Isec fully exposed, lying on cushions placed on her father's desk.

This morning, Tash waited for nothing. She flung apart the curtains and marched inside. Her father was standing beside Isec, who had a sheet covering his lower body. The Baron was gently blotting the young man's arms with a wet cloth.

"How is he?" Tash asked.

"He survived the night, I'm happy to say," her father replied, turning to look at his daughter. He noticed the food in her hand. "I'm sure he'll appreciate something to eat."

Tash came closer. Isec watched her every move. His expression seemed more alert, though behind his eyes, she could still read his pain. She glanced at his chest, where the Baron carefully wiped away the green paste that had dried on his skin. The pustules beneath no longer looked on the verge of bursting. "He's healing," she said, trying to give Isec a look of encouragement.

"Yes, it appears so," her father replied.

"I bet you're hungry," Tash said to their patient. The young man nodded ever so slightly.

She peeled back the fuzzy skin of the peach, then bit into the sweet flesh, pulled out the chunk, and placed it into Isec's mouth. "It's a nice juicy one," she said. "Should go down easily."

Isec nodded again and chewed carefully before swallowing. Tash continued feeding him until only the peach pit remained. She then tore apart a small piece of the bun, but with his first mouthful, he choked on the seeds and crumbs.

"Maybe bread isn't a good idea when he's lying flat," suggested the Baron.

"Then I'll find him something else to eat." Tash made a move to leave but her father gently caught her by the arm.

"Stay. We'll need your help," said the Baron.

Her father wiped the last of the paste from Isec's abdomen. He handed the stained towel to his attendant, but didn't take another. "I'd like the three of us to move him onto his stomach. Tasheira, you hold up the sheet for privacy as we turn him."

They carefully lifted Isec and flipped him over. Once he was repositioned, the Baron resumed his work, removing paste from the young man's back. When he was nearly finished, Tasheira's father turned to his servant. "We're almost ready for the suit."

"You don't need to add more paste?" asked Tasheira.

"The medicine has done all it can for now."

The Baron's attendant went around the desk to the woven chairs suspended from the rafters, where a blanket was draped over a large object sitting in one of the seats. When the blanket was yanked away, Tash saw the white, heavily stuffed suit they had retrieved from the crash site. The reflective glass globe was still perched on the shoulders. Tash caught her breath, excited that Isec would wear this outfit when he was finally introduced to the Royal Court. She couldn't imagine a more dramatic entrance. The court would be spellbound.

The light inside the tent brightened as the younger of Tash's cousins, Fimal, entered carrying a pair of fine cotton trousers. "As requested," he said to his uncle. He handed the garment to the Baron and then winked at Tasheira. "I had to steal the pants from Neric." He looked down at their patient. "Shall I put them on him?"

"Yes," the Baron replied as he lifted the sheet off Isec, exposing his white, bare bottom.

Tash didn't blush, but still turned away, knowing she was expected to, otherwise she'd be forced to leave. She swung back only when Fimal had finished.

"No shirt for him?" Tash asked.

"We should allow his poor skin to breathe as much as possible, especially if he's going to be sealed up for the entire journey," said the Baron. He then pointed to the suit. "Now let's get that thing on him without causing further injury to his wounds."

They turned Isec again, ever so carefully, until he was face up. Tash noticed him lift his head to peer down his body. He looked astonished — and worried — as the cumbersome gear was brought to him. "No, please," she heard him murmur, but her father apparently caught nothing of his protest.

"Tasheira, I'll get you to direct his feet into each leg of the suit," instructed the Baron. "And try to prevent the trousers from bunching." He then nodded at his attendant and Fimal. "You two, lift him by the shoulders as I pull it on."

Little by little, the padded suit was pulled higher. Isec cringed as it passed his waist to cover his chest. Then, with the Baron's servant on one side and Fimal on the other, they slipped his arms inside. Once the heavy outfit had reached his shoulders, they supported Isec while Tash's father fastened the clasps along the back to seal the young man in.

Isec's forehead was sweating, and Tash gently patted it with a damp towel. "He's already hot," she said uneasily. She now doubted her original plan. "Will this really work?"

"It will. I tested it last night. The suit seems to be a self-contained unit. If I'm correct, overheating shouldn't be a problem." The Baron held out his hand to his attendant, who was holding the spherical helmet. "And once this thing is secured in place, it seems to activate the suit's cooling system. I can't explain how, but it appears to be a marvelous design."

Just then, Tasheira's other cousin entered the tent. He seemed startled to see Isec's head poking out of the massive suit. "The stallion brigade has been spotted on the horizon," said Neric, shifting his gaze to the Baron. "We estimate their arrival in the next twenty minutes. Except for your tent and Tasheira's, everything else is ready for loading."

"Good," said the Baron. "Tasheira, you should leave to make sure all your belongings are packed."

"I will," Tash replied, stepping away from the desk.

She paused at the door, however, to watch her father lift the glass globe over Isec's head. He lowered it onto the metal collar, then twisted it to one side. The globe locked into place, followed by a gasp of pressurized air.

The suit was sealed, with Isec now trapped inside for the duration of the long trip ahead.

Chapter 27

HOLDING HER PILLOW UNDER ONE arm and Nym in the other, Elia stepped into the desert's morning light wearing the fresh nightgown she had been given the previous evening. Directly across the camp, she saw Tasheira simultaneously exit the tent where Hokk was being kept. She tried to gauge the other girl's expression, but as Tash moved closer, her face surrendered no clue of his condition.

Elia lowered the fox to the ground and clutched the pillow to her chest. Her intestines felt like coiling ropes by the time Tasheira reached her. "How is he?" she croaked.

"Seems to be doing fine," Tash replied with a relaxed smile as she lowered herself into a shaded chair beside a tray of food. She must have noticed Elia's concern, because she continued with a reassuring tone. "I was just as worried as you, which is why I got up early. But his blisters are down, and we were able to get him clean and ready to go."

"Can I see him?"

"There's really nothing much to see. Not anymore."

Elia cocked her head, and her brow wrinkled. "How can that —"

"He's wearing his suit. He's completely sealed up inside, but perfectly safe and comfortable."

"Oh . . . that's good," Elia replied hesitantly. Tasheira had mentioned this suit several times, yet Elia couldn't imagine what made it so special.

Tash pointed to an empty chair. "Sit and have some breakfast."

As Elia settled into the seat, Marest arrived and greeted her politely, inquiring if she had slept well. "And if you are no longer needing it, Miss Elia, shall I go ahead and strip the bed?"

Feeling herself flush with guilt, Elia held up her pillow. "I'm so sorry, but my forehead bled onto the pillowcase. I guess the bandage leaked during the night." She turned the pillow over and revealed the dark spot smeared on the other side. "But I'm sure I can scrub it out," she added earnestly.

"My goodness, no!" Tasheira snorted with a laugh. "Don't worry about that. Marest will just throw the thing away."

"But the fabric is still perfectly fine," said Elia, shocked by such a wasteful suggestion. "I know what to do with bad stains. Perhaps, Marest, if you have some soap pellets, I can . . ."

"Nonsense!" Tasheira cried out as if Elia's suggestion was the craziest thing she had ever heard. "I'm not putting you to work. You're my guest." She reached for Elia's arm and gave it a comforting squeeze. "My very distinguished guest. I'd say you've been through enough lately, wouldn't you agree?"

Suddenly realizing her dangerous lapse in judgement, Elia could only nod in agreement. To play this part convincingly, she must not offer to help with chores. There were servants now for that.

Tasheira coaxed the pillow from Elia's grasp and tossed it to her attendant. "Just get rid of it, Marest. And hurry up with your work too." Her voice grew firm, sounding almost irritated. "Neric says the horses have been spotted, so they will arrive shortly. I'm sure you still have plenty to organize."

"Yes, indeed, Miss Tasheira," replied Marest with a modest bow before disappearing into the tent.

"How is that wound on your forehead, anyway?" Tasheira wondered as she leaned closer, squinting at Elia's brow.

"It's crusted over." Elia touched the spot self-consciously.

"No, don't pick at it again!" Tasheira exclaimed, playfully slapping away Elia's hand.

"I'm not," Elia said with a shy grin as she promptly lowered her arm.

Preparing for bed the night before, Tasheira had insisted Elia change the lace headband for a true bandage. But when the scab was exposed, the girl had looked at it, seemingly puzzled. Elia feared her tattoo was showing through, so she hastily scratched the wound to make it bleed again. And though Tasheira wanted to first dab it clean, Elia quickly applied the sticky bandage before the girl could get another look.

Perhaps she should get a fresh bandage now. But before she could ask, she realized Tasheira's attention was drawn by something behind them.

Turning, Elia saw a very strange sight. Tasheira's two cousins had emerged from the Baron's tent carrying an object stretched horizontally between them. Like an oversized doll made of thick, white pillows, it had limbs and a massive round head that reflected the sunlight. Elia assumed the thing was lifeless until she saw an arm fall toward the ground, then lift itself up unaided, to rest again on its chest. And then Elia realized. This could only be Hokk.

"That's the suit?" Elia asked in astonishment. She watched the two young men bring Hokk to the shady slope of a nearby sand dune, where they propped him up, wedged into the bank. "Won't he overheat?"

"The suit is specially designed not to. In fact, my father says he'll stay cooler in there than by any other means we can provide. It's quite the design."

"I've never seen such a thing."

"Neither had any of us until I discovered it," Tasheira replied proudly as she took two buns from a plate and passed one to Elia.

While they ate, she described everything: how the many flaming pieces of the moon had fallen onto the island days before; how the most unusual metal vessel was included in the shower of debris; how she had found the wreckage in the desert, as well as clues that at least one person had been on board.

The girl had so convinced herself with this intriguing tale, Elia decided not to explain that Hokk was actually from Below. The truth would only lead to more awkward questions, which she wasn't prepared to deal with.

But what if Hokk had already said things this morning that revealed too much? Tasheira might start testing Elia for holes in her story.

"So, I assume you've been able to confirm all this with him?" Elia asked.

"Unfortunately, no. Isec has said very little. I'll give him a few more days to recover before I press further. Of course, everyone at the palace will want to know all the details, especially since we've been separated so long from our ancestors on the moon."

"Yes, they'll be fascinated," Elia replied grimly.

She gazed at the suit now sitting motionless in the sand — so still, it seemed impossible Hokk could be inside. Nym had wandered over and was standing in front of it, but keeping a safe distance.

"So, how do you know to call him Isec?" Elia asked.

"It's on his suit. Spelled out on a name badge."

"I'll have to look for that." It dawned on Elia that using Hokk's name was another major slip-up she couldn't afford to make going forward. She hadn't been successful avoiding the name in front of Roahm, but now, with Tasheira, Hokk would *always* have to be Isec.

• • •

Thirty or more stallions soared far overhead as they approached the Isle of Drifting Dunes. Many horses didn't have riders, their saddles empty for the passengers they would have to carry back. Some animals were tied together in teams of four, pulling stone barges, like shipping platforms, which were essentially small floating islets that had once been part of larger islands before they broke off.

"I'm surprised they fly at such a high altitude," said Elia, craning her neck. She remembered how her home had been towed back to Kamanman, skimming just above the clouds. "Why don't they fly lower?"

"To avoid Scavengers!" Tash exclaimed as though it was the most obvious answer. "Surely you haven't forgotten about Scavengers!"

"Of course not," Elia replied, pretending to look flustered. "I wasn't thinking."

"Those monsters are notorious for clinging to the sides of these freight islands as stowaways so they can be brought to more populous areas of the System. And we can't have that!"

Elia sucked on her lower lip to prevent herself looking smug. Naturally, Tasheira wouldn't know any better, but Elia now found the idea of Scavengers such a naive fear. It was a fear shared by everyone who lived on the islands of Above — except for the few Imperial Guards who had ventured to Below and now knew better. Would Tash believe the truth without seeing for herself? Unlikely.

The stallions circled above the camp before spiraling down to land on the desert. The flat rocks they were hauling hovered just above the ground, similar to the way all the other islands floated in the clouds. Servants immediately began loading the islets with heavy crates, wooden support beams, stoves, the two remaining sleighs with their masts removed, and all the other household belongings that the Baron and his family had brought to the island.

All the while, Elia kept an eye on Hokk. He hadn't changed position since he had been left in the sand, but once the last of the cargo was loaded, Fimal and Neric directed servants to move him. They squeezed Hokk into a spot between two shipping containers and strapped him in around the waist to make sure he was secure. There he sat, almost regally.

The Baron and Baroness mounted their horses. Two more were brought forward for Tasheira and Elia. Tash seemed excited to see hers, as if they had been separated for a long time. Elia's horse was not large, but it was spirited, tossing its head and pawing the ground.

Elia nervously tugged the waistline of her new dress, one that Marest had set aside for her to wear. Although fashioned to fit Tasheira's measurements, Elia found the garment comfortable. It was a bit baggy in the chest, but she was pleased the sleeves were long enough. However, as she watched Marest approach her now, Elia anxiously eyed the shoes she was carrying.

"Let's see if these are the right size, Miss Elia," Marest said as she handed them over.

"I'm fine," said Elia, pushing the shoes away and trying to speak with the same force she always heard in Tasheira's orders. "I don't need anything."

"It will make the ride so much easier, especially so your feet can stay in the stirrups."

Elia glanced at Tasheira, hoping the girl would tell her servant to back off. Instead, Tasheira studied Elia as if suddenly unsure. "You *do* still remember how to ride, don't you?"

"Of course!" Elia snorted, wondering if her indignation was believable. "I'm sure I've ridden many, *many* times. All my life, in fact." She caught the reins of her frisky horse as it tried to rear up on its hind legs. "Riding is a skill I'd never lose!"

Now she just had to prove it.

Chapter 28

THEY HAD BEEN AIRBORNE FOR a few hours already and Hokk was getting weary.

He kept forgetting about the curved glass surrounding his head. If a sore on his face started itching, he would reach up with his padded arm to scratch it, only to smack the side of the helmet with his bulky glove. But while the painful itch might persist, he was extremely grateful to have the protection of this transparent globe — this entire suit, for that matter. It alone kept him safe as he rode this islet barge being towed to wherever they were going.

The tinted glass spared his eyes from the blinding sunshine and finally allowed him to take in the amazing view without hiding behind his hands. Again, he was overcome with the immensity of the sky and the vast expanse of clouds that passed by *below* him. But the sun! The sun was most incredible of all! Such an intense ball of fire! He could glance at it just long enough to see radiating beams of light dancing around its edges. And though he was sitting beneath its rays, miraculously, Hokk felt no heat. Instead, he sensed the touch of cool air wafting across his skin.

Was the suit producing this draft? It seemed the only possible source since he was sealed so tightly inside. As soon as the helmet had been locked into place, the outfit came to life, automatically filling with air until the internal pressure made the entire thing grow stiff. From that moment on, the suit had continued to hiss and whir, ever so faintly, as if breathing.

But the gear was extremely cumbersome. Hokk sat like a lump on the floating rock platform, supported on either side by wooden crates that kept him from toppling over. Clearly, he was much too heavy to ride one of the stallions, though he would have preferred to join everyone else flying around him. He still had no recollection of how he'd ended up recovering in the camp on the desert, surrounded by strangers, but as he had gradually regained consciousness, he had been comforted to know Elia was among them. They must be members of her family. He had finally succeeded reuniting Elia with those she had been so worried about.

A horse now dropped lower to fly beside him. He recognized Elia sitting in the saddle. She was wearing finer clothing than he had ever seen her in, and most surprisingly, shoes on her feet. Nym was in her lap, and Twister flew just behind, his little wings flapping vigorously to keep up with the horse.

Elia stared at Hokk, looking worried, yet seemed unable to actually see him through the glass. He turned his head, tried to smile and nod; however, the suit did not shift with him. With great effort, he forced his shoulders around and raised his hand to wave, though he clumsily punched the helmet — *thunk* — before his arm lost strength and dropped. Yet it was enough. A relieved grin spread briefly across Elia's face. Then, after looking around as if to confirm no one was watching, she placed a finger to her lips.

Hush.

"Why?" Hokk asked out loud, his voice trapped by the helmet.

The other girl, Tasheira, who had shared food earlier that morning, brought her horse alongside Elia's. Elia quickly dropped her finger and turned. They appeared to be talking. They both glanced in Hokk's direction again — Tasheira's face curious; Elia's face serious, her eyes intense as if to reinforce her earlier gesture.

But Hokk was confused. Though she obviously wanted him to stay silent, what could he possibly say trapped inside this suit?

• • •

Throughout the day, the sun's movement in the sky had seemed almost immeasurable. Now, though, as it dipped into the clouds, Hokk watched it slip away, bit by bit, until just a glowing speck remained. Then it was gone completely. In its absence, the white of the clouds transformed into varied hues, and Hokk felt tempted to tear off his tinted helmet to see the true colors. But even behind the darkened glass, the oranges and pinks that blended upon the surface of the swirling mist looked almost . . . delicious.

Their journey had lasted many long hours, and Hokk wondered how far into the night they would continue traveling. They had stopped only once in the afternoon, landing on a small, desolate island with stunted trees and shrubs. It was a chance to rehydrate the horses and allow everyone else to stretch and relieve themselves in the bushes. Other than this break, they spent the entire time in the air and saw no more islands suspended in the cloud cover below.

Now, as the darkness deepened, Hokk noticed a single growing point of light on the horizon and assumed it was their destination. The spot resembled the countless twinkling lights that spanned the evening sky, like the burst of sparks above a fire. They were little more than specks, however, in comparison to the much larger pieces strewn overhead, which he assumed had once been Elia's moon. She had explained the moon, but nothing about these other tiny lights. How could there be so many of them?

As if sensing they were reaching the end of their journey, the animals began flapping their wings with greater force. Hokk trained his eyes straight ahead. What he had guessed was a single light at the bottom of the sky became many more. They were advancing toward an island that seemed to be ablaze with fire — not uncontrolled flames, but rather the contained fire of glowing lanterns as well as torches, which he began to distinguish as they moved closer.

Compared to the huge chunks of rock Hokk used to observe drifting over the prairies, this island was relatively small. It appeared to be the estate of one family. Their home — a massive structure with multiple tiers and columns along its front — sat in the middle of the property, with fields and gardens that stretched beyond the flickering lights.

A brightly lit front courtyard was ringed with massive candelabras, each as tall as a man, with candles as thick and long as Hokk's arm. Servants awaiting their arrival stood in two rows and only broke formation to grab the reins of horses as they touched down on the cobblestones. Footstools were carried forward to allow the lady and gentleman of the estate to dismount first, then the rest of the family. Elia, Tasheira, and a female servant who had been flying with them were surrounded by other staff in skirts and aprons who whisked them along a walkway strung with paper lanterns that swayed in the wind. They were escorted up wide stone steps before disappearing into the house.

Hokk was certain he would be forgotten and left behind with the rest of the cargo, but the two well-dressed young men he had seen in the tent, along with the older man they called the Baron, ordered several staff members to climb up and carefully remove him from his perch. Once Hokk was lowered to ground level, the Baron held his helmet between his two broad hands and twisted it off. The rigid suit deflated as the air escaped.

"Journey's over," declared the Baron. "You were able to manage all right?"

"I'm fine," replied Hokk, his voice hoarse. The quality of the outside air seemed drier and thinner than what he had been breathing all day.

"Yes, you look well," the Baron decided. "And you stayed conscious the whole time?"

"I did. Or at least, I think I did."

The man nodded with satisfaction. "Good. You're not as red as yesterday, and your skin is already starting to peel. That's a positive sign. Another day, and you'll look more like your usual self. I can see you are tired, though, so we'll take you inside and get you out of this suit. I suggest applying some more medicine before we send you to bed. You'll feel even better by morning. And then after breakfast, you'll join me in the library. I'm curious to know every detail about where you have come from and why you fell out of the sky."

Chapter **29**

"YOUR NAME IS ISEC, OK?"

"What?" Hokk asked with a start. Elia was suddenly beside his bed. He hadn't seen her enter. He sat up and glanced from her to a side door where the Baron and his attendant had stepped into an adjoining room.

Elia's gaze swung in the same direction before her eyes darted back to Hokk. She appeared anxious, as if expecting the two men would soon return, which was a very safe bet. "Just be careful what you say!" she hissed.

"Is that what you were trying to signal to me earlier?" he whispered. He was no longer wearing the padded suit, but was instead bare-chested and lying under a lightweight bedspread pulled up to his waist.

"I have to make this quick. They think you fell from the moon. That your name is Isec. I haven't corrected them."

"But why would they —"

"Shh." Elia looked behind again. "And they know nothing about Below, nothing about how you and I are connected. I want to keep it that way for now."

"Really? You're not going to tell your family?"

Elia flinched, suddenly caught off guard. "They're . . . not family," she replied in a somber tone.

"I just assumed —"

"I don't know who any of these people are."

"Who's got my sack?"

"I do."

Her apprehension was contagious. "Are we in danger?" Hokk asked grimly.

"No."

"Then how did they find us?"

"I found them. They have ties to the palace. They'll be traveling there soon, and the Baron's daughter, Tasheira, says we will be joining them. Which is perfect, because —" She paused when the sound of commotion rose in the outside hallway. The household was still in turmoil with the family's arrival less than thirty minutes earlier, and Elia seemed to be waiting in case the door abruptly opened.

"It's perfect because . . . ?" Hokk repeated, prompting her.

Elia returned her focus to him and lowered her voice. "Because it gets me even closer to home. Hopefully, I can learn what's happened to the rest of my *real* family. And maybe, by returning to the palace, I can find out why the telescope is so important that people are willing to risk their lives for it."

"By risking your own? Returning to the palace might be too dangerous. Why not just forget about it and carry on as you did before any of this happened?"

"I can't. I want to, but unfortunately, it's not as easy as that. I don't see how my life can ever be the same again now that I've been implicated in this whole mess. Though I'm afraid what might happen, I have to see this through to the end, whatever that end may be. Perhaps I can use the telescope, or the secrets it reveals, as a bargaining tool if my life is ever threatened."

"And I want to help you. You can count on me."

"I know I can," Elia replied. "So then, don't be surprised if they call you Isec. Go along with it. And make up some story about being a descendant of our ancestors from the moon." She grimaced and shook her head. "I don't really know what you can say, however. Tasheira says she found your vessel crashed in a crater. Something about you falling out of the sky."

"The Baron made the same comments to me."

Elia nodded. "I'm not surprised. They're very interested to hear our stories."

"So, what's yours?"

"I'm pretending to be suffering from memory loss. I found you unconscious in the desert, suffering from sunstroke. Then they rescued both of us and brought us here. But whatever you decide to tell them, don't include me in any way. I find keeping things simple is best. It stops them asking too many —"

As she had been anticipating, the hallway door opened. Elia jumped back from the bed just as one of the younger gentlemen walked in, carrying something folded in his arms.

"Oh," the young man said with surprise. "I thought I would find my uncle in here."

"He just stepped into the other room," Hokk quickly replied with a nod to the side. "He mentioned getting the ingredients for more medicine."

"Of course," said the nephew. "That paste has done a marvelous job treating your blisters." He placed what he was carrying on an elegant bureau that matched the lavish decor of the room and then approached Hokk. "Now that you're more alert and settled, I can properly introduce myself." He reached out his hand. "I'm Fimal. Very pleased to meet you, Isec."

Hokk shook hands. "I'm very grateful to you and your family."

"We're just fortunate Miss Elia, here, was able to find our camp and then help my cousin, Tasheira, locate you again on the desert." Fimal turned to Elia. "I trust your journey today was satisfactory, my dear."

"Long, but uneventful. I'm looking forward to another good night's sleep," said Elia, showing no trace of her earlier anxiety. She pulled an object from her pocket. "I actually stopped by to give something to Isec before it goes missing."

Between her fingers, she pinched a polished orange stone. As she passed it to Hokk, he recognized it as the one she had retrieved as a keepsake from her grandfather's meager collection.

"I'm sure you recognize this," Elia continued. "When I found you unconscious, it was clenched in your fist. I was afraid you'd lose it in the sand."

"Ah, yes, thank you," replied Hokk, understanding her ruse as he took the stone. "It has great meaning."

"And I've brought back the rest of your things too," said Fimal, indicating the small pile sitting on the cabinet. "Your trousers, and the little waist pouch. I'm curious about the feathered darts inside it."

Hokk's eyes flicked toward Elia, who gave no more than a casual glance in the direction of the bureau. Thankfully, she didn't seem to realize the significance of the stolen projectiles.

The Baron re-entered the room, grinding the mortar and pestle. Seeing Elia, he gave a wide grin. "I hope your accommodations are acceptable, Miss Elia, though you'll find the household will take at least a full day before it begins functioning like normal again."

"Absolutely. Your home is incredibly beautiful, and your hospitality is beyond what anyone could hope for. I feel very fortunate."

"I'm so pleased," replied the Baron, his smile unwavering as he dipped his fingers into the mortar for a gob of paste.

"In fact, Tasheira is probably waiting for me," said Elia, taking a step backward. "We have our rooms next to each other just down the hallway, so I won't bother you any further."

Elia gave her two hosts a respectful nod before moving toward the door. The Baron began smearing paste onto Hokk's shoulder and Fimal stepped closer, yet Hokk could still see

Elia where she had paused behind them. Her gaze swung to the side of the room. With a frown on her face, she drifted toward the bureau. Hokk swallowed nervously and watched as her hand shot out. Snatching the leather pouch, she tucked it into the folds of her dress and slipped silently from the room.

Chapter 30

SURELY THE EQUIVALENT OF EVERY morsel of food
Elia had ever eaten was spread out before her: fruits of all
colors; biscuits dripping with butter and honey; eggs that
were poached, baked, or hard-boiled in their shells; trays of
sliced meats and cheeses; amber-, rose-, and green-tinted
teas in glass vessels that steamed over burning candles. It was
definitely too much food — too much choice — for the five
people assembled. So far, neither the Baron nor Hokk had
shown up, and probably none of the servants who hovered
against the walls, including Marest, would enjoy this breakfast
— unless they snuck some later for themselves surreptitiously.

Elia filled her plate with a heaping pile, taking more than
even Neric and Fimal who sat opposite. Her instinct was to use
her hands and immediately devour everything, but instead, she
resisted, observing first how others were using their utensils.
Ineptly maneuvering her knife and fork, she shoveled the food
into her mouth, relishing flavors she had never experienced.
Though the rest of the people in the room were probably
noticing how quickly she was eating, she couldn't slow herself.
She was starving and too tempted by the many tantalizing
items still waiting to be tasted.

Seated beside her, Tasheira had taken much smaller por-
tions, which she was only picking at. "Breakfast gets so boring,"
the girl sighed.

The Baroness was slumped in a chair at the end of the table.
When she had arrived, shuffling her feet, she offered only a
few mumbled greetings, which prompted similarly indifferent
replies from the rest of the family. Elia hadn't actually met
the woman, except for seeing her at a distance on the Isle of
Drifting Dunes, so she was expecting somebody to make an
introduction this morning. Surprisingly, no one bothered. A
few times already, Elia caught Tasheira's mother glancing in
her direction, yet the woman would quickly look away with
an awkward smirk on her face.

Even with such a bountiful selection, the Baroness refused
food as the platters were offered. "No," she pouted like a child.
"Bring me my incense."

Tasheira snorted and tossed a spoon onto her plate. The
clatter made the Baroness look up with a start. "Do you have
to do that now?" Tash complained as her mother's personal
servant lit a flame at the tip of a very long, thin stick.

"Really, Tasheira, you must learn better manners." When
the Baroness spoke, her eyes seemed to drift independently of
each other. "You will be leaving in a few weeks —"

"Thank goodness!"

"— so don't make things worse around here than they
have to be."

"The smell of your so-called *incense* makes me sick!"

"Well, I'm already sick," her mother spat back. "And this
is the only thing that makes me feel better."

The servant blew out the flame, causing smoke to curl up
into the air. The Baroness then took the stick and waved it
below her nostrils, inhaling deeply with a contented sigh. For
a woman who appeared legitimately ill and weak, she seemed
remarkably revitalized by the incense. Elia wondered why Tash
would want to deny her mother this comfort.

As the smoke drifted in Tasheira's direction, the girl blew it back toward the Baroness and fanned her hand in front of her wrinkled nose. "Keep that stuff away from me!"

The Baroness frowned and pointed at Tash. "How many times have I told you? You must remember to behave properly; otherwise, you'll embarrass the family, especially when you're at the palace."

"*I'm* the one embarrassing the family?" Tash asked incredulously. "You must be joking!"

Elia glanced across the table at Tasheira's cousins, who looked just as awkward as she felt. Neric took a few more bites of his meal, then tossed his napkin onto his plate, which still contained plenty of food. He pushed back his chair and stood. "Come on, Fimal," he muttered. "Let's get out to the stables."

Fimal popped a last tidbit into his mouth and then got to his feet as well. The two brothers left the dining hall without another word.

"You're chasing everyone away," Tasheira accused her mother.

"Nonsense."

"Father never eats with us anymore."

The woman's expression seemed to glaze over and she crumpled even further into her chair. The incense stick hung so limp in her hand her servant had to retrieve it.

Tasheira spun on Elia. "Are you almost finished? I want to leave too."

Elia quickly swallowed what she was chewing, but almost choked. "No, not yet," she sputtered, wiping her mouth with the back of her hand. "Though, I'm sorry," she added sheepishly, holding her stomach. "I think I took more than I should have. I'm slowing down."

Tash dismissed Elia's concern with a wave of her hand. "Doesn't matter."

Elia couldn't fathom being so wasteful, but when Marest pulled back Tasheira's chair so she could stand, Elia feared being left behind with the Baroness. "What shall I do with the leftovers?"

"Just leave it. Find Nym and then come out with me to the stables,"Tash ordered, firing a final glare at her mother before storming past Marest and exiting the hall.

Elia rose, but hesitated. "I hate to waste anything." She looked down on her plate, then at Marest. "Perhaps you can enjoy it?" she suggested.

Marest appeared mortified. "My goodness, no. It wouldn't be appropriate."

• • •

Elia sat in direct sunlight, balancing on top of a fence with her feet hooked around the lowest rail as Nym sniffed around in the grasses and chased wandering chickens.

The fencing around the property divided the lush green pasture land into plots for grazing, separating the much smaller herds of sheep and cattle from the estate's significantly large horse population. Right now, the majority of the winged thoroughbreds were actually airborne, swirling overhead, and tended by mounted stablemen. While the animals would touch down in the fields when they grew tired, thirsty, or hungry, the horses were soon flying once more, diving and soaring on the air currents, their shadows playing catch-up below.

Elia was observing everything with the lady-in-waiting's telescope. The enlarged images sprang toward her with amazing detail. A few times, she spotted Tasheira riding her own steed, yet Elia would quickly lose sight of them as the animal changed directions. But it didn't matter. The real reason for removing the telescope from its protective box was to see what secrets it could reveal. Though Elia still wasn't sure how the device exposed the truth about things, she suspected it would finally prove itself useful when she returned to the palace. In the meantime, there seemed to be plenty of conflict here with Tasheira's family, so she was intrigued by what the telescope might show.

She pointed the instrument at the Baron's colossal home. She could see every feature of the strange, stone-carved beasts adorning the roofline, each leaf on the vines that climbed the walls, individual bricks in the chimneys, movement at one of the windows, just behind the curtains. Was somebody attempting to peer outside without being seen?

Elia tried refocusing the lens when suddenly, a blurry, bright red image blocked her view. Recoiling, she lowered the telescope to discover the Baroness standing in front of her.

"I startled you," said the woman.

"It was my fault. I didn't hear you approach," Elia replied as she quickly collapsed the three sections of the telescope.

The Baroness was wearing a red cape and a fancy black hat perched precariously on her head. In her hand, she clenched the last remaining two inches of an incense stick. Her attendant stood behind.

"You've decided not to join Tasheira?" she asked with an upward flick of her wrist, though Elia noticed her inquisitive gaze linger upon the telescope in her lap.

"No, I didn't feel like it." Elia was worried the Baroness would want a reason, so she turned the question back to her. "Are you going for a ride yourself?"

"I spent enough time on a horse yesterday." She surveyed the property. "Is Marest out here too, or up at the manor?"

"I believe she's still unpacking everything."

Tasheira's mother grunted and flicked her incense to the ground. Elia's eyes followed it, watching as the small ember at the tip smoldered in the grasses. Nym approached with interest, his nose twitching.

Looking up again, Elia saw the woman's attendant pull out a fresh stick.

"Light two of them," the Baroness ordered coldly, and her servant obeyed.

Once the flames were snuffed out and replaced with tendrils of smoke, the Baroness held one out to Elia. Remembering Tash's reaction to the incense, Elia thought it best to be cautious, but before she could decline the offer, wisps of the spicy scent tempted her nostrils. It's a harmless fragrance, she told herself as she took the stick, not wanting to insult the woman.

One tentative sniff — she was too curious to resist — and Elia felt a faint calming sensation. Another whiff made her shoulders relax as though she might be able to let down her guard. This stuff didn't seem to be so bad after all. Maybe Tasheira simply enjoyed overreacting to it, just to spite her mother.

Noticing the smoke's therapeutic effect on Elia, the Baroness gave a half smile, though it quickly faded. "I'll be losing Tasheira for good in a few weeks," the woman said sadly.

"When she leaves for the palace?"

"That's right. And I'll be left here all alone."

Elia thought this was an odd comment since the property employed so many staff. "Won't you be able to visit her?"

"I hate being among the Royal Court. I never accompany my husband when he leaves to sell our stallions. Tasheira thinks she'll love it, but time will prove otherwise, I'm sure."

Elia didn't know how to respond. She simply stared up at the horses.

"Of course, Marest will be going with her," the Baroness continued, giving a side glance at Elia. "I think she plans to take you too."

"So I understand."

"But I wonder if you wouldn't prefer to stay here."

Elia's eyes flared for an instant before she masked her shock. "No, I think it's better that I go. I need to be reunited with my family, whoever they are. My memory is still failing me. My parents are probably very worried."

The Baroness pinched her lips, studying her before she spoke. "I don't believe you."

"What?" Elia gasped, feeling instant perspiration glisten across her forehead. Had this woman figured out the truth about her already?

Tasheira's mother pressed a hand on Elia's breastbone. "I understand pain. I can read pain when others are suffering. And *you* are a person who's suffering. You're unhappy."

"I'm fine," said Elia. She caught herself breathing in the incense again, which seemed to calm her pulse.

"I fear life in the palace will be too much for you. I believe you'll be better off with me. Tasheira already has Marest. You can be *my* companion. Doesn't that sound like a better plan?"

Elia collected herself. "I still feel —"

A blaze of irritation twisted the Baroness's face. "You will be terrorized by the other women in the court. Trust me. It will happen, regardless of your family's ties. You're ugly, which for some reason, you don't seem to realize. Your hair's much too short and you have that horrible bandage on your forehead. You lack womanly curves, and to make matters worse, you have a clueless air about you that will make you an easy target."

Elia's mouth hung open. She was too dumbfounded by the woman's attack to respond.

A sudden gust of wind surged above their heads, disrupting the uncomfortable silence. The woman ducked her head and reached up to hold her hat. As Elia stepped down from the fence rail, a horse landed beside them, and Tasheira launched herself from the saddle. Nym scurried out of the way as Tash strode angrily toward Elia. She yanked the incense stick from her hand and mashed it into the ground with her boot. "Get rid of that!" she shouted before spinning on her mother. "And you stay away from us!"

"Tasheira, my dear. You're such a tyrant," the Baroness

sneered, holding a shaky hand up to her nose as if to ward off a foul smell.

"I despise you!" Tash yelled, then turned back to Elia, pointing an accusatory finger toward her mother. "Don't listen to a single thing this woman says! She can't be trusted!"

Chapter 31

AS HE WAS ESCORTED INTO the library, Hokk immediately shielded his face against the glare of sunlight streaming in through the floor-to-ceiling windows.

The Baron was standing right beside him. "Get those drapes drawn," he commanded. The *swish* of curtain rings dragging across their rods quickly followed and the room darkened.

Hokk dropped his arm, though his eyes still had to adjust before he could make out Fimal sitting on a sofa and the Baron taking his seat behind a large polished desk. Servants, who had lowered two chandeliers to floor level, were removing the stubs of old candles and installing new ones. Once the wicks had been lit, the room grew brighter and the crystal fixtures were hoisted back up with ropes and pulleys to the lofty ceiling, the lines tied securely into place.

"Will Tasheira be joining us?" asked the Baron. "I'm sure she will find this very interesting."

"She was supposed to be coming," replied Fimal. "Neric too, though I don't know what's keeping them. We all went out to the stables after breakfast."

Hokk was only half listening as he scanned the cavernous room. When Uncle Charyl had begun teaching him how to read and write — prior to Hokk's exile from Ago, when his uncle was living in great comfort with Auntie Una — Hokk had learned about the massive book collections that the Ancients had assembled in what they used to call *libraries*. Hokk had never been to one because they existed long ago, before their printed volumes were misplaced, stolen, or destroyed over the centuries. Now, given the Baron's obvious wealth, he was keen to see how many books the man had managed to accumulate.

Yet for all the cabinets lining the walls of this personal library, Hokk could see very few books. A quick count and he estimated less than two dozen. Instead, the shelves were filled with a multitude of artifacts, many of which were difficult to identify, though unmistakably old. The items reminded him of the debris he had found almost a month earlier, dug up from the ancient garbage dump buried beneath the prairies. As Hokk now approached the shelves for a closer look, he recognized a number of things: all manner of rusted tools, knives, and metal gears; colorful glassware and ceramic bowls; row upon row of battered shoes; numerous jars filled with keys, and another set filled with coins. To his great surprise, Hokk also saw a lot of plastic objects, from brushes and utensils to toys and containers. Since Elia had mentioned on the plains of Below that she had never seen plastic, he had assumed no such thing existed in Above. But now here, clearly, was further evidence that his world and Elia's used to be one.

Hokk's eyes settled on several stacks of very thin, flat rectangles of stiff plastic with rounded corners. Identical in size and about as long as his palm, there were probably two to three hundred in total. He picked up a handful and shuffled through them. They had various colors and designs, and each had a row of raised numbers on the front, stamped through from the back. Below the numbers were similarly embossed but smaller words, which appeared to be names.

"I found many more of those things during this most recent excursion," said the Baron. "I'm still trying to determine what they are."

"They're plastic."

"Plastic?" the Baron repeated as if having never heard the word before, just as Hokk expected. "And what does a plastic do?"

"No, I mean it's the material they're made from."

"That's the name for it, is it? I've always wondered."

"Actually, a lot of the things on your shelves are composed of plastic." Hokk fanned out the objects in his hand and held them up. "Same with these cards — or whatever they are — though I'm not sure what they would have been used for." He returned them to their pile, then swung around with open arms. "But I must say, I'm very impressed with your collection. I used to collect quite a lot too, items I found abandoned. How long has it taken you to assemble everything?"

The Baron seemed pleased by Hokk's admiration. "I've been an archaeology enthusiast since my teenage years."

"Arky — lodgie . . . what?" asked Hokk. Now he was the one hearing a new word for the first time.

"Ar-chae-ol-o-gy," the Baron repeated, carefully sounding out the syllables. "It's the historical study of human activity. When I travel to dig sites, I recover what people from our past have left behind. It allows me to piece together their stories."

"And all these plastic items were found on the islands of Above?" Hokk asked, lifting a plastic doll with ratty black hair and skin as pale as his own. "Nowhere else?"

"Yes, of course, on the various islands of the System, though I've made most of my discoveries on the one where you landed. The Isle of Drifting Dunes. The area has remained undisturbed and often proves to have some of the best-preserved artifacts." Suddenly curious, the Baron raised an eyebrow. "But why do you ask? Where else were you thinking?"

Hokk shrugged.

"The moon, perhaps?" asked the Baron.

JASON CHABOT

"There's much to learn about the past and how we've come to be here," said Hokk, evasively.

"Yes," the man replied, gesturing for Hokk to sit in a plush chair in front of his desk. "Which is why I wanted to spend time with you today, Isec."

"My name is actually Hokk," he replied as he settled into the seat.

The Baron cocked his head. "It is?"

Silent until now, Fimal chuckled. "All this time, we've been calling you Isec because of the name badge on your suit. Tasheira had us convinced."

"Isec is actually my *last* name," Hokk lied. "So you're not far off. Just thought I'd correct you in case you hear me called something different."

"Well, Hokk it is," said the Baron. "But you *are* from the moon, are you not? We didn't get that wrong, did we?"

Hokk shifted in his chair and rubbed his thighs to flatten the material of his borrowed trousers. "No, that's right," he said with a nod. "From the moon."

"So what's your story?" Fimal asked eagerly.

"Yes, how did you manage to be among us?" wondered the Baron.

Hokk gave a wry smile. "I'm curious to hear your theory first. Tell me what you've pieced together and I'll share whether you're right or wrong."

He hoped the Baron would take the bait. When Hokk saw a broad grin spread across the man's face, he knew it had worked.

The Baron stood up and started pacing while he stroked his chin. "Our people in the Lunera System have been separated from your people on the moon — who are descendants of the ancestors we share — for centuries, with apparently no ability to reconnect across such a vast distance. But you're part of the first successful attempt that has been made to change that."

Hokk nodded, hoping to encourage him.

The Baron began speaking faster. "A specially designed

craft was constructed to bring you here to re-establish the link between our two worlds — your world, which we see as pieces high in our sky, and our world, which was created from the remaining moon fragments that now float in the clouds around us."

"I'm impressed," said Hokk, trying to sound believable. "Your explanation is incredibly accurate."

"But why did your vessel crash-land?" the Baron wondered.

Hokk thought quickly. "As you said, this was the first attempt at contact. The mission failed. Or rather, it would have failed if you hadn't rescued me."

"And what about the other burning pieces we saw falling out of the sky?" asked Fimal. He was frowning, looking almost skeptical.

Hokk prevented himself from squirming in his seat. "Unfortunately, I guess I'm the only survivor. The other crafts in our fleet must have all burned to cinders. But at least there's still one of us to deliver our message."

"What's your message?" asked the Baron.

"I'm sorry," said Hokk, bowing his head respectfully. "I received strict orders about who I could deliver the message to first."

"The Twin Emperors," Fimal concluded.

"Twins?" Hokk replied, pretending to sound surprised. "If that's the case, then yes, the two of them."

"We're actually taking a trip soon to visit the emperors to sell the horses that have matured since our last visit. But the whole family isn't going. Just Tasheira and me. My wife and my nephews," the man added with a nod toward Fimal, "will remain at the estate to oversee the newest generation of foals. They'll start to be born any day now."

"I would be most grateful if I could join you on your journey."

"That was always the plan. Though, regrettably, it will mean another uncomfortable trip. As before, you'll need protection from the sunlight," the Baron added.

"Actually, Uncle, I thought of an alternative to make things easier for Isec — um, I mean Hokk," said Fimal. He rose from his seat and approached the farthest wall. "If I'm not mistaken, I seem to remember something from one of your digs a few years ago. It reminded me a lot of Hokk's helmet, but *much* less cumbersome."

Both the Baron and Hokk were intrigued as they watched Fimal scour the lower shelves, then stand on his tiptoes. When he still couldn't find it, he went to the corner of the room and pulled a ladder along a track that followed the edge of the ceiling. He climbed higher and looked on both sides until he found what he wanted. Grabbing it, he returned to the floor and brought the object forward.

"This should help you see better," Fimal announced.

He held a pair of spectacles between his fingers. The two lenses were tinted black.

"That's a brilliant solution!" said the Baron. "Try them on."

Hokk hooked the spectacles around his ears and his view of the room immediately dimmed.

"Until now, these particular glasses always seemed so useless. The lenses don't actually magnify anything and they are much too dark," the Baron explained. "But they might be exactly what you need." He stood and pulled apart the drapes behind his desk.

Hokk automatically squeezed his eyes shut, but opened them when he realized the glasses were reducing the sun's intensity. He came around the desk and stared outside, where he could see the pastures and the flying horses swirling in the air. "They work perfectly!"

The Baron turned to his nephew. "I'm impressed you remembered them. With so much stuff on these shelves, I often forget what I have. Or how some artifact might be put to use."

Still wearing the shaded glasses, Hokk returned to his seat. There was no need to close the curtains.

"Well, I'm glad that problem is solved," said the Baron. "Yet it makes me wonder once again who in the past would have ever needed to wear such things." He drummed his fingers on his lips, studying Hokk. "And while we're on the subject, I must confess — I'm puzzled why you have such a severe sensitivity to the sun. I've never seen anyone with your pale skin color. And most curious of all, you have only an outer eyelid, no secondary membrane. No wonder your eyes are so troubled in the sunlight. How did that come to be?"

"Would you believe that until recently, every person I've ever known had skin as light as mine and only one set of eyelids?"

The Baron seemed astounded. "Is that true?"

"It's a fact. Have you really *never* seen anybody as pale as me?" Hokk asked. He was interested whether someone like the Baron, with such an inquiring mind, had ever questioned the notion that his origins could only be traced to the moon. Did he have absolutely no concept — no inkling whatsoever — of Below and its inhabitants?

"Well, there has been one other person," said the Baron.

Intrigued, Hokk sat straighter.

"Empress Faytelle," the man continued.

"An empress?" Hokk replied, pulling back with surprise.

"That's right. The woman who married Emperor Tohryn. She was much paler back then when they first wed." The Baron looked at his nephew. "I don't believe you've ever seen her in person, have you?"

"No, I haven't," replied Fimal. "Only her portrait."

"Yes, her portrait!" the Baron exclaimed, quickly rising and coming around his desk. "Come with me," he ordered.

Hokk and Fimal followed the Baron out of the library and into the long hallway that stretched beyond the double doors. Massive framed paintings hung along the walls on both sides.

"From what I had always understood, Empress Faytelle came from a very distant island, one that drifts on the outskirts of the System, making it extremely difficult to travel to," the Baron explained. "Supposedly, it drifts close enough only every few decades. The last time was when the empress arrived to become Tohryn's wife."

Hokk removed his dark glasses to look at the people painted in their stiff, regal poses, staring out through the windows of their ornate, gilded frames.

The Baron gestured to the portraits with a wave of his hand as he strode along. "Thirteen generations of nobility on these walls. My great-great-great-grandfather started collecting these paintings, and I've kept up the tradition." He led the way to the end of the hall and pointed to the last two pictures. "And these are the most recent additions, installed about twenty years ago."

Hokk gazed at the first canvas. Newlyweds. A young emperor and empress, both very serious, sat side by side on thrones in front of their Royal Court, their hands clasped between them.

"This is Empress Faytelle," said the Baron. "As I was saying, you can see how pale her skin was at the time. But now it makes me wonder —" He cut himself off to consider it further. "Perhaps it was never true that she came from a distant island. Perhaps she's from the moon too, and for whatever reason, it's never been revealed."

As Hokk stared at the empress's image, he realized the Baron had failed to mention her obviously dark hair. Compared to the blond courtiers surrounding her in the painting, this feature made the woman very striking and distinct. And her features confirmed what Hokk had been suspecting — she was undeniably from Below.

A female servant came running down the hall toward them. "Baron Shoad," she called out breathlessly.

"What is it?" snapped the Baron, unhappy with the interruption.

"A messenger has arrived."

Listening, but not removing his gaze from the wall, Hokk shifted down to the last painting. This could only be a portrait of the first emperor's twin — it appeared to be the same man sitting beside a different wife.

"And what news does this messenger have to deliver?" asked the Baron.

As Hokk scrutinized the face of the second empress on the canvas, his hand shot up to cover the startled gasp from his mouth.

"He didn't share his message," said the servant. "But he's from the palace."

"The palace? We weren't expecting them so soon."

Hokk felt light-headed. He clutched the wall for support.

Fimal must have noticed his reaction. "Are you all right?"

His words caught the Baron's attention as well and the man turned to Hokk. "What's wrong?" he asked with concern.

Hokk struggled to speak. He pointed to the couple in the last painting. "Who's this?" he sputtered.

The Baron looked at the image. "This is Tohryn's twin brother, Emperor Tael, as a young man."

"No, the woman," said Hokk.

"His wife, Empress Mahkoiyin."

"Mahkoiyin?" Hokk repeated, staring into the woman's clear, serene eyes. "Koiyin?"

There was no mistaking the three moles that formed a triangle above the empress's parted, slightly smiling lips.

Chapter 32

"WHAT WAS MY MOTHER TALKING to you about?" Tasheira demanded as they entered the stables.

"Nothing much," Elia replied, following behind with Nym.

Tash turned and her eyes narrowed. "You're lying." She threw open a stall door with a crash before leading her horse into the empty enclosure.

"She mentioned how she'll miss you after you leave."

"Did she say it in those words?"

"Basically," said Elia. She saw a grooming brush hanging from a peg, so she took it and began brushing the horse's glistening coat.

Tash was intent on digging deeper. "There was more, I'm sure of it. It was written all across your face when I found the two of you together." She slid her back down the wall until she was sitting on the ground, then wrapped her arms around her knees. "Now tell me what my mother said. Honestly, I'm not angry with you, but I know you're withholding something."

Elia sighed before reluctantly answering. "The Baroness suggested I stay here when you leave for the palace."

"What?" Tash exclaimed in disbelief. "Here on the estate? Why?"

"She thought I might prefer to be her companion instead of yours."

"That woman's even more insane than I thought. I can't believe —"

Tash stopped talking as a stable hand arrived carrying a bale of hay. While he pulled it apart for the horse to eat, Elia focused on her brushstrokes. Carefully combing around the base of the animal's wings, it was not lost on Elia that her grandmother had performed this same task every day of her life — or at least until the woman's mind began to fade. Omi's work had always seemed so ideal compared to being stuck underground in the palace laundry.

The pounding of feet along the stable corridor announced Marest just before she ran into the stall. "I'm glad I found you!" the girl wheezed. "We have to leave!"

"Leave?" asked Tasheira. "What — this very minute?"

Tash's attendant shook her head, trying to catch her breath. "No, not *right* now. And not tomorrow either. But the day after, absolutely, otherwise it will be too late."

"You're not making sense."

Marest noticed Elia brushing the horse and frowned. She turned back to Tasheira. "A messenger from the palace arrived less than an hour ago. The house is all abuzz."

"So just tell me already!"

"The air currents have changed. We don't have to wait the three weeks until the Noble Sanctuary drifts close enough to start our journey. It's close now."

"Now?" Tasheira repeated with surprise as she quickly stood. "You've just finished getting all my stuff unpacked!"

"I know," Marest replied, a hint of annoyance in her voice. "But the Drift Master's predictions had to be recalculated. A messenger was sent last week with the new coordinates, but of course, we weren't here. Now we have even less time to ready ourselves."

The stable hand spun around with a concerned expression. "Does that include preparing all the horses that the Baron plans to sell?"

"I assume it does," said Marest.

"Well, at least we don't have to wait *longer*," said Tasheira. "The sooner I can get away from here, the better."

• • •

A full afternoon and evening of frenzied preparations had left Tasheira's bedroom in shambles.

Her room was very large, with a plush, intricately woven carpet that ran the entire length. Lounges, tables, and stuffed chairs along one side faced an immense fireplace; on the other, a bank of glass doors opened upon a balcony with stone balustrades, and a view of the gardens, the edge of the island, and the sun, which was now close to setting.

A huge, four-poster bed sat at the farthest end of the room, and from the ceiling, cascading swaths of fabric hung around the thick mattress as if the drapes protected an enchanted realm within. Behind the bed, additional layers of curtains obscured a passageway that led to Tasheira's huge walk-in closet. Marest had been coming back and forth from there since they had left the stables, hauling out clothing, shoes, and boxes, and leaving them around the bedchamber wherever she could find space.

"What about this?" asked Marest, looking frazzled as she held up yet another dress.

"Everything! I need *everything* packed!" Tasheira said adamantly as she picked through and inspected items.

"I don't think it's your size anymore."

"Doesn't matter. It's all coming with me. Whatever I don't need, Elia can use for the time being." Tash turned to Elia and pointed to a jumbled pile of clothing on a sofa. "I'm setting all this aside for you."

"I appreciate whatever you can spare," Elia replied.

"Not a problem. Until we can sort things out for you, you've got to be perfectly presentable. I won't have it any other way."

Tasheira's generosity gave Elia only a faint sense of relief. After receiving such harsh criticism from the Baroness, she couldn't shake a burgeoning fear about facing life at court. The Baroness was right — even with Tasheira's support, how did Elia think she could possibly survive the ruthless, intimidating environment of the Mirrored Palace?

"I'm actually quite nervous," Elia now dared to admit.

Tash raised one eyebrow. "About what?"

"Going back." Her voice tightened. "Having to meet the Twin Emperors."

Tasheira lowered herself sideways into a chair where Nym was curled up beneath it, asleep. She kicked her legs over the armrest. "I bet you've met them before. You just don't remember."

"Yes, perhaps," Elia said. She picked up a piece of clothing and began folding it to keep her hands busy and her nerves in check. A part of her would have welcomed the more tranquil state she had experienced — though it had been tantalizingly brief — when she'd inhaled her first breath of incense. She could imagine why the Baroness always kept her medicine close by. "But I'm sure I've forgotten all the rules of protocol," Elia continued. "Don't be surprised if I make a fool of myself."

"Just don't mix up the emperors' names when you address them and you'll be fine. They look identical, but it's actually easy to tell them apart. Emperor Tael is the blind one. You can remember if you think *tail* and picture him holding on to somebody's *tail*coat as he's guided around the palace. And Emperor Tohryn is the one with all the children, as though he's *torn*, not knowing which one of his kids he should spend time with. Not surprisingly, it's Crown Prince Veralion who gets most of his attention. Then there's Faytelle, his wife, who you'll know immediately. There's no mistaking her. Other than that, they should be simple to keep straight."

"Yes, that makes it easier," Elia replied. "*Tail* and *torn*."

"I'm certain it'll all come back to you."

"We'll see. But I'm also worried I won't fit in. That my hair's too short. Even the Baroness said so."

"Nonsense. You're letting my mother get to you. If you wear a turban around your head, no one will notice. I can help you wrap it before we arrive."

"You seem very calm about going, especially if you'll be leaving here for good."

"I've been waiting a long time for this to happen. Ever since Neric and Fimal's half sister, Jeska, became a lady-in-waiting for Empress Faytelle, I've been eager for the same opportunity. Until now, I was too young."

"I didn't realize you had another cousin."

"A half cousin. She's much older, and better connected. She's never lived with us."

"But you'll be joining her?"

"Yes. Upon her recommendation, I've been invited to be a lady-in-waiting for the empress too."

"How fortunate," said Elia as she added another folded piece of clothing to the growing pile.

"It's certainly prestigious. Naturally, there will be many more experienced women there, but I don't plan to stay at the bottom for long, if at all. Sooner than later, I hope to marry well, and I'll have a better chance if I can gain Empress Faytelle's favor."

Marest arrived with another armload. "We're getting close to the last of it."

"Good. It's getting late," said Tasheira as she stretched in her armchair and yawned. "Tomorrow, you can finish getting it all packed and loaded, right?"

"Yes," said Marest. She stepped toward Elia and yanked away the blouse that Elia was about to remove from a hanger.

"I'm sorry," said Elia, startled by the servant's rough manner. "There's still so much to do, I thought I could help."

"There's no need. I'm plenty capable of doing my job," Marest said through clenched teeth. She flung the blouse onto a chaise lounge and marched back to the closet.

Embarrassed, Elia turned to Tasheira and shrugged. "What did I do?"

Tash snorted with a laugh. "Ignore her. Marest can get jealous about the craziest things. But don't lose sleep over it. I promise you, she's harmless."

Chapter 33

TWENTY MINUTES. THAT'S ALL IT would take. Nothing more.

And then at least he would know.

Wearing his tinted glasses, Hokk stood at the window of his room. It was the morning after his interview with the Baron, and he was gazing upon the estate grounds as dawn broke over the horizon. He noticed a few servants already in the gardens, and one stableman pushing a wheelbarrow, but otherwise, the property was quiet.

Go now! He could be back in time for breakfast. Nobody would notice him missing.

Hokk opened his bedroom door just a crack to check before slipping into the empty hallway. He silently descended several staircases until he reached the main floor, then cut across to the rear of the house, where he found a back door leading outside. As he was about to exit, a servant came through and nearly ran into him. Startled, she murmured a shy apology, bowed, and stepped out of his way.

His heart was beating rapidly as he ran toward the stables. The cool freshness of the early morning air felt wonderful on his skin, but this temperature would not last long. He had to be back before the day's heat began to build.

Just twenty minutes, he reminded himself. At the very most.

He couldn't get Koiyin out of his thoughts. All night, he was haunted by the portrait of her as a happy young woman. It was such a contrast to the wild eyes and tangled hair of the person who had yelled at him to pull her over the ledge of the cliffside cave, moments before she plummeted into the water. How could he have deliberately let go?

That's why this morning, he felt so compelled to see if he could find her, presuming Koiyin had indeed survived. He remembered how Elia's two islands had circled over the same area of the prairies before she fell, as if the floating masses were caught in an unusual vortex, until finally drifting off. Maybe this very island, the Baron's estate, was now hovering over Torkin territory. The possibility certainly existed. Hokk would only have to dip below the clouds for a brief moment to know for sure.

But then what? Could he actually fly down and save Koiyin? That would take much longer than twenty minutes. And though Hokk wanted to clear his conscience, he wondered if she was really meant to be rescued at all. Maybe he had done the right thing letting her drop into the river. She could have been an unwanted criminal, banished from Above all those years ago just as he had been exiled from his own city. Besides, he could not retrieve the fallen empress on his own. While the Baron might be able to arrange a large enough group, how would Hokk explain how he knew Koiyin's whereabouts? Saying anything would only reveal the truth that he wasn't actually from the moon, a fact that would surely ruin Elia's plans. And would the Baron even attempt coordinating a rescue party when the fear of Scavenger attacks was so prevalent?

Hokk had almost talked himself out of going, yet he knew he should not let anything stop him. He'd descend quickly, just far enough to see where the Torkins' village might be.

Then he could return, tell Elia everything, and let her decide the next move.

Hokk entered the stables and was relieved to be alone. The familiar smell reminded him of prairie grasses and soil. He could hear a soft whinny, the rustle of feathers, a creak from the wooden rafters, a hoof clomping on the ground, and the whisper and crunch of a mouthful of hay being pulled from a manger.

The sprawling building was on a single level, but it probably covered the same area as all the rooms in the manor. Hokk paused, deciding where to start looking first. Moving quietly down the closest passage, he inspected the enclosures on both sides, trying to find the pen for his injured stallion — he'd know it by the silver ornaments in its mane and tail.

But where was it? Peering into one stall after another, Hokk had no luck finding the animal. His anxiety grew. He was wasting time. When he came upon Twister, he was positive the stallion would be close by, yet after searching the length of two more passageways, he had still found nothing.

Just choose one and get going!

Hokk looked over the railing of the nearest pen; the older mare inside seemed approachable. Thankfully, it remained calm as he opened the gate. He fitted the animal with its reins and, after ensuring nobody else was around, led it outside, safely beyond the view of anyone who might be watching from the manor.

As if anticipating the flight, the horse opened its wings. The animal didn't have a saddle, which Hokk preferred, since he had always ridden a gazelk bareback. Hoisting himself up, he nudged his heels into the mare's ribcage, and it took to the air.

Hokk kept the beast at a low altitude. They flew over the pasture, just clearing the fences, and soon they were approaching the edge of the island. When the ground dropped away to white nothingness, Hokk leaned forward. The horse understood the command. It tucked its wings behind into a diving position and plunged into the clouds.

The thick layer of mist grew darker the farther down they went. As his steed emerged through the underside of the cloud cover, Hokk realized immediately they had arrived in a realm he didn't recognize. He removed his dark glasses. Having prepared himself for the odds of not locating the Torkinian Mountain Range, he had tried to imagine what the ocean, the prairies, or the City of Ago would look like from such a height. Yet he saw none of this below him.

Ice. Solid ice as far as he could see. In some spots, the whiteness gave way to a bluish tinge; other areas had deep crevices of black. There were mountains too, but not the Torkinian range dusted with snow. No, these ragged, frozen hills were like the waves of an ocean that had solidified before hitting the beach.

The horse was still descending rapidly, so Hokk pulled back on the reins. The animal backpedaled its wings, and Hokk encouraged his hovering steed to gradually turn around, only to be shocked by an even more amazing sight behind them. In the distance, a massive wedge of rock had impaled itself into the ice.

An island of Above.

Hokk didn't see any long gouges to indicate that the island had dragged across the surface, as he had first witnessed weeks ago when he'd found the prairies ripped open. Instead, this piece, like an upside-down mountain peak, had somehow dropped straight down to Below, as if the clouds had suddenly released their hold. Flying closer, he could tell that upon impact, the tip must have crumbled, because large fragments of snow-covered rock were scattered around the base. And though the island was sticking into the ice and hadn't fallen over, it was still not fully upright either; rather, it tilted dangerously — seemingly balanced for the moment on a precarious center of gravity, yet quite possibly on the brink of collapsing to one side.

The sight was truly unbelievable. How could this have happened? And what did it mean for the other islands of Above?

Tossing back his head to look skyward at the base of the Baron's estate, he saw the point of it poking through the mist, floating as he'd expected. However, he was shocked to see something else up there — something falling straight toward him.

Wait — it wasn't falling! It was flying! Seconds later, Hokk could distinguish wings and the underside of another horse.

He had been followed!

Both rage and dread boiled within him, but Hokk could only watch as Fimal directed his horse to hover beside him.

"You shouldn't be here!" shouted Hokk.

"What about you? Are you insane? Scavengers could be after us at any moment!"

"That's true. So then let's leave right now!"

The young man surveyed the land of ice beneath them. "What is this place?" he exclaimed.

Hokk didn't answer.

"This is incredible!"

"I wish you hadn't followed me."

"It's a whole other world!"

Hokk growled with frustration. "This is Below," he said, deciding to share as little information as possible. "But we should return to your uncle's estate."

Fimal seemed too spellbound to pay any attention to him.

"Are you listening to me? We have to get back!" yelled Hokk. "It's too dangerous down here!"

Fimal whipped around and studied him with the same suspicion Hokk had observed in the Baron's library. "I was certainly curious to see you sneak away, but when you flew off and then dove into the clouds — well, it was the craziest thing I had ever seen!" Again, he scanned the sheet of ice below, as well as the shaft of the island impaled in the frozen ground. "Craziest thing until this very moment. I knew there was more to your story than what you were telling us, I just wasn't expecting this."

"Obviously, I'm not from the moon," Hokk grumbled, though Fimal didn't seem to hear his words.

"I followed to warn you about Scavengers," the young man said. "But there don't seem to be any around at the moment. You're fortunate. You could have easily been killed by now!"

"There are no such monsters."

"What are you talking about?" Fimal's eyes narrowed to a frigid stare. Then they widened and his brow rose as he came to a sudden realization. "You've been here before," he decided with excitement. "I'm right, aren't I? Otherwise, you'd never have risked it. I almost didn't myself."

"This is where I come from," Hokk replied. He felt a sinking feeling. This was surely going to ruin everything Elia had hoped to accomplish. "But I mean what I just said. We should return before anyone realizes we're gone!"

"No!" Fimal yelled. "Go back if you want, but not me. Not now after seeing all this! I never fully believed all those stories about monsters anyway. I should have trusted my instincts long ago."

"That doesn't mean it's safe."

"I'm continuing on. I want to explore. I have to!"

"I'm warning you!" Hokk shouted, but Fimal's horse was already spiraling down to Below.

Chapter 34

THE CURTAINS OF ELIA'S BEDROOM were suddenly yanked open and morning sunshine streamed in.

Still gripped in the depths of sleep, Elia groaned. She attempted to roll over, away from the light, but someone pinned her shoulders beneath the covers, preventing her from moving.

"What's going on," Elia mumbled through a drowsy haze, though her pulse began to stir.

"You've slept long enough." It was Marest's voice. "They're going to start breakfast without you."

Elia struggled to sit straight. The next moment, she felt Marest's fingers on her forehead, picking at the edges of her bandage. "No!" she protested, trying to reach up, but she was too slow. The bandage was ripped off.

"I knew it!" said Marest.

Elia threw off her sheets. Marest quickly backed away, a silhouette in the sun's brightness. Launching herself out of bed, Elia charged, but the girl stepped aside.

Elia turned to face her assailant, now bathed by the light from outside. "What are you trying to do?"

"Find out the truth."

"How dare you be so disrespectful!" Elia challenged, hoping her outrage would intimidate a servant who was supposed to remain obedient. "I don't deserve this treatment!"

"Everything about you is a lie. Your tattoo confirms all I need to know. All that I suspected from the start," Marest said with contempt.

Elia's mind was racing. This couldn't be happening. Her plans. Her mission. She had been so careful.

She grabbed a nearby chair to steady herself and sat down. "I don't know what you're talking about," she said, trying to sound confident.

"You're a servant, like me. No, not like me — your status is obviously much lower."

Elia took several deep breaths, trying not to panic. "What could possibly make you think this?" she finally asked in a deadpan voice.

"It was easy to figure out."

"How?" Elia demanded, glaring up at her.

"You apologize too much. I've never heard Miss Tasheira say sorry for anything in her life. You do it all the time."

"That means nothing. I—I simply have . . . better manners."

"No, there's much more. You could never have been born into a high-ranking family like you claim, or rather, like you allow Miss Tasheira to assume. You give yourself away with everything you do and say. Whenever you offer to help. Whenever you suggest sharing your leftovers. I noticed it right away. That first morning, you were so worried about the blood stain on your pillow, you wanted to wash it off yourself! I couldn't believe it!"

"That shouldn't matter when —"

"Then there was yesterday: brushing the horse, folding the clothes. Those are the jobs for servants. It seems no matter how hard you try, you simply can't break your old habits."

Elia wanted to explain, yet wondered how much she could risk sharing. Maybe confiding in another servant was a safe choice. Maybe Marest would understand Elia's situation and her struggles. Perhaps she'd even offer to help if she knew the full story.

"What if I admit everything?" Elia finally asked. "Then what will you do?"

Marest seemed momentarily taken aback by Elia's apparent willingness to confess; however, she quickly bolstered herself. "I'm going to first tell Miss Tasheira."

Elia cringed. "No! You can't! You have to let me explain."

"Explain all you want, but ultimately, I serve my mistress. I can't trust your motives."

"The situation is more complicated than you could possibly imagine."

"I don't care. I have my loyalties. I put Miss Tasheira's best interests above all else."

"Just give me some time," Elia pleaded. "Then you'll see."

Marest held up her palm as if to block Elia's words. "I'm telling her when she gets back from breakfast."

"I beg you —"

"Then it will be up to her to decide what to do with you. I suspect Isec, or Hokk, or whoever he is, isn't telling the truth either."

Elia bit her lower lip.

Marest noted Elia's hesitation. "So, I'm right about that too," she concluded, looking almost surprised with herself. "Miss Tasheira will certainly be made aware of this as well."

With that, Marest gave her customary curtsy — although this time with a smirk on her face — then exited the room, leaving Elia sitting in despair.

Nym appeared around the foot of the bed and stared up at her.

"No warning from you about our intruder this morning?" she asked miserably, but the fox simply licked his muzzle.

Elia stared out the window. Blinking back tears of anger and hopelessness, she strengthened her resolve. She knew exactly what she had to do. And time could not be wasted.

She put on a new bandage over her scabby tattoo, then hurried to the dresser to open the top drawer. Tucked out of sight beneath bed linens, her fingers felt for an item that was now going to prove very useful. Grabbing it, she shoved it into a pocket of the robe she had pulled on over her nightgown. She stepped over Nym, who was still watching her, and moved quietly to the door. Seeing the corridor empty, she slipped out and crept along the wall toward Tasheira's bedchamber.

As she peeked around the door frame, she caught a glimpse of Marest passing through the curtains at the far end to enter the closet. Thankfully, no other servants were in the room, and Tasheira was nowhere to be seen. She was probably still at breakfast.

Elia took a quick look down the hallway to confirm she was not being watched, then she ducked into the room and ran silently on her tiptoes across the plush carpet. Last night's mess was everywhere, still waiting to be packed into the crates delivered for this final day of preparations.

Elia paused out of sight behind the bed, holding back one of the curtains to listen. She heard rustling, but guessed Marest was alone.

Do it!

Elia reached into her pocket and flipped open the leather pouch that she had earlier had the foresight to steal from Hokk's room. She pulled out a dart. If she could trust its white feathers, then the dart's poison would cause sleep, not death.

She silently stepped into the deep closet and let the curtain fall back into place behind her. The spacious chamber was lined with shelves that were practically bare; empty hangers hung on the rails, except for one outfit waiting to be worn. A large mirror was angled toward Elia, though she tried to avoid catching a glimpse of herself.

Marest was pulling something off a shelf when she spotted Elia's reflection and spun around to face her. The girl's face contorted with disdain, but the look was instantly replaced with alarm as Elia lunged, her weapon clenched in a fist.

Hand held high, Elia swung down and stabbed the dart into Marest's back until the needle could penetrate no farther. The servant fell to her knees, gasping, clawing at Elia in vain as she seized another projectile, jabbing this one into the girl's neck. As Marest's legs collapsed, Elia caught her and deftly lowered her to the floor.

So what now?

Her eyes flitted about. Elia hadn't worked out her plan past this point.

Hide the body.

But how long would Marest stay unconscious? Hopefully until after tomorrow morning, when Tasheira and Elia would finally leave for the palace. Elia's attacker at the lagoons had used four darts to take her down, but she had been revived. Otherwise, how many hours might she have been out?

Looking in the pouch, Elia counted five darts remaining. Guessing two more would keep Marest asleep for the rest of the day, she poked both into the skin above her elbow, leaving the barbs buried deep to ensure all the poison was absorbed.

Now to move the body before they were discovered.

But Marest was deadweight. Straining and grunting, Elia could barely lift her. She began to panic, knowing that Tasheira might return from breakfast at any moment. Ideally, Elia wanted to get Marest away from the house, but that would be impossible to accomplish on her own. If only she could just return to her room and hide the girl there.

She would never be fast enough. Elia needed Hokk's help, yet there was no way she could leave the body to go find him.

Dragging Marest by the feet, she slowly pulled the girl from the closet and out past the curtains into Tasheira's bedroom. The stretch of carpet before her seemed unbearably long. Her only option was the bed. She would have to hide Marest beneath it.

The girl did not stir as Elia struggled to haul her closer. She lifted the skirting and pushed Marest under the mattress as far as she could, making sure no limbs were sticking out.

Breathing heavily, Elia straightened her back and scanned the room. This could work, she decided. This could actually work.

But what if they dismantled the bed so they could take it with them to the palace?

The thought stopped Elia cold. She began biting her thumbnail.

Surely they wouldn't do that until tomorrow morning. Tasheira would need the bed for her last sleep here at the estate, which meant Elia would have to return with Hokk in the middle of the night and get Marest out of the house before dawn. It was risky, but the only solution — so long as Marest didn't wake up in the meantime.

Reaching under the bed, Elia pulled out the girl's leg and stabbed another dart above her ankle, just to be safe, then shoved her back in as far as she could go.

Chapter 35

AS HE FLEW THROUGH THE band of near-zero gravity that split the atmosphere between Above and Below, Hokk saw Fimal's horse land on the frozen ground beneath him, the animal's hooves skidding on the slippery ice. By the time Hokk's own steed touched down, Fimal had already dismounted and was exploring among the strewn rocks in the shadow of the island that loomed at an alarming angle overhead.

"Damn fool," Hokk mumbled angrily. So much for keeping this expedition under twenty minutes. He wanted to get back to Above more than anything. Up in the stormy sky, the Baron's island was floating farther away, and Hokk feared losing sight of it completely. How would they ever find it again if they didn't leave right away?

A cruel wind blew across the frigid wasteland, colder than Hokk had ever felt. He was sure this alone would convince Fimal to return home, but he seemed oblivious to any risks.

"There are huge cracks everywhere," Fimal called out.

"Don't get too close in case an edge breaks away," warned Hokk, apprehensively gazing up as his voice echoed off the overhanging rock, which blocked out a large portion of the sky.

As if to reinforce Hokk's warning, the ice below their feet groaned. Small bits of stone rained down from the island, causing both of them to shield their heads.

"I want to get to the top of this thing!" said Fimal.

"Let's leave before something bad happens. Before everything comes falling down on us!" Hokk exclaimed, grabbing him by the arm.

"Don't touch me!" shouted Fimal, breaking free.

"If the Baron knew about this —"

"I don't care," Fimal scoffed. "Tash was able to find you and whatever that thing was that made the crater in the desert. But this is *my* discovery. Everything else my uncle has found pales in comparison to what I'll be able to share!"

Hokk threw his hands up in exasperation as Fimal raced back to his steed. As soon as he was in the saddle, the horse rose into the air and quickly disappeared over the top edge of the island.

He's going to kill himself, thought Hokk. If he wants to be an idiot, is it really up to me to stop him?

Swiftly returning to his own horse, Hokk saw the animal stomping its hooves as if not wanting to spend a single moment longer standing on a sheet of ice. "I agree," said Hokk as he hoisted himself onto its back. "Let's get out of here."

Hokk was glad to be airborne again, watching as the ice fell away from him. Gaining altitude, they flew up to the top of the island, where Hokk could now see the remnants of an abandoned village. The homes were just shacks, and though they were built far enough back from the rocky edge, the island's unnaturally steep tilt made it look as though the structures could slide right off. Snow had not accumulated on their roofs, but rather on the upward-facing walls. In several areas, debris from damaged buildings had slid toward their neighbors, forming piles of rubble, also partially covered with snow.

Hokk saw no signs of life — no bodies, neither human nor animal — except for Fimal's horse, which had been left standing on the side wall of a dilapidated home. Did Fimal have no sense at all? While there certainly wasn't any level ground for the animal to land on, Hokk was sure the horse's weight could cause the feeble wall to collapse.

And where was Fimal anyway?

Hokk flew closer. "Where are you?" he shouted down, though his voice seemed to be swallowed up by the empty sky around him.

Below, Fimal's horse turned its head toward an open door that was still swinging on its hinges, hanging down toward the inside of the building. The next moment, a box was pushed up through the entryway until it rested on the wall; then hands appeared, clinging to the door frame. Fimal pulled himself outside wearing a coat he must have found within the home. He flipped open the box's lid and began removing the contents, tossing items aside as if scavenging for treasure.

"Are you coming?" Hokk asked loudly one last time, though Fimal either heard nothing or was ignoring him on purpose. Hokk shook his head at the young man's foolishness. "Well, you're on your own then," he muttered begrudgingly before loosening the reins and nudging his horse to climb to the dark, misty upper limits.

● ● ●

It took longer to return to the Baron's island than Hokk would have guessed. He stayed below the cloud cover until he had reached the island's tip, then directed his horse to soar straight up through the fog. Hokk slipped his dark glasses on just before they emerged into the bright sunlight. Fortunately, the air above the estate was filled with many other flying horses, and he was able to easily blend in with them as he guided his steed toward the stables. He didn't return the animal to its stall, however, but rather lingered near the pastures for a short while, hoping to see Fimal riding back to the property.

Minutes passed without any sign of him, so Hokk gave up waiting and hurried to the manor.

He was panting as he climbed the first of the staircases to return to his room. Starting up the second set, he heard Tasheira call out from the floor above.

"Marest!" she shrieked.

Tash quickly descended the stairs, her hand just barely touching the curved banister. Hokk wished he could duck out of sight, but she had spotted him. Her furious expression softened.

"Well, at least I found *you*," she said. "But where's everybody else? Have you seen my servant?"

"No, I haven't."

"She has me worried," said Tasheira. She then looked at him quizzically. "Your face is flushed."

"Yes, I was outside," he replied. Elia appeared behind Tash on the spiraling stairs, and Hokk gave her only the briefest glance. "I decided I needed some exercise."

"Good to hear." Tash then cocked her head in a flirtatious manner. "You know, I still intend to sit you down, just you and me, so I can learn more about who you are. You're very fascinating, Hokk."

"Hokk?" Elia repeated the word, looking shocked. "Isn't it Isec?" she asked — almost demanded — her wide eyes betraying her concern.

"That's my last name," said Hokk before facing Tash again. "Yes, I would be pleased to meet with you."

"My father shouldn't have proceeded without me. He knows better, especially since I lay claim to you. And I hope you didn't tell him *everything*, that you kept back a few tantalizing details, which you'll kindly share only with me."

"Yes, of course. I am at your disposal whenever you choose."

"Well, it will have to wait, unfortunately." Her frustration flared to its previous level. "Everything's in such a horrendous turmoil right now given that we're leaving for the palace tomorrow. And I don't know what's happened to Marest!" She stormed past Hokk and continued down the stairs as if she could not afford another minute of talking. "*Come on* everyone, where are you?" Tash shouted out as she rushed away and her voice grew fainter. "Marest? Neric? Fimal?"

Hokk flinched to hear the last name reverberating through the corridors.

Elia had paused on the stairs, but started to pass him. Hokk caught her by the elbow, though she resisted. "I'm sorry. I have to keep up with Tasheira," Elia said nervously.

Hokk pulled her closer. "I really must speak with you," he whispered. Only now did he register her haggard expression. "Wait — are you all right?"

She gulped. "I need to talk to you too. Urgently!" she whispered. She shot a glance in the direction where Tash had gone, then back up the stairs toward the bedrooms before anxiously looking again at Hokk. "Where will you be this afternoon?"

"I'm not sure."

"If we don't meet up sooner, come to my room tonight. But make sure everyone else is asleep before you do."

"Why? What's happened?"

She anxiously ran her fingers through her short hair. "I need your help. I'm afraid everything might start falling apart!"

Before he could question her further, she wrenched herself from his grasp and hurried down the polished steps, the patter of her slippered feet fading away to nothing.

Chapter 36

ELIA WAS TIGHT-LIPPED AND silent as she sat at the end of Tasheira's bed, guarding what lay beneath. She did not move from her spot — and certainly did not offer to help — but simply watched the activity in the room.

She and Tash had returned about an hour earlier after pulling three servants away from their work in other areas of the house. They had been busy organizing Tasheira's belongings ever since. Tash was darting about, wringing her hands, ordering her staff to pack and repack boxes. Elia, however, was too concerned about Marest waking up and raising an alarm to find any amusement in it. "I'm leaving tomorrow," Tash kept reminding everyone. "First thing in the morning. We still have a lot to get through!"

The servants did not appear bothered by her bossy demands, but rather worked at a steady pace. As the afternoon progressed, the crates were filled, sealed with lids, and removed from the building. At one point, the Baroness appeared through the doors at the other end of the bedroom, and Elia stiffened, clenching her fingers around the pillow in her lap. Tasheira had spotted her too. "I don't want you here complicating things," she barked, and her mother backed out, leaving a curling trail of incense smoke in the air.

Elia was too far away, but she could imagine that lingering fragrance. A smoldering stick of incense was suddenly so appealing. Maybe if she had one, its sedative effect would help eliminate her fears about stealing Marest from this bedroom tonight without getting caught.

•   •   •

Dinner was long and unpleasant. Once again, there was plenty to eat, but Elia felt too worried to taste anything. She devoured her food, hoping they could return as soon as possible to Tasheira's room, where they had left the three servants working.

Tash, on the other hand, had accepted a large portion and appeared ready to enjoy a leisurely meal. She was also in a more agreeable mood because her father had decided to join them.

"I couldn't miss your last dinner at the manor," said the Baron.

At the other end of the table, the Baroness sniffled. This briefly caught her daughter's attention, though Tasheira showed no sign of hostility before turning to her father. "But now, Fimal's missing out," Tash pouted. She nodded toward the empty chair between Hokk and Neric. "Has anyone seen him today? Have you, Neric?"

"No, I haven't," Neric replied.

"It's not like him," said Tasheira. Her lip quivered ever so faintly. "I'm going to miss him most." She seemed to regret this comment as soon as she said it. "Except, of course, for you, Father."

Her mother whimpered again, and waved her incense below her nostrils.

Making eye contact with the Baroness, Tash opened her mouth but hesitated before saying, almost reluctantly, "I'll miss everyone, actually."

The Baron nodded. "We all feel the same. Fimal as well. Perhaps he's taking this harder than any of us expected. The two of you have been almost inseparable since you were toddlers."

"Which is why he should be here," said Tasheira.

Elia noticed Hokk had stopped chewing, a lump of food stuck against the inside of his cheek. He stared down at his plate.

"Fimal will show up," said the Baron. "He won't miss his last chance to say goodbye."

Hokk's fingers drummed the stem of his glass. Elia couldn't guess why he seemed so nervous all of a sudden. How would he react when she shared her plans for Marest?

●　　●　　●

Tick. Tick.

A candle burned on the nightstand beside Elia. Dressed in her sleeping gown, she was sitting upright in bed, staring at the clock on the opposite wall. Though she couldn't tell time, the thinnest arm on the device, which counted off the seconds, had made enough revolutions for her to know she had already waited far too long.

Isn't he coming?

Tick. Tick.

She tugged on the hem of her sleeve until the stitching came undone.

Had the Baron or Tasheira waylaid him? Had Hokk fallen asleep?

Tick.

Maybe his lies have been discovered too!

Elia threw back her bedspread. The moment her toes touched the carpet, she heard a creak from her door. It slowly swung open. A shadow slipped inside, then the door closed behind it.

"Where have you been?" Elia whispered, shoving her legs back under the covers.

Hokk moved into the circle of candlelight. "You said to wait until everyone was asleep," he answered defensively.

"Are they?"

"As far as I can tell."

Nym came around the bed. Hokk picked him up and placed the fox in his lap as he sat on the mattress beside Elia. "You've had me worried. I was tempted to come much sooner so you could tell me what's wrong."

Elia sighed as she hugged herself. "Marest found out who I am."

"What? How?"

"She saw the tattoo on my forehead and put the pieces together."

"Has she told anyone?" asked Hokk, absentmindedly petting Nym.

"I don't think so."

"But Tasheira was looking for Marest when I ran into the two of you on the stairs. She must have eventually found her."

"I made sure she wouldn't."

Hokk gave her a side glance. "How did you accomplish that?"

Elia reached under her pillow and produced the pouch of darts. "I stabbed her."

"Stabbed her!" Hokk exclaimed, his voice rising.

"Shh," Elia replied, tilting her ear toward the door to listen for sounds in the hallway.

Hokk continued in a hushed tone. "So she's unconscious?"

"As unconscious as the poison from five darts can make her," Elia replied proudly.

"Then there must be a body." Hokk scanned the room, his eyebrows high on his forehead. "Where did you hide her? In here somewhere?"

"Under the bed . . . in Tasheira's room."

"Under *her* bed!" he gasped, then covered his mouth, realizing he had been too loud again. As he lowered his hand, his shock turned to confusion. "I don't understand. If Marest is out cold, shouldn't everything be fine for you now?"

"Only if we can get away tomorrow before she's discovered. Before she's revived and can tell Tash everything." Elia leaned forward and held Hokk's wrist. "But as an added safeguard, we have to move Marest out of Tasheira's bedroom. Out of the entire house, for that matter. I'm afraid she could still be found in the morning if they dismantle Tash's bed. Then what would I do?"

Hokk grimaced.

"I can't let her wreck my plans," she continued. "We have an amazing opportunity here to get to the Mirrored Palace that we can't afford to jeopardize."

Elia noticed Hokk's jaw clench, and his gaze dropped to Nym. She went rigid. "What is it?" she asked.

He brushed away dry skin that was still peeling from the back of his hand, but he said nothing.

"Tell me," she urged as her stomach began to cramp.

"The whole situation is even trickier," said Hokk, looking up with a frown. He began explaining about his excursion to Below and being followed by Fimal, about how all the land was covered with ice, and how Fimal had refused to return with Hokk to the estate, preferring, instead, to explore the fallen island that tilted so dangerously above the ground.

"I can't believe you'd be such a fool," Elia spat out, her voice now at a dangerous volume. "What were you thinking to leave? Are you completely insane?" Closing her eyes, she pinched the bridge of her nose and shook her head with frustration. "Fimal knows too much now. He could come back at any moment and ruin our plans just as easily as Marest! Either one of them could expose us as imposters ... and then what?"

"I didn't intend for any of this to happen. I assure you. I had a very good reason to go to Below. I had no other choice."

"No other choice? I can't imagine why."

"I found out new information about Koiyin."

Elia's back straightened, and she eyed Hokk suspiciously. "How? From who?"

"From the Baron." Hokk took a deep breath before continuing. "I think Koiyin might play a much more important role in everything than you could ever possibly imagine."

Chapter 37

"I CAN'T BELIEVE IT," SAID Elia. She stretched up on her tiptoes and held a candle closer to the portrait hanging farthest from the library doors.

"But you can see the three moles, can't you?" Hokk whispered. "That unmistakable triangle above her lips?"

"Yes, it's definitely Koiyin," Elia replied quietly.

Though she'd resisted coming here to see for herself, Hokk had been adamant, practically pulling her out of bed and dragging her down the stairs. The two of them had moved silently through the dark corridors and down the stairs with their bobbing candlelight casting long shadows on the walls.

"Surely you can understand now why I went to Below," said Hokk. "If there were any way of rescuing her, I had to take that chance to find out — in the very least so I could report back to you."

Elia nodded as if only half listening. She seemed unable to pull her gaze away from the painting, but she finally turned and looked into Hokk's eyes. "I just can't get over it," she murmured. "Koiyin . . . an empress?"

"I know. It doesn't seem possible when you see who she's become."

"We were always told she was dead. Pulled over the side of the island one morning while strolling in the palace gardens with her husband."

"This man?" asked Hokk, pointing to the picture.

"Yes, Emperor Tael. He was blinded when the Scavengers attacked and stole Koiyin."

Hokk scrunched his face. "You do remember no such monsters have ever existed, don't you? That there must have been some other explanation all along."

"Yes, of course, I realize that *now*."

"So when you were with Koiyin, she gave no indication of who she was?"

Elia considered the question. "I guess, looking back, there were clues. She knew I used to work at the palace. She recognized the telescope and was aware that looking into it could reveal secrets."

"Yet you didn't find it surprising that she —"

"I did, absolutely! I was amazed how much she seemed to know. But she said the telescope had a long history, so I simply assumed she had heard rumours about it in the past."

"I would have thought she'd look familiar to you, maybe from seeing her at a public celebration or during a parade."

"No, I never saw her. Neither in person, nor in pictures. The incident that supposedly took her life happened a few years before I was born. I only heard stories. But really, it all adds up. The Torkins said Koiyin fell to Below about eighteen years ago. That would have been around the same time the empress went missing."

"And her name itself didn't trigger anything? Make you think twice?"

Elia sighed as if she was tiring of Hokk's questions. "We knew her as Empress *Mah*koiyin. Nothing made me suspect I should make a connection, certainly not to the woman I met. You saw her — she's on the brink of madness. For years, she's been terrified of being found."

Hokk's brow furrowed. "Makes me wonder if the telescope is somehow related to her disappearance."

"Yes, you're right," Elia said, wide-eyed. "That could actually explain quite a lot." She thought for a moment. "In fact, Koiyin warned me to never let the telescope get into the wrong hands — but when she said it, I sensed there was . . . something else. As if she knew more she didn't want to tell me."

"The telescope's still safe?"

"I have it hidden in my room." She glanced down the hallway.

Hokk followed her gaze. "Don't worry. I don't think anybody has seen us."

"No, but we should return," she replied, grim-faced, clutching her nightgown tighter around the neckline. "We still have the problem of Marest. Let's get this over with."

Together, they climbed the stairs and stopped outside Tasheira's bedroom. Elia rested her ear on the door to listen. "I don't hear anything," she whispered.

Reaching past her, Hokk grabbed the knob, but Elia put her hand on his chest. Something in her palm was pressing against him. Looking down, he saw the pouch of darts.

"I should go first, just in case she's awake," Elia whispered. "I don't want her seeing you."

"And these?" Hokk asked with a nod toward the leather bag.

"We can't wait for her to fall asleep if she isn't. You may need a dart to speed things along. I have a plan."

"While you keep her distracted?"

"That's right. But try to give Tash the smallest dose possible. Though we don't want her to see us carrying Marest out of her room tonight, she must still wake up as usual tomorrow morning."

"I'll try my best," said Hokk. "But no promises."

Elia blew out the flame and placed the candle holder on the floor before taking a deep breath. She turned the knob. The door opened with a loud creak. She paused, as if expecting a reaction to the noise, then stepped inside.

Unfortunately, the room wasn't dark like the hallway. It was lit by a faint glow. Hokk peered around the door frame and saw Elia moving toward a bed draped like a cocoon. Candlelight shone from within. Making out Tash's voice, he strained to listen but caught nothing.

"It's just me," he heard Elia reply.

More words were mumbled from the sheltered bed.

Elia spoke again. "I couldn't sleep either, so I thought I'd check on you."

Hokk noticed Elia gesturing behind her back for him to enter. He slipped inside and flattened himself against the nearest wall.

Elia parted the curtains on one side. "We're both feeling too excited about leaving tomorrow."

Hokk darted forward and took cover behind an armchair, where he could hear Tasheira's response.

"I've waited so long for this," the girl said. "And now that it's all about to happen, I'm almost . . . scared."

"It's understandable. I would feel the same," Elia replied.

"I have such a bad headache too. After today's craziness, with all the packing, Marest missing, and Fimal not showing up for dinner — my mind can't stop racing," said Tash. "I'm really worried about what's happened to them. And if I don't get any sleep, I'll be a mess in the morning and for the rest of the day. What kind of first impression will I make?"

"We have to calm your thoughts. Perhaps if you blow out the candle, close your eyes, and focus on your breathing."

"That won't work."

"Then just try closing your eyes and —"

"Perhaps if you read to me," Tash abruptly suggested.

Silence.

Knowing Elia had never been taught to read, Hokk peeked over the chair to see if she looked panicked. Although he could not see Tash's face, her arm was sticking out past the drapes, holding a book toward Elia, who was frowning. He had seen so few books in the library, he was surprised Tash had one of her own.

"This is my favorite," said Tasheira, still hidden behind the curtains. "I almost have it memorized."

Hokk watched Elia reluctantly take the book and open it, flipping a few pages in. What felt like a minute passed.

"If you're so familiar with the story," Elia finally replied, closing the cover and placing the book on a nightstand, "then I'm going to make up a new one for you. But this story will be unlike anything you've ever heard, and you'll have to shut your eyes tight so you can picture it." She took the candle from Tasheira and, without extinguishing the flame, left it beside the book on the same table. "Now just lean back on your pillow and try to relax." Elia peered into the shrouded bedchamber as if waiting for the other girl to settle into place. "Got them closed?"

"Yes."

"Tight?"

"They are."

"Good. Now, this is a story about —"

"Massage my head while you tell it," said Tasheira, "to stop the throbbing."

"Of course."

As Elia climbed onto the mattress, she gestured to Hokk once more. Without making a sound, he crept forward until he was standing near Elia beside the bed. He held open the curtains and gazed down upon Tash, who was lying face-up in shadows, all her eyelids shut.

Elia cleared her throat. "I want you to imagine a world with no sunlight." Her fingers began massaging circles against Tasheira's temples. "Dark, threatening clouds hang high overhead, forever blocking out the blue sky above. From these clouds, countless drops of water fall through the air to soak the ground below."

Tasheira snickered. "Sounds bizarre."

Hokk froze, afraid the girl's eyes would open.

"Shh. Just listen or you'll never fall asleep," Elia said firmly. Glancing at Hokk, she gave him a nod to proceed.

Opening the pouch, he removed one of the two remaining darts.

"The land is perfectly flat," Elia continued, massaging with earnest. "It stretches to the horizon in every direction. It's cold. Tall grasses ripple in waves with the relentless wind."

Hokk carefully stretched over Tasheira's body, looking for a place to poke her.

"This is the world where a young man survives all on his own," said Elia. "He lives in exile, wrongly accused, banished because of an unfortunate accident with fire . . . but it wasn't his fault."

Feeling a sharp twinge of guilt, Hokk flicked his eyes toward Elia. She still didn't know the truth about his past sins.

Elia repositioned her hands on Tasheira's head. "Now, don't be startled, Tash," she said, interrupting her own storytelling, "but as I begin to massage between your eyebrows, you might feel a sudden pain."

"That's fine," the girl replied, sounding completely alert.

Elia pressed her thumbs together and pinched the skin above Tasheira's nose.

Recognizing his opportunity, Hokk lightly pricked the girl's flesh at this spot with the tip of his dart, then quickly withdrew it.

Was it enough?

They both waited for a reaction, but Tash hadn't even flinched.

Staring down at her, Elia waited a few moments. "Tash?"

No response. A speck of blood seeped from the tiny wound.

Hokk and Elia looked at each other, both worried.

"Tash? Are you awake?" Elia asked.

Nothing.

Elia sat back. At the same moment, Tasheira's mouth slowly fell open. She was unconscious.

"What a relief," Elia sighed, her shoulders relaxing. "I'm always so glad when that stuff works."

"And so quickly, too," said Hokk.

Elia promptly climbed off the mattress. Crouching beside the bed, she reached under the skirting.

"Can you feel her?" he asked.

Elia pushed her arm in deeper. As she concentrated, the tip of her tongue stuck out from the corner of her mouth. She seemed to be struggling.

"What is it?" Hokk asked, nervously glancing over to make sure Tasheira wasn't stirring.

Elia yanked out her arm, concern written across her face. "I can't feel anything —"

"Is Marest gone?" The speed of Hokk's pulse doubled as he dropped to the floor beside Elia. "She can't be!"

How could Tasheira's servant be missing? Was all this simply a trap to catch them in the act?

"No, she's still under there," Elia replied calmly as she shifted to give him space. "I just pushed her in too deep. I can't grab hold."

"Then move over and let me try," Hokk snapped, his relief coming across as irritation. With his longer arms, he had no difficulty feeling Marest's elbow, and he slid his hand down until he could wrap his fingers around her wrist. "I got her," he said, his voice now composed.

He hauled Marest out from under the mattress. Compared to Tasheira, who looked almost serene as she slept, her servant appeared dead.

Five darts. That was a lot of poison. Perhaps Elia had killed her.

Elia must have been worrying about the same thing. "Is she all right?" she asked.

Hokk placed two fingers on the artery in Marest's neck. He felt a very faint heartbeat. "She's still alive."

"Good. Then let's get her out of here."

Elia lifted Marest's feet and Hokk grabbed her under the shoulders. As they headed toward the door, Elia glanced back to make sure Tasheira wasn't watching. Hokk checked too, but all he saw were the curtains hanging down and the candle still burning on the nightstand.

They stopped briefly in Elia's room to wrap Marest with a bedsheet, then returned to the hallway and moved quietly through the house, carefully descending to the main level and out into the back gardens. The luminescent pieces of the moon lit their path, as well as the bundle they were carrying. Swathed in white fabric, Marest's body looked no different from the discarded corpses Hokk used to find fallen on the prairies.

"Are we throwing her over the edge?" he asked, walking backward.

Elia looked up at him, horrified. "I'm not that wicked. I don't want her dead!"

"Then where?"

"The stables."

"Won't somebody —" Hokk began to ask.

"Not right away. Not where I have planned."

The farther they went, the heavier Marest seemed to become, and they were both out of breath by the time they reached the building. It was dimly lit with only a few scattered lanterns left burning inside. Passing the stalls, they could see many of the animals had been prepped for sale, their manes and tails braided.

That reminded Hokk. "By the way, where are they keeping our stallion?" he asked. "I couldn't find it yesterday, and I saw no sign of it when we left the desert and flew here to the estate."

"It's dead," Elia grunted, changing her hold on Marest's ankles to maintain her grip.

Hokk was taken aback. "How can it be dead?"

"It didn't survive after we landed in Above. It succumbed to exhaustion and dehydration."

So how did I survive? wondered Hokk.

Elia led the way to the farthest corner of the stables, through wide double doors, and then into a large shed stacked high with hay bales. "We'll hide her behind all this."

There was just enough space to tuck the body between the piles of hay and the back wall. Before shoving her in, however, they unwrapped her, and Elia tore three strips of fabric from the bottom of Marest's uniform. She used separate pieces to bind the girl's wrists and ankles. The third was used as a gag. As it was tied into place, Marest let out a low moan.

"Give me another dart," Elia ordered.

Hokk reluctantly handed over the last one. "No more left after this. You don't think she's had enough?"

"Can I risk it?" Elia plunged the needle into the girl's neck and waited a few seconds before pulling it out and tossing it far away, to land somewhere high up in the hay. Then she ripped a final strip of cloth from the girl's outfit. "Now help me wedge the body into place back here."

Hokk was perplexed. "Why tear off more fabric?"

In the faint light, Elia focused on Hokk, her eyes void of any emotion. "I need this last piece to create a distraction."

Chapter 38

LAST NIGHT'S THROBBING BEHIND HER eyes was gone, but this morning, Tasheira found it difficult to lift her head off the pillow. She had obviously overslept — her drapes and windows were already open to let the fresh air and morning light pour in. Thanks goodness. Marest must be back.

She pulled herself up onto one elbow, her vision swimming. She closed her eyes until the wave of dizziness subsided. Had she ever slept so deeply? Or found it so agonizing to wake up? Whatever technique Elia had used to make her fall asleep had worked incredibly well. In fact, Tash could only vaguely remember the previous evening: the book she had been reading; the creak of her door opening; the strange story about dark clouds overhead and water falling out of the sky; Elia's fingers pressing against her skull to relieve the pain.

Tash groaned now as she climbed out of bed. On the nightstand, she noticed her book sitting beside the candle holder, with only a small lump of cold wax remaining. It must have burned all night. Why hadn't Elia blown it out before she left? The girl always seemed so keen not to waste anything.

Tasheira unlaced the ribbons down the front of her nightgown and let it slip off her shoulders. The garment landed at her feet, and she stepped out of it. Naked, she approached the windows and looked out upon the property, which was already bustling with activity. As she undid the braid in her hair, she watched men herding horses into teams outside the stables. Primped and dancing about, these young animals were slated to be sold to the Royal Court.

This is your last morning in the manor, she reminded herself. She turned and scanned her room, trying to memorize every detail. She would never see any of it again. Only her clothes were coming with her. The bed would not be dismantled. All the furniture would remain. She was leaving this life to start a brand-new one.

Was she ready for it? A shiver traveled down her spine to her toes.

Tasheira walked into her closet behind the bed. She expected to find Marest, but the space was empty, except for one outfit that hung on a hanger. She put the dress on and stepped into the matching slippers. Standing in front of the mirror, she ran her fingers through her hair to loosen the cascading curls and admired the reflection. Then she frowned when she noticed the red pimple in the very center between her eyebrows. Typical. Of all the days, she would have to break out with a blemish today. At least she didn't have that big ugly wound Elia had in the middle of her forehead — which was a reminder. Tash had offered to hide the crusty scab with a turban. She should check on Elia now and just get it done.

Tash left her room, strode down the hallway, and opened Elia's door without knocking.

Elia was already dressed and looking out the window. She turned as Tasheira walked in. "I'm so glad to see you're awake," said Elia, almost with a sense of relief. "How did you sleep?"

"Like the dead."

"But you're rested?"

"I feel ready to take on the day," Tash lied. "You too?"

"I suppose."

"Good. Now, before we leave, I've come to tie that turban like I promised. Got a scarf?"

Elia shrugged and glanced around her room. "I don't think so."

"I'm sure you have something that'll do the trick. All my stuff is packed."

Tasheira searched through drawers filled with linens but found nothing appropriate. She scrutinized what Elia was wearing — a simple, flowing dress of white that Tash could no longer fit into — and then scanned the room until she spotted a pillowcase on the bed with a fancy beaded trim. "This should do nicely," Tash said as she yanked out the pillow. She pulled the empty casing over the top of Elia's head and wrapped it low enough to cover the girl's bandage, but without getting the fabric caught in her eyebrow piercing. She finished by twisting a knot at the back.

Tash held Elia out at arm's length for inspection. Just as she was about to comment, she suddenly heard running foot-steps in the hallway.

A male servant ran past the door, then doubled back after noticing Tash in the room. "Miss Tasheira?"

"What is it now?" she asked impatiently. From his clothing, Tash could tell he wasn't a member of the household staff, but rather worked in the stables. "Should you be in here?" Tash inquired.

"I've got news. It's about your attendant," he said with trepidation.

Tasheira bristled and could feel Elia go rigid too. "Tell me."

The servant gulped, his hand on his heaving chest as he tried to stop panting. "We've discovered what's happened to Marest."

"Take us!" Tash demanded as she grabbed Elia. Together, they hurried from the room and followed the young worker down the stairs, then out one of the back doors of the manor. Tasheira ran as fast as she could as they headed toward the stables. Her hand squeezed Elia's, who was trying to keep up.

What's really happened? Tash wondered. *If Marest has been found, why couldn't she come find me herself?*

Tash shot a worried glance at Elia, who appeared equally concerned.

They raced past the assembled horses and entered the building, where all the stalls were now empty. Tasheira felt her slippers step into small mounds of manure that had not yet been cleaned up. She was also sweating heavily through the outfit she had specially selected for her grand arrival at the palace, but she kept running, undeterred.

They sped to the far end of the building, then out again into the open air and the pastures behind. Older horses not for sale, plus the ones being kept behind for breeding purposes, were either grazing or flying overhead.

But the stableboy leading the way did not stop here. They continued toward a group of workers who were clustered around a spot along the fence built right by the edge of the island.

Dread tightened like a fist in Tasheira's gut when she saw a section of the railing missing. The gap opened up to the swirling mist that pressed against the property. Even more shocking, she noticed a torn piece of Marest's uniform hanging from a bent nail on the last post, where the fence disappeared.

"Oh my goodness, no!" Tasheira exclaimed, clapping her hand over her mouth. The assembled workers looked at her with a mixture of sympathy and fear.

One of the older men spoke up. "We just discovered this spot."

Tasheira shook her head in disbelief.

"She must have been pulled over by a Scavenger," said the same man, his voice somber.

"Yes," Tash croaked. Wringing her hands as she surveyed the scene, she noticed scratch marks in the soil, where Marest must have tried to cling to the island.

Didn't anybody hear her screams?

"Can you think of any reason why she would have strayed so close to the edge?" another stableman asked.

Tash could only shrug. Her throat was choked up with grief. Turning away from the men, she faced Elia, who was still holding her hand. Elia's look of anguish made the magnitude of the situation all the more real and horrifying. Tasheira felt wetness catch in her eyelashes, and her legs began to tremble.

Over Elia's shoulder, she saw the Baroness striding purposefully through the fields toward the group. In an instant, Tash pulled free of Elia's grasp and started running toward her mother. The Baroness threw a stick of incense to the ground just as Tasheira launched herself into the woman's arms.

And then the tears flowed.

The Baroness held strong. Tash did not feel her mother go rigid with embarrassment or unease. Instead, she caressed Tasheira's hair, trying to soothe her. "Hush now. Everything will be all right."

Though it helped to hear this, Tash knew it wasn't true. Her devoted attendant had been killed and nothing could change that. And even more devastating, Tasheira suspected another tragedy — Fimal had been taken by the Scavengers too.

Chapter 39

FOLLOWED BY A TRAIL OF servants, Elia supported Tasheira on one side, the Baroness on the other, as they helped the distraught girl up the stairs to her room. She collapsed on the bed and allowed her mother to fuss over her: fluffing the pillows, rearranging blankets, giving her sips from a waterball, pulling back the surrounding drapes to let the breeze through.

Neric arrived when he heard the news, and Baron Shoad was summoned as well. "Tragic," the Baron said. "Simply tragic. That poor girl."

"And they took Fimal too," Tash sobbed, which made everyone in the room, family and staff, shudder with horror.

"We don't know that for sure," said the Baron, though he didn't sound convincing. "We've seen no evidence."

"So where is he?" his daughter demanded. "He's been missing just as long as Marest."

The Baron frowned and dropped his head. Neric crumpled onto a sofa, his face in his hands to hide his grief. Elia lingered at the side of the room, stone-faced, standing beside curious workers who apparently saw no need to give the family privacy. Elia, herself, certainly didn't want to leave — someone might come racing in to announce that Marest had indeed been found . . . alive!

Squirming uncomfortably on the bed, Tash reached out to touch her mother's hand. "Perhaps just a little whiff today," she said pitifully. "To calm my nerves."

"Of course, my dear," the Baroness replied. She snapped her fingers and her servant provided a burning stick of incense, which the woman held under her daughter's nose. "It's exactly what you need at a time like this."

Elia was surprised to see the girl take such a deep breath, then hold the smoke in her lungs at length before finally exhaling. As she reclined back onto her pillows, her eyes were already starting to glaze over.

The Baroness turned to the others. "We should leave her in peace. She needs a chance to recover."

"We have no time for this," Baron Shoad protested firmly. "We should have departed by now."

"And is everything absolutely ready to go?" his wife spat back.

"Not quite, but —"

"Then surely you can spare one hour," she growled. "At least give your daughter that much before she leaves us."

The Baron opened his mouth as if to argue, then closed it. He spun on his heels and left the room. Neric, looking miserable, followed him out, as did everyone else. Only the Baroness stayed, pulling up a chair next to the bed.

Elia made sure she was the last to exit, falling into step behind the Baroness's attendant. Once in the hallway, she caught the servant's arm and held her back until certain no one was within earshot.

"Do you have any more?" Elia asked quietly. "More incense, I mean. Just in case Tasheira relapses during the journey?"

"I have plenty," the servant replied, producing a handful from a deep pocket in her uniform. "How much do you think you'll need?"

Elia eyed the sticks hungrily. "I'll take all you've got," she said, startled by her own response.

As if simply following orders, the servant surrendered every piece she was carrying. Elia felt a mixture of delight and shame, but she wasn't sure why. Was it because the thought of incense was now always hovering at the back of her mind? Or because she was willing to make up lies to get some? She tried to reassure herself. *I have nothing to be guilty about!* Incense has *helped* the Baroness, not made her the way she is. And the stuff has to be safe — even Tasheira's using it now!

With the incense clenched tightly in one fist, Elia darted toward her bedroom, certain she had enough time to enjoy burning one stick in private so she could be better prepared to face the rest of the day. However, she found her door ajar. Cautiously, she pushed it open. Hokk was waiting inside, already wearing his dark glasses.

Elia swiftly hid the sticks behind her back, knowing he wouldn't understand. He hadn't been through what she had endured.

"I poked my head into Tasheira's room to see what was going on," said Hokk.

"I didn't notice you," Elia replied, her voice catching slightly.

"I don't think anybody did. But it sounds like your plan has worked out just as you intended." He seemed impressed.

"So far. But I'm not in the clear yet." Elia took a step toward the bureau, where she had hidden the telescope in its carved box. "We now have over an hour to wait before we leave. The Baroness insisted on more time for Tash to rest."

"I heard. But at least it's still happening. They could have postponed the trip much longer." He noticed the one hand tucked behind her back, then pointed to the one hanging at her side. "Were you able to get that splinter out after we parted ways last night?"

Elia looked down at the small wound on the fleshiest part of her palm. She had gotten the sliver from pulling the fence apart and throwing the rails over the edge of the island. Only after washing away all the traces of dirt under her fingernails had she finally succeeded in removing the tiny dagger. "It's healing fine. I had actually forgotten about it. There's been so much commotion this morning keeping me distracted. What about you? Have you been watching the preparations outside?"

"Yes. Your view of the courtyard is much better than the one from my room."

As she had hoped, Hokk turned now to look out her window, giving Elia the opportunity to open the middle drawer and hide the incense sticks in the box with the telescope.

"They just started loading Tasheira's belongings onto another floating rock barge like they use for transporting things," he said. "I suspect that's where I'll be riding again, towed behind the team with the rest of the freight."

Elia closed the drawer and joined Hokk by the window. The stone platform was hovering just above the cobblestones. In one area, poles had been driven into the rock to support a silk canopy overhead. "You'll have plenty of shade," she noted.

"Anything to avoid wearing that bulky suit."

"We'll just have to be careful you don't get too much sun again," said Elia as she looked at the side of Hokk's head and noticed a few remaining flakes of dry skin on his ear. Rubbing them off, she was impressed once more how quickly his skin was healing with the Baron's medicine. It wouldn't be long before Hokk had fully regained his pale complexion.

"How long do you think it will take us to get there today?" he asked.

"I'm not sure. But I'll be relieved when we finally arrive. I never thought I'd see those two islands again," said Elia. She felt a sudden sense of gratitude. "You know, I didn't properly thank you."

Hokk kept staring outside. "For what?"

"For last night. You took a big gamble."

"You needed help. I owed it to you."

"You owed me? Why would you say that?"

Hokk sighed, then tilted his head toward the ceiling and

dropped his shoulders. "I feel like I have . . . so many regrets."

"Who doesn't?"

"I wish I could go back and make up for every bad thing I'm guilty of."

"You're always too hard on yourself," Elia said gently.

"I just know there's more I could have done." He gazed at her with heartache. "Even now, for Koiyin and Fimal. I shouldn't have left them in Below. They're probably both dead because of me."

Elia put a hand on his shoulder. "Those were just unfortunate circumstances. You had no choice in the matter."

"Didn't I?" he replied with a grimace before turning and leaving the room.

Chapter 40

EVERYTHING AND EVERYONE WAS ON standby, waiting in the oppressive heat for Tasheira to emerge from the house. Hokk sat in the shade with the cargo. Nym rested in his lap. The white padded suit was stretched out behind him, tied down to one of the many crates. Hokk watched the Baron and the stable manager work through a checklist as they performed a final inspection of the assembled livestock. A few other men were sitting patiently on horses that stamped the ground with their hooves, eager to get airborne. Nearby, he saw Elia had already mounted too, sitting slouched in her saddle, holding her telescope and his old sack.

She looked very exotic wearing her white turban, with her metal eyebrow piercing catching the sunlight. Her eyes, however, lacked focus in an unsettling yet somehow familiar way. What had changed since being alone together in her room? He tried to catch her attention, but she looked right through him. Remembering her dazed expression at the Torkin bonfires, he hoped she wasn't starting to feel sick again.

Tasheira took much longer than the hour her mother had insisted upon. When the girl finally emerged from the manor, she wore a fresh outfit and her thick curls had been piled in an elaborate fashion on her head. In stark contrast to such finery, however, her manner was slow and clumsy, and her eyes seemed especially vacant — in fact, she had the same look as Elia, only to a greater degree.

A servant placed a footstool beside Tasheira's horse. Showing no sign of emotion, Tash hugged her mother and Neric goodbye, then climbed onto her saddle without so much as a final farewell glance toward the house, the staff, or the rest of the estate. Instead, her head flopped forward as though her neck had no strength. How was the girl going to manage the trip?

But at least they could finally leave. As soon as the Baron had mounted, a trumpeting sound was heard, and all the horses took flight. Hokk stretched beyond the overhead canopy to look over the edge of his floating barge and watched the shadows of flapping wings grow smaller as they rose above the ground. Soon, the island property was behind them, and they were flying with only brilliant clouds below.

• • •

They flew for hours. They found no islands en route upon which to set down for a break, but there was enough space on the platform behind Hokk for several horses at a time to land, rest their wings, and rehydrate. As riders dismounted to stretch their stiff limbs, Hokk overheard conversations about the team's progress. He learned that the palace messenger who had arrived a few days earlier was now helping to lead the expedition. While there were no landmarks out here, Hokk assumed the man knew his way with the same sense of direction Hokk had counted on all those years traveling across the prairies.

When the horses being ridden by the Baron and the messenger finally rotated through for their own break, Elia and Tasheira touched down at the same time. Hokk was pleased to see both girls looking more alert. But little was said between any of them. Everyone was becoming exhausted. Hokk was beginning to feel the same. Luckily, he did not have to worry about staying upright in a saddle, so as the afternoon wore on, he eventually dozed in his place.

When he awoke much later, the light was less intense, but the sun had not yet set. He leaned out past the canopy to get a view of the horses in the air. He spotted Elia's, flying at a slightly higher altitude. She was sitting erect, peering through her telescope. His curiosity piqued, Hokk stretched his neck to follow her line of sight. He stood up and moved to the edge of his stone platform, feeling the sun's rays warm only half his face. He had to squint, even behind his glasses, but he made out two massive bulks materializing along the shimmering horizon.

Elia's islands!

As if she had felt his surge of excitement, Elia looked over at Hokk. She waved, then pointed ahead. Hokk nodded.

As they flew closer, Hokk could make out more details. The largest island had a mountain that rose to an imposing elevation. On one side, its steep slope fell away into the clouds; on the other, the gentler incline was covered with trees. Beyond the forest, the terrain flattened into what he assumed was agricultural land, and then, past this, he could distinguish low-rise buildings making up the outer limits of a city. What was its name again? Had Elia called it Kamanman? No, that was the name of the island. The city was called something else.

According to Elia, Kamanman was joined to its smaller neighbor by a large, arching bridge, and Hokk knew this other island was the Noble Sanctuary. From this distance, however, the palace's mirrored exterior reflected the clouds and the color of the sky, making it difficult to distinguish the two towers. But as the team of horses started to fly over the city, Hokk began to see the impressive structures more clearly. They had what looked like seamless glass panels spanning their entire surface, and though Hokk had never seen such pristine examples, he knew, without a doubt, exactly what he was looking at.

The two towers of the Mirrored Palace were actually identical skyscrapers, undamaged, but undeniably designed and constructed in the same manner as the buildings that soared high into the sky within the City of Ago.

Chapter 41

AS THEY FLEW OVER THE City of Na-Lavent toward the Mirrored Palace, Elia twisted in her saddle to look behind one more time. Unfortunately, they had approached Mount Mahayit and the Noble Sanctuary from a direction that prevented her from seeing her family's home floating at the end of its suspension bridge. She still couldn't catch a glimpse of it on the far side of the forest, so she gazed down instead upon the ramshackle buildings passing directly below and noticed the market where she used to shop with her mother. Elia wondered if her father continued to struggle in its filthy back lanes, scrounging for morsels of spoiled food. Maybe he was dead. Or, perhaps, he was Elia's only surviving relative.

She faced forward as they drew closer to the palace. Though she had stared up at the two towers every day of her working life, Elia looked at them now as if for the first time. *They're practically scraping the sky!* She was stunned by how similar they were to the tall buildings in Hokk's city — or at least to how Ago's skyscrapers must have looked in the past.

Led by the Baron's steed, the horses soared above the Grand Bridge, then began to descend, banking sharply to glide over the many acres of manicured gardens. Elia had never seen this area of the Noble Sanctuary before, and she was awestruck by the vast array of trees, flowering plants, pavilions, and statues scattered throughout the grounds. And she saw people everywhere, as if the entire Royal Court had emptied from the palace. Elegantly dressed ladies and gentlemen were strolling along the garden's many paths, sampling food laid out on long tables and enjoying the entertainment of jugglers, dancers, and groups of musicians who filled the air with their blended melodies.

Too preoccupied with their merriment, no one appeared to notice the Baron's entourage as it flew overhead, and Elia didn't anticipate a receiving party when their horses finally touched down in a large courtyard. But their arrival must have been expected, because they were swarmed by a brigade of servants, all with those small, familiar tattoos on their foreheads. They immediately set to work unloading cargo, helping riders from their saddles, and tending to the animals with water and brushes.

Elia dismounted. In one hand, she carried her sack with the telescope and carved box inside. Tasheira grabbed her other hand and squeezed it as they were whisked away. Elia craned her neck, but failed to see Hokk for all the people buzzing about his floating barge. She would have to try to get back to him as soon as possible. At the very least, find out where he would be staying.

The two girls moved toward the palace's front reception hall. The outside was clad in the same reflective glass, and it rose several stories high to connect the two towers. In the maturing twilight, the flicker of candlelit chandeliers and torches could be seen shining from within. Along the front, servants pushed against the large panels of several revolving doors that spun completely around, allowing people on either side to simultaneously enter and exit. Making sure her dress didn't get caught, Elia pressed into the same tight enclosure as Tasheira, yet they almost tripped each other as they shuffled forward. A half revolution and they were inside a massive, vaulted atrium rising high above them, with plants everywhere as an extension of the outside gardens. Again, this was a view Elia had never seen, having always entered the palace from the back.

"Any of this look familiar?" Tasheira asked.

"Vaguely," Elia lied.

Footsteps echoed in the cavernous lobby. Each tower had its own spiraling staircase that disappeared into the interior, and the servants were approaching the one on the left.

"Tohryn's side," said Tash.

Not far from the staircase, Elia noticed two sets of double door panels and instantly recognized what they were for — *elevators*. She was absolutely certain. They looked the same as the ones she had seen inside the Board's skyscraper in Ago. These doors, however, probably didn't have functioning carriages behind them since large vases with flowers had been placed directly in front to block access. Gazing skyward through the glass ceiling, Elia could see Tohryn's tower rising outside, and she wondered how high they would have to climb without the benefit of an elevator.

Tash seemed to read her thoughts. "Guest quarters are just a few flights up," she said. "They're reserved for visiting dignitaries. That's where I used to stay when I came in the past."

"But not now?" asked Elia.

"Now, I'll have a permanent room of my own on a higher level. Hopefully, I can be on the same floor as my cousin."

"Have you been in Lady Jeska's room before?"

"No, but I'm sure it's impressive. She's lived in the palace for almost a decade."

"I look forward to meeting her."

"I wouldn't count on it tonight. You saw what was going on in the gardens. I suspect she'll be busy attending to Empress Faytelle's needs throughout the evening."

"I'm curious what they're celebrating."

"Yes. I was wondering the same."

They began to ascend the steps. Illuminated by candlelight from sconces, the staircase was not nearly as narrow as the one Elia had climbed with Roahm and his Torkin warriors when they stormed the Seed Keeper's storeroom. In contrast, these stairs at the palace had been built wide enough to accommodate the ladies of the Royal Court wearing voluminous dresses.

Tash and Elia reached the first landing. A massive door blocked entry to this level. To the left and right of it, two Imperial Guards stood at attention. Elia's heartbeat doubled at the sight of them, but thankfully, the servants leading the way continued to climb.

"What are those men guarding?" asked Elia.

"That's Emperor Tohryn's private quarters," Tasheira replied. "In their respective towers, each emperor gets the first floor above ground level all to himself. Then the next floor, in this particular building anyway, is for Tohryn's wife, Faytelle. Keep going higher and you get to the levels where visitors and the Royal Court stay."

"Is that where your father and Hokk will have rooms?"

"Probably. However, they could end up on Tael's side, depending on what's already occupied."

The second level was not guarded, but had a similar closed door. Subsequent floors, however, had corridors leading off from the landings.

"This is Jeska's level," said Tash after a few more flights. "I assume we'll be staying here."

A servant just steps ahead overheard and turned around. "No, you're much higher."

"Higher?" Tash repeated sternly. "How high do we have to go? At this rate, we'll be at the very top."

Tash and Elia climbed on with two servants in front and a small army of staff behind, each loaded down with Tasheira's belongings. They continued, floor after floor, until the staircase ended. Everyone was panting heavily. Elia's body was sticky with perspiration. Though Tasheira had nothing to carry, she sounded the most winded of all. "This is ... unbelievable," Tash sputtered between gasps for breath. "I can't be . . . climbing this . . . every day."

One of their guides proceeded halfway down the corridor that stretched before them and unlocked a door. "This is your room," she said, handing both Elia and Tash a key. Another servant gave Tasheira a candle holder with the wick already burning.

Tash stared down at what she held in her hands as if ready to protest, then seemed to reconsider. She pushed open the door with her shoulder and stepped inside. Elia followed right behind, but bumped up against Tasheira, who had halted in her tracks.

The room, bathed in candlelight, was about a quarter of the size of Tasheira's old bedchamber at the manor. It was completely unadorned. No furniture or place to sit. No wardrobe. A bare mattress sat on the floor along with a thin blanket and a single stained pillow.

Tasheira whirled on the servant who had let them in. "This can't be right! There must be a mistake! This room is a disaster."

"This is the only one available," the servant replied with a deadpan face.

"But this space is too plain and dirty. Look!" Tash pointed to a number of holes in the walls. "These walls are damaged. What am I supposed to do about that?"

"Cover it with art, perhaps?" the staff member replied.

"Art?" Tash shouted. "This room should be properly furnished. What happened to the person who had this room before me?"

"The girl's gone. She disappeared about a month or two ago."

"Why?"

"She ran off to get married. Supposedly to some commoner."

"No wonder she ran off if this is where she had to stay. So where do I put all my clothes?" Tasheira angrily asked as the rest of the people carrying her possessions filled the room.

The servant shrugged. "You have all these boxes. Can you perhaps use those?"

J A S O N   C H A B O T

While Tasheira continued to erupt with outrage, Elia was drawn to the huge window that filled the entire wall opposite the door. From up here, the garden below seemed so far away. Lanterns, lighting numerous pathways, shone like luminescent pearls strung along a necklace, providing just enough light for Elia to make out the people who had assembled. Elia swallowed hard, however, knowing that soon, either Tasheira or the Baron would be canvassing this crowd to find out just who in the Royal Court might know her.

"Tashi!" Turning, Elia saw a young woman, perhaps ten years older than Tasheira, standing in the doorway. She wore a layered dress swirling with all the colors a sunset has ever painted.

"Jesi!" Tasheira replied, and the two of them embraced. But Tash quickly pulled back and swung her arms in disgust around the room, spilling wax over the edge of her candle holder. "Can you believe it? Look at the miserable condition of this room! They say it's the only thing available."

"Hmm," said Jeska as she scanned the space. She looked surprised. "I don't know why it's so empty. I'm sure we can find something better."

"I just assumed every square inch of the palace was richly decorated."

"It's only like that on the lower floors, or wherever the emperors might find themselves," Jeska explained. "Everywhere else, the rooms are noticeably plainer. Well, maybe not *this* bad," she said with a frown. "But don't worry about it for now. We'll try to track down some furniture for you, which will make a difference. And soon, you'll find it doesn't really matter. You'll spend most of your time outside this room, accompanying Empress Faytelle."

"It's just very disappointing. Definitely not what I was expecting," Tash sulked.

"I can understand, but you must remember, it's an honor for us just to be selected to serve our empress."

Tasheira sighed. "Perhaps," she said, though she did not sound convinced.

"Give it time. You'll see it's all worth it in the long run, no matter what we left behind to be here."

"Why aren't you with Empress Faytelle right now?"

"She wanted to take a short nap. It gave me a chance to slip away when I found out you had arrived. But you should go down to the gardens ahead of us to enjoy the night's festivities."

"And do the stairs again?" Tasheira complained.

"You'll get used to them too. I promise. But I'll see what I can do over the coming days to get you moved to a lower floor. In the meantime, you need some food and drink. That will make you feel better."

"What are they celebrating anyway?" Tasheira asked.

"Crown Prince Veralion's birthday," Jeska replied. "He's turning sixteen. The empress, his mother, has missed the start, though she'll make her appearance soon. Listen, I can't stay much longer, but I'm eager to hear news about my brothers."

A sudden explosion just outside made the windowpanes shake as if they might shatter into the room. Elia shrieked and shielded her head as three more explosions followed. But the windows stayed intact. On the other side, sparks of red, yellow, and green cascaded through the air like a dripping flower burst, accompanied by cheers from the audience below.

Had Elia been the only one who screamed? She turned and saw both Tasheira and Jeska grinning with amusement.

"Don't worry. Those are just fireworks. They set off a few at the start to announce more to come," said Jeska. "You must be Marest, I presume."

"No, Marest is dead," Tasheira bluntly replied. "This is Miss Elia. My apologies, I should have introduced the two of you earlier."

Elia nodded. "A pleasure to meet you."

"And you," said Lady Jeska with a gracious curtsy.

"Miss Elia is from a noble family," Tasheira explained,

"but somehow, she got lost or separated from them and she has suffered an accident. Now she can't remember anything about her parents. Our hope is that we can determine what family she belongs to."

Jeska's face lit up with a sincere smile. "No fear, Miss Elia. Between Tasheira and me, we can personally introduce you to everyone in the Royal Court, if that's what it takes. In fact, I'll start first thing in the morning after I officially introduce both of you to Empress Faytelle. And I'm sure she'll agree you can stay at the palace as long as necessary to sort everything out."

Though Elia tried to look appreciative, she was clutching her bag so tightly, it felt as if her knuckles might tear through her skin. She was becoming less and less confident of her plan with each passing minute. Perhaps she could stay within the palace for a day, maybe two, but any longer and her lies would be discovered. Someone would surely recognize her as the laundry girl who had escaped — the same person Imperial Guards had hunted in Below, looking for the very telescope she had now smuggled back into the palace.

A day, two at the most, she reinforced in her mind. Then she'd have to get out. Get out, give up, and go into hiding.

Chapter 42

HOKK CLUTCHED NYM CLOSE TO his chest. He had lost sight of Elia and Tasheira almost as soon as they had arrived, so now he stood waiting to find out where he would be taken. But he remained alert. A nagging sense of unease had surfaced and was building. Though he didn't know why he felt so cautious, he knew to trust his instincts. Then he saw Imperial Guards enter the courtyard, and every strand of muscle fiber in his body tensed.

Their presence alone was ominous. The last time he had seen Imperial Guards was in the City of Ago after he and Elia had been pursued across the prairies. That one commander with the mutilated nose and the metallic wings on his helmet — the man Elia was so terrified would capture her — had been a monster.

They're probably all monsters, hiding behind those reflective masks — every one of them with ravaged, hideous faces!

Around him, palace staff continued to unload cargo, their glances darting back and forth between Hokk, the converging guards, and the puzzling white padded suit still resting on the floating rock barge. A few servants peered into the suit's spherical headpiece — even tapped on the glass — and debated in whispers about the best way to carry it. They worried someone might be unconscious inside, or worse, already dead.

"It's empty," Hokk said, which quickly silenced their concerns.

But a guard had noticed the fussing. Intrigued, he marched closer and the workers dispersed. He examined the outfit from head to toe. "What's this thing supposed to be?" he demanded.

"It's my survival suit," Hokk brusquely declared.

The guard scrutinized Hokk, then the heavy garment again. "For surviving what?"

Hokk's eyes narrowed. "Why should I have to tell you?"

He heard the leather of the man's glove stretch and groan as the guard formed a fist.

Wait, why am I arguing? While his defensiveness came as no surprise — Hokk had reacted the same way each time he had appeared before the Board — showing such defiance now could be downright dangerous. It was unwarranted, too, since he had only just arrived. He was here to help Elia, not make matters worse. "This suit kept me alive during my fiery freefall from the sky," he offered in an attempt to cooperate. "I landed on one of your neighboring islands."

"Fiery freefall?" the man grunted.

"Even with the suit, I still got burned and have the wounds to prove it," said Hokk. He lowered Nym to the ground, then pulled up his sleeves to show the rippled scars from his injuries years earlier and the skin that was still peeling from his sunburn.

The man stared at Hokk through his expressionless sculpted faceplate. "Who the hell are you?"

"My name is Hokk."

"And why are you hiding your face?" the guard asked suspiciously, before reaching up and yanking off Hokk's dark glasses.

That's a question you should also be asked, Hokk thought. Instead of such a confrontational response, however, Hokk merely gazed at the guard wide-eyed, then blinked several times in a deliberate manner to show he had only one set of eyelids. "In case you can't tell, I'm not from here."

The guard snorted. "No kidding."

"I have been brought to the Sanctuary specifically for an audience with the Twin Emperors," Hokk explained, suddenly aware of a drop of sweat slowly trickling down the back of his neck.

The guard shook his head. "Nice try, but that's not going to happen," he said severely. "No one is granted access to the palace without the appropriate clearance." He grabbed Hokk by the wrist and twisted, prompting Nym to growl a warning. The guard ignored the fox at their feet. "And certainly nobody the likes of you will *ever* get inside."

Hokk shot a quick glance at the Baron, who was nearby, reviewing his checklist of livestock as animals were being led away to the Royal Stables. "Baron Shoad!" he called out, and when the man looked up from his records and saw Hokk beckoning with his free hand, he strode over. The guard released Hokk's other wrist before the Baron could notice anything.

"I'm being denied entry to the palace," Hokk complained as he snatched his glasses from the guard. "Though I've been trying to explain —"

The Baron's face instantly went rigid with rage. "This is nonsense!" he bellowed. He spun on the guard. "Are you an absolute fool?"

Hokk brimmed with satisfaction as the man behind the metal mask shrank back. Servants stopped what they were doing to stare in their direction.

"Do you not know who I am?" the Baron challenged.

"I do indeed, Baron Shoad," replied the guard with a catch in his voice. "But for security purposes, we must interrogate all questionable visitors to the Sanctuary."

"Questionable? We are invited guests! We come every year."

"Please be assured I didn't mean you or your family. But it's a different matter for this . . . this . . ." The guard was struggling to describe Hokk. "Stowaway. Or whatever he is."

Shoad was seething. "Where is your superior officer?"

Before the man could answer, they were joined by a guard with a metal spike protruding from the brow of his helmet. This feature was a unique embellishment and somehow one that Hokk felt certain he had seen before.

"Is there a problem here?" the second guard inquired.

"Officer Blaitz, is it not?" questioned the Baron, who apparently recognized him.

"It's actually Commander Blaitz now," said the guard. "As of a few weeks ago."

"You've been promoted, have you? Then I guess congratulations are in order," Shoad conceded. Yet the lull in his anger was short-lived. He pointed an accusatory finger at the first guard. "This man should be *de*moted for his insulting charges."

The two metal faces looked at each other. Then Commander Blaitz did a most unexpected thing — he removed his helmet and tucked it under his arm. Hokk was startled to see not a grotesque face, but rather a handsome, square-jawed, serious-looking man who was probably a few years older than the Baron, with the same dark skin and thick blond hair as all the residents of Above.

"Your subordinate, here, has been grilling my very distinguished guest, throwing around allegations that he is a stowaway and a trespasser," the Baron continued with a huff. "And I will tolerate none of it!"

"If there has been a misunderstanding," said Blaitz, "then I offer our apologies. Security around the palace has been ramped up a hundredfold recently, much tighter than you've likely encountered during past visits. But of course, you, your family, and your guest are most welcome and free to come and go as you wish." Commander Blaitz then turned to Hokk. "And may I ask, sir, is this your first visit to the palace?"

"It is," Hokk replied.

"Then a special welcome to you. Where are you travelling from?"

Before Hokk could say anything, the Baron answered for him. "He's actually from the moon."

Hokk could see that both Blaitz and the other guard were jolted by this revelation. "The moon!" the commander repeated. He looked up to the scattered lunar pieces trailing across the night sky. Eavesdropping servants close at hand followed his gaze. "The *actual* moon?" wondered Blaitz.

"The very one above our heads," Shoad replied proudly.

"Incredible!" said the commander, now examining Hokk more closely and nodding as if his appearance explained everything. "But can it really be true after all these years of separation?"

The Baron smiled. "Hokk is part of a special envoy sent down to the Lunera System to reach out to us and finally bridge the gap."

"Yes, I have come with a very special message to share with the Twin Emperors," stated Hokk. "After I crash-landed, I was rescued by Baron Shoad, and he promised to do whatever necessary to make sure a meeting takes place."

"I offer the same guarantee," said the commander with a respectful bow. "And I hope you enjoy your visit, for however long you stay with us. Again, my apologies for any offense you may have experienced. Now, to prevent further delay, I'll have you shown to your rooms immediately."

Escorted by Commander Blaitz and a group of palace staff, Hokk carried Nym toward a bank of revolving doors at the base of the palace's colossal glass facade. Drawing closer, Hokk gazed up at both sides of the soaring skyscrapers, and almost failed to notice as the servants ahead of him abruptly split apart, halted, and bowed their heads. He wasn't sure why until he spotted a man, regally dressed, pushing against a revolving door to exit into the courtyard.

Hokk recognized the man from his portrait hanging outside the Baron's library. He was one of the Twin Emperors, though with less hair and a rounder stomach than the youth depicted in the painting. He wore a finely tailored, brocade jacket of yellow and deep blue. His silk trousers hung perfectly creased above a pair of tightly woven gold shoes that curled up at the tips. He projected a sense of sovereign confidence, but it was his unusual gait, vacant eyes, and the thin white cane he swung along the ground as he stepped outside that gave him away. This was the blind emperor Tael.

"Your Excellency," said the Baron, bowing from the waist.

Tael stopped and turned in the Baron's general direction as the rest of his royal entourage began spilling out behind him, followed by a few more Imperial Guards. "That voice," the emperor said with a smile. "I recognize it but can't match it to a name."

"It is I, Baron Shoad, just arrived with this year's delivery of horses."

The emperor's face lit up even more. "Ah, yes, my dear Baron. Has a year truly passed by already?"

"It has."

"Amazing. I'm so pleased you could join us once more at the Sanctuary."

Tael held his hand forward and Baron Shoad took it. "The honor is always mine," said the Baron, bowing once again, then pressing the emperor's knuckles to his forehead as a sign of respect.

"I always enjoy your visit, and this year, I suspect I'll end up buying your whole herd again. That is, if I can beat my brother to it! I don't think he's ever fully forgiven me for that last time when I purchased the entire lot."

"I have brought an even greater selection this visit, which I'm sure will please you both," the Baron said with a chuckle.

"And have your lovely wife and daughter joined you too?"

"Just my daughter. She has already retired to her quarters ahead of us."

Commander Blaitz leaned close enough to whisper something into the emperor's ear. "Is that so," Tael said with a nod, turning slightly, but still facing neither Hokk nor the Baron precisely. "I understand, Baron, there's someone else who has also traveled with you this trip."

"Yes, I would like to introduce you to Hokk Isec," said the Baron.

Emperor Tael held up his hand, trying to judge where Hokk might be standing. Hokk shifted Nym in his arms so he could take the man's hand, then he performed the same gesture to his forehead that he had witnessed just minutes before.

"It's an honor to meet you, Your Excellency," said Hokk.

Tael cocked his head. His unfocused eyes stared over Hokk's shoulder. "You have an accent," noted the emperor. "An accent I'm not familiar with. That's most intriguing. You must be from a very distant island, if I'm not mistaken."

Again, the Baron responded for Hokk. "Yes, he's traveled a very great distance, but not from where you might guess. He has actually come from . . . the moon! He's here specifically to see you."

"The moon!" Tael gasped, leaning heavily on his cane to keep himself balanced as if the shock had made his legs wobbly. "I knew . . . I knew this day might come," he sputtered as the surrounding courtiers murmured with hushed excitement. He stretched out his arm as before and Hokk took his hand again. "Let me feel your face," said the emperor, his dead eyes staring right through him.

Hokk felt uncomfortable as Tael's fingers started at his forehead, then worked their way down, feeling the shape of his nose, his lips, his chin. When he was done, the emperor didn't pull away. Instead, his hand lingered upon Hokk's neck as if giving him the gentlest of choke holds.

"I want to know everything about you," said Tael.

"He has a phenomenal story to tell," added the Baron. "Plus a message to share."

"Yes, an important matter that I look forward to sharing with both you and Emperor Tohryn. *Together*," Hokk stressed, stepping back just enough to be beyond the emperor's reach.

Tael lowered his arm, looking thoughtful. "If it's business to discuss, then I agree, let's save it for a more opportune time when my brother and I are officially holding court. However, I will make sure that happens as soon as possible tomorrow. If it were not for this evening's festivities — which I'm obliged to attend — I'd much prefer to steal you away this very minute."

A burst of piercing lights erupted overhead, followed by a thunderclap that echoed between the two towers. Nym yelped. Everyone, except the emperor, looked up as fire rained down in searing trails, burning with a multitude of colors. There was an audible gasp of surprise.

"The warning shot," Tael shouted with a flourish of his hand, looking amused. "The fire show will be starting soon. We are celebrating my oldest nephew's birthday tonight." He turned to the Baron, but again, his aim of address was off. "I would be delighted if you and Lord Isec would join us, though I understand completely if you choose to decline. Don't mind my observation, but I can hear the exhaustion in your voices."

"You are most generous, Your Excellency, and you are right," replied the Baron. "We have had a long, full day of travel, and I am beginning to feel weary. I also plan to be up at dawn to make sure the horses are fully prepared for your inspection."

"Absolutely," said Emperor Tael. "Rest well, and we will see you in the morning." He summoned Commander Blaitz with a snap of his fingers and murmured something only the guard could hear.

"Of course. Understood, Your Excellency," Blaitz replied with a deep bow.

Tael smiled, then boldly tipped back his head and strode forward, his cane swinging left and right to clear a path as his entourage followed him to the gardens.

• • •

Hokk placed his ear against his bedroom door. He listened. He heard the Baron say a few words to someone in the corridor — probably one of the servants — followed by the sound of a door closing farther down the hall. Then silence.

Hokk didn't move. After waiting a few minutes longer, and hearing no other noises outside, he turned the handle quietly to open his door and look out.

The Imperial Guard, who had followed them to this floor, was standing against the opposite wall. "Can I help you?" the guard asked gruffly.

"No, everything's fine," Hokk murmured as he closed the door again and locked it.

He's not just out there to ensure my safety. He was ordered to keep watch over me. Hokk had seen Commander Blaitz talking to the man just after Emperor Tael and his group departed for the celebration. The guard had then immediately fallen into step behind Hokk and the Baron as they entered the palace. He had been with them ever since, monitoring Hokk's every move.

Unless I'm being more paranoid than usual.

"I'm always so suspicious," Hokk confided softly to Nym, who was still cradled in his arms. He scratched behind the animal's ears, glad to see the fox had stopped trembling from the earlier blast of fireworks. Nym was now starting to doze, but with the scratching, he opened his eyelids just a slit and licked his muzzle.

"But what to do with you now?" Hokk wondered.

The palace wasn't a suitable environment for the fox. Someone might even try to steal him.

It was obvious. Nym could not be allowed to leave the room.

Hokk approached a cabinet with drawers and opened the lowest one. He grabbed a blanket from his bed and curled it into a nest before lowering the fox into it. He then stepped back and watched the animal fall asleep, its small chest rising and falling with each breath.

"The next couple of days will be very fascinating. For all of us," Hokk whispered, more to himself than the fox.

He scanned his room. Elia must be staying in one similar

to this. It was beautifully decorated, just like the room where he had slept at the Baron's estate. He blew out a candle on a nearby table and walked in the darkness over to a wall of windows. He looked down upon the throng below. Since he was only a few levels above ground, Hokk could easily distinguish the revelers. Couples danced. Acrobats tumbled. Clusters of women whispered among themselves and waved for others to join them. Groups of men seemed engaged in heated debates as they demanded more wine to fill their glasses. Imperial Guards were watching everything.

And then he saw Elia. She was moving through the crowd with Tasheira, who appeared to be introducing her to one person after another. Even from this distance, Hokk could easily read the anxiety on Elia's face, which mirrored his own. Now that they were both at the palace, her plan had been set into motion and there was no way to stop it.

Pinpricks of light shot up into the air, catching his attention. The twinkling spots, like flaming bumblebees, climbed high into the black sky before exploding into blooms of pink, red, and purple. *Boom. Boom.* The window shook. Nym yelped. *Boom.* The bedroom blazed with color. Simultaneously, Hokk felt himself surrendering to his old fascination with fire — it was as if his pupils and every vein in his body had dilated to resurrect him. He felt alive! He wanted more!

With the next flash of lights, Hokk tried to suppress his irresistible stirrings. *Boom.* Digging his fingernails into his palms, he looked down, hoping to find Elia once more, even just to see her turban bobbing among the crowd. But she had disappeared, swallowed up in a mob of faces, all staring skyward.

Chapter 43

CURTAINS! THAT'S WHAT HER ROOM needed before any furniture or decorations. Curtains! The top floors of the palace were the first to be hit by the rising sun, and as light started to stream in, Tasheira knew it was too wretchedly early to wake up. Especially after getting to bed so late. She wished she could throw a cushion over her head to block out the glare, but unfortunately, Tash was sharing the room's only pillow with Elia.

But why was she being so accommodating? She should just yank the pillow away and let Elia's head hit the hard mattress. Tash still felt frustrated by how awkward and shy Elia had been the previous evening when they had joined the party outside. She had introduced the girl to everyone she knew — practically dragging her around by the wrist — yet Elia had made no effort to be friendly. Instead, she'd held back from each group as if ready to bolt into the shadows, always clutching that ugly, old sack she carried everywhere. By the time they returned to their room, Tash was livid, steaming with anger from both the hike up the stairs and Elia's lousy attitude. Yet, despite her irritation, Tasheira had reminded herself not to do or say anything she'd regret. Elia might still have the connections to improve Tash's position at court, and at the moment, that was her highest priority. Because if Tash couldn't change her situation, she would have nothing more to do with this palace.

It's an honor for us just to be selected to serve our empress.

Such nonsense. Surely Jeska didn't really believe this. She was no better than a servant. Why hadn't she warned Tash what it would be like here?

I'll return home with my father if necessary, thought Tasheira. He won't make me stay if he finds out how unhappy I am.

Unhappy, yes, but nervous too. Staring at the holes in the dingy white walls, Tash realized just how extremely anxious she felt, partly from not knowing what was in store for her today, but more so because acute anxiety was a side effect from inhaling the noxious, addictive smoke from incense sticks. That's why her mother was obsessed with the stuff — the Baroness couldn't handle the irrational fears that accompanied coming down from the high, so it was easier not to stop at all. Even now, Tash felt a strong urge for another dose to calm herself. But she knew better and should have known better yesterday. Like a fool, she had been too weak to resist. Then again, dealing with the death of both Marest and Fimal on such an important yet stressful day — well, the timing couldn't have been worse.

A latch clicked and Tasheira turned her head toward the door. Between the stacks of boxes, she watched the handle depress slowly before the door opened and her cousin's head peeked inside.

"Good, you're awake," said Jeska as she entered and maneuvered around the crates.

"I shouldn't be," Tasheira grumbled. Beside her, Elia stirred.

"You should actually be dressed, ready to go," Jeska half scolded. "Though maybe I wasn't clear about it last night. Now hurry and get out of bed. Elia can sleep longer if she wants, but you'll have to come down with me."

Tasheira's expression hardened as she sat up and pushed curls away from her forehead. "No, Elia's getting up too!"

• • •

Curtains. Everywhere. That was the first thing Tash noticed. Every window in Empress Faytelle's sprawling quarters was covered with tightly drawn curtains.

Jeska led them into the darkened boudoir that took up the entire floor, just one level above Tohryn's suite. Tasheira followed right behind, walking arm in arm with a still-drowsy Elia. Besides the shadowy bulk of furnishings, Tash couldn't see much else in the gloom except the silhouettes of other women waiting patiently for their mistress to wake up.

As it turned out, Jeska had made sure they arrived just in time.

"Have I slept too long?" asked a disembodied voice drifting out from within the tasseled drapes surrounding the bed.

The empress's voice spurred the women into action.

"It is your usual hour of the morning, Your Grace," one of the ladies-in-waiting replied as several others started opening curtains to let in the sunshine.

"Good. Today, of all days, we cannot afford to dawdle," said the voice that Tash now recognized as Faytelle's.

The empress swung out her legs and planted her feet on the floor. As the woman emerged and the lavish room quickly brightened with the curtains drawn, Tasheira was surprised how downright ordinary the empress appeared at this time of day.

She wore a billowy nightgown as white as her astonishingly white skin. Instead of her typical long, blond locks, her natural hair was dark and cropped short. Her wrinkled face was plain, and she lacked eyebrows above her pale eyes. She unabashedly disrobed and let the gown fall to her feet. Her belly and breasts had the fullness of a middle-aged mother, but her weight was well proportioned to her sturdy limbs.

Jeska leaned close. "Feel free to simply observe things this morning," she whispered. "But you'll be expected to help out tomorrow. It's the best way to learn what needs to be done."

If I'm still here tomorrow.

Yet Tasheira's fascination grew as she watched the empress's preparations for the day. And the more Tash saw, the more she had to admit these ladies-in-waiting were less like servants and more like confidantes. They hummed melodies and read poetry, but mostly, they shared gossip, which Faytelle particularly seemed to enjoy.

The mood in the room grew steadily more serious, however, as the empress dressed, as if each new piece of clothing added a layer to her imperial persona. After stockings, underskirts, and a camisole were put on, any exposed skin that remained was darkened with makeup, including her ears and the backs of her hands. Next, a blond wig was placed on the empress's head and carefully attached, then styled with ribbons, gemstones, and long twisting braids. Other women painted eyebrows onto Faytelle's face and outlined her eyes in black and her lips in dark red. Her corset was mercilessly cinched to reduce her waist and push up her jiggling bosom, and by the time a green dress was put on, the empress had taken on a stern demeanor, as if any trace of her earlier, more amiable personality had completely vanished. Now *this* was the woman Tasheira was familiar with — a person who embodied power, who fiercely commanded the attention of all those in her presence.

As a full-length mirror was brought forward, Empress Faytelle finally noticed Tasheira and Elia in the reflection, hovering nearby.

"You're the Baron's daughter," the empress decided as she shifted her wig to sit more balanced on her head.

"I am, Your Grace. We arrived last night."

"With that young man from the moon your father found."

"Yes . . . uh . . . Hokk," Tash sputtered, stunned not only that the empress had already heard about him, but that she believed the Baron was the one who had found him. How utterly annoying! Hokk was *her* discovery to share with the court.

"Everyone's abuzz about him," said the empress, "though hardly any of us have seen him yet. But that won't be for long. An audience with this young man will be arranged as soon as possible."

"First thing this morning?" Tash wondered.

"No. First we go to the stables. Otherwise, my crazy brother-in-law will snatch up every animal there before we've had a chance to make our own selection." She stared at Tasheira through the mirror, examining her more carefully. "As I understand, you'll be my new lady-in-waiting."

"That's correct," said Tasheira, yet suddenly feeling as if she had betrayed herself by agreeing so quickly.

"Your name again?"

"Tasheira."

"And you have no plans, Lady Tasheira, to disappear on me? To foolishly run off and get married?" Faytelle asked, her voice surprisingly severe.

"No, not at all."

"You want to stay with me, then?"

"I do," Tash croaked, begrudgingly committing herself.

"And as for your companion — I don't believe we've ever met."

"I was actually hoping you had. Your Grace, may I present to you Miss Elia. She's joined me here, hoping to be reunited with her family."

"Which family?"

"That's what we're trying to determine."

Faytelle seemed irritated. "Has she no voice to speak for herself?"

"I'm recovering from an accident that caused me to lose my memory," said Elia.

"And I'm just trying to help her," Tash added.

"Come closer, my girl." As Elia approached, the empress

turned to inspect her without relying on the reflection in the mirror. "No, I don't recognize you at all."

"Unfortunately, no one seems to yet," said Tash.

"Why the turban?"

"She has little more than an inch of hair on her head," Tasheira replied again on Elia's behalf, wondering at the same time if the girl kept it so short, like the empress, because she too used to wear a wig.

"Well, we'll have to learn more. To make sure her claims are legitimate. It should be easy enough to confirm."

Tash noticed a flash of alarm cross Elia's face. It sparked a similar reaction within Tasheira, forcing her to consider something she hadn't thought about until now — was Elia telling the truth?

"And that thing in your eyebrow. Is it a piercing?" asked Faytelle.

"It is," Elia replied.

"And why did you decide to put a piece of jewelery there, of all places?"

Elia frowned. "I honestly don't remember."

"No, of course you don't." Empress Faytelle turned back to her mirror as if she had tired of the conversation. She touched the base of her bare throat. "Now, where are the rest of *my* accessories?" she huffed. "We should have left by now. My husband is surely waiting for us."

A lady-in-waiting fastened a necklace around the empress's neck and slipped a matching bracelet on one wrist. From the bracelet dangled a long, delicate chain, and a tiny clasp at the end of it was attached to the leg of a small yellow bird. A woman held the bird securely in her hands; however, when she released it, the bird didn't settle nicely on Faytelle's arm as expected, but instead tried to escape, losing a few feathers and defecating on the empress's sleeve.

"Who's fed this thing?" Faytelle raged.

Before anyone could capture the wildly flapping bird, the

empress yanked on the chain. As the startled animal fell out of the air, Faytelle quickly grabbed it in her fist and squeezed. Pulling the bracelet free from her wrist, she tossed it and the bird over her shoulder. The poor creature landed dead on the floor.

Though none of the other women, including Jeska, seemed shocked, Tash was shaken. She could feel Elia flinch beside her.

"I need a fresh outfit!" Faytelle shouted. "And a new bird. One that doesn't need to empty its bowels!"

Tasheira felt a pit of dread in her stomach as she watched the ladies-in-waiting strip away the empress's outer garment, then carelessly toss it away, where it landed over the lump of feathers on the ground.

This was clearly a woman who shouldn't be crossed. But was this really the kind of person Tash wanted to spend her days with?

Definitely not.

Chapter **44**

THOUGH IT WAS STILL QUITE early, Hokk was dressed for the day and waiting expectantly by the door of his room. When the knock came, Nym poked his head above the edge of the drawer where he'd been sleeping.

"Shh. It's okay," Hokk said to soothe the startled animal.

He opened the door and greeted Baron Shoad. The previous evening, Hokk had asked to accompany him in the morning, hoping to see Elia with Tasheira at the stables. Now, putting on his dark glasses, he joined the older man in the hallway. He wasn't shocked to see a guard still standing out there too — but could it be the same man from last night?

Hokk and the Baron descended the few flights of stairs, followed by the guard, until they reached the main floor. They didn't exit through the revolving doors, but rather headed in the opposite direction, cutting diagonally across the front reception hall to move deeper into the palace. They entered a separate wing and came upon a huge dining room with the same ceiling of glass and view of the towers rising into the sky. Inside the banquet hall, a number of people — likely members of the Royal Court, Hokk guessed — were seated at long, extravagantly adorned tables, while servants carried platters with the day's first meal. Looking up from their plates, a few people spotted Hokk and excitedly began whispering among themselves.

"Early risers like us," said the Baron as they passed by. "Although, if it's fine with you, we'll skip breakfast to check on the animals first. We can make up for it later."

"Absolutely," Hokk replied. He was well accustomed to missing meals.

But two tables of food were already being laid out when they got to the stables. Hokk wasn't surprised — the palace staff must have been aware of the Baron's plans to start the day here, and Hokk suspected the privileged class always had something available to eat no matter where they were. The stable workers clearly knew none of it was for them, however. They ignored the food as they hurried around, taking horses out into the courtyard and grooming them one last time. Hokk could sense how much stress they were under preparing everything for the arrival of the Twin Emperors and their noble contingent.

Emperor Tohryn arrived first. Alone. He was wearing a fitted black and gray suit, with a cap on his head and a single white horse's feather stuck in the side. Since the emperor was dressed like this and had no entourage, Hokk wouldn't have recognized him as a monarch if he hadn't already met his identical blind brother.

"I knew he'd be the first to show up this morning," the Baron murmured to Hokk, before striding forward and bowing in front of Tohryn.

Hokk didn't want to stand out unnecessarily. Something had crossed his mind during the night, and he couldn't stop worrying about it. Presumably, a number of elite, specially selected Imperial Guards had received orders several weeks ago to search for Elia *beneath* the clouds. It was therefore very possible a few of them had shared information that could allow Tohryn — the emperor with full use of his eyesight — to recognize that Hokk's dark hair and pale skin marked him as an inhabitant of Below, rather than someone from the moon. Hokk had to delay this realization as long as possible, so he moved behind one of the animals, where he could be less conspicuous, yet still have a good view. Of course, the guard shifted closer in order to keep him in sight.

"Your Highness," said the Baron, pressing the emperor's hand to his brow, then standing straight again. "I trust you slept well after last night's festivities."

Pinching his lips, Tohryn said nothing. He slowly scanned the livestock on display. Stable workers stood beside each animal, clutching short reins to ensure none of them became unmanageable. The emperor patted the hindquarters of the closest horse, slid his hand down the animal's leg, and lifted a rear hoof to inspect underneath. He released the leg, gently stretched out a wing, rubbed the horse's neck, and finally pulled back its lips to examine its teeth.

Emperor Tohryn nodded with approval. "A worthy specimen," he said simply, his face expressionless.

The Baron was pleased. "You have a keen eye, Your Excellency. This particular horse has a superb pedigree. Our breeding strategy ensures we choose only the finest."

"And it shows," Tohryn flatly replied. "As it has in the past."

"Do you have a specific trait or purpose in mind so I can assist you with your selection?"

"I want a first-class thoroughbred for my son, the Crown Prince. He turned sixteen yesterday. I also want to provide each member of my personal guard with new steeds. I require at least twenty to replace the current animals that are past their prime."

"We can certainly accommodate whatever you are looking for."

"And my wife, Empress Faytelle, will have her own requests too."

"Yes, of course," replied the Baron.

The sound of approaching flutes, cymbals, and drums

wafted in the distance. The fanfare grew louder, announcing the arrival of Emperor Tael.

This morning, he wore a long, colorful robe, as if he had merely put it on over his nightclothes upon waking. He held his white cane but wasn't using it, preferring to be escorted by a pretty young woman. She skipped along beside him, giggling, and Tael's face was beaming. Behind them, a retinue of ladies and gentlemen all exhibited high spirits — perhaps their party from the previous night had not yet ended.

The young woman whispered something to Tael. He smiled, then theatrically flung his arms wide. The musicians following him stopped playing as the emperor breathed deeply through his nose and loudly declared, "Ah, my nostrils fill with that unmistakable equine fragrance!"

The girl giggled again. Hokk saw Tohryn frowning, obviously irritated by his brother's performance.

"Where is the Baron?" asked Tael. "Is he here?"

Baron Shoad stepped in front of him. "Yes, good morning, Your Majesty."

"It's a *marvelous* morning!" Tael replied enthusiastically, turning his head in the direction of Shoad's voice. "Now, the question is, did I beat my brother?"

"No, I've already arrived," said Emperor Tohryn in an icy tone.

"What a shame!" Tael laughed. "I guess I shouldn't have been carousing until the wee hours of the morning." He sniffed the air once more. "And I do believe my lovely sister-in-law is coming right up behind us."

His impressive sense of smell was correct. A group of women glided within view along the same path leading from the palace to the courtyard. Hokk was eager to see Empress Faytelle in person for the first time, so he stepped a little farther into the open.

Though she was neither tall nor beautiful, her regal manner easily set her apart from the women accompanying her. Yet she wasn't nearly as pale as Hokk had expected from seeing her portrait — in fact, her skin had an unnatural shade and was slightly streaked, as if makeup had been applied to make her look darker. Wearing a bejeweled amber dress, she moved with grace, expertly balancing the pile of blond hair heaped upon her head. She also held one arm raised and slightly akimbo as she walked. From the bracelet around her wrist, a fine chain rose into the air, attached to a live bird. The little creature flapped its wings but could not escape.

Faytelle passed Tael, a look of contempt on her face. She nodded at her husband, Tohryn, and continued right up to Baron Shoad before stopping, her arm still extended.

The Baron took her hand, kissed it, then touched her knuckles to his forehead as the bird flew circles above him. "Always a glorious vision, Your Grace," he said.

She rewarded him with the slightest smile. "Unfortunately, we're late," she said, looking around. "But not too late, it appears."

Behind Faytelle, her ladies-in-waiting held back. Hokk stretched his neck and spotted Elia's turban. Tasheira stood beside her.

"These are some of the purest white horses I've ever seen," observed the empress, admiring the animals. She glanced behind at Tael with a smirk of wicked intent. Her brother-in-law's head was tilted as if listening carefully. "And since I love white horses so much, I absolutely *must* take them all!" she announced, prompting Tael to nod as if accepting defeat. Her ladies cooed their support. The empress swung her head forward again. "But I'll leave the financial matters . . ."

Faytelle's voice trailed off and she froze, staring hard at Hokk, her hand upon her chest as if to calm her heartbeat. Her reaction didn't go unnoticed. All faces turned in Hokk's direction. Regrettably, Tohryn's somber face showed interest now too.

Everybody seemed to be waiting. Only seconds passed, yet it felt like minutes. Then the empress collected herself with a deep breath and pulled her eyes away, turning back to the Baron. She spoke, but sounded rattled. "As I was about to say, I'll leave the financial matters for my husband to deal with."

Though Hokk had not moved a muscle, his pulse was beating rapidly.

She's seen me. And now she knows my true origins!

• • •

Less than an hour later, all the livestock had been purchased. Once Faytelle's order of white horses was completed, the Twin Emperors proceeded to select their own animals — Tael choosing his with input from the giggly young woman — and then what remained of the herd was offered up to the rest of the Royal Court, who had arrived after breakfast. The sales were brisk, and sometimes heated; but in short order, the horses were tagged with the names of their new owners, and the appropriate payments made to the Baron.

The courtyard outside the stables was now packed with animals and people. Nobody wanted to leave, preferring to socialize instead. Hokk had lost track of Elia, but when he spotted Tasheira mingling by herself, he decided Elia must have slipped away. Time for him to do the same.

The guard who had been following him was lingering at the edge of the crowd. Hokk casually worked his way deeper into the throng, nodding politely whenever he caught the attention of others. He thought he'd appear less suspicious if he was standing with the Baron, so he continued until he found him holding the reins of a large stallion, enthusiastically explaining the animal's lineage to the person who had purchased it. With a discrete glance behind him, Hokk confirmed that the guard did not seem troubled with his movements, though it was hard to tell if he was paying attention.

Hokk ran his hand across the horse's hindquarters as if admiring it, then slowly wandered around to the other side until he was entirely blocked from the guard's view. When another horse passed by, heading toward the stables, he ducked behind it and followed the animal for a short distance before meandering through the assembled courtiers as nonchalantly as possible. He reached the farthest side of the courtyard and continued along the periphery until he found a path that led into the gardens.

Was this the way Elia had gone, or had she returned to the palace?

Looking over his shoulder one last time, Hokk's throat clenched. His attempt to escape had not gone unnoticed. The guard was now pushing through the congestion toward him.

Hokk dashed down the path. Fortunately, he was the only one on it. Around the first bend, he knew he was out of sight, but he kept running. A little farther along, he entered an orchard and stopped to quickly get his bearings, knowing the guard could appear at any moment.

Maybe trying to outrun the man was foolish, especially since Hokk was so unfamiliar with the Sanctuary grounds. He had no clue which direction he should go from here. Where could he hide?

"Hokk!"

He twisted around, yet the path was still empty.

"*Hokk.*" he heard again. This time, he could tell it came from above.

He looked up into the nearest tree, and despite the leaves and hanging apples, he noticed a slippered foot on one of the limbs. Stepping closer to the trunk, he gazed overhead and saw Elia perched in the branches.

"What are you doing there?" asked Hokk.

"Just get up here," Elia ordered.

With his heart racing, Hokk hoisted himself onto the lowest bough and climbed higher until he was sitting beside Elia. She had bunched her dress up around her waist and he recognized his old sack in her lap. In her hand, she held the telescope, fully extended.

"I'm being followed," he whispered, trying to calm his breathing.

"Really? When did that —"

"Shh." Hokk placed his finger on Elia's lips. Below them, the Imperial Guard ran past. Thankfully, he did not look up.

"I've had a guard tailing me since we arrived last night!" he said quietly.

"Why?"

"That's what I'd like to know."

"This should be as safe a spot as any," said Elia, leaning much closer to Hokk. "It actually reminds me of the last time we were in a tree together." Her breath tickled his ear.

"Why are you even up here?" Hokk asked, sounding more annoyed than he had intended. "You're going to be seen!"

"*You* didn't know where I was hiding," Elia retorted, appearing a bit hurt.

"I thought you'd go somewhere with more privacy than this!"

Elia held up the telescope, looking exasperated. "I can't waste time," she answered. "I've got to use this damn thing to figure out what's going on."

"Yes, I've been trying to find you so I can ask — have you seen anything?"

"No. Nothing! But I thought this vantage point might at least show me something."

"Can I have a look?" he asked. Elia handed him the instrument and Hokk held it to one eye. Peering through the leaves, he had a clear view of the stable area and the towers beyond. The images jumped forward as if he could reach out and touch them. He noticed Commander Blaitz had arrived in the packed courtyard, with several guards now talking to him.

"The telescope's not showing what it's supposed to," Elia complained.

"It seems to be working as it should."

"I don't just care about seeing objects up close. I need

more than that! I'm supposed to look inside this thing to discover secrets."

"I'm sorry, I have no idea." Hokk lowered the telescope and frowned as he passed it back. "So, what are you going to do?"

"What can I do, except keep trying? Maybe it only works when it's meant to. I'll have to continue pointing it at things until it finally reveals what I'm supposed to see."

"Just promise me you'll do it without getting caught."

"I won't get —"

Elia stopped. Both she and Hokk stared down again at the ground. A horse had appeared beneath the tree, but they couldn't see who was riding. Hokk nervously pointed to Elia's dress, which had slipped from her grasp and was now hanging much lower. As she frantically pulled it higher and hid the telescope within its folds, the horse took a step forward, revealing a man in the saddle. Though his face was turned up, as if having spotted them, Hokk quietly sighed with relief. Tael's blind eyes were looking right at them, but could see nothing.

"Am I wrong, or did I hear voices?" Tael asked. "Young voices."

Hokk looked at Elia with concern. The emperor's hearing must be as sharp as his sense of smell.

A second horse stepped into their line of sight. The emperor's young escort was riding with him.

"Yes, there are two people in this tree," said the girl.

"Up in the tree?" Tael exclaimed. "How odd."

"I like to climb," Hokk called down. "I can never resist getting up into the branches. I should have been born a cat," he added, hoping any response, even a ridiculous one, was better than none.

"Is that Lord Isec I hear speaking? The young man from the moon whom I met last night?" If he thought it strange that a man from the moon would be perched in a tree, he gave no indication.

"It is," Hokk replied, sounding awkward.

"I'm so glad I found you. I want to invite you and whoever's up there with you to my private suite this afternoon. I always hold a reception for the Baron whenever he visits, but with you here, it is going to be an extra special affair. I'm asking only a select few. Of course, I insist that you join our gathering."

"It would be my pleasure."

"Excellent. Then I look forward to seeing you *both* later on, right after lunch. My brother will be there too. It's high time to finally learn what you've come here to share with us!"

Chapter 45

AFTER THE CROWD AROUND THE stables had dispersed, Elia and Hokk came down from the tree and agreed to meet later at Emperor Tael's reception.

Elia was glad for some time alone. Since she was certain Tash would avoid climbing the horrendous number of stairs to their shared room unless it was absolutely necessary, it gave Elia a chance to sneak back up to enjoy some incense in private. Her last stick yesterday morning seemed so long ago. She had started to feel jittery and all her fears were creeping back again, which tempted her to light two of them in a row. Yet she resisted overindulging. Just twenty-three sticks remained. What would she do when she had finished them all?

Elia spent an hour or so in a semi-dream state before she was able to rouse herself from the mattress. She retied the turban around her head, then stood in front of the window until she felt steadier on her feet.

When she guessed lunch was over and it was time to go to the reception, Elia put on her shoes, grabbed her bag of belongings, and departed, though she only made it a few steps down the hallway before returning to her room. Having journeyed too many miles to risk anything, she decided that carrying

Hokk's worn-out sack all over the place might draw too much attention. So she removed the telescope and strapped it to her calf for safekeeping with some silk ribbon she had found in one of Tasheira's crates. The carved box, however, she decided to leave behind as a decoy in case somebody broke into the room to look for it. Staying vigilant was essential. Her enemies were everywhere. Though the incense had made her mellow, it was also working its wonderful magic on her — everything was now so much clearer. The threats against her were very real, and with so many people in the palace, surely someone had already recognized her and knew what she was hiding or why she was here.

Elia descended the many levels until she reached the ground floor. She crossed the reception hall and began climbing Tael's tower. At the top of the first flight of stairs, she saw two Imperial Guards protecting the door to the emperor's private suite. With each nervous step, she felt the telescope press against the back of her knee. Could they tell something was amiss just by the way she walked?

This will work! Elia tried to convince herself. After all, this was how the telescope had been smuggled out the first time.

A memory flashed into her mind — the terrified face of that desperate young woman Elia had met at the clotheslines. She must have been one of Faytelle's own ladies-in-waiting. Had she received a direct order from the empress to make sure the telescope ended up in safe hands, or did she get her instructions from someone else?

I can't let that poor woman's fate be my own.

Then a question struck Elia that made her halt in the middle of the staircase. Was that same lady-in-waiting the girl who had previously occupied the room now assigned to Tasheira?

Elia felt weak-kneed at the possibility. She was sure one of the staff had mentioned something about the previous occupant disappearing a month or two earlier. The servant said a girl ran off to get married, but perhaps she had not. Perhaps that was only a rumor intentionally spread to hide the truth. And if Elia's suspicions were correct, it would explain the damaged walls and missing furnishings — the young woman's room had been ransacked and stripped in order to find the telescope!

Elia was so preoccupied imagining the scenario that she didn't register the sound of footsteps on the stairs behind her until a split second before someone grabbed her by the elbow. She jumped, but thankfully did not cry out — it was only Tasheira.

"Where have you been all this time?" Tash demanded angrily. "Don't forget, I'm responsible for you here at the palace. You have no business wandering off on your own! How do you think that makes me look?"

Elia tried to quickly compose herself. "I was in the gardens."

"Why?"

"To enjoy the sunshine."

"I don't believe you. What's really going on?"

Elia glanced at the two guards. They stood so still, she wondered if anyone was actually behind those mirrored masks.

"I'll tell you, but not out here," Elia whispered.

"Fine," Tash snorted. "Follow me." Tasheira tightened her grip as they climbed the last few steps. "We're expected," she boldly declared to the guards as she pushed the door open. Fortunately, the men did nothing to stop them.

Inside Tael's suite, the reception had already commenced. The room was filled with music and laughter, most of it coming from Emperor Tael, who was seated on a lounge covered with cushions. A young woman — not the one Elia had seen with him earlier at the stables — sat on the back of the couch massaging his temples. His eyes were closed, but he was nodding as he laughed, listening to Baron Shoad share a story with everyone who had gathered around the emperor.

Hokk was there too, drawing curious stares from people throughout the room. Elia hoped Tash would join him, but the girl had her own plan as she led Elia to a table of desserts and handed her a plate. After they had selected a few sweet pastries, Tasheira wasted no time resuming her interrogation.

"So, what's really going on?" Tash demanded again as Elia took her first bite. "I'm trying to help you, but you're doing nothing to cooperate. You're either unfriendly to whomever I introduce you, or you're off hiding somewhere. Are you avoiding me?"

Elia wiped away crumbs from the corner of her mouth. "No, I —"

"Then what is it?"

Elia sighed and glanced around to make sure no one close by was listening. "It all started last night," she began, having worked out her lie shortly before Hokk found her in the tree. "When we went down to that party, I thought I caught a glimpse of someone I knew."

"Really?" Tasheira asked, her frustration instantly shifting to intrigue. "Who was it?"

"I'm not sure. But the person looked very familiar. Then suddenly, something inside me, a deep foreboding, made me feel so afraid, I didn't know what to do. I just knew I was in danger and had to stay away from him."

"It was a man?"

"Yes. And I saw him again this morning at the stables. I left as soon as I could, before I had the chance to tell you. I'm sorry. I disappeared into the gardens and found a spot to hide so I could think and try to remember things."

"And did you?"

"No. But I'm absolutely certain he has something to do with my past. Something bad."

"At least he didn't see you."

"Thankfully not, though now I'm afraid to go anywhere. He might catch me — and then what?"

"It's a frightful thought," Tash replied grimly. Then she bristled. "He's not in this room right now, is he?"

Elia pulled Tasheira in front of her and pretended to cautiously peer over her shoulder. "No, thank goodness." She noticed Hokk glancing over at them.

"What does he look like, so I can be on the lookout?"

Elia kept her description vague. "Average height. Blond hair. Very well dressed."

Tash frowned. "That could be anyone."

Just then, Elia saw Empress Faytelle enter the room, surrounded by her ladies-in-waiting. The new bird was still flying above her extended wrist.

Tash noticed them too. "I can't think who you might be describing, but we should tell Empress Faytelle immediately that you are in danger."

Horrified, Elia caught Tasheira's arm. "No, please. You can't!"

"She should hear about this! She'll be able to help."

"Don't tell her anything," said Elia. She did not want to involve too many people in her lies. At least not yet. "It's too soon," she continued. "I just need . . . I want to be absolutely certain before making any accusations. Maybe my memory is playing tricks on me."

Tash looked skeptical.

"Listen. Give me some more time," Elia added quickly. "By the end of tomorrow, I will know better. Then we can tell the empress. I promise. Between now and then, however, don't be surprised if I have to investigate matters on my own, even if that means you don't know where I am. Can I count on you to cover for me?"

Tash glanced at Faytelle and the group of women who were now being served wine. Jeska was waving her over.

"Will you be able to do that?" Elia asked firmly, trying to hold Tasheira's attention. "Will you make up an excuse for me if necessary?"

Tash was still listening. She turned back and placed her hand on Elia's shoulder. "Yes, of course. If anyone wonders where you are, I'll simply say you're not feeling well."

"Perfect," Elia replied. "That's all I need."

"But be careful. And no matter what, we bring this to the empress tomorrow night," Tash insisted. "Agreed?"

"Agreed."

"Good," said Tash with the hint of a smile. She was enjoying the mystery. "Now don't look so worried. It will all work out in the end, you'll see," she added before squeezing Elia's arm. Then she walked away to join her cousin, leaving Elia alone by the desserts.

Elia was relieved to have curbed Tasheira's curiosity. But what should she do now? She would prefer not to be here, though she knew it would look bad if she tried to leave. Since people were still arriving to join the reception, she decided to wait for a better moment to slip away.

Elia popped her last pastry into her mouth. As she chewed, she gazed around Emperor Tael's quarters, taking in details of the room that she hadn't focused on earlier. While Faytelle's suite in the other tower was open and uncluttered, Tael's space was crowded with pillars, art, and large pieces of furniture. Ornaments, ticking clocks, candelabras, and documents covered every flat surface.

Elia's eyes lingered on a pile of scrolls tossed randomly on a nearby desk. Official decrees? she wondered. Personal correspondence? Poetry? Even if she dared to open one, she wouldn't be able to read what was written on it. Emperor Tael would need somebody to read the pages to him, too. Whatever information they might contain, they probably didn't reveal any secrets if they had been left lying around like this.

Yet something about the parchments was utterly intriguing. Elia could not resist. She checked first to make sure nobody was watching before casually picking up a document for closer inspection.

Then it hit her like a slap to the face. It wasn't the scrolls themselves that were so interesting, but what held them together! The rolled pages were bound with ribbons to prevent them from unraveling. Blue ribbons! Identical to the one tied to the bone Elia had discovered in her washtub that same fateful morning Mrs. Suds was hauled to the dungeon.

As if the scroll had burned her fingertips, Elia flung it back onto the desk. Her body temperature soared. Again, she looked around the room, but people were thankfully too engrossed in their conversations to notice her.

Her thoughts were reeling. That bone tied with blue ribbon had been the start of everything in her life falling apart. But what did it all mean? Had the bone been sent from this very room as a warning? Was the ribbon a clue pointing specifically to Emperor Tael, or could ribbon like that be found anywhere in the palace? And how did any of this relate to Mrs. Suds, and more importantly, to Elia's family?

Elia's intuition told her that Emperor Tael must have played a key role in the mystery, especially since it was his wife, Empress Mahkoiyin, who had been presumed dead, only to miraculously turn up alive in Below. And he was supposedly blinded by a Scavenger attack, but obviously, since no such monsters existed, there had to be a different explanation.

No doubt, this room was the best place to start searching for answers. If only she could tear it apart right now to see what might be hiding here! Elia's thoughts turned again to the scrolls, strangely left out in the open for anyone to see. Unless their secrets could only be revealed with the telescope! Yes, that had to be it! Somehow, she had to return to this room on her own, with the telescope, when she knew it would be empty. But while it might be possible to track Tael's where-abouts, whether he was in the palace or strolling through the gardens, getting past the guards stationed outside his door would be impossible.

Well, perhaps not *impossible*. Though she hadn't thought about him for a long time, there was that Imperial Guard with the metal spike centered over the forehead of his helmet. He had found her twice on the prairies, yet he'd never turned her over to Commander Wrasse. She could only assume he was looking out for her best interests. But she had seen no sign of the man — or rather his unique helmet — since arriving yesterday. And she wasn't sure she could actually trust him if she needed help to get into this suite. He might have his own twisted agenda.

Now her brother, Rayhan, on the other hand, would have been her best option of all. She imagined the advantage she'd have if he had actually become an Imperial Guard after waiting so long to make it happen. He'd be a palace insider, someone who could help her, no questions asked, and who would stop at nothing to keep her safe.

Don't think about Rayhan! Even if he's still alive, he can't help you now. Accept that!

At this very moment, Elia wanted more than anything to hide in a dark corner with an incense stick. Her hands were starting to tremble. She felt flushed. It wasn't that long since enjoying her last one, but her mind was struggling as if it were about to become unhinged. She needed to get to some incense again soon.

"What are you doing over here on your own?"

Spinning around quickly, as if to confront an assailant, Elia almost punched Hokk in the stomach.

Hokk blocked her. "Whoa, whoa," he said. "What's gotten into you?"

With fists still clenched and her muscles charged, Elia found it hard to pull herself back. "I'm sorry," she sputtered. "But you shouldn't have snuck up on me."

"I wanted to talk to you." A perplexed look suddenly crossed Hokk's face. He leaned closer to Elia and sniffed the air just above her head. "You smell funny," he said, crinkling his nose.

Elia winced. "How dare you!" she spat at him, feeling her cheeks flush. "How can you say something like that?"

"No, I don't mean you stink. There's just something different. I think I smell . . . smoke. Like a spicy, fragrant smoke."

Elia was stunned. If he could catch a whiff of the incense, had Tash noticed the smell too? "Is that why you came over here? To insult me?"

Hokk sighed. "No, of course not. I just wanted to make sure you were okay. I was watching you earlier. What were you saying to Tasheira? You both looked so serious."

Elia was still scowling. "I was making up lies to keep nosy people from prying into my business."

Hokk seemed to take this personally.

"No, I don't mean you," Elia quickly added, trying to soften her tone. "But I now know what I need to do."

Curious, Hokk cocked his head. "And what's that?"

"Break into this room to look for clues. To see if my tele- scope can produce results."

Hokk raised his eyebrows. "That's your plan? I don't like the sound of it."

"It's my only option."

"That may be true, but you'll never succeed. And why this room in particular?"

"I've already seen enough to suspect this is probably the best starting point."

"This place is too heavily guarded."

"I know," said Elia, fretfully biting her lower lip. "But I'm hoping there's a way."

Emperor Tael suddenly sprang up from his couch on the other side of the room, momentarily distracting both Elia and Hokk. "Yes? Is he here?" Tael asked. Then he clapped his hands. "Excellent. My brother has arrived," he called out to everyone. "Let's open more wine!"

A sour-looking Tohryn had entered the room and was standing beside a teenage boy. The Crown Prince, Elia realized. There had been too many people last night crowding around Veralion, offering birthday greetings, for her to properly see him. Even now, people were starting to swarm the prince.

Hold on! Just over Veralion's shoulder! By the entrance.

More people were entering the room, obscuring her view. Elia waited impatiently until they eventually moved out of the way.

Yes! She was right. Two pairs of door panels like she had seen throughout the towers. Instead of vases, however, each set had a statue in front of it.

Elia grabbed Hokk's shirt and pulled him closer. "See, by the entrance. Behind the statues. Those are elevator doors, aren't they?" she whispered with excitement.

Hokk looked over and nodded. "Yes, most definitely. I've noticed two sets on every floor."

"Me too!"

"So what? I don't think the carriages behind them are ever used."

Elia's eyes penetrated deep into Hokk's. "I know how I'm going to sneak back into this room!"

Chapter **46**

"YOU LOOK WORRIED," ELIA WHISPERED.

"I guess I am," Hokk admitted. "For your sake."

"This is going to work. It has to."

Her expression was so earnest that Hokk knew she was being serious. Sneaking down either one of the elevator shafts to break into Tael's suite appealed to his inclination for taking risks — but could she really pull it off?

"Though I hate having to ask for your help again," Elia added.

"I'll always help you, no matter what. However, we need a more solid plan. Like, when are you going to attempt it? And how will you know the place is empty?"

"Surely, he's not in his suite all day long. He has to leave at some point," she said quietly. "I think I should try first thing tomorrow morning when Emperor Tael heads down for breakfast. I bet after he eats, he'll go for a stroll in the gardens, when it's still early enough to avoid the midday heat. Even if he doesn't, I'm positive I can get in and out quickly before he returns. But I'll need someone to keep watch for me. That's where you fit in."

Hokk glanced warily at the carefree Tael, who was nearby yet oblivious to their scheming. "Let's do it."

"What floor are you staying on?" asked Elia. "Tash and I are at the very top of Tohryn's tower. I hope you're not that high."

"My room is just two levels above this one."

"Perfect. Then I won't have to climb too far down the shaft, and it will be easy to get back up again when I am done. The only question is, do you think I can pry the doors open?"

"Yes, but the real problem is going to be the guards."

"That's the beauty of my plan. They're only going to be —"

"Not the ones outside this room," Hokk interrupted. "I'm talking about the guard who's following my every move."

"Still?"

"That's him over there," Hokk said with a slight nod toward the far side of the room. "He found me again shortly after I left the orchard. We'll have to get rid of him first." *Though this time, it will be even harder to elude him*, Hokk had to admit to himself.

Elia casually glanced over.

"He's watching us now," Hokk continued. "We shouldn't talk much longer."

"It's like Tael already knows to be suspicious."

"Is anyone watching you?" he asked.

"Probably. My enemies could be everywhere, but I'll be extra careful," Elia replied. Then something at the entrance caught her attention. "Look. Here they come. I hope you're prepared for this."

Hokk turned and saw several staff members carrying the padded white suit into the room as if it were a lifeless body. Behind them, another servant held a large chunk of — actually, Hokk had no idea what it could be. The suit was lowered into a chair while the other object was placed on the floor in front of it.

Hokk frowned. "I hope I'm convincing," he murmured.

"I have faith," said Elia. "I've heard you talk your way out of trickier situations."

"You're right. If only I could forget," Hokk replied with a tinge of guilt in his voice, thinking back to the lies he had spun in front of the Board back in Ago, hoping to save Elia's life, yet at the same time making Elia believe he had intended to betray her all along.

"Lord Isec?" Emperor Tael called out now, swinging his head around as though hoping his ears would pick up Hokk's voice in a conversation somewhere nearby. "Lord Isec? Is he still with us?" he asked the person beside him.

Hokk hurried to the emperor's side. "I was just checking out the dessert table, Your Highness," he responded, though he had no plate in his hand.

"Excellent," said the emperor. He swiveled to face the rest of the room. "Everyone!" Tael commanded, clapping his hands for quiet. "Please, silence everyone." The music stopped and people found seats for themselves. When the general commotion had subsided, Tael smiled broadly. "My ladies and noblemen, the moment has come that we've been waiting for with much anticipation since his arrival last night. Emperor Tohryn and I are so pleased to host our very prestigious guest, Lord Hokk Isec, who has come to visit us from the *moon*."

There was applause and whispered excitement as Hokk stepped forward. He bowed graciously and took a deep breath. If he had twice survived arguing his case before the Board when he was tried for his crimes, then he should be able to handle speaking to this group. Yet he felt nervous and couldn't be entirely sure he wasn't on trial again today. *This had better work.*

"Thank you both, Emperor Tael and Emperor Tohryn, for such gracious hospitality," said Hokk. "Since I arrived at the Sanctuary yesterday with Baron Shoad and his daughter, Lady Tasheira, the warm welcome I have received has been greatly appreciated." He shot a furtive glance at the guard still standing within clear view. "And, yes, I have indeed come from the moon, as you've all likely heard by now, and what a great honor to finally have the chance to share a message from my people."

As he said this, his eyes settled on Empress Faytelle. Her piercing glare bore into him, and Hokk faltered for an instant, though he quickly recovered. "Before I get to that message, however, I want to mention how challenging my voyage was to get here. I was one of a contingent of messengers dispatched to make this long-awaited trip to reconnect our worlds. Unfortunately, I am the only survivor. As we descended, our craft suffered crippling damage. It broke apart, raining burning debris across the sky. I survived only because of the suit that protected me — the one you see before you now." Hokk paused as he pointed to it.

"Is there any chance there were other survivors?" asked Tael, his empty eyes gazing just to the side of where Hokk was standing.

"I wish I could say it was possible. But even I would have been doomed, if I hadn't been fortunate enough to be discovered once I landed. I am alive thanks to —" He scanned his audience until he spotted her. "Thanks to Lady Tasheira."

Applause and murmuring followed, and Hokk could see Tash was extremely pleased to be given credit, just as he knew she would be. Her pride prompted her to speak.

"The vessel Lord Hokk was traveling in smashed into the desert on the Isle of Drifting Dunes," Tash explained. "It left a huge crater in the sand. That's a piece of the wreckage there on the floor, which I brought back to show my father."

Wreckage — so that's what that chunk was supposed to be. Hokk picked it up and showed the audience the charred metal on one side and the crumbly yellow foam on the other.

"I risked the scorching heat of the desert to rescue Lord Isec," Tash continued, "and nursed him back to health day and night at our camp."

More clapping.

Hokk glanced at the emperors. While Tael seemed enthralled, the much more disagreeable Tohryn appeared to be impatient.

"I understand this suit you were wearing has your name on it," Tohryn grumbled. "Isec, is it?" he asked skeptically.

"Yes, my last name is written on the front."

"Then why are there periods separating the letters?" the man challenged.

Hokk's mind began to race, trying to determine what the man was getting at and how he should answer.

"Does the word perhaps stand for something else?" Tohryn added, unwilling to let the issue drop.

"No, Isec is my last name," Hokk replied firmly, though he was sure Tohryn knew something he didn't.

The emperor grunted, but thankfully, his blind brother spoke up before an awkward silence could settle in. "To me, how a name has been written is an inconsequential detail," said Emperor Tael. "The suit obviously did what it was designed to do, and that was to save a life. But what I really want to know now is this message you have for us."

"Yes, of course, Your Excellency," Hokk replied. "The message is actually quite simple." He took another deep breath. "It's a message of unity. We have been separated too long. Your people and mine must live together as we once did in ancient times."

Tael nodded in agreement, which encouraged Hokk to continue.

"And it's an appeal for all of us to open our eyes to our reality. To learn the long-forgotten truth about the origins of our people, both Above and Below. Everyone living in the Lunera System must reject the old lies that have become so deep-rooted they are now taken as fact. It's vitally important to reconnect all mankind, regardless of the ground they call home or whoever's sky they happen to live in."

He stopped to gauge the impact of his statements. Everybody was silent, sitting perfectly still in their seats. Tael's cheerful expression had vanished and he looked as forlorn as his brother had earlier. Tohryn, however, was smirking as if he had just heard nonsense. Baron Shoad and Tasheira seemed confused, and Elia a little worried. As for Empress Faytelle, her lips were pinched so tightly that Hokk knew, without a doubt, she understood exactly the point he was making. She likely appreciated it more personally than anyone. And she clearly did not like it.

"Interesting," Emperor Tael finally said, sounding disappointed after such a buildup. "So when you say . . . your suggestion that . . ." He let out a long sigh and shook his head with frustration. "What role, specifically, should my brother and I be playing to achieve what you're asking?"

As Hokk considered his answer, he thought back to the Imperial Guards who had been ordered down to Below, into a realm that Elia said no one from Above was supposed to know about. "Be honest with your subjects. Don't hide the truth."

Tohryn chuckled, though he did not sound amused. "I need more wine," he said dismissively, holding out his glass. A servant quickly began pouring some from a decanter.

"Yes, I think we all need our glasses refilled," said Tael. "You've given us much to think about, Lord Hokk." He flicked his hand in the air. "Let's have some music while we discuss it."

The music began again, and people slowly rose and reassembled into groups, looking unsure about what had just happened. Tohryn downed his wine and requested another as Tael stood up and felt his way across to the other side of the room, using people's shoulders and the backs of chairs to guide him. The guard who had been following Hokk joined the emperor and they spoke quietly together.

Hokk then saw the Baron approaching him. The man's mood seemed somber.

"I don't think that went very well, I'm afraid," said Hokk.

"Messages that speak the truth are often hard to swallow," said the Baron. "I can see why you had to wait and share this directly with the emperors. Only they can fully grasp what you request. You've traveled such a distance, risked so much, and your message is so profound, it demands careful consideration. The emperors have clearly taken it very seriously."

"I hope so," said Hokk, amazed by Shoad's response. He was so accustomed to his efforts backfiring in situations like this that he was pleased to have the Baron's support.

One of Faytelle's ladies-in-waiting appeared beside the Baron.

"Lady Jeska," said Shoad, warmly greeting her. "I haven't yet had the chance to talk to you this visit."

"Hello, dear uncle." The woman kissed him on his cheek. "I must say, you and Tasheira have brought such fascinating people with you to the Sanctuary this year." Her comments were accompanied by a flirtatious wink at Hokk.

"This is my niece, Lady Jeska," said the Baron.

"And I am Hokk."

"So I've heard," she said with a laugh.

"Jeska is the half sister of Fimal and Neric, whom you met at the estate."

"Oh, so that's the family connection," Hokk replied.

Lady Jeska lightly placed her hand on her uncle's arm. "Uncle Shoad, I've heard no news yet concerning my brothers; however, I trust they are well." Though the Baron's face saddened, she didn't seem to notice. "But you'll have to tell me all the details later. First, I'm keen to learn more about Hokk," she continued. "We all are. In fact, the empress, just a moment ago, sent me over to see you, Hokk, with a special request."

Hokk's eyes darted toward Faytelle, but the woman wasn't looking in his direction. "What does she ask?"

"She would like to meet with you. Just the two of you."

Of course she would, he thought.

"Empress Faytelle says she has a private matter she wishes to discuss."

"I am happy to oblige. Would she like to see me in her suite later this evening?"

"No. Tomorrow morning, when everyone else is having their breakfast and the gardens are quiet. She'll meet you at the stables."

Hokk wanted to decline — tomorrow morning was when Elia needed him to help break into this room. Unfortunately, he had no choice but to agree.

Jeska must have noticed his hesitation. "She plans to take you on a guided tour of the Sanctuary," she added.

"Then I look forward to meeting her at the stables," Hokk confirmed. "Anything for the empress."

Chapter **47**

IT WAS JUST AFTER DAWN the next morning when Hokk swung open the door of his bedroom. The guard in the hallway seemed startled that he was up so early, yet the man still fell right into step behind him as Hokk hurried down the stairs. And Hokk wasn't surprised to be followed, but not just because he had tried escaping surveillance at the stables. What he had said at yesterday's reception had obviously given the Twin Emperors all the more reason to keep him under close scrutiny.

Hokk wanted to arrive in the banquet hall before anyone else. Though filled with palace staff who were preparing the tables, Hokk was glad to see only a few courtiers in the room. He chose a seat where a young scullion was laying out cutlery.

"Good morning, My Lord," said the girl. Like all the other workers, she had a tattoo in the middle of her forehead that resembled the one Hokk had seen on Elia. "Would you like to start with a selection of fruit or would you prefer fresh pastries today?"

Hokk was more interested in getting information than something to eat. "I didn't realize it was so late in the morning.

I guess everyone has come and gone from breakfast and already started their day."

The girl was surprised. "My goodness, no, it's still very early. You're actually one of the first to get here."

"That's a relief," said Hokk, noticing that the guard had positioned himself at the entrance — the only way in and out, except through the kitchens. "I was afraid I had missed seeing the emperors. They hosted a fine reception for me yesterday, and I want to thank them again."

The girl seemed to be fighting shyness as though not used to speaking with the people she served, yet still keen to talk. "You won't have long to wait," she said. "I suspect both emperors will arrive here in the next hour."

"Do they not sometimes have their meals in their own suites?"

"Occasionally in the evenings, but never in the mornings."

"Is that so?"

"If you ask me, I think the emperors like to make their presence known to the Royal Court as soon as possible each day, as well as to one another. It's as if they're always in a race to see who can show up first." Her expression suddenly clouded as though she had said too much and now regretted it.

But at least Hokk had confirmed what he wanted to know. "If you could bring me something hot to drink and a few warm biscuits with jam, I'll start with that."

The servant curtsied. "Right away."

When she came back a few minutes later, she was carrying a silver tray with a steaming teapot, a cup and saucer, a selection of jams, and a plate of biscuits. She was about to place all the items in front of Hokk when he stopped her.

"Actually, if I could just take everything away with me, that would be better," he said. Though she hesitated, he swiped all his cutlery off the table, dropped the utensils on the tray, and then took the tray from her hands. "I'm going to bring this up to my room, although I'll return later for a proper meal once the emperors have arrived. You see, I traveled to the Sanctuary with a beloved pet who I'm sure would be happy to get something to eat too."

"Yes, of course," she replied.

But Hokk did not return to his room. He didn't even head toward Tael's side of the palace, where he was staying. Instead, he started climbing the staircase of Tohryn's tower, where he hoped to find Elia on the top floor.

As he carried the tray, the dishes rattled, and hot water spilled from the teapot's spout. He reached the second landing and continued on. Before he made it to the third, however, he ran into Tasheira coming down. She was startled to see him.

"Hokk!" she exclaimed. "You're up so early!"

"My empty stomach forced me out of bed," he replied, hoping she couldn't detect his disappointment over their chance encounter.

"So, why are you here?" Tasheira asked.

"What do you mean?"

"This is Tohryn's tower," she said with a curious chuckle. Her gaze shifted over Hokk's shoulder. Without looking, he knew she saw the Imperial Guard, who must have halted just a few steps below him. "Your room is on Tael's side, isn't it?" she asked while scanning the items on his tray.

"Have I gotten it wrong?" Hokk wondered, pretending to be befuddled. "I guess I've not paid close enough attention since I'm always letting your father lead the way. Are you heading over there now too?"

"No, I'm joining my cousin, Lady Jeska. You've been introduced to her already, haven't you?"

"Yes, at Tael's reception."

"I'm meeting her in Faytelle's quarters. This is my first morning in my new role, and I understand the empress has a special appointment with someone in the gardens before breakfast. We have to get her ready in time."

Hokk decided not to share who she'd be meeting. "I shouldn't delay you then," he said, moving out of the way.

"Wait. Not so fast." Tasheira reached over and placed her hand on his chest. She must have felt his body tense up. "I want to thank you for what you did yesterday," she said as a curl of hair happened to loosen and fall onto her brow.

"What did I do?" Hokk asked, feeling his cheeks radiate heat. He realized the dishes on his tray had started to rattle ever so slightly. *Don't start shaking now!*

"No, I don't mean what you did, but what you *said* in front of everyone," Tash clarified. "For telling the court it was me who saved your life, not my father."

"Well, it was the truth."

Tash bit her lower lip. She took a breath as if she was about to say something else, then suddenly leaned forward on her tiptoes and kissed Hokk fully on the mouth.

"I . . . um," Hokk stammered when she finally pulled away, too stunned to think of anything more coherent to say. He had never been kissed before. Certainly not like this. It felt so . . . tender. Intimate. Intimidating. Invasive. And while he had certainly been blushing moments earlier, Hokk was sure his skin was now an even deeper shade of red.

"Just know that I appreciate it," said Tash.

"Thank you," Hokk croaked.

Tash smiled. She reached around, sticking her thumb into a belt loop on the side of his trousers, and started to lead him down the stairs. They passed the waiting guard, who turned around and descended after them. Arriving at Faytelle's floor, Tash released him. Still flustered, Hokk tilted his head away from her and held the tray higher, suspecting she might try to kiss him again. Yet she only smiled before opening the door and entering Faytelle's room.

Hokk looked at the guard as if for an explanation. The man did not move or say anything. He only stared through his metal mask. He did, however, brace himself as though expecting to be knocked over when Hokk started back up the stairs toward him.

"Start climbing," said Hokk as he brushed past.

Still carrying the tray, he mounted the stairs as quickly as he could, hoping the guard would struggle to keep up. Unfortunately, the man seemed to have no problem with the pace.

Finally reaching the top floor, Hokk realized he didn't know which one of the doors in the hallway belonged to the room Elia shared with Tasheira. He debated asking the guard, but luckily, another lady-in-waiting emerged and drifted along the corridor toward him.

"Lady Tasheira's room?" he asked.

The young woman must have recognized him, because she grinned knowingly and pointed behind her. "Two doors down and on the left."

"Thank you."

As the guard assumed his position on the opposite side of the hallway, Hokk turned the handle, found the door unlocked, and entered. Yet no sooner did the door close behind him than he decided he must have walked through the wrong one. Though there was an odd scent in the air, it was the state of the room he found so surprising. Holes had been smashed into the dirty white walls, and he saw no furniture — in fact, it appeared there weren't any adornments whatsoever to make the space attractive. Crates were piled in the middle and some had been opened, with clothing pulled out and tossed all over. As he looked around the corner of a stack of boxes, he noticed a crooked leg limp on the floor, bathed in a patch of morning sunlight.

Filled with instant dread, Hokk darted around the boxes and saw Elia lying face down. Her body was half on a mattress, half off it. She had on the same white dress he had seen her wearing the day before, but her clothing looked rumpled and she had no turban on her head. Most distressing of all, he couldn't tell if she was breathing.

"Elia!" he shouted. "Elia! What's wrong?" He dropped to his knees, leaving the breakfast tray on the floor, and flipped Elia onto her back.

His shouting roused her, and she raised clenched fists to fend off an attack.

"Stop it," Hokk demanded, grabbing her hands as she tried to fight him. He pinned her wrists to the mattress as he straddled her.

That's when he saw something thin pinched between her fingers, trailing smoke into the air. And then he recognized what he had been smelling. Incense smoke.

Releasing his grasp, Hokk pushed himself off the mattress and stood up. He ran his hand over the short stubble on his scalp. "Is this what's been making you look sick lately? How much have you had?" he asked angrily.

"Not that much, I swear," Elia whimpered, cowering on the mattress and looking up at him pitifully. "I just started this one."

But her eyes already had that telltale glassy look.

"Damn it Elia! Of all mornings!"

"I'm sorry," she mumbled.

"You chose to do this now! What about our plans? *Your* plans?"

"I couldn't help it. I'm scared. The incense calms me."

"That's utter nonsense," Hokk spat out with disgust. He reached down and snatched the smoldering stick from her hand. He broke it apart before grinding the pieces into the floor with his boot. "This has got to stop!"

"I will. I won't do it again."

"It's absolutely unacceptable. And it's disgusting. This isn't who you are! Is it addictive? Are you already addicted to this stuff?" As he said it, Hokk's voice cracked with emotion. He dropped down onto the mattress beside her and took her trembling hand.

Elia glanced at him sheepishly. "That will be my last."

"I hope so," Hokk sighed, remembering his own struggles to resist uncontrollable urges — the impulses to play with fire when life seemed too challenging to cope. "Believe it or not,

I know what you are going through. But you've come too far to ruin everything."

"And I agree. I don't want to. Not after all this."

"So what do we do now?" Hokk asked.

"I'm ready to follow through with the plan we agreed on," said Elia, sitting up and rubbing her eyes. "I swear I'm capable. I feel fine."

Hokk wondered if he could believe her.

"All I need is to get into Tael's room and just get on with it," she added.

Hokk studied her face. Now that she was upright, her expression seemed less bleary. But he still wasn't sure. He took the teapot from the tray. "Here. Drink this. All of it."

Elia drank directly from the spout. When she was done, she passed the teapot back and Hokk opened the top to make sure it was empty. "Do you have your telescope?"

She pulled up her dress to show it tied to her lower leg. "It's all ready."

"Good." Hokk looked at the door, then back at Elia. "Now, sprawl out on the mattress like you were when I found you and close your eyes until I come back."

"Why?" she asked. "Aren't we doing this together?"

"Yes, though first I have to create a distraction," he replied. "But don't let it scare you. Just keep lying there until I tell you to get up. Understand?"

"I will."

Elia followed his instructions. Once in position, with her short hair and the bandage still on her forehead, she looked roughed up and broken — perfectly believable.

Hokk took the tray with all of its dishes, and lifted it above his head. He then threw everything onto the floor with a tremendous crash. Elia's body recoiled, but she stayed silent.

Hokk raced to the door and flung it open. "She's collapsed!" he shouted at the guard. "Get in here!"

The guard charged into the room as Hokk rushed to the mattress, crunching over shattered glass.

"She's unconscious!" yelled Hokk.

The guard hesitated.

"Don't just stand there!" Hokk screamed. "She could be dying!"

"What do you want me to do?" the man shouted back.

Shoving the guard aside, Hokk crouched beside Elia and felt her neck for a pulse. "Her heart's still beating, but just barely!" He glared at the biscuit pieces and jam containers spilt on the floor. "Someone must have poisoned her food. I'll race downstairs to find help, but you have to stay and try to revive her!"

"I don't know how!"

Hokk sprung to his feet and raged at the guard. "Then *you* go and I'll stay here! But hurry. We might not have much time! Every minute counts!"

The guard raced from the room, and Hokk went to the door to watch the man disappear down the stairs. Then he hurried back to Elia. "He's gone. Get up!"

Elia leapt off the mattress, and Hokk was glad to see she seemed steady enough on her feet. He picked up a dinner knife from the cutlery strewn on the floor and clenched it in his fist. "Now, let's get out of here before anyone returns!"

Chapter 48

ELIA'S LEGS FELT SHAKY AS she and Hokk rushed down the stairs. Fearing she would trip, she focused all her attention on each step and took deep breaths to clear her head. She felt so humiliated that Hokk had caught her smoking incense — and he seemed so disappointed. She had thought she'd have plenty of time to finish and remove all traces of the stuff before he arrived, but that wasn't a legitimate excuse. Elia now wanted to make up for it. Anything to prove she could accomplish what she had set out to do. To restore his faith in her.

They encountered a few staff and courtiers in the stairwell, but no one stopped them. When they reached a landing about a third of the way to the bottom, Hokk pulled her into the adjoining corridor. They crouched and waited, trying to calm their breathing. A minute later, several Imperial Guards and one older courtier — was he a doctor? — charged up the stairs. After they had passed, Hokk murmured, "All clear," and the two of them continued to race down to the ground floor.

They slowed their stride, hoping to be less obvious as they crossed the front reception hall to the other tower. However, it was then that Elia realized she had forgotten to wrap the turban around her head. The bandage was still there below her hairline — she reached up to touch it to make sure — but unfortunately, she could not go back now to cover it completely.

At the base of Tael's tower, they started their ascent. Outside the door to the emperor's quarters, the pair of guards thankfully ignored them, apparently unaware of the commotion stirred up on Tohryn's side of the palace.

Two more levels and they were on Hokk's floor. The corridor was quiet. But would it remain that way? People would soon start heading to breakfast in greater numbers.

"You'll be able to stay and be a lookout for me, won't you?" Elia asked in a whisper.

Hokk grimaced. "Actually, there's been a change of plans," he replied just as quietly. "I've been asked by Empress Faytelle to meet her at the stables before breakfast. She wants to take me on a tour of the gardens, just the two of us."

"What? Why didn't you mention this earlier?"

"Because you and I can still pull this off. Look —" He pointed to the elevator doors, which on this particular floor were blocked by tall pedestals. "We can pull one of these stands forward and get behind it to pry the doors apart, just enough for you to slip through. I'll show you how. If they're opened just a bit, and with the pedestal in front, I bet nobody walking by will notice any difference."

"As I start climbing down, can you at least go to the banquet room to see when Tael shows up?"

"Yes, that's what I was planning to do. Once I've confirmed he's there, I'll come back to let you know, then I'll head off to meet Faytelle. But after that, it will all be up to you alone."

Elia nodded. "I can handle it. Don't worry about me. I won't need you once I hear back from you that Tael's at breakfast," she said, trying to ignore the prickly fingers of anxiety creeping up her spine.

Together, they inched the heavy pedestal forward, scraping it across the floor. The distance between it and the door panels left room for only Elia to squeeze in. Hokk was completely exposed as he coached her from the side.

"All you need is to create adequate space to hook your fingers in. Then it gets easier after that," Hokk explained as he handed her a simple dinner knife. "Give it a try with this thing to get it started," he encouraged.

The knife didn't seem strong enough, but Elia jammed the blade between the panels and pushed against its handle. Though the knife began to bend, the doors separated, albeit with a gap of no more than half an inch.

"Now grip the opposite edges and pull the two halves apart as hard as you can," said Hokk.

Elia did as he directed, and was relieved to feel the panels surrender. Slowly they separated until there was a slim space for Elia to slip through. "Will the doors slide back if I'm not holding them?"

"Try it."

Elia removed her hands. The doors did not move.

"Good. Now wait here a second," said Hokk. He returned a moment later with two burning candles he had taken from the stairwell. "I'll pass these to you once you're inside."

Elia stuck one foot into the dark shaft and felt around until she found a foothold. She angled her shoulders and shimmied through, finding spots to hold with her hands. Hokk stepped behind the pedestal where Elia had been standing. He reached in with a candle, and its light illuminated the surrounding area. Elia took it and wedged it between metal support bars. Looking down into the shaft, she saw a dark pit below.

Hokk gave her the second candle, which she purposefully let fall. Its flame flickered as it dropped, but thankfully it did not go out as it landed on what Elia guessed was the outer hull of the elevator carriage. The extra light gave her a much better sense of how far down she'd have to go. And judging from the distance between her and where the candle was resting, the carriage was fortunately stopped on the main level, just below the spot where Elia planned to enter Tael's suite on the next floor above. Perfect!

Elia put the handle of the knife into her mouth to keep her hands free for climbing.

"Just do the same thing with the door panels into Tael's suite once you get down there, right?" said Hokk.

She nodded.

"But don't open them until I come back and tell you everything's good to go," he added.

Elia gave him a thumbs-up. Determined and allowing no room in her mind for fear, she felt unstoppable. Since she had successfully stormed a seed room in a skyscraper of Ago, she could certainly do this.

Chapter 49

TASHEIRA WAS PLEASED WITH HERSELF. She couldn't help smiling.

"What are you so happy about?" Jeska whispered in the semi-darkness. The empress was still sleeping.

"Nothing," Tash replied quietly. "I'm surprised you can even see me."

"I can see the white of your teeth virtually lighting up the room."

Tash pressed her lips together, not wanting Jeska to dig for more details.

"Have you seen Lord Hokk this morning?" her cousin asked.

"No," Tasheira lied, feeling the urge to smile again.

"I haven't been able to stop thinking about him."

Tash clenched her jaw. Since arriving, she had heard much gossip among the ladies-in-waiting about Hokk, and after yesterday's reception, he dominated their conversations.

"Though I'm still not sure I understood the significance of everything he said to the emperors," Jeska continued. "But it must have been important. They seemed almost disturbed by his message. I haven't figured out what it all means."

Tash had been wondering the same thing. Hokk's

comments had come across as too vague to provoke such a noticeable reaction from Tael and Tohryn. But that's what she loved about the situation — the mystery. It made Hokk all the more irresistible.

"I guess there's no word yet how long Hokk will be staying at the Sanctuary," said Jeska.

"Not that I've heard," Tash replied, though she knew he had nowhere else to go in the meantime. Certainly returning to the moon would be a tremendous challenge.

"When is the Baron leaving?" Jeska asked.

"He usually stays a few days." A few more days for Tasheira to decide whether or not she would remain at the palace or go back home with her father.

"So long as Hokk doesn't leave too soon," her cousin murmured. "But I guess that's why Empress Faytelle wanted to see him so suddenly, otherwise she might miss the opportunity."

Tasheira bristled. "When are they getting together?"

"This morning," Jeska replied, sounding surprised that Tash didn't know. "He's the person she's meeting at the stables. Though it's getting a bit late. I wonder why she isn't up yet."

Tasheira did not like hearing this. It seemed unnecessary for Faytelle to request time alone with Hokk. Or was Tash just being jealous? And why hadn't Hokk mentioned it?

Another ten minutes passed before the empress awoke and was ready to get out of bed. "Open the curtains," she ordered.

This morning, Tasheira did not wait in the wings. Instead, she helped pull back the drapes, then joined Jeska and the other women beside Faytelle's bed.

The empress held her hand over one side of her forehead as if experiencing pain. As she lowered it, Tash was stunned to see a large gold loop piercing her eyebrow.

When had that been done?

"Is it swollen?" asked Faytelle. "Any bruising?"

"It looks perfectly fine," replied one of the ladies.

"It's truly a spectacular spot for a piece of jewelery," said another. "You'll be able to do so much with it."

The empress made eye contact with Tasheira. "Tell your friend, Miss Elfa, or Elsi, or whoever she is, to remove hers. It's too crude and does not flatter her face."

"Yes, of course," Tash answered, trying hard not to smirk. So, she thought to herself, I'm not the only jealous woman in this palace. "I'll tell her as soon as I see her."

Faytelle stepped out of her flouncy nightgown and stood naked in front of a mirror, arms held to the side, as she waited for the women to dress her. Today's gown was pink and her makeup was applied to complement its shade. Other women styled her hair with live butterflies attached to strings threaded into the cap of her wig.

Again this morning, the empress seemed willing to engage in some idle chatter. So when there was a gentle knock at the door, no one seemed to register the sound.

The knock came again, with more force this time.

"Who's disturbing us at this hour?" the empress complained.

Another knock.

"Somebody please get that!"

With her skirts rustling, the closest lady-in-waiting moved serenely to the entrance and opened the door. Tash glanced over but couldn't see past her. Before long, the woman scurried back.

"What did they want?" Faytelle demanded.

"It's someone for Lady Tasheira."

All the women, including the empress, were surprised, but none more so than Tash. With one eyebrow raised quizzically, Tasheira left to find out who was looking for her.

A middle-aged servant stood on the other side of the door. "Lady Tasheira?" the woman asked.

"I am," Tash replied.

"I've been sent to find you right away. You have a special guest who's come to see you."

"Who?"

"I wasn't told. But whoever it is has traveled all the way from your father's estate and is now asking to speak with you. It seems urgent. About what, I don't —"

Tash held up her hand to cut the servant off. Not bothering to check first with the empress, she stepped into the corridor and closed the door. "Take me immediately!"

Chapter **50**

ELIA KNEW SHE COULD FALL at any moment. Though she didn't have far to drop, her injuries could be severe if she landed on top of the elevator carriage. If that happened, how would she ever be rescued without incriminating herself?

Don't rush! Take it slow.

While her flowing white dress got in the way and made it difficult to descend, her shoes helped. The soles gave Elia traction against the walls as she worked her way down, her body wedged into one of the corners of the elevator shaft as she tightly gripped the vertical metal rails that ran all the way to the bottom. When she reached the next set of door panels, the frame around them provided no more than an inch of ledge for the tips of her shoes, but it was enough to give her arms a rest before cautiously continuing on. By the time she finally stepped onto the carriage, her fingers, legs, and toes were cramping.

But at least she had made it!

Stretching far above her into black nothingness, the passage was silent except for her labored breathing. Fortunately, the candles were still burning — the one beside her feet on top of the elevator and the other two stories up — giving her all the light she needed. Looking straight ahead, she could easily distinguish the door panels that she would soon be prying open after Hokk returned with the all-clear.

Yet something was bothering her, gnawing at the back of her mind. She wished she could figure out what. Was she worried because Hokk had been gone so long? Or was she simply scared and second-guessing herself?

Elia stepped back and stared up at the opening in the shaft where she had entered, concentrating hard as if to will Hokk's head to appear. If he didn't return soon, he'd probably be late for his meeting with the empress, which could raise suspicions. Yet the whole scenario was already suspicious. What couldn't Faytelle say to him yesterday at the reception that had to wait until they were alone today? And why tour the gardens so early in the morning, when the grounds would be empty?

Unless the empress has an ulterior motive. Could she want to get rid of Hokk?

The sudden realization made Elia bite down hard on the handle of the knife still clenched in her mouth. She could taste metal — or was it blood? She took the knife out and rubbed her tongue over her teeth and gums.

She couldn't erase this new worry. The more she thought about it, the more certain she became. She debated climbing back up to warn Hokk, but where would she find him if he wasn't in the banquet room? Besides, leaving now would surely jeopardize this opportunity to break into Tael's suite.

Moving closer to the wall, Elia put her ear to the crack between the panels. She could hear nothing coming from the room on the other side.

Maybe she should just do it!

Then she heard a muffled voice. She couldn't tell whether or not it was the blind emperor speaking or somebody else with him. However, when the words were repeated, louder and clearer this time, Elia realized they were actually floating down to her.

Praise the sun! It was Hokk! He had made it back! She could see him looking over the edge. "Hokk!" she called out.

"I said, can you hear me?" he replied softly.

"Yes! I can hear you now," Elia answered, lowering her voice. "Are you all right?"

"Just waiting for you."

"Well, Tael arrived for breakfast a few minutes ago. You're safe to proceed."

"Thank you."

"Good luck. I'll come find you again after I'm done in the gardens."

"Hokk, wait. Before you leave, I must warn you."

"What?"

"Don't trust the empress. I don't have a good feeling about this."

"I'll be careful."

"Be more than careful. Be alert. And don't let her lure you too close to the edges. She could shove you off."

This was what had been bothering Elia — her mind had now pieced it all together. Everything about Faytelle's arrangements today seemed eerily similar to what Elia could imagine had happened that morning almost two decades ago when Mahkoiyin had fallen — or been pushed — over the edge of the island. Faytelle's pale skin alone was enough evidence that the woman was from Below, and obviously she must have quickly figured out the same about Hokk. Someone like the empress would never allow any threat to endanger her powerful position, so naturally Faytelle would do whatever necessary to protect herself. Surely Hokk could see that too.

Yet Hokk only gave a strained chuckle and waved. "Like I said, good luck. To both of us." And with that, he pulled back his head and disappeared.

Elia sighed, wishing he had heeded her warning with greater seriousness. But she couldn't waste more time or energy fretting about it. He was on his own, just as she found herself now.

Before allowing herself any chance to reconsider, Elia slipped the knife blade between two of the panels and slowly pulled them apart as she had done earlier. Rolling on their tracks, the doors separated without excessive noise. She opened them only as far as she needed to squeeze through sideways. The statue in front of her blocked any view of the room, but at least she could easily step inside. She peered around the stone sculpture to confirm the suite was empty and glanced at the entrance where the doors were closed. As far as she could tell, she was alone. *Now to get started!*

She loosened the straps around her leg and removed the telescope, extending it to its full length. Before she raised it to her eye, Elia scanned the room, which looked so different compared to yesterday when it had been full of people. But where should she start searching in such a sprawling space?

Let the telescope decide.

Elia moved to the middle of the room and slowly pivoted, peering through the eyepiece at the walls and the art covering them. Not a single thing stood out as important, so she examined every piece of furniture, as well as the carpets and fireplace before moving deeper into Tael's personal quarters, which had been off-limits to his guests. She followed hallways that branched off into his massive bedchamber, a huge walk-in closet, a luxurious bathing area, and finally, his private dining room with its sweeping vista that encompassed the gardens, the Grand Bridge, and the City of Na-Lavent beyond. It was an incredible view wasted on a man who couldn't appreciate the beauty.

Elia's frustration was escalating. So far, the telescope had revealed nothing. And the farther she moved away from the main entrance, the more anxious she felt. She decided to return and focus her telescope's lens on the papers Emperor Tael had collected on his desk near the front. They were what had caught her attention in the first place.

The scrolls seemed to be even more randomly tossed about since she had last seen them. One especially large parchment,

which was covered with lines of small writing, had been fully
unrolled and was held open by bottles of ink, one red and the
other black. To Elia's disappointment, the telescope revealed
no further clues as she studied the page, though she worried
maybe she was missing something important because she
couldn't read.

But she couldn't give up yet. There were many more scrolls
to open. She untied the blue ribbon around one of them and
spread the paper flat with one palm. This document had a few
diagrams, not just text, although once more, none of it meant
anything to Elia.

On to the next one. Yet as she started to undo the scroll,
something made her stop. She raised her head. She listened
carefully. Breathlessly.

Voices again! This time, without a doubt, they were coming
from outside the room, where the Imperial Guards were
stationed.

Elia's eyes darted in panic toward the elevator shaft. She
could just barely see the gap in the panels behind the closest
statue.

Hearing unmistakable laughter from the outer hallway,
Elia frantically snapped her attention back in that direction.
She froze, staring at the doorknob just a few feet away.

The handle was lowered, followed by a *click* as the lock
released.

Then the door swung open and Emperor Tael stepped into
the room, vigorously sweeping his white cane from left to right.

Chapter 51

TWO HORSES, FLAWLESSLY WHITE, WERE already saddled and standing patiently in the courtyard of the Royal Stables. Hokk assumed the pair had been requested by Faytelle for this morning's tour, but as far as he could see, the empress had not yet arrived. Good. He preferred to be the first to show up. He had run to get here on time after leaving Elia, guessing that almost thirty minutes had passed since Tasheira entered the empress's room. He did not want to face the consequences if Faytelle was forced to wait.

Rather than stand out in the open, however, Hokk scanned the area for a spot to conceal himself. He feared his dark glasses gave him away too easily. So far, he had avoided detection, with no Imperial Guards following him, and though he hoped to keep it that way for as long as possible, he knew the guard he had tricked would eventually raise the alarm.

Noticing the stable's portico and the amount of shade that it cast, Hokk hurried across the courtyard until he was standing beneath one of the arched entryways. He took cover behind a stone column. From here, he could keep a close watch for anyone who might suddenly appear looking for him.

Approaching the stables now, he was intrigued to see a horse in apparent misery. It struggled to walk as it was gently led along by a young stableboy holding its reins. The animal's hide was soaked with perspiration and its wings hung limp beside its body, with the tips of its feathers dragging on the ground.

Then the horse's back legs gave out, unable to go any farther. As the animal's hindquarters dropped, its front limbs faltered, and the horse crumpled to the cobblestones with a painful-sounding thud.

"Some help here, please!" shouted the stableboy.

Hokk watched several workers run into the courtyard to assist. The oldest in the group seemed to be the stable foreman. "What's happened to this animal?" the man asked.

"It's absolutely exhausted," the boy replied.

"I can see that, but why?"

"It was driven too hard by its rider to get here. The poor thing likely hasn't had a break or water for who knows how many hours."

The foreman looked appalled. "Who would do such a thing?"

"Someone who has just flown in from Baron Shoad's estate."

Hearing this, Hokk stiffened. He strained now not to miss a single word.

"The rider is in rough shape too, completely worn out," the boy continued while some of the other men tried to coax the animal to rise. "Whoever it was has been flying continuously since yesterday afternoon."

"Alone?"

"Yes, alone. I guess something urgent has come up that couldn't wait for the Baron's return."

Hokk had heard enough. He bolted across the courtyard toward the palace, startling the stablehands as he charged past. Forget the empress and her tour of the Sanctuary grounds! All Hokk could think about was warning Elia immediately of this sudden complication to her plans — a complication that could ruin everything. Because if there was anybody who would travel such a long distance from the Baron's estate with crucial news to share, it could only be one person.

Marest.

Tasheira's servant must have traveled all night to warn her mistress about Elia.

Chapter 52

AS TASH FOLLOWED THE SERVANT, she felt uncertain — concerned, in fact — about how she would react to seeing her mother here at the palace.

Part of Tasheira was touched to think the Baroness had been so worried about her daughter's well-being that she would have flown such a great distance to check up on her. It would now give Tash the chance to share all the things about palace life that were so unappealing. Surely her mother would then demand better, or at least talk to her father. On the other hand, the very idea of the Baroness interfering had the potential to just as easily spark Tasheira's temper. What if her mother had arrived in her silly, drug-induced state, acting so inappropriately that Tash would be mortified to admit any connection to the woman?

"Where are you taking me?" Tasheira asked impatiently as the servant led her into a section of the palace opposite the wing that housed the banquet hall.

"Your guest is waiting in one of the private meeting rooms reserved for official business."

Perfect, thought Tasheira. She would have the privacy she'd need to either unburden herself to her mother or scold her for being an embarrassment to the family.

After passing several closed doors, the servant halted beside one, opened it, and stepped out of Tasheira's way. "If you'll be pleased to enter, My Lady," the woman said with a bow.

Tasheira swept past and walked into a plush sitting room. So convinced she would see her mother, she stopped abruptly and had to grab onto the back of a chair to steady herself as she did a double take.

The person waiting for her — it couldn't possibly be!

"Fimal!" Tash cried out as she raced forward.

Fimal rose from his chair just in time to catch her in a tight embrace.

"I can't believe it!" Tasheira half sobbed. She released her hold just enough to look into his face. "Is it really you?" she wondered incredulously. "Are you back from the dead?"

"You could almost say that."

Somehow, Fimal's face had aged in the few days since Tash had last seen him. "Sit down," she encouraged. "You look ready to keel over."

"You're right. I'm truly exhausted," her cousin replied with a weary sigh. He slumped onto a couch. "I flew nonstop to get here after I learned that you had already left the manor."

"I was so upset to leave without the chance to say goodbye to you — and thinking you were dead! — well, that was too much to bear. But where were you? Hiding somewhere on the estate grounds?"

"I was neither hiding, nor at the estate."

"Then what were you doing?" Tasheira asked as she took a seat beside him.

"I was exploring."

"Where could you possibly explore if not —"

Though Fimal's face was sagging with fatigue, his eyes managed to twinkle. "Tash, there's a whole world out there that you and I could never have imagined."

Tasheira's brow furrowed. "What do you mean?"

Fimal shook his head and rubbed his temples as if he were

still struggling to comprehend it himself. "If anyone had told me, I would have thought they were lying. But I know you'll believe me, though I can't say the same for my brother or the Baron."

"Of course I'll believe you." Tasheira's whole body prickled with anticipation.

Fimal looked into her eyes with such intensity that her throat tightened.

"Our world is not what it seems," he replied. "All these years, we've been told something that isn't true. Instead, we've lived in fear about things that don't even exist. And what does exist, well . . . it's almost too hard to fathom. It has now made me question everything about the Lunera System. About the shattered moon in our skies. About our very origins."

Tash found it fascinating yet unsettling how similar Fimal's story was sounding to Hokk's message for the Twin Emperors. "What exactly did you see?" she asked.

"I've been to *Below*!" Seeing the shock on Tasheira's face, he nodded solemnly. "And there's so much more down there than either of us could have ever dreamed. It makes our islands up here seem incredibly small and insignificant in comparison."

"You must be mistaken. It couldn't actually have been Below. What about Scavengers? They would have killed you! I didn't think you'd be foolish enough to take that risk."

"Scavengers don't exist," Fimal flatly declared.

"Everyone knows —"

"They don't!" he insisted. "Beneath our clouds, there are no such monsters. Only miles upon endless miles of land. It's incredibly cold and dark, and when I first arrived, the terrain was covered everywhere with white. But when I flew back to the estate, I could see soaring mountains in the distance. Even flying now to join you at the palace, I dipped below the clouds a few times, and everything looked completely different. I saw meadows that stretched to the horizon and then what turned out to be a body of water that was so massive —" He sighed with frustration. "I wish I could describe it properly."

Tash found it all too incredible. Her shoulders slouched. "Have you been smoking incense?" she asked. "Did you hallucinate or something?"

Fimal was insulted. "I'm stunned you don't believe me! *You* of all people!"

"I want to, but how can I?" She rose from the sofa as if all of a sudden she needed to create distance between herself and her cousin. "What you're saying is impossible!"

"We've been told it's impossible, but it's not," said Fimal, grabbing her wrist and trying to pull her closer. "Just ask your friend Hokk."

Tash stopped cold. She sunk once again onto the couch. "What do you mean I should ask Hokk?" she murmured, pulling her hand back to rest it in her lap.

"Hokk doesn't come from the moon as he claims. He's from Below."

Tash gazed blankly at her cousin, struggling to process what he was saying.

"And the only reason I know this," her cousin continued, "is because I followed him down there. I thought I had to rescue him. I wouldn't have dared to go beneath the clouds otherwise."

Fimal proceeded to tell Tash everything: how he had watched Hokk leave the manor so early that particular morning; how Hokk had taken a horse, then flown off; Fimal himself in pursuit, too curious not to chase after him; how he had been astounded to see Hokk dive down through the clouds as if something had gone wrong. Her cousin described the dark cloud cover overhead and the frozen wasteland, as well as the island that had somehow fallen to Below with the remnants of a village on its top slope, yet with no traces of life.

Tash listened to it all. She forced herself to try to accept every word he said as fact. And the more she heard, the more his story seemed to answer questions she had ignored not just recently, but all her life.

"I want to take you down there with me," Fimal finished off. "So you can see for yourself. It will be an adventure! Will you join me?"

Tash shuddered. "I still associate the place with death. It's going to take a lot for me to shake that feeling." A thought suddenly blindsided her. "Wait! How do you explain what happened to Marest? We saw the damage to the fence where she was attacked by Scavengers and pulled over to her death. How do you explain that?"

"You interpreted what you saw based on what you've been taught to believe. But it was all staged."

His suggestion was preposterous. "That can't be! She's dead."

"Like you thought I was dead?" he challenged.

"But —"

"It was all planned as a clever trick by this girl Elia who you've been helping."

"How can you make such an accusation against Elia?" Tash demanded, though she felt a sinking feeling all the same.

"Because Marest is very much alive."

Chapter 53

ELIA STOOD COMPLETELY STILL. SHE held her breath, afraid that Tael's sensitive ears might somehow hear her heartbeat.

As a guard outside the room closed the door, Elia glanced once again at the open elevator panels. Could she sneak back into the shaft without making a noise?

The blind emperor turned his head in her direction.

He sniffed the air.

Elia shuddered. He could probably smell the incense smoke still clinging to her clothes. Damn her stupidity!

Tael seemed to be staring just over her shoulder. He sucked another deep lungful through his nostrils. "Don't think for a second I don't know you're in here," he said.

Elia felt light-headed.

The emperor took a step toward her.

She resisted making a move.

"I could so easily call in a guard and have you dragged off to the dungeon."

He can't see you, Elia reminded herself. And if he did call for help, she could always run to the elevator shaft before anyone else arrived in the room. It would likely take the guards a while to figure out where she had disappeared — long enough for her to climb back up to Hokk's floor and blend in with the rest of the Royal Court enjoying their breakfasts.

The emperor moved between Elia and her only escape route. It was as if he had guessed her plan. Or maybe he could sense a draft coming from the dark, silent passage.

Tael chuckled. It was a wicked laugh. "Perhaps you heard. This morning, there's been a scare in the palace. Some nonsense about an attempted food poisoning," he said, closing the gap between them. "It has shut down the dining room and canceled my breakfast. I wonder if you might have had something to do with it."

Elia glanced at the telescope in her hand. She didn't want to risk damaging the instrument by using it to defend herself. She needed something else.

On the desk beside her, she noticed the bottle of red ink and picked it up. Upon doing so, the bottom of the parchment began to curl back up again into a roll. Elia cringed. The sound was so obvious.

"I'm curious what you have in your hand," said Tael.

He knows I've grabbed something.

Another step forward.

"Stay back," Elia warned, though she immediately regretted it. Now he would be able to recognize her voice.

As she feared, the emperor's face twisted with a sinister smile. "I know who you are, my dear."

Elia squeezed the makeshift weapon in her fist.

Tael moved closer still.

"Don't take another step!" she demanded. "You'll regret it."

"Will I?" he mocked, disregarding her threat and taking another step forward.

Elia threw the inkpot, aiming right for the blind emperor's head.

His reflexes were instant. His hand shot up and grabbed the bottle in mid-air.

For a split second, even the emperor seemed surprised by

his reaction. Gone was his fiendish smile. The man's eyes narrowed, focusing angrily on Elia.

"That was very unwise," he seethed.

Though somewhere in her head, Elia was shouting *He can see! He can see!* she was too dumbfounded to do anything except gawk in amazement.

Tael looked at his hand where the lid of the bottle had opened and red ink was dripping through his fingers and down his arm. Elia stared as well.

Then the emperor dropped the bottle and lunged at her. But his hand was too slick to get a firm grasp, smearing her with the ink instead.

Elia broke free. She fled toward the entrance with the telescope still in her hand.

"Guards!" Tael shouted, sounding as if he was right at her heels.

Elia flung open the door.

"Stop her!"

But the men reacted too slowly. Elia dashed past them and flew down the stairs, two steps at a time.

Chapter **54**

"MAREST IS ALIVE?" TASHEIRA GASPED. The news was staggering.

"And Elia tried to kill her," Fimal said gravely.

"You've actually seen Marest? You talked to her?"

"Yes. Marest told me face to face everything that happened. Or at least what she can remember. She would have joined me here to tell you herself, but she's still recovering."

Numb, Tash stared at the floor.

"Do you know who Elia *really* is?" Fimal asked. "Not who she pretends to be?"

With trepidation, Tasheira looked back up at her cousin. "Who?"

"A servant girl. Nothing more than a lowly servant girl."

"That can't be!"

Fimal nodded. "She has the tattoo to prove it, just like you see on all the staff around this palace."

"Maybe Marest is mistaken and —" but Tash stopped herself. It all made sense now: the wound on Elia's forehead; how she kept making it bleed; how she always needed a bandage, then the turban to cover it. "I was blind not to realize," Tasheira muttered, shaking her head in dismay. "Everything's suddenly starting to add up so clearly."

Fimal squeezed her arm. "Don't feel bad. We all fell for it. What else were we supposed to think?" Then her cousin's expression turned grim. "The question now is, where is she?"

"I don't know."

"I assume, though, she's somewhere in this palace."

"Yes, she is," Tash replied, dreading to imagine what the girl's hidden agenda might be.

"Then we have to find her. And warn the emperors. Who knows what she's planning? Lives could be at stake."

Remembering Elia's request to be left alone to deal with her own matters, Tash leapt from the couch and pulled her cousin to his feet. "Come with me! Quickly! We have to fix this right away!"

Because if Hokk wasn't from the moon, and Elia was a servant — and a potential assassin no less! — then there was more on the line than just saving lives. Tasheira's reputation was threatened too.

Chapter 55

AS HOKK RAN BACK INTO the palace, he saw Empress Faytelle approaching a short distance away, gracefully strolling through the wide corridor with her ladies-in-waiting. Fearing he'd be spotted, he slipped among a group of gentlemen who had just emerged from the dining room. The men looked surprised to see him in their midst, yet after only a slight pause, their conversation continued. Hokk kept his head lowered. He nodded as if in agreement with whatever they were discussing — something about the kitchens inconveniently shutting down. Only when he was sure the empress had passed did he leave the group just as abruptly as he had appeared.

He raced into the front reception hall, arriving just in time to see Elia fleeing across the open expanse, dodging people in her way.

"Elia!" he cried out. His shouting made courtiers turn toward him with alarm.

Yet Hokk was unconcerned with their reactions. He was instead horrified to see the bright red that was splattered on Elia's arm. She was bleeding badly. "Elia, stop!" he yelled after her again, but she paid no attention.

What could have gone so wrong?

Hokk started running to follow her, but abruptly held back, skidding to a halt as several Imperial Guards suddenly appeared, in obvious pursuit of Elia.

Don't hesitate, damn it! She needs you!

As he was about to give chase again, someone grabbed his shoulder and violently spun him around.

First he saw Tasheira. Then Fimal beside her.

"You!" said Hokk in amazement to the young man. "You made it back!"

Tash shoved him in the chest. "Everything you've said is a lie!"

Hokk shook off his surprise to see Fimal. He glared at Tasheira. "I've got no time for this!" He pointed in the direction where he had seen Elia escape. "Elia's in danger. She's covered in blood!"

Tasheira's expression blazed with horror. "What has she done?"

Hokk didn't answer. He tore off as fast as he could across the hall, hoping to catch up.

Whether or not the pounding feet behind him were those of Fimal and Tasheira, or more Imperial Guards, he did not look back to find out.

Chapter 56

ELIA CHARGED TOWARD THE REAR of the palace. There were no courtiers here. Only palace staff.

She arrived at the stairs leading deep underground to the kitchens, the laundry room, and the dungeon. But she did not go down these familiar steps. Instead, she burst outside into the open air.

The Grand Bridge was in front of her. It was her only means of escape.

How are you going to get past the gates? They're guarded!

Though her mind demanded an answer, Elia could only keep running. She knew she was being chased. Behind her, she heard shouting.

"Stop that girl!"

She glanced over her shoulder and saw Imperial Guards storming out of the palace.

"Stop her!" one of them called out again.

Ahead, Elia noticed a guard standing beside a winged horse. He was preparing to block her from getting onto the bridge.

She couldn't avoid him. He lunged and grabbed her around the waist.

Frantic, Elia fought back, kicking as hard and screaming as loud as she could. "Let go! Let me go!"

With one hand, she punched the man in the stomach. With the other, she smashed the telescope against his metal faceplate. She heard the instrument's glass eyepiece crack from the impact.

And then, somehow, the guard loosened his grip. Elia pulled away until he was clutching her only by the elbow. Behind his dead mask, the man stared down at her. Elia looked at his gloved hand holding her arm and could see the wet red ink that had stained her sleeve.

Elia took advantage of his hesitation. With a final burst of energy, she tore herself free and darted up the incline of the bridge.

At the crest, more Imperial Guards swiftly appeared, having come up from the gate on the city side.

Elia stopped. Panicking, she spun and saw guards closing in just below her. Some were on horses.

She was trapped.

Panting.

Exhausted.

Mind racing.

She had no hope.

But by no means would she ever allow herself to be captured.

The Grand Bridge had low walls on both sides, spanning the entire length. She climbed onto one of them, still clutching her telescope. Balancing on top, she peered over the edge into the clouds.

Jump!

But jump to what? It would be impossible to survive another fall to Below. She had only survived the first time because the island had dropped lower and she had the bedsheet to slow her down.

The guards, both above and below, were almost upon her.

JUMP!

Elia was drenched with sweat. She gazed back for a final look at the palace.

Her heart seized to suddenly see Hokk. Their eyes met. His expression was pure terror. "No, Elia!" she heard him scream. "Don't do it!"

But Elia turned away. She focused only on the swirling clouds just inches from her shoes.

Then she stuck out one foot and closed her eyes.

Chapter **57**

DAZED, THE IMPERIAL GUARD FLIPPED up his visor and stared at the blood on his glove.

Then he glanced up to where he saw his sister climbing the wall of the Grand Bridge as other guards ran to get closer.

Rayhan had no idea how Elia had suddenly appeared in his arms, or why she was coming out of the palace dressed in the clothes she was wearing, bleeding so badly, and with so little hair on her head. She was transformed. But he recognized her instantly. Her eyes!

And now she was preparing to leap off the bridge.

Everything started to move in slow motion.

Rayhan watched his sister look over the edge and hesitate before glancing back in the direction of the Mirrored Palace. He followed her gaze and saw what — or rather who — she was looking at. A young man, a nobleman, about Rayhan's own age, who was extremely pale and wearing dark glasses. Whoever he was, the young man shouted out, "No, Elia! Don't do it!"

Hearing her name snapped Rayhan into action. He flung off his helmet and began sprinting up the bridge toward his sister.

But each step he took felt sluggish, as if he were struggling in mud that had risen to his knees.

Elia stretched one leg out over the clouds.

"No!" Rayhan shouted.

She leaned forward, on the verge of losing her balance.

He almost reached her. His hands were just inches away from grabbing her waist. Yet he clutched only air.

Elia had stepped off.

She was falling.

The clouds swallowed her up.

His sister was gone.

Chapter **58**

ELIA LANDED WITH SUCH FORCE, her ankle twisted painfully, and her breath was knocked from her lungs. She gasped for air.

Yet she had fallen for what seemed like only a few seconds. She had not emerged through the underside of the cloud cover. She had not seen Below racing up toward her.

So where was she?

Although surrounded by white mist, she knew she couldn't be floating — she felt solid ground beneath her.

Gazing upward, the clouds were not as gray and heavy as she would have expected. In fact, they were bright, with the faintest rays of filtered sunshine. And then, to her amazement, her eyes adjusted and she could make out a long shadow stretching above.

The Grand Bridge! She was right below it!

But how was that possible? The bridge joined two completely separate islands — two land masses that would drift apart if not for the man-made crossing that connected them.

Unless that too was a lie!

Perceptions deceive. The voice of Elia's grandmother resonated in her head, though it seemed like a lifetime ago since Omi had uttered that advice. *Things are often not as they seem.*

How true those words had proven to be over the past few weeks.

Elia could hear muffled commotion overhead. Men shouting. It sounded as though fighting had broken out.

Then she saw the dark silhouette of a flying horse swoop over and plunge down through the clouds to Below. The mist prevented Elia from distinguishing any details, but whoever the rider was, he must have been ordered to search Below for her body.

Would anyone ever discover what had actually happened to her? That she had landed only a short distance away, under the arched bridge? Maybe somebody already knew what was down here and would arrive to start searching. She might not have much time.

Limping because of her injured ankle, Elia began to explore the rock shelf upon which she found herself. It was double the width of the Grand Bridge above. She had landed on an area of gravel and dirt, but other spots were covered with damp patches of moss. At one end, the ground had large cracks, and Elia discovered pieces of cobblestone directly below where the bridge had crumbled that morning when the earthquake forced workers to evacuate the palace. Down here, however, the damage didn't look too severe. It was definitely not enough to cause the two islands — or rather the *one* island — to break apart.

But at least she now had a means of escape! She'd hike up the opposite slope to reach the city and disappear into its alleyways. Then she'd return to her tiny home at the end of its suspension bridge. While the house would likely be empty, she'd have somewhere to hide until she could sort out what to do next.

What about Hokk? Elia hated to leave him behind after everything he'd done for her. Unfortunately, any attempt to reunite with him now could be dangerous for both of them. He would have to fend for himself. Although a proven survivor, how would he fare being stuck in a world so foreign and hostile compared to what he was used to in Below? What kind of life awaited him?

What about her own future? This was not the way events were meant to unfold. Elia felt more alone than ever. After such an effort to get back to the islands of Above, she had learned nothing about the fate of her family. Then, taking the huge risk to return to the Mirrored Palace, she had failed to discover whatever secret she was supposed to reveal. And despite finding out the shocking truth that Tael was not actually blind, in the end, relying on the telescope had been futile.

Where was the telescope anyway? The instrument was no longer in her hands. It must be somewhere close by.

As the sounds of turmoil continued above, Elia searched until she found the telescope not far from where she had landed. The round piece of glass at its widest end was badly damaged. Now the damn thing would never work!

Look inside and this telescope can reveal a truth that would topple the monarchy.

Total nonsense. Again, another example of how things were not as they were made out to be.

Was it pointless to still carry the telescope with her? She had no practical use for such a device, and now that it was broken, it had no real value. But still, she was reluctant to just abandon it. A young woman had died for this thing!

She stared at the instrument, thinking about all she had been through to keep it safe, about the many times she had come so close to losing it to the wrong hands.

Look inside.

Elia peered through the eyepiece one last time —

Then she smashed the end of it on the ground. She continued until the glass shattered completely and all the pieces fell away.

She peered into the hollow shaft and discovered something — *inside!*

Filled with a surge of exhilaration, Elia jammed her hand

into the metal cylinder. She fiddled with trembling fingers until finally catching hold of the edges of some papers. Gently, she eased out the documents.

The pages were rolled like the much larger scrolls she had found on Tael's cluttered desk. She flattened the sheets against the ground. She could read nothing, but recognized the royal seal — matching her tattoo — stamped upon each piece of paper. It was the last document, however, that she found especially intriguing. The page had a pair of small handprints, as well as a set of similarly sized footprints, presumably belonging to a baby.

No, it's not over! Far from it!

She carefully kicked off her shoes, glad to be alive and glad to be barefoot again. Though her ankle was swelling, the cool dirt and gravel felt good between her toes as they curled with excitement. She rolled the documents and carefully slipped them back into the telescope, then hobbled through the mist to the far slope that climbed to the surface of Kamanman and the city built right up to its edges.

No doubt about it now. Elia was absolutely certain she finally possessed the secrets that could topple a monarchy. And maybe . . . just maybe, solve the mystery surrounding her family.

She simply needed to find someone who could decipher the pages.

End of Book Two

Acknowledgments

MY DEBUT NOVEL, *BELOW*, WAS written over many years when I had to juggle my responsibilities as a chartered professional accountant with my dreams of becoming an author. My encore, *ABOVE*, was nurtured and produced in a personal creative environment afforded by the amazing opportunity to focus full-time on my writing. Now, as I anticipate my third volume, *BEYOND*, I look forward to continuing my collaboration with a remarkable group of people.

I owe the ultimate realization of my goals to the efforts of my literary agent, Daniel Lazar, from Writers House in New York City. Thank you, Dan, for your steadfast commitment and enthusiasm.

In this tremendous industry of book publication, I have been very fortunate to work with a world-class team from Turner Publishing Company. My sincere appreciation goes to my exceptional editor, Jon O'Neal, for everything that has been done to make The Broken Sky Chronicles such a success. I am also very grateful for my publicist, Jolene Barto, who has coordinated superb launches for the release of every one of my novels.

Throughout my creative writing career, I have learned a

ACKNOWLEDGMENTS

great deal from true experts in their fields. Thank you many times over to Hadley Dyer, Maria Golikova, Catherine Dorton, and Catherine Marjoribanks. Your thoughtful feedback has always been appreciated and has helped my storytelling to flourish.

Above all, a deeply heartfelt thank you to those who I cherish most in my life. You each mean more to me than I can truly express with just words. Much love to Shawn Shirazi; my parents, Jo-Ann and André Chabot; my brother and his family, Jeff, Jennifer, Jack, and Kate; and my long-time friend Jazz Rai. Faced with the challenges of life, when my spirits have dipped to Below, everyone's love and support has allowed me to not only set my sights on Above, but to also soar to Beyond.

THE BROKEN SKY CHRONICLES

WILL CONCLUDE IN . . .

BEYOND

MAY 2017

FROM

TURNER
PUBLISHING COMPANY